Family
Trust

ISABELLE HOLLAND

Family Trust

PIATKUS

For Peggy Brooks, with thanks.

I would like to thank Virginia Terhune,
Ralph Brozan and Edith Van Slyck
for their invaluable help.

PROLOGUE

The little boy sat in the pickup truck between the man and the woman.

After about a mile he said suddenly, "Where's Mom?"

"I told you," the woman said. "She said we were to take you with us. We're your family now."

They drove another mile or so.

"I wanna go home," the boy said.

"That's where we're going," the woman said.

"I want Mom," the boy said. "I want her now!"

"Look, Sarah," the man said. "I must have been crazy to let you do this. Let's go back. Let's go back now, before it's too late."

"No!" There was something in her tone that made the little boy shrink toward the man.

"But—"

"No!" the woman said again. "God gave him to us, to make up for losing Mickey. This time he won't get away."

THE
SUMMONS

CHAPTER

1

The letter arrived in the morning mail in the last week of September and was brought into the breakfast room by the housemaid, interrupting an angry exchange.

"I'm sorry!" Graham said. "Really sorry. What more can I tell you? The girl was there paying attention to me in a flattering way. It had been a long time since you and I—"

"That was not of my choosing," Elizabeth flashed back with quick anger. She was a slender, attractive woman in her late thirties with hazel eyes and waving auburn hair cut stylishly short around her head.

"Wasn't it? Granted, you didn't put up a 'No Admittance' notice on your bedroom door, but short of that you made it clear you wanted no part of me."

"What I made clear was—" She stopped as Paget appeared in the doorway, mail in hand. "You can put it on the side table, Paget," she said, trying to ignore her husband's abrupt departure from the dining room. This was followed almost immediately by the sound of the front door slamming as Graham flung himself out of the house. "I'll look at it as soon as we finish breakfast."

Duncan came in to spend a few minutes with her before his departure for school. "I'm ready to go, Mummy," he said importantly.

Elizabeth took in the seven-year-old in his blazer, with his neatly tied school tie and his cap clutched in his hand. "Yes, darling. You're looking very smart." Duncan blushed. "Please, Mummy." But he didn't look unhappy.

At that moment Pamela, a pleasant-looking, squarely built young woman, came in with five-year-old Ailsa pulling at her hand.

"Good morning, Pam," Elizabeth said. "I think Duncan is all set." She looked at her daughter. "How are you this morning, darling?"

Ailsa tugged at the nanny's hand. "I want to go to school like Duncan!"

"Good morning, Lady Paterson," Pam said. Then, glancing down, "Now be patient, Ailsa. You'll be going to school next year."

Ailsa stamped her foot. "I want to go now!"

Pain flickered through Elizabeth as an old memory echoed in her mind. She heard her own thirteen-year-old voice: "Can't you wait, Mark? We'll go back to the toy department in a minute!"

"I wanna go now!"

The memory was twenty-six years old and three thousand miles away, but it still had the power to wound and accuse.

Pam glanced at her employer. "Ailsa and I will walk Duncan to school. Is there anything we can get you on the way back?"

"No. I don't think so. I'll be leaving myself in a minute." Elizabeth turned toward her daughter. "What are you going to do today, darling?"

Ailsa, staring mutinously at the floor, said nothing.

"Answer your mother, Ailsa," the nanny said.

Elizabeth felt a stab of irritation, which rapidly became guilt. Ailsa so often rubbed her the wrong way. Was it because she reminded Elizabeth so often of Mark and of her role in his tragedy?

"Go to the park," Alisa muttered unwillingly.

"That's nice," Elizabeth said.

Pamela said quickly, "Your coat's out in the hall, Ailsa, I put it on the hall chair. Go and get it and I'll help you into it." Then, as Ailsa started to run out, she added, "But first say goodbye to your mummy. She has to leave, too."

"Goodbye, Mummy," Alisa said, her voice defiant with anger.

As though, Elizabeth thought, I beat her soundly every night. She held out her hand. "Come here, Ailsa."

For a moment Ailsa didn't move. Then she glanced up at Pamela.

Elizabeth, catching the nanny's swift glance, shook her head slightly. Ailsa might be only five, but she already knew the art of playing her nanny off against her mother. Where does she get it from? Elizabeth wondered. Graham had once protested, "Darling, you're projecting far too much into the motives of a five-year-old." For a moment she wished he were here to handle the situation. But of course he'd already left this morning and, anyway, was more often than not away, all the more so during the last months as the shadows had lengthened across their marriage.

Pamela's quiet voice broke in. "Run and say goodbye to your mummy, Ailsa."

Obediently, Ailsa ran over to Elizabeth. Not because I asked her to, Elizabeth thought exasperatedly, but because Pamela did.

Then she leaned forward and hugged the little girl. "I love you, darling. Now go along with Nanny!"

Ailsa had neither replied nor hugged her back. I wish I knew what to do with her, Elizabeth thought, getting up and watching the two children trot across the hall with Pamela. Duncan, sandy haired like his father, was uncomplicated, happy and good at whatever he undertook, from schoolwork to cricket and rugby, and Ailsa was so different in every way.

When they'd gone out into the square Elizabeth collected her own coat, bag and tote bag from the hall coatroom. After a brief pause she placed them on the hall chair and went through the door that led down a flight of stairs to the kitchens.

Mary, the tall Irish cook, was staring into a large round pot on the stove. Ellen, the second housemaid, was sitting at the table under the window giving onto the area way, drinking her tea and reading the tabloid *News of the World*.

In answer to her "Good morning," Mary turned and Ellen stood. "Good morning, my lady," they said.

"I just came to remind you, Mary, that Sir Graham will not be back tonight, as he had originally thought, so I'll be eating alone."

"Yes, my lady. I was planning an Irish stew."

Elizabeth smiled. "As you know, I always like that."

As she was retrieving her coat and bags from the hall chair, she remembered the letter that had been left in the breakfast room. She hadn't paid much attention to it, but the letter carried an American stamp, and even at that distance across the room, the handwriting looked familiar.

Reentering the breakfast room, where Paget was busy clearing away, Elizabeth picked up the envelope from the side table. On closer inspection there was no question about the sharply angled handwriting. She would have known it anywhere even if the envelope had not carried the familiar College Hill address in Providence.

"Anything I can do, my lady?" the maid said.

"No, thank you, Paget, I just remembered I wanted to take this letter with me."

Hailing a taxi, Elizabeth gave the driver the address of the publishers, Houghton and Lord, off St. James's Street, where for nearly twenty years she had worked. Then she sat back and opened the letter.

Dear Elizabeth:
    I have just been told by our lawyer, Jon Treadwell, that a living trust established by

my father sixty-five years ago is due to be
opened on October 26th. I expect you, Robbie, Caleb, and Terry to be present along with
your mother and me and, I am told, my cousin
James Beresford and his wife and children.

I have known for years that a trust such as
this existed, having been informed of it by my
father before he died. I asked the obvious questions, of course, but have never been told
what is in it. I am, however, reasonably sure
from occasional hints and dropped information that the trust represents a considerable sum
of money to be distributed to the family,
something I am sure we can all use.

The one rule laid down is that we are all to
be there, so I will expect you at Summerstoke
on or before October 26th. An identical letter is
being sent to your sister and brothers. I look
forward to seeing you.

Your father,
Robert Beresford

Well, Elizabeth reflected, sitting back and staring at
the familiar Belgravia streets they were passing, with
things as they were between herself and Graham, the
money would be welcome. If there were a divorce,
she thought with pain and anger, she was reasonably
sure Graham would be generous. He always had been.
But she didn't want to have to depend on his generosity. She wanted something she'd never had before: her
own money. She would, therefore, do what in twenty
years she'd never done despite the pleas of both parents in their different ways: go back to her own country and her childhood home.

As she made the decision, she felt the buried anger
at her father surge within her. For two decades it had
kept her from even considering a return home. But
now there was the trust—and the independence it
promised.

Her next thought, as the taxi neared St. James's Street, was that a trust that old—sixty-five years—must surely have accumulated a lot of money.

Robbie's letter was sent to his law office in downtown Providence and was brought in with the rest of the morning mail by his secretary. Recognizing his father's handwriting, Robbie wondered why it hadn't been sent to his home. When he finished reading he sat there for a moment. He had known that such a trust existed because his father had told him, but he had also known that none of the other siblings had been told. "You're here, the others aren't, and you're the oldest, which is why I'm telling you. I don't know what's in the trust or when it's going to fall due, and I'd just as soon you'd keep this information to yourself." And, of course, Robbie had.

His first thought was: Now maybe I'll really have enough for the campaign.

He had announced his candidacy for the governor's race more as an act of faith than anything else and because his wife kept urging him to run. "Rhode Island needs some honest public officials," Jenny had said. "I think if you put your heart in it, you'd have a good chance of winning. I'll do everything I can to help." And Robbie knew she would. Behind the soft, pretty southern girl he had married was a woman of drive and ambition.

With the promise of money from the trust he could augment his publicity, appearances, commercials, ads ... On an impulse he picked up the phone. With her numerous activities, and with both their children in boarding school, Jenny would most probably be out. God knows, he thought, she was on enough committees, and that wasn't counting her shelter and feeding the homeless schedules connected with St. Michael's. Still—

"Hello," he heard her voice.

"Jenny? Guess what I just got." He read her the

letter. When he finished he heard her short, characteristic intake of breath.

"Robbie, that's wonderful! With that coming up, you'll be able to hire a decent political staff for the first time!"

He laughed. "You're right. I could use somebody—maybe as a consultant or something—who really knows the political ropes." His thoughts immediately went to Kate Malloy, a local and very savvy columnist whom he and Jenny had met at a benefit.

"Who did you have in mind?" Jenny asked.

He hesitated. "I'm not sure. I'll have to think about it." He stopped, astonished at his lie. He had never before lied to Jenny or, except for the odd white lie, to anyone else.

Her voice was warm and approving. "You do that—think about it, I mean. It could make all the difference!"

Robbie's instinctive caution came to the fore. "Of course, I don't know, and I'm sure Dad doesn't know, how much the windfall amounts to. Still, after sixty-five years—!"

"Go for it, Robbie!"

When he hung up he thought about asking his secretary to get him the newspaper where the reporter's column appeared. Then he reached for his own directory. When a cheerful male voice answered "Providence Times," Robbie asked for Kate Malloy without really thinking he'd get her. Somehow he thought that anyone who wrote in the tough, smart way she did about the people in local politics would be out interviewing and digging up the dirt. So he was mildly surprised when a female voice said briskly, "Kate Malloy."

"Miss Malloy? I'm Robert Beresford Junior—"

"The aspiring Republican candidate in person!"

He hesitated, then said mildly and with a smile in his voice, "Liberal Republican."

"Ah yes. Pro-choice, anti-new tax, less waste, but somehow more money for schools."

Robbie was amused. "You've been reading our literature."

"I read all the candidates' literature."

"Of course. By the way, I think we've met."

"At that ghastly benefit!"

Robbie found himself slightly shocked and then amused. The benefit in question was one of the truly sacred causes to Rhode Islanders. But she was absolutely right. The road-show company of a Broadway musical that had provided the excuse for the benefit had been a letdown. "I think that's a fair estimate. Can we meet for a drink?"

"That sounds like a proposition."

"It is."

"All right. Where and when?"

He was about to suggest one of his clubs, then suddenly switched to a popular but rather raffish bar not far from his office. "How about Peter's Pub? Do you know it?"

"Very well."

"This afternoon at five?"

"I'll see you then."

Robbie replaced the receiver with satisfaction and a hint of excitement. What was it he'd heard one of his legal colleagues say recently apropos of a piece of dirt Kate had written in her column about one of his clients? Something like "There's not a cockroach—nor its place of burial in Providence—that that gal doesn't know about, damn her!"

Robbie linked his hands behind his head and stared out the window at the river, at College Hill rising above it on the other side, and at the roofs of the buildings of Brown University. For the first time his run for the governorship actually looked promising.

The hole in his back was healing nicely, but Caleb still felt weak and knew that if he stood up too quickly, as he had before, he could be hit with tremors and sweating, a legacy of the fever that had followed the wound.

He glanced around the room—not much more than a cabin—and wondered where he was. It was no use asking, he'd tried that. Even after all these months with the guerrillas, writing their proclamations and posters and letters, marching with them, hiding out from the soldiers and police who seemed to have informers everywhere, after all the nights with Julie— even after all that they still didn't trust him.

Well, he argued to himself, why should they? His commitment to their cause, however cataclysmic in his life, had come after more than two years of serving as a loyal priest, keeping his growing radicalism and disaffection from the Church under wraps from Father Matthew and the government officials and soldiers that had a way of dropping by the mountain parish, unannounced. From the point of view of his fellow revolutionaries, his conversion to their cause could so easily be yet another clever device to betray them, as they had been betrayed before.

The door opened and the man he had heard addressed as José came in carrying what looked like a letter.

"*Buenos días,* José," he said. "*Que pasa?*"

He didn't really expect a reply and he didn't get one. José had been one of his nurses and had been gentle and thorough. But he never answered any of the many questions Caleb had thrown at him. "You have to realize," Julie had said when he complained to her a few weeks previously, "that they're intensely aware you could betray anyone you saw—what he looked like, how his voice sounded, what he said. And if you did, they—and probably their families—would be killed and everything we are all working for destroyed."

"Is that what you think of me?" he'd asked angrily.

"That I'm some kind of traitor? That I've left the priesthood and the church only to become a Judas?"

"No, Caleb, it isn't. But if anybody wanted to infiltrate the movement it'd be one of the best ways of doing it. You have to see that." When he didn't reply, she came over and rubbed her cheek against his.

As always, his body responded even when he didn't want to. "I don't even know where we are," he grumbled, glancing through the window at the moist green undergrowth and wet earth. "We could be anywhere between the capital and the coast."

"Better that you don't." She pressed her slender body against his. "The less you know the safer you are."

They'd moved him twice since then. At a guess, looking at the foliage, sniffing the drier air, he knew they'd gone back up, away from the coast, nearer to Guatemala City. He hadn't seen Julie for a week.

He stared at the letter José was holding out and recognized with astonishment the handwriting on the envelope. Robert Beresford Senior's handwriting, angular and elegant, was unmistakable. Caleb wasn't as surprised that his father had written to him as the fact that the letter was being delivered to him here—wherever here was. He had been out of the Church for more than eight months. No other letter, addressed to him at the community where he had served, had been brought to him.

He snatched it from José and tore it open.

When he had finished reading it he sat back in the bed. Money, he thought. They were always in desperate need of money in the movement. There was never enough for arms, medicine, sometimes even food. He'd go back up to Providence and collect his share of the trust and come back down.

His next thought was, if he gave his entire inheritance to the movement, maybe then they'd start to trust him.

The door opened. He glanced up and his heart gave a leap in his chest, causing him both pain and joy.

"Hi," Julie said, coming in, carrying a satchel stuffed with paper. She was tall, blond, and leggy, the complete Californian in appearance. She had penetrated his guard as no other woman ever had. And it was not what he sometimes called her surfboard good looks that had done it. It was the passion she brought to the cause they now both served.

He waved the letter at her. "Guess what!" he said.

She came over and kissed him. "Tell me."

He handed her the letter.

She scanned it quickly. "Wow!" she said, and glanced up. "Do you have any idea how much it will be?"

"None. I didn't even know it existed. But whatever it is will go to our work here."

She leaned over and pressed her lips against his, then lay against him on the bed.

After a while they drew apart, and she sat up. "I have two bits of news." Leaning toward the floor, she fished a newspaper from her satchel there. "That's your brother, isn't it?"

It was the *Providence Times*. The headline sprawled the width of the first page: BERESFORD JR. THROWS IN HIS HAT.

"Yes," Caleb said. "That's Robbie, and it's no big surprise. He's a straight arrow: liberal Republican, vestryman of his local Episcopal Church, member of all the right clubs in Providence, Boston and New York. In other words," Caleb added bitterly, "the favored son, the family success story."

"I always thought your family was Catholic—like you!"

"Only half of it. My old man, in a moment's oversight, fell in love with a Catholic." Caleb scanned the article. "Where did you get this?"

"At one of those newsstands that carry half the important papers in the world."

"Then you must have been in the city."

"I have. We had business there."

Caleb wanted to ask, what business? And who's "we"? But he wasn't sure she would tell him, and he didn't want the discomfort of knowing she was lying to him. So he said, "What's your second bit of news?"

"Did you know that at least some of your family's wealth is invested in our own dear Guatemala, thus propping up the regime and policies of the *presidente* we love to hate." She paused. "Considering the recent furor in the States over the government-ordered killings here—like the uproar over the murder of the priests in El Salvador—I wonder what would happen to your brother's run for governor if that came out."

Terry picked up her father's letter along with the rest of her mail when she got back to her apartment building in Boston and opened her mailbox.

Her first thought, accompanied by the usual mixture of irritation and guilt, was that the inevitable had at last happened to her mother. Sighing, she opened the envelope on her way up the stairs to her apartment and then stopped. There on the carpeted steps, she read her father's news about the trust.

Holding the open letter in her hand, she proceeded up one more flight and slipped her key into her door. A doctoral student and a teaching fellow in women's studies at Boston University, she was also heavily involved with her activities as secretary of the Women's League, one of the coming organizations in the national women's movement.

As she turned on the light a ginger and white cat jumped off her sofa, stretched and came toward her at a stately pace, and the. phone started to ring.

"Greetings, Emily," she said, bending down and scratching the cat behind her ear. Then she picked up the phone on one of the bookcases serving as tables at the ends of the sofa.

"Hello?" She leaned over, holding out her finger to

Emily, who took a rather deliberate attitude toward her owner after she had been out all day. Slowly, Emily sniffed at the finger, then rubbed her jaw and neck against it. Terry felt the purr beginning to vibrate inside the small, soft body. "Yes, I'm sorry, Emily," Terry said. "Everything took longer than I thought." Then, aware that she had gotten no response on the phone, "Hello?" she said again into the receiver. When there was still no response, she put the receiver back. "Wrong number, I suppose."

But as soon as she started taking off her raincoat, the phone rang again.

"Yes?" she repeated impatiently, wondering which of her students was trying to get in touch with her, if it was a student.

"Terry?"

Terry recognized the slurred voice immediately.

"Hello, Mom." She tried hard to sound welcoming.

"How are you?" As if I didn't know, she thought.

"All right. Did you know Elizabeth might be coming from England? For the reading of the trust. And Caleb from Guatemala. You'll be here, won't you?"

"Of course."

There was a pause. I should think of something else to talk to her about, Terry thought.

"What do you plan to do with the money?" Her mother's voice sounded, if anything, thicker. Terry wondered if she'd taken a swallow of her drink during the pause. And then she knew she didn't have to wonder. Of course she had.

"I don't know. I haven't thought about it," Terry said. It was weird, but she hadn't. And then as though the mere mention of the money had galvanized her, the idea hit with full force: She'd establish a home where girls who found themselves pregnant could go for counsel and a time to think, without being constantly bugged by parents and priests harping on the wickedness of abortion. Of course there were branches of Planned Parenthood and other similar organizations, but not the kind of long-term place she herself would have been so glad for eight years ago.

She became aware that the phone was registering nothing but a dial tone. "Mom? Mom?" With exasperation she pushed down the button and then dialed the number of her parents' home in College Hill. Her father picked up the phone. "Hello?"

"Hi, Dad. I got the letter. I'll be there. October twenty-sixth is—what?—two months off. Mom called and said Elizabeth and Caleb would be coming."

"Money is a powerful attractor." Robert Senior's voice had a dry, slightly satirical note.

"That's true," Terry said. She decided she wouldn't discuss her plan with anyone for the moment, not until it was better worked out and she knew how much money was involved for each of them. But she couldn't resist asking, "Do you have any idea how much money we'll get?"

"None whatsoever. However, if my father put some in a trust sixty-five years ago, what with inflation and even the most modest return, it should by now be a gratifying amount for all of us."

And then, because she still felt guilty, Terry asked, "How's Mom?"

"Didn't you talk to her a few minutes ago? I picked up the phone down here and thought I heard you. How was she then?"

Terry paused a moment, then said bluntly, "Drunk."

"Are you surprised?"

"I suppose not. But for God's sake, how many rehabs has she been to?"

"The last time I bothered to count, about six."

"They work for other people. AA works for other people. Why not Mom?"

"I don't know the answer to that, Terry. As you can imagine, I've wondered about it myself. By the way, the meeting for the trust will be in Summerstoke."

"Yeah. The letter said that."

"Just thought I'd remind you. Anything else?"

"No. Thanks." And Terry hung up. Any other father, she thought angrily, would ask, How's the work
coming? How's the dissertation shaping up? How
far've you gotten with it? Then she pulled herself up.
That was one of those myths that girls believed: that
fathers were loving creatures concerned about their
daughters' careers.

One of her earliest memories was hanging over the
stairs, listening to her father on the phone to her
older—much older—brother.

"That was pretty outstanding, Robbie! Magna cum
laude! We're all proud of you!" As always when he
spoke to Robbie, his voice lacked the faintly satirical
and/or sarcastic undertone that was otherwise present.

Six-year-old Terry, coming down the stairs, said
loudly, "I'm going to get a magna ... magna—" She
couldn't remember the rest.

Her father, replacing the receiver, looked up.
"We'll see."

When Terry had brought home her summa cum laude
and shown it to her father, what had he said? "Ah,
in women's studies." And then he had changed the
subject.

Robert Beresford put down the phone after his conversation with Terry and waited while one of his wife's
golden long-haired dachshunds darted across the floor
toward the front door, followed by two others, one of
them elderly, wheezing and waddling. All three were
brought up in the rear by Maureen, Matilda Beresford's maid. And/or keeper, Robert thought cynically.

"How is Mrs. Beresford this evening?" he nevertheless asked politely.

The young woman from Ireland took some dog
leashes from the hall closet. "Not bad, sir," she said.

They both knew what she meant.

Finally Robert said, "I'm glad she has you,
anyway."

"Aye," Maureen said, putting leashes on the two younger dogs. And then she surprised her employer's husband by saying, "She needs someone on her side."

Robert watched her while she opened the front door and let the three dogs and herself out. For a moment he wondered if she was being deliberately impertinent, feeling secure in the knowledge that Matilda Beresford, that wreck of a woman, would be helpless without her. Then he shrugged. The matter wasn't worth worrying about.

His mind shifted to his favorite child. The money would mean that Robbie could make his run for the governorship. His heart quickened as he thought of it: Robbie, so like him in every way, but without the taint, the curse, that had distorted his own life. The great wealth that the first Beresford, his grandfather, had made from his invention and then invested wisely was still keeping them all in reasonable comfort. But the money wasn't quite as plentiful as it used to be. Running two houses, one on College Hill and the other in the country, was taking more and more each year. Some of the principal had been used. The trust would help a lot. Even so, even if it meant pinching, he'd give his own portion to Robbie if it would make the difference between winning and losing first the nomination and then the election.

Robert decided he might as well go into dinner alone and take a book to read.

Earlier that evening, Matilda Beresford had sat in the sitting room next to her bedroom, her hands on the arms of her armchair, her legs sprawled out under her full-length robe, her on-the-rocks glass on the Sheraton table beside her. She knew she ought to have a coaster under the glass to protect the table, for which her in-laws had once paid a vast sum. But she did not feel like getting up, and she had no wish to attract the attention of Maureen, who was tidying up the bedroom and would make some comment about the dark, undiluted whiskey in the glass.

"Won't you be wanting a dash of soda in that?" she'd say, bringing the soda over, knowing perfectly well that Matilda wanted no such thing, but counting on shame to make her acquiese.

Matilda kept her eye on the glass because she knew if she withdrew her attention for more than a minute Maureen would slip in and somehow manage to tip out some of the whiskey and put in water or even, God help her, some ginger ale, which was near enough the same color. And if Matilda woke up or came to or suddenly took notice and asked her what she thought she was doing, she would answer that she was just freshening the drink.

"In Al-Anon they tell you not to do that to the family member who's drinking," Matilda once said to her.

"And how would you be knowing that," Maureen replied, "seeing as how you won't go to AA, as the doctor keeps telling you?"

In front of Matilda the television screen showed a man, a haunted look on his face, being chased by another holding a gun. Matilda had no idea what she was watching, but by keeping her eyes on the screen, she warded off unnecessary conversation.

After a minute or so Maureen came into the room and started making minor adjustments to books, pictures and ornaments. Matilda knew she was simply marking time until she could remove Matilda's glass and put her to bed, and most of the time she liked having Maureen there. It kept at bay the terrible sense of isolation that could so devastate her. Also, Maureen was Irish, not Irish–American, but the real article from Ireland, and Matilda found that infinitely comforting. Maureen did not sit in arrogant WASP judgment like her husband.

"Maureen, that'll be all now. There's nothing really more to be done. Tell Mr. Beresford I won't be down to dinner, that my headache has got far worse and that you'd given me a pill and put me to bed."

Maureen hesitated, wondering whether she should suggest that the mistress should make an effort. But she knew Matilda was in no condition to do that. And ordering coffee from the kitchen was already useless.

At that moment Maureen spied the naked glass on the table. "Ach!" she said and picked up a coaster from the desk. "You know you shouldn't put the glass down without this."

As she came over, Matilda snatched up the glass and held it in her hand where it would be safe. Maureen slapped the coaster down, first ostentatiously wiping the surface where the glass had been.

"I don't need you anymore," Matilda said coldly. "You can go."

"Very well, ma'am. Shall I take the dogs?"

"Yes, all right. If ... after they've eaten and been out, they want to come back, then you can let them in.

It was a risk. She didn't know what condition she might be in. But the dogs were the only beings—with the occasional exception of Maureen herself—whom she wanted around when things had gone this far.

When Maureen and the dogs had gone, Matilda pulled the letters the three older children had written saying they would be at the summer home, Summerstoke, on October 26, and reread them. For the first time in years they'd all be together. All, of course, except Mark. Matilda poured some more into her glass from the bottle hidden in back of the cushion behind her. With all her might she tried to hold the agony at bay, summoning the fantasy ...

It always started the same way. She would see Mark again. He would be older, often only a little older, perhaps nine, sometimes twelve or sixteen, occasionally a young man in his twenties, although as he got older in the fantasy, his face would be less clear. His hair would be the way it had been—dark and wavy— and his eyes would be blue. Those were things that wouldn't change. Since he was so plainly a Beresford rather than a McGarrett, he would also be tall for his age—whatever his age happened to be—and lean.

She would be in a strange city somewhere, sitting in a hotel lobby or on a promenade and would know that the young male figure coming toward her was Mark, her son, that he was alive and well and undamaged by the monster who kidnapped him. He would recognize her even before she recognized him. He would hold out his arms and run toward her, and he would tell her that what had happened in Shephard's, the big department store, that day a week before Christmas twenty-six years ago was in no way her fault. . . .

But as always when she came to that part, no matter how much she had drunk, she knew how untrue her fantasy was, and the corkscrew knives of guilt started twisting in her.

It was her fault. All her fault, and all the drink in the world couldn't blot that out. . . .

He arrived in Providence in the early morning. The appointment was for ten o'clock, and the managing editor had given him instructions on how to get to the paper. He was disappointed it was not Providence's leading newspaper. The main thing was, it was in Providence. Stopping the car, he stared up at the state house and across the muddy trickle below to the houses rising up College Hill, waiting to see if some fragment of the past would look familiar, if anything would jog his memory. But, as so often before when he tried to open the locked doors of those early years, there was only a blank, nothing.

They hadn't promised him the job, but his experience on other papers and the clippings he brought with him were good. As a teacher had once said to him, whatever else he was or was not, he was a good writer. The paper he'd just left was sorry to lose him, though, as one of his colleagues said as they were having a last drink in the bar, he hardly qualified as a warm, fuzzy friend. But then the person who said that—a woman—had, like others before her, tried to make him into just such a friend, only to encounter the seamless wall that had, as long as he could remember, served to keep the rest of the world out.

"It makes a person wonder what the hell is going on behind it," the woman said.

Untouched, he stared at her. "You wouldn't want to know."

He could, of course, have told her: It was a consuming rage that had enabled him to survive a brutal upbringing and had driven him to seek out those whose arrogant carelessness had brought about the catastrophe in his life. His driving ambition was to prove who he was—and to pay them back a hundredfold.

THE
FAMILY

CHAPTER
2

Her first thought was he was the handsomest man she'd ever seen—tall, lean, blue-eyed and patrician looking.

"Who is that?" she asked her friend and hostess, her roommate from Wellesley.

Ginny turned her head. "Oh, that's Robert Beresford. Obviously back from the wars, since he's still in uniform."

"God, he's good looking!"

Ginny glanced at her friend and smiled a little. "Yes, he is. He's also rich and Beresford's a good name around here. Want to meet him?"

Matilda hesitated, the ever-present question in her mind: Would he find her attractive? Her father, Patrick McGarrett, a true Irishman, had never believed in mincing words: "You're going to have to watch your weight, Mat, me girl. Fat runs in our family, and it's beginning to show in you already."

"It is not," her mother replied indignantly. "Matilda's got a lovely figure—shapely and curvaceous, we used to call it."

"Yes, well, a few pounds more and fat is what people will be starting to call it."

Matilda had fled from the room so she could cry and burn over her humiliation in peace. But her mother joined her almost immediately. "Pay no attention, Mattie! All you have to do is think of all those young men who are forever calling you up and wanting a date."

"Why does he always make me feel so . . . so ugly?"

"Because he may be a brilliant engineer and made pots of money building bridges and God knows what else around the world, but about people he's got the brains of an ant. I should know! So stop thinking about your father and start remembering Jeff O'Banion and Brian Mahaffey and George Mulroony. If we didn't have such a big living room, we'd never fit in all the flowers they send you with their little love notes!"

It was true. There were not only Jeff and Brian and George but quite a few others, graduates of Notre Dame and Boston College and St. John's, all until recently in the army, the navy, or the air force, helping to defeat the Germans and the Japanese. So she did what her mother wanted and cheered up a little. But she also went on a diet and made sure she had no more than three glasses of champagne at the New York deb dances she went to during the season. It was hard, because she loved wine even more than she did food. Food made her fat, but wine made her feel attractive, sexy, and witty.

Then Ginny invited her to Providence for a dance. And she saw Robert Beresford.

"For heaven's sake," Ginny said now, "if you think he's that good looking, why are you hesitating? What've you got to lose?"

What Matilda couldn't quite explain was that Jeff and Brian and George and the others were a known quantity—Catholic boys from good Catholic colleges. After she'd gone to Wellesley, she'd met other kinds, of course. But none of them had caused her heart to beat. She knew already that Robert Beresford would be another matter altogether.

"All right," she said. "Let's go meet him."

But he was coming across the room toward them. "Hi, Ginny," he said, his eyes on Matilda.

"Matilda, this is Robert Beresford, an old friend of our family's. Robert, this is Matilda McGarrett from New York."

Robert held out his hand. "Hello, Matilda from New York. I'm glad to meet you."

She put her hand in his and smiled, her doubts assuaged. "And I'm glad to meet you."

Robert was the best dancer she'd ever glided around the floor with.

"You're very good," she murmured at one point during their fifth dance, her cheek against the top button of his uniform.

He smiled down. "Only because I'm with you."

She knew it wasn't true, but she loved him saying it. After the dance they went to a nightclub and after that to a popular, crowded bar.

"I should take you back to Ginny's," he said at some point, "but I don't want to."

"Neither do I."

At his request she stayed with Ginny an extra week. She and Robert went out every night. One evening they had dinner with his parents in their beautiful home on Benevolent Street in College Hill, not far from Ginny's family home. The Beresford house made a lasting impression on Matilda. She had grown up in New York in a sprawling co-op on one of the most expensive blocks on Park Avenue, and had visited many town houses and apartments of her school friends. But she had never been in any home as elegant as Robert's and, confronting for the first time the distance between mere luxury and elegance, was a little awed by it.

The walls were filled with large and small portraits dating back two hundred years. In addition to those, there were other paintings.

"What beautiful horses!" she exclaimed once, standing in front of an oil painting.

"Yes, they are nice, aren't they?" Robert's mother said. A slender, distinguished woman, she reminded

Matilda of the old-fashioned meaning of the word *lady*. "He does them well."

Who was "he"? Matilda wondered. With anyone else she would have asked. But she found the question freezing on her tongue.

The older Beresfords were courtesy personified and did their best to make Matilda feel welcome. Nevertheless, for the first time since she'd met Robert, she felt, rather than simply knew, the difference in their backgrounds.

"You're Protestant, aren't you?" she asked suddenly on the way home.

"Yes." Robert, who was driving, glanced at her. "Does that bother you?"

"No," she said, and knew she was telling the truth. "It doesn't a bit." But she also knew the problem would bother her father. I'll worry about that later, she thought, and then forgot all about it, because Robert turned down a side road and stopped the car. Putting his arm around her, he pulled her to him and kissed her. It was a long, passionate kiss.

"This sounds insane," he said, breathing rapidly. "A week ago I didn't know you. But I—I've fallen in love with you, Matilda."

"Oh, Robert! And I've fallen in love with you!"

He didn't paw her or fumble at her dress the way Jeff and Brian had. But there was no doubt how he felt. Their kisses grew longer and more passionate. Much, much later on the way home, cuddled inside his arm, she asked suddenly, "Robert, who painted that picture of the horses in the dining room?"

"Stubbs. The English painter, George Stubbs."

She didn't get back to Ginny's until nearly morning.

When she returned to New York, Robert followed her and stayed there with a friend for ten days. The McGarretts, of course, invited him to dinner, and Matilda sat pridefully and watched how impressed they were. At the same time she also knew that her father, who had always had cozy conversations with her previous boyfriends, full of references to shared Irish and Catholic jokes, was far stiffer with Robert.

"Why doesn't he call himself Bob?" Patrick grumbled the next morning.

"Why should he?" Margaret McGarrett said. "Robert's his name."

"And mine's Patrick, but my friends call me Pat or Paddy."

That evening, the night before he had to go back to Providence, Robert proposed and Matilda, beside herself with joy, accepted.

Predictably, Patrick McGarrett was not that happy. "Yes, I know he's got money and had a good war record and comes from one of those posh WASP families that have been grinding the Irish down for the past eight hundred years!"

"This country isn't two hundred years old yet!" Matilda's mother protested.

"And what did his ancestors do for ours a hundred years ago when the Irish were dying on the roads during the famine? Bloody all!"

"But what's that got to do with Robert?" Matilda protested. She knew she'd have a hard time with her father, and she was having it.

"There's something about him I don't like," Patrick said, switching ground.

"And what would that be, Patrick McGarrett?" Matilda's mother asked. "Other, of course, than the fact that he's a Protestant!"

"I don't know. If I knew, I'd tell you. And you're right about the Protestant bit. I want my girl to marry a Catholic. At least then you know what the rules are and what to expect. With these Protestants you never know!"

"You sound like a bigot!" Matilda protested.

"You want to know about bigots? Listen, me fine lady, sometime when you can spare a moment, go to the library and look up some of the fashionable magazines of eighty or ninety years ago. I've seen copies!

Cartoons—famous ones by some feller named Thomas Nast—with the Irish drawn with the faces of monkeys and apes and all speaking with a brogue!"

"I don't believe it," Matilda's mother said. "Where did you see those?"

"At a book convention of some sort. I was visiting in the town and got a pass, so I went."

"And they were showing anti-Irish cartoons?"

"No ... well ... some Jewish organization was there with a booth and they were showing what prejudice was, and I guess they wanted people to know they weren't the only ones that got it. Anyway, I saw those cartoons there, and I'm not liable to forget them!"

"This has nothing to do with Robert and me!" Matilda said.

"I knew something like this would happen when you talked me into sending you to that fancy Protestant college instead of a decent Catholic one."

"You were perfectly willing for her to go," Matilda's mother pointed out. "In fact, you boasted about it to all our friends!"

"More fool me!"

In the end, though, he gave in. And Matilda knew that for all his bluster some small part of him was proud of the fact that his daughter, the granddaughter of an immigrant hod carrier, was going to marry into the New England aristocracy.

"Actually, sir, we aren't really," Robert said to his future father-in-law that night when they were all at dinner, "not like the Adamses or the Aldriches or the Eliots who go as far back as the country does. My grandfather invented a device connected with mill machinery that earned a lot of money and made it easy for his descendents."

"You're near enough for us," Patrick said grudgingly.

Not long before the wedding, he asked Matilda suddenly, "Does he treat you well, Mat? I mean, with love and that kind of thing?"

She was surprised at the question. If anything, she would have expected him to worry about whether the Protestant outsider had tried to "go too far." "Of course, Daddy. Are you still worrying about him being a Protestant New Englander?"

Patrick didn't answer right away. Then, "It's not that."

"Then what is it?"

"I don't know! I told you, I don't know these people!" Then he added suddenly, "He seems to me cold."

Matilda, remembering the ardent kisses, wanted to laugh. But she knew—or thought she knew—what her father meant. "In some ways he's much more reserved than the boys I've known. But I like that. He isn't always trying to swarm all over me."

Her father's face grew red. "Do you mean to tell me you've—"

"No," Matilda said. "You know I wouldn't, not before the wedding. Anyway, I thought you were worried about his being cold. Now you're ready to get a gun if we'd ... we'd gone all the way before the wedding."

"That's no way to talk to your father."

Since that was always Patrick's final resort after being rousted in an argument by either his wife or his daughter or both, Matilda didn't pay much attention. But she did go over, put her arms around him and give him a kiss.

"Get along with you," Patrick said. But he hugged her back.

The wedding was in St. Ignatius Loyola Church on Park Avenue at 84th Street in New York City, and there was a bishop, a friend of Patrick's, among the clergy.

When Robert had been confronted with the papers he'd have to sign, agreeing that all the children of the marriage should be baptized and brought up in the

Catholic Church, he looked at Matilda and said dryly, "I take it this is a crucial part of the bargain."

"Yes, I'm afraid it is," she replied anxiously. If he balked they would have to elope, and if they eloped and were married before a judge or an indeterminate Protestant minister, how could it be a real marriage like one blessed and solemnized before the high altar?

Robert gave her the look—cool, a little distant— that sometimes reminded her of her father's strictures about Yankee aristocrats being a different breed. Then he signed.

She could never remember with certainty the moment when she knew beyond a doubt that something was wrong with the sexual aspect of their marriage. For one thing, she had no basis on which to make any sort of judgment. She had always taken her own parents' marriage for granted, as, indeed, did most of the girls with whom she'd gone to school at the Sacred Heart Academy. Divorce was something you read about in the papers, something that people in Hollywood were always getting. But not people she or her family knew.

Although she'd never discussed it with anyone, sex was a subject she knew almost nothing about. Her mother had given her a Church-approved book that outlined the facts: he did this, she did that, nine months later out came a baby. What the book mostly discussed was the holiness of the sex act, which was God's way of providing human beings with children, and the wickedness of contraception, which divided the sex act from its only lawful end.

Her father, as usual, had summarized the whole teaching in his blunt way. Shortly before the wedding he wandered into the room when she and her mother were edging up to a discussion of the book's contents. When he came in, their comments became even more oblique.

"Ach!" Patrick said after a few minutes of walking

around the room and listening and fidgeting. "It's simple. If you don't want the responsibility you can't have the fun!"

"Patrick!" Margaret indignantly said to her husband. "That's no way to talk to a bride!"

Patrick walked up to Matilda. "Listen, me girl, your husband will tell you and . . . and show you everything you ought to know. There's no need to bother your head with it now!"

So, relieved, she'd let the subject go. Robert would teach her.

And she was sure he'd done his best, making love with tenderness and passion. The trouble was, it was always over before anything happened to her. She loved what went before: the long, passionate kisses, the closeness, the love talk. But for her it seemed unconnected with what followed. Shy, living with unfamiliar people, she couldn't bring herself to discuss the matter with anyone. It'll get better, she told herself. But as time passed, she became aware that Robert was growing a little less patient. The lovemaking became more hurried, and the nights when he made love grew further apart.

Then Robert, Jr., forever after called Robbie, was born.

Matilda never forgot the look on Robert's face when he came into the hospital room. She was immensely tired and a little woozy from the painkiller they had finally given her once the baby was definitely on its way out, but she didn't fail to notice the wonder, joy, and pride on Robert's face as he caught sight of his son in the crib beside Matilda's bed.

An added joy of Robbie's advent was that somehow the marriage seemed restored. Robert stood proudly by when the local priest poured a few drops of holy water on Robbie's forehead and christened him Robert Anthony. As the drops hit his face, the baby let out a bellow.

"That'll be the devil coming out of him," Patrick

said with satisfaction. He and Margaret had been invited up for the christening.

The priest glanced up. "Quite so," he said with a small, wintry smile.

Robert didn't look up, just kept his eyes on his son.

He and Matilda became happy and fulfilled young parents, absorbed in discussions about school, prep school, even college.

"But Robbie's not yet two!" Matilda said, laughing, one evening at dinner when they were entertaining other young parents of their group.

One of Robert's Harvard friends, now a close business associate, spoke up. "It's never too early, Matilda. I've already entered Jack in St. Paul's."

"Robbie might want to go to Princeton," Matilda quipped. One of the guests had brought an excellent and expensive wine, and, as always, it gave her self-confidence.

Robert looked up at her, amused. "Certainly not," he said.

With the death of Robert's father a year later, they moved into the family home in College Hill and, during the summers, into Summerstoke, the rambling, ambitious mansion Peter Beresford had put up on Narragansett Bay. For a few years Robert's mother, Elizabeth Beresford, shared the houses with them. For all her native reserve, she was always kind, happily baby-sat at any hour of the day or evening and took immense care never to seem in the way. But Matilda remained a little in awe of her, fearful of seeming naive or ignorant in front of her mother-in-law with her air of breeding, her dry humor, and witty tongue. Robert and his mother, Matilda noticed, though noticeably undemonstrative with each other (in contrast to the McGarretts), could spend hours at the dinner table exchanging quips, quotes, and amused, often faintly derisory, comments about anything from politics and society to religion and motherhood. Often one or the other would try to draw her in, but her fumbling

contributions would more often than not come off
sounding clumsy rather than clever. There would be
a silence, then Elizabeth would invariably say, "Yes,
of course, you're quite right," and Matilda would instantly feel stupid and inept.

Once she said to Robert, "Your family's not very
demonstrative, is it?"

"No, we don't go in much for hugs and kisses."

"Not even when you were a little boy?"

"No, we never found it necessary. We knew how
we felt."

Matilda wondered how a little boy would know that.
But she said nothing.

Nevertheless, a daughter was born two years after
Robbie. Matilda, who had secretly wanted to name
the little girl Margaret after her own mother, acceded
readily to Robert's request to have her christened
Elizabeth. Unlike Robbie, Elizabeth arrived early
when Robert was still on the West Coast examining
family investments and real estate.

When he got back and walked into the hospital
room, his new daughter was enjoying a snack, suckling
noisily at Matilda's swollen breast. Matilda looked up
and smiled. "Welcome back, darling. I'm afraid Elizabeth got ahead of our schedule." Then, a moment
later, after she saw the strange look on his face,
"What's the matter?"

"Nothing." Recovering himself, he strolled over and
sat down on the bed. "I'm just sorry not to have been
here for the blessed event. How are you, m'dear?"

"Fine. Everything went like clockwork. Even
though she was earlier than Robbie was, she seems
bigger and noisier, although the nurses tell me she's
a shade lighter. As a girl should be, shouldn't you,
darling?" Matilda gazed lovingly at the scarlet-faced
baby, who suckled greedily and then gave a burp. Matilda glanced up and caught the expression she'd seen
before on her husband's face. "The trip go all right?"
she asked, concerned.

He got up abruptly. "Fine. I wasn't entirely happy with what the West Coast people were doing, but I think I got them straightened out." He gave a stifled yawn. "I'm sorry, but what with one thing and another I didn't get much sleep last night. I'd better go on home. I'll be back first thing in the morning!" He leaned over his wife and child and kissed Matilda on the cheek. Then he left, smiling and waving from the door.

My God, my God, he thought as we walked quickly down the hospital hall, as though his wife and new-born child could pursue him. But in an odd way, he felt as though they were indeed following behind, re-proaching him for his moment of unguarded revulsion at what had to be one of the most natural scenes of mother and child. He'd seen women with children at their breasts during the army's long progress up the Italian peninsula. And—he combed his memory— what had he felt? Nothing in particular, except that such pastoral simplicity was something to be expected of a Mediterranean people in a sunny climate. But his own wife?

Back inside, Matilda, her baby now in its crib, found herself upset. Why had her husband recoiled when he walked in? Reaching under the pillow, her fingers encountered a rosary. Saying a decade or so, she thought, would calm her down and do the trick, and she started off. But intermingling with the Hail Marys came a curious brew of memories, like snapshots, among them her father's face, and the face of a girl with whom she'd gone to school who whispered to her one day that it was an established fact that Protestants hated babies.

"What rubbish," she murmured sleepily. All she had to do to contradict that was to recall a choice collection of scenes of Robert with his son. He wasn't the kind of father who got on the floor and played horse or wrestled eye to eye with the little boy, but no one seeing them could have the slighest doubt as to how Robert felt, least of all Robbie himself.

Before sleep came, her last thought was clear and definite. Whatever was bothering Robert had to be about the family business affairs on the West Coast, and she must remember to ask him about them and show an interest.

Given her husband's relationship with his son, Matilda assumed the same sort of affection would exist between him and Elizabeth. But from the time she could toddle around it was obvious that Elizabeth and her father were not a good mix, though not for want of trying on her part.

"Don't run after him like that, Elizabeth," Matilda said, holding her tearful six-year-old daughter in her arms. "You know he ... he doesn't respond well to it."

"I just showed him my picture," Elizabeth sobbed, holding out a sheet of paper with a crayon drawing of a cat on it.

"Yes, but I think he was busy, darling. He was ... he was reading the paper."

"He liked Robbie's picture, the one that he brought home from school."

Matilda, her heart torn, knew exactly what her daughter was talking about. When Robbie approached his father about anything, his father perked up right away.

She tried to reason with her husband. "Robert, I know you don't mean to, but sometimes the way ... well, sometimes you treat Elizabeth as though ... as though you didn't care for her. I know that's not true," Matilda rushed on. "But when she tried to show you her cat drawing—"

"She only went and hastily drew it because she had seen me admire Robbie's drawing. She was doing it to get attention, Matilda, that's all." What he thought of that was plain in his voice.

"But she's only a child wanting some approval from her father—is that so terrible?"

"Perhaps not, but it's certainly not behavior that should be encouraged in any way. At six it's not particularly attractive. At sixteen—it would be nauseating!" And Robert terminated the discussion by walking out of the room. Matilda had learned by now from experience that this was the way he handled anything unpleasant. He didn't stoop to fight, he rarely lost his temper, he just left the room.

She sat by herself staring out the window, across the wide lawn to Benevolent Road outside, wishing that her mother-in-law, who had died a year after Elizabeth was born, was still alive. Though Matilda knew now she had not sufficiently valued her at the time, her mother-in-law had often served as a link, a pacifying agent, when misunderstandings between Robert and Matilda had occurred.

"I'll look after the children! They're such fun to be with! Why don't you and Robert go out to dinner? You both need a break."

Increasingly of late Matilda had found herself sitting alone in the living room staring out, her husband somewhere else, the children upstairs being looked after by a nanny of some kind. None of her mother's friends had had nannies, but nannies were common in College Hill. Her father, she found herself thinking, had been right. They were a different breed.

After a moment Matilda got up and went to the cabinet where Robert kept his liquor. Five o'clock was two hours away, but she wanted a drink now. More and more that seemed the only thing that held at bay a queer depression that had the power to immobilize her.

She had thought she might name the next boy, born two years after Elizabeth, after her father, Patrick Sean. But at the very moment she and Robert were actually discussing the name for the new baby, she put herself at a disadvantage.

"I thought we might call him Caleb," Robert said.

She took a swallow of her drink. "That's an odd name. I was thinking of Patrick, Patrick Sean after Daddy."

"There's nothing odd about the name Caleb. It was the name of an ancestor of mine—one killed in the Civil War."

"I thought your grandfather came over from England after the Civil War."

"Peter Beresford, my paternal grandfather, did. I'm talking about my mother's grandfather, Caleb Mathers. He didn't have to go to war, but he was a strong abolitionist and volunteered."

Matilda took another swallow from her glass. Promptly at five Robert had arrived home from his office and fixed them both a drink. Matilda accepted it gratefully, not considering it necessary to tell her husband that it was not her first.

Without thinking she said, "Mother's grandfather, Michael Leahy, was involved in the Civil War draft riots in New York."

Robert lowered his glass. "What do you mean by involved?"

"He was part of a crowd that hanged a Negro."

A look of distaste came over Robert's face. "Not, I think, a very distinguished role."

The anger that had been surfacing in her of late erupted. "Why should the poor Irish go and fight a war that had nothing to do with them? They hadn't enslaved anybody!"

"I thought the Irish always enjoyed a fight."

"Only of their own choosing. It was the rich WASPS who paid three hundred dollars to keep their precious sons from being drafted."

She saw that Robert was looking at the glass in her hand. In a foolish gesture that gave her away, she covered it protectively with the other hand.

"How many drinks did you have before I got home?"

"None," she lied, and could see that he knew she was lying.

"You're drinking too much," he said evenly, "and you're beginning to show it."

"I don't know what you mean. I never touched the stuff when I was pregnant. Well, I didn't take much. Now the baby's here, I have a right to celebrate." She could hear the stridency in her voice, knew that she was wrong, wrong, wrong. She closed her eyes.

Robert stared at her, then looked down at his own drink. "We still haven't decided what to call our son— our new son. And we have to if he's going to be christened tomorrow. What about Caleb?"

"Yes, all right," she said.

In the years that immediately followed, whenever she thought about her drinking she reassured herself that she had it under control. She never drank too much in public—at parties or dinners or any other affairs. And she learned to watch it at home, so that never again would her husband have reason to ask how many drinks she'd had before he arrived home.

Caleb had been the result of what she called to herself a one-night stand with her husband. He now occupied a separate bedroom most of the time. Increasingly seldom he crossed the hall to her room. But there were such occasions, however rare. Caleb was the result of one of them and, five years later, Mark of another.

From the beginning Mark was the child of her heart. Tall for his years, he was, like Robbie, a Beresford, with his father's lean build, dark hair, and blue eyes. But he had a warmth and eagerness that reminded her of her father. From the time he could walk Mark was lively and full of curiosity and, unlike Elizabeth and Caleb, seemed also to possess his older brother

Robbie's self-confidence. Perhaps this was the reason that he was able to approach his father with ease, and Robert, amused, showed him the affection and attention that he had given Robbie but had been unable to give his two middle children.

How long had Mark lived with them?

Matilda could recite not only the years but the months, weeks and days.

The week before Christmas when he was five she took him and thirteen-year-old Elizabeth to the big department store, Shepard's, on Westminster Street, that was featuring a well-advertised spread in the children's toy department.

Mark was entranced with the toys, going from Winnie the Pooh to Eeyore and Piglet, to a black-and-red model train engine to a car and a stuffed puppy, wanting them all, yelping with delight, bringing them all over to show his mother and sister, unable to make up his mind.

"Darling," Matilda said, trying not to sound impatient, "you can't have all of them, so try to decide which one you want the most."

"I want this!" He held up the engine.

"All right!"

"And this!" He picked up the stuffed puppy. "And this!" In the same hand he tried picking up Eeyore.

"You can't have them all, darling. Just one. You'll have to choose."

Elizabeth's attention, she noticed, was focused on the makeup department several aisles away.

"I want them all," Mark yelled.

At what point did she decide she couldn't keep on standing there without some kind of pick-me-up to give her a boost and take away that weak feeling in her knees?

"Elizabeth, this should take care of at least one." Groping in her purse she got out some bills. "Buy the one he wants most, will you? I have to get something from the car."

As she left she heard Elizabeth say to Mark, "All right, Mark, pick one out. I'll get it for you, then let's go over to the makeup department for a minute."

As Matilda walked away she had the thought that if she stayed, Elizabeth, who had reached the age when anything to do with makeup was of absorbing interest, would be free to go play with the lipsticks and mascara to her heart's content and she herself could remain with Mark and buy the toy he wanted.

She knew that was what she ought to do, but the bottle hidden in the glove compartment of her car was too powerful a lure.

When she reached the car in the parking lot in back of the store, she got in and closed the door. Then she opened the glove compartment. With the first few gulps the anxiety that seemed always to ride her retreated. Relaxation flooded through her. The pain in her knees stopped. . . .

After a while she put the bottle back behind the gloves and Kleenex and maps and returned to the store. Elizabeth, lipstick in hand, was at the makeup counter, staring at herself in the mirror the smiling salesgirl was holding up in front of her. Matilda couldn't see Mark anywhere, not with Elizabeth, not in the toy department.

She never saw him again.

After a year of the police, the FBI, of private detectives, of guards watching the remaining children, of the endless, endless waiting to no avail, Matilda's drinking increased dramatically and whatever had kept the family together lost its hold. They were flung apart as though by some centrifugal force.

"What do you mean, you're not going to be home for dinner?" Matilda shouted into the phone late one afternoon. Then, because she heard the strident note in her voice and feared the question she hated most— how much have you had to drink?—she got a grip on herself and said in a more normal tone, "Robert, you were out to dinner last night and the night before."

"But on Tuesday we had a very pleasant evening with the Bradleys, and on the Friday before that with the Eliots."

"But—?"

"And when we discussed it last weekend, you agreed with me that the family business could stand a little closer overseeing. This means working with the West Coast, which doesn't close for three hours. You were the one who pointed out that our income is not stretching as far as it used to, and I must remind you that it was also you who urged me, as head of the family, to do something about it—particularly in view of ... should the need arise ..." His voice ended abruptly. "I'm sorry, Matilda, I have to go. I'll see you later."

Everything he said was true, but Matilda knew she was being manipulated, as she had been in that apparently casual conversation over the weekend, and his dragging in now the phrase, "should the need arise"—a code meaning should they hear from whoever had Mark, demanding ransom. She was the one who worried constantly that if a ransom demand were made, they wouldn't have enough money to rescue him.

On one occasion, when they were talking with one of the federal agents, Robert, his patience gone, had snapped, "If they—or he or whoever—had taken Mark for a ransom, they'd have demanded the money by now."

Not wanting to believe it, Matilda had turned to the agent. "That's not true, is it?" When he didn't reply immediately, she pushed, "Is it?"

"I'm sorry to say, probably yes. It's been more than a year. If it had been done for money, if Mark were still alive, then we've have heard, I think, by now."

The agony of those words, "if Mark were still alive," was like another dagger.

These days Robert was away more than he was home. All three children were in boarding school, Robbie because he had been entered in his school almost at birth, Elizabeth and Caleb at their own insistence.

Unexpectedly, unbelievably, because they had not slept together since Mark's disappearance, Robert suddenly came into her room one night and, she thought afterward, as though she were a whore hired for an hour, took her. Neither one referred to it the next day or afterward. Why he did it she never knew, nor could she bring herself to ask. But the act was not without consequence. Almost nine months to the day later Terry, christened Margaret Teresa, was born.

"Is this after the big Teresa or the little Theresa?" the priest asked quizzically when she told him what the new baby was to be named.

"What—?" Robert started.

The priest turned to the baby's non-Catholic father. "The big Teresa is, or was—she lived in the sixteenth century—Teresa of Avila, one of the great saints and doctors of the Church. The little Theresa, spelled with an h, otherwise known as the "Little Flower," lived in the last century and was often called the little Theresa."

"I see," Robert said.

The priest turned back to Matilda. "Well?"

"The big Teresa," Matilda said, trying not to breathe out. She had fortified herself for the occasion.

"The little Theresa would have liked that," the priest said equably.

"Robert signed the papers," Patrick said one day not long before he died when he was visiting them in Providence during the Christmas holidays. "But two out of three of your older children have left the Church." He looked severely at his daughter, his gray-green eyes dulled and clouded because of the cataracts he stubbornly refused to have operated on. "Is this Robert's doing?"

"No, Dad," Matilda said tiredly. She knew she wouldn't have much longer to see her father, and was deeply ashamed of the fact that these days she dreaded seeing him at all. His eyes might be failing, but his ability to see into his daughter was undiminished.

"Then why is Caleb the only one of the three to remain in the faith? If there's such a thing as being born a Protestant, then Robbie fills the bill. And Elizabeth, she goes when she has to, that's all, and makes no bones about it. I'm glad to see that Caleb is an old-fashioned Catholic, goes to mass, says the rosary, is planning to belong to Opus Dei."

"Then he'll have to pray for the rest of us, Dad, that God will be merciful and let us into heaven despite all our sins."

Her father glanced up with a pained look. "Ah, Mat, I wish you didn't drink so much. I know it's the curse of the Irish, and your uncle ended up on skid row, but it hasn't touched your mother or me, and I wish to God it hadn't started with you. If you'd just married the way we wanted you to—"

"It wouldn't have made any difference, Dad." She had to say that to save her own face. But she secretly agreed with him.

"That's what you say, but—"

Matilda couldn't stand any more. She did what she'd always dreaded she'd do. She stood up and screamed. "Stop! Stop it! I can't stand any more. Go away, Dad. Leave me alone. Let me go to hell my own way!"

He didn't say a word. Just stood up and left the room. He called a taxi to take him to the airport and left. When he got back to New York he had a stroke, and a month later was dead.

CHAPTER
3

So often it was her father who caused her the most misery. Her earliest memory was trotting after him, her broken doll in her hand, begging him to fix it.

"But you don't even like dolls," he had said, his impatience showing. This was true: She far preferred her older brother's soldiers or younger brother's stuffed animals. Getting Daddy to fix her doll was not for the doll's sake. It was a way of capturing Daddy.

But her attempts were never any use. Occasionally she tried to climb onto his lap, as she had seen her friends do with their fathers. Sometimes he'd endure her presence, but she knew, young as she was, that he wished she wouldn't bother him that way. More often he'd say, "No, not now," and remember something he'd have to do somewhere else.

Once, only once, Elizabeth said to her father: "Why don't you like me the way you like Robbie?"

"Don't be absurd, Elizabeth. I love you equally."

"No, you don't!"

Her father sighed. "If it seems as if I don't, then perhaps it's because Robbie doesn't subject me to scenes like this. I really can't abide them! And if you're so concerned about comparing yourself to Robbie, then let me tell you he'd never, ever go around whining to be loved."

She ran from the room to her mother, who held

her and murmured reassurances that neither of them believed. Later Elizabeth heard her try to appeal to her husband. Even though she couldn't quite hear her father's reply, she knew that it wasn't any use.

After that she stopped trying to get his attention.

It was just before Christmas the following year that Matilda said, "I think we ought to take Mark to the shopping center. They had a huge ad about their toy department, and he's been nagging me about his present. I know his father's bought him something, but I thought you and I could maybe get him something extra."

Elizabeth's immediate reaction was resentment that her father had already got Mark his present. "Of course Daddy's got Mark's present! Mark's a boy."

"He's got you one, too, Elizabeth," Matilda said exasperatedly.

"Yes? What?"

"You know perfectly well I'm not going to tell you. It'd spoil the surprise."

"Probably a lab set, knowing how I feel about science."

Matilda didn't say anything for a moment. Then, "I know you ... you and your father don't ... well, don't have a good relationship, but I wish ..." She sighed. "I wish you did, or something could be done about it."

"I don't think anything can. And anyway, I don't care!"

Mark, sitting between them, chatted all the way there. When they got to the toy department, he ran ecstatically from one toy to another. For a while Elizabeth enjoyed watching him, then she grew bored and her eyes strayed to the displays of the makeup department across the store. She heard her mother's voice: "Buy him the one he wants most, Elizabeth, will you? I have to get something from the car."

"Yes, all right."

Elizabeth's attention returned immediately to the cosmetics department. None of the girls at school were supposed to wear makeup. A couple of the teachers let it be known that makeup on anyone under sixteen would be considered tacky and common. But for Elizabeth, perennially worried about her appearance, it always looked like the door into a glamorous world, a world where at last she would have perfect skin and a perfect figure. . . . And when her mother came back, Elizabeth thought, she'd buy the toy Mark wanted and then they'd have to leave.

She turned to her young brother. "All right, Mark, pick the one you like best and I'll buy it for you."

"I like them all," Mark repeated, but was finally persuaded to choose the red-and-black toy engine. Elizabeth handed the money to the salesgirl, then said, as Mark tried to hang back, "Let's go over to the makeup department, Mark, for a minute."

"I'd rather wait here for Mom," he said, examining his shiny new engine upside down.

"This'll only take a minute." Elizabeth took hold of his hand. "Please, Mark. I want to have a present, too!" And, pulling his hand, she dragged him over.

The girl at the cosmetics counter, who wasn't doing too much business, grinned and took an interest and held up a mirror as Elizabeth brought the sample lipstick near her face to see how the color went with her skin and eyes.

"It looks like it was made for you!" the girl said. "It's especially good with auburn hair like yours!"

No one, to her knowledge, had ever called her hair auburn—red, or dark red, or just plain dark. But never auburn. It sounded mysterious and sophisticated.

She leaned forward, absorbed, only dimly aware of her young brother, bored and impatient, tugging at her jacket, yelling that he wanted to go back to the toys.

"We'll go back in a minute, Mark," she said.

"I wanna go now!"

"In a minute," she repeated.

After that she looked at various shades of blush and mascara. Time—she never knew how much—passed.

Then, as she was drawing a soft black pencil along the line of her eyelid, her mother appeared beside her, screaming, "Where's Mark? I left him with you!" The breath that poured out of her was whiskey drenched.

They spent what seemed like hours searching the store and the surrounding stores. Later, when the police had been summoned, they said she and her mother had lost valuable time searching one store after another, as either Matilda or Elizabeth would say, "He's nuts about ice cream, let's go in here. He's probably gorging on a cone," or "Let's check out the pet store. He'd never pass it up!" instead of immediately informing the police.

Mark was gone. Mark, her little brother who sometimes drove her nuts but whom she loved and with whom she shared a dog, Macdougal, and a cat, Muffin.

In the terrible days and months that followed, Muffin ran off and Macdougal, neglected, died under the wheels of one of the many cars sweeping up to Summerstoke.

There were guards and police and FBI men and private detectives, some of whom had been hired to guard Elizabeth herself and her two remaining brothers. They swarmed all over the place and asked persistent questions:

"How soon after you went to the cosmetics department did your brother leave?"

"I was only there a second!"

The government agent's voice was gentle but implaccable. "The woman at the counter said you were there at least fifteen or twenty minutes."

"Then why don't you ask her?"

"Elizabeth!" Her father's voice shook her up as it always did.

"Leave her alone," Matilda said. "It was my fault."

The FBI man turned to her. "It's not a question of alotting blame, Mrs. Beresford. We're trying to narrow down the time when your son could have wandered away or somebody could have ... could have accosted him."

"I don't know when Mark left," Elizabeth, near tears, said loudly. "I didn't notice. One minute he was hanging on my jacket. The next he wasn't there!" And she started crying.

None of it did any good. There was never any word about Mark—no calls, no letters, no ransom notes.

Deep down, Elizabeth believed Mark's disappearance was at least partly her fault. If she just hadn't been so self-absorbed at the cosmetics counter! Then her defensive voice would rush in: But I was only thirteen!

On a more accessible level she blamed her mother, whose drinking, after Mark's disappearance, became more frequent and more obvious. But the two levels never seemed connected to each other.

When she was fifteen, she insisted on going to boarding school. Matilda didn't like the idea. "After what happened, I want my children around where I can see them."

"You can't keep us locked up forever. It's bad enough being watched over by those guards whenever we walk out the front door. And I want to go somewhere new where people are different!"

"They'll know your little brother was kidnapped. It was in all the papers and on television. Everywhere you go they'll know."

"But that was years ago!"

Finally Matilda gave in and agreed that Elizabeth could go to a convent.

"Why do I have to go to a convent?" Elizabeth argued.

"Because you're a Catholic!"

Elizabeth opened her mouth to say she was no longer a Catholic—a decision she'd made recently.

"It's either the convent or you go on at day school here."

Reluctantly, because she had to get away from home, Elizabeth chose the convent.

She hated it because she felt the Catholicism was being forced down her throat, an accusation she made to one of the nuns.

"I'm sorry you think that," Sister Catherine said. "Forcing anything on anybody never works." The sister, nobody's fool, gently led the conversation around to Elizabeth's family. She knew, of course, about Mark's disappearance.

A few questions later, answered by Elizabeth's somewhat evasive replies, the nun thought she had a fairly clear picture. Her mother was an alcoholic and her father rejected any attempt on her part for attention or affection.

"You and your family have had a very hard time indeed," the nun said. "The hardest. They've had to endure the unendurable." She glanced at the stormy fifteen-year-old. "Perhaps, Elizabeth, you can become the family healer. Not now," she added hastily as signs of total revulsion appeared on Elizabeth's face. "But sometime."

"How do I do that?"

"I really can't tell you. Maybe it'll come to you. You might consider praying about it."

"I've given up prayer. It doesn't work. We all prayed and prayed and prayed Mark would come back. And what good did it do?"

"I don't know. But perhaps—"

"No! I don't believe in a God who doesn't answer prayers."

"Perhaps not on your time schedule." Then, seeing the mutinous set of Elizabeth's mouth, she said, "Run along now or you'll be late for class."

When during vacation Elizabeth discovered that thirteen-year-old Caleb had become an altar boy, her scorn knew no bounds.

"What a good little Catholic you are!"

"And what's wrong with that?" Matilda asked. "It's

a great pity you're not a good Catholic yourself. You might be a lot nicer to your family."

Elizabeth turned on her in anger. Then they both stopped, Matilda because whenever she confronted Elizabeth could never forget that terrible day in the store, and Elizabeth because something in her mother's face was so defeated and frightened. The nun's words about her being a healer came back. Elizabeth thrust them away angrily, as she always did.

By the time she was seventeen, Elizabeth had experienced her own miracle. Without her doing anything to assist it, the skin on her face cleared, she grew an inch or so, and she suddenly found it easy to lose weight. At parties boys no longer looked past her. She heard herself described by two adults, gossiping in a corner at one of the dances, as a beauty. She didn't believe it, but it gave her pleasure and confidence and a sense of justification. Some of her anger, so much a part of her life, retreated. She started enjoying herself. She even seemed to get along better with her father, who, when she no longer demanded something he couldn't give, relaxed.

Then one weekend Robbie, now at Harvard, invited her to a get-together in Cambridge. At some point the party adjourned to a local bar and grill filled with students drinking to celebrate that exams were over or to drown out the foreboding of poor grades. Elizabeth looked up and saw Robbie bring over a tall, fair-haired young man.

"This is Nigel Conway," Robbie said. "Having tried Cambridge in England, he's trying Cambridge, Massachusetts."

Elizabeth looked straight into the angular, attractive face and fell in love. "How does it compare with the English Cambridge?" she asked.

He smiled a lopsided, engaging smile. "Most favorably. Now, especially."

He was flattering her, of course, but couched in the

English accent the words were not only charming, but sounded sincere.

"You're English," Elizabeth said when he sat down. It was a fairly obvious statement, but she felt desperate with a desire that he like her, and she was in such a turmoil she couldn't think of anything else to say.

"Half. My father's English. Mother's from the States and now lives here."

Robbie had already discovered somebody at another table and left them alone. Elizabeth didn't know whether to feel pleased or angry about this. Being alone with Nigel was heaven, but she was terrified she wouldn't be able to think of anything to say.

But he was easy to talk to. Afterward, she could never remember what they talked about. But whatever it was kept flowing.

Elizabeth had never been in love before. Perhaps because she was in a girls' school, she'd never even developed a crush on a boy, so she was unprepared for the way that everything in her life seemed taken over by it. She couldn't stop thinking about Nigel. He called her several times during that first week, and they met the following Saturday at the bus station where he picked her up.

"I should have come to the convent for you," he said.

"Absolutely not. I'd have hated you to see such a dreary place. And I don't want the nuns fishing around for who you are."

"What did you tell them?"

"That I was coming into Boston to see Robbie, of course."

Nigel laughed. "And what happens if they call him up and ask for you?"

"Oh, Robbie'll back me up."

"If he doesn't, I'll call him out!"

"Call him out?"

Nigel glanced at her as he wove his way through

the traffic. "Challenge him to a duel. Swords or pistols, that kind of thing!"

Elizabeth was enchanted.

They went out at least once a week, and would have more often if Elizabeth hadn't been forced to study before final exams.

"I wish I'd known you last year," she said wistfully.

"So do I. But why? Any particular reason?"

She sighed. "I could have thought then of trying to get into Harvard—or at least some place around here. Not that I'd have made it, probably—studying hard has never been my thing—but who knows?"

"Where are you going?"

She made a face. "Tulane. But I'm going to see if I can change that. There must be some college reachable from Cambridge where they'd welcome a medium-bright student with medium-good grades."

He grinned. "I'm sure you're better than that."

"Probably would have been if I'd studied. But—"

"You had other and better things to do."

She grinned back. "Or so it seemed at the time. Are you coming to Robbie's twenty-first bash at Summerstoke?"

"Yes, indeed. I've already been invited. I gather it's to be quite a party."

"The twenty-first of the oldest son's always been celebrated like that—well, anyway, for the last two generations. It's always seemed to me a little unfair not to do the same for the rest of us. But the original Peter Beresford wanted to do it the British way." She paused. "There was some talk at home this year about maybe ... because of ... well, of what happened to Mark, we ought to give the party a miss. But Dad insisted. He felt it was not right not to have Robbie's party."

"I think he was right," Nigel said. "However awful what happens, life goes on."

"Yes." She hadn't been sure before, but now she

was. "It does." Everything in her life, she thought later that night, was better because of Nigel.

They saw plays and musicals together, went to Tanglewood, attended the symphony because Nigel had season tickets and dropped by any new nightclub act that opened. Plainly, Nigel didn't lack money. Elizabeth, used to boys whose main object was to get her alone in the back of a car or, better still, in their rooms, was surprised that Nigel didn't follow the usual pattern. But she liked his more laid-back style and put it down to his being English. Then one evening he did casually suggest they drop by his room, and there he made up for any lost opportunity. He was a tender lover and before Elizabeth knew what had happened, she found herself lying naked in bed with him. She couldn't believe how marvelous it felt or the pleasure it brought.

"I gather this is new for you," Nigel said, sliding his fingers slowly up and down her chest.

"Completely. I had no idea it could be this wonderful."

Finally, school finished, she was given her diploma, and she went back to Summerstoke to wait the week before Robbie's party. She didn't see Nigel before then, but did talk daily on the phone.

"Who are you talking to?" her father asked once.

"Nigel Conway. Robbie introduced me. I think you and Mom'll like him."

"Remembering the last boyfriend you brought home, there's nowhere to go but up." But it was said dryly and with a smile, and Elizabeth merely grinned.

"Wait till you meet him."

The party was to be given (weather cooperating) on the lawn leading down to the Bay, and a huge tent was erected, containing tables, chairs, serving areas, and a place for a small orchestra.

"Who are you bringing?" she asked Robbie. "Anybody I've met?"

"I don't think so. She's a southern girl. From Memphis."

"Oh." Elizabeth, her mind on Nigel, wasn't really interested. It'll be a wonderful party, she thought, a turning point in her life. Secretly she thought Nigel might propose.

The festivities were well underway when he arrived. She was standing in the front hall, waiting for him. Her father, passing through, said, "I take it you're waiting for your young man—Nigel something."

"Conway."

At that moment Nigel walked through the front door.

"Nigel!" Elizabeth exclaimed and ran over and kissed him. Then, seeing her father, she proudly introduced Nigel, knowing he was by far the most personable young man she'd been associated with.

"How do you do?" Robert said slowly, putting out his hand. His eyes were on Nigel's face. "Glad you could come."

"Wasn't I right?" Elizabeth asked proudly, her hands around Nigel's arm.

Neither man seemed to be paying any attention to her.

"Well, wasn't I?" Elizabeth persisted.

The silence stretched. "Hey—!" Elizabeth said.

"I hope you have a good time," Robert said, withdrawing his hand.

"Thank you, sir." Suddenly Nigel sounded very English.

"You have to ignore Daddy," Elizabeth said as they walked through the house to the back lawn. "He can sometimes seem awfully formal."

Nigel didn't say anything.

The party remained in her memory, a searing recollection, forever dividing her childhood and adolesence from the rest of her life. Even so, there were stretches of the evening—when they were toasting Robbie, when they met his date, a very pretty girl with a pronounced southern accent and amber eyes, when they were nibbling from the buffet table—when all the memories seemed to blur together.

"What are you going to do for the summer?" she asked Nigel once.

"Probably go back to England," he replied vaguely.

"To see your father?"

"Yes, I think so."

"Maybe I'll go to England, too," she said, slipping her hand through his arm. "It would be a nice graduation present."

He smiled but didn't say anything. In a few minutes he excused himself to seek out a bathroom.

"We have loads of those up at the house," she said cheerfully. "Would you like me to show you the way?"

"Absolutely not. I'll be back in a minute."

As she watched him walk across the lawn and enter through the wide porch, she had the strong impression he wanted to be left alone for a moment, and wondered if some of the canapés they'd nibbled had upset him. He was longer than she thought he'd be, and she was beginning to get worried when he suddenly appeared at her elbow.

"Everything okay?" she asked a little anxiously.

"Absolutely. Sorry to have kept you waiting." His cheeks were slightly flushed, she noticed, and decided tactfully not to query him anymore about the state of his health.

When he left she expected him to nail down their next date, as he had invariably done before. But he just kissed her and said, "I'll be in touch." Then he got into his car before she had time to say anything.

She didn't hear from him the next day or the day after. She told herself that everything was all right, that he was simply involved in trying to arrange his summer plans. But she didn't believe it, and even if he were, why didn't he call? She stayed close to the house in case he did, refusing to go out sailing, or to lunch with school friends in town. She did go out in the evening with a couple of her local boyfriends, mainly because she didn't want to be in at that hour if Nigel phoned. But there was no message when she returned. In the past she had never called him unless he had phoned first and left a message for her to do so. Besides, there was no need. He had called frequently—until now. Elizabeth was aware of a liberating spirit abroad in the land regarding male-female conventions. Even so, she didn't want to initiate a call. Her nerves grew tight.

"Haven't you had enough to drink?" she snapped once at her mother, who was helping herself from the liquor cabinet.

"How dare you speak to me like that?" Matilda replied, but her righteous indignation was somewhat nullified by her shaking hand. "Just because your fancy Englishman hasn't bothered to telephone—"

She hit a nerve. "He's waiting to find out about his summer plans," Elizabeth almost shouted.

"Lower your voice at once," Matilda said. "And why should that prevent his calling you?"

Since Elizabeth, sick at heart by now, had been also wondering that, she shifted ground. "Mom, why don't you do something about your drinking? You were staggering around the tent at Robbie's party."

"I was not!"

"Yes, you were. I saw you around ten-thirty, and I think a lot of other people saw you. Why don't you go to AA or a hospital or something?"

"My drinking is not a problem. I have it under perfect control."

"Like you did that day in the store?" Elizabeth stopped, horrified. "I'm sorry. I shouldn't have said that."

Matilda put down her drink and stormed out of the room. Elizabeth heard her going upstairs. "Oh God!" she said aloud. Remorse filled her. She followed her mother upstairs. "Look," she said, going into her mother's private sitting room, "I'm really sorry." She stopped. Her mother was standing in front of the mantelpiece, her hands gripping its edge, her eyes on a framed snaphot of Mark grinning, his hand clutching Macdougal's collar. When Elizabeth moved around she saw the tears trickling down Matilda's face. "Mom? I'm really—"

"Oh my God," Matalida said. "Where is he? What's happened to him? What did they do to my little boy?"

"Mom ..." Elizabeth went up to her mother and put her arms around her. "I'm sorry," she whispered. "I'm sorry," as her mother sobbed in her arms.

The letter from Nigel arrived the next morning. Elizabeth, recognizing the handwriting, pounced on it with joy and bore it off to the study, where she could be alone.

It was quite short:

Dear Elizabeth,
    I'm sorry, but I cannot see you again. I'm afraid whatever we had is over. I find that I am deeply in love with someone else. You're a wonderful girl and I wish you the best.
                                        Goodbye
                                        Nigel

Elizabeth read it again and then a third time. And then, as though the meaning hit, gave a cry. "No!"

"What's the matter?" Caleb asked, passing by the study. He was just home from boarding school.

"It's not true," Elizabeth cried. "It can't be true!"

Caleb went into the room. "What are you talking about?"

But Elizabeth, staring at the letter, seemed beyond answering. "I don't believe it," she said. "It's not true!"

"What's not true?"

But it was as though he weren't there. Elizabeth,

still clutching the letter, went past him into the hall toward the telephone. She knew the number by heart and dialed it. There was no answer. Just to make sure she had the right number, she dialed a second time. There was still no reply.

Every hour during the day she dialed the number. Then, when she continued not to reach Nigel, she called Robbie in Cambridge. The term, of course, had ended, but he had signed up for some summer courses.

"Where is Nigel, Robbie?" she asked over the phone.

"I thought you knew. He left yesterday for England."

Slowly, not thinking, Elizabeth put down the phone. Then she dialed her brother again. "Did he leave any address or phone number?" she asked.

"Liz, if you don't have it, I certainly don't. What's going on?"

She couldn't bring herself to tell him. "Nothing," she said, and hung up.

The next day she remembered that Nigel had said something about his mother having an apartment in New York. The telephone company was perfectly willing to admit that a Mrs. Desmond Conway had a residence in New York, but said that at her request her number was unpublished. Refusing to let herself be defeated by that, Elizabeth racked her mind to remember the phone numbers of one or two of her closer friends at the convent who came from New York. She started calling around. Another friend, the owner of a social register listing phone numbers, was called in. Finally, armed with a phone number, Elizabeth dialed. This time there was a woman's voice saying she would be away for the summer. Any messages could be left care of the Carlton Club. Elizabeth called the club and learned what genteel stonewalling could consist of: They would be delighted to take any message they could pass on to Mrs. Conway when she returned. No, they had no idea where she would be during the summer. Was there anything else?

Elizabeth felt bewildered, abandoned, and desperate. She had friends in Providence, but after her all too obvious pride in showing Nigel off at the party, she couldn't bring herself to admit what had happened. Unable to contain her misery any longer, she decided she had to talk to someone.

Crossing the hall to the stairs, she met her father.

Catching sight of her face, he stopped and asked casually, "Anything wrong?"

Elizabeth looked up at him. "Yes," she blurted out. Then the floodgate opened. Faintly, dimly, another voice was cautioning her to remember previous times she had gone to her father for understanding and sympathy, but it was drowned out.

"I got this letter from Nigel. I can't understand it. Why is he doing this? It's not fair. He loves me. I know he does. Daddy, what on earth can have happened? I know he loves me—" As her voice rose, she took hold of her father's lapel.

He unloosed her fingers. "For God's sake, Elizabeth, get control of yourself! Whatever's happened, it's not an excuse for you to sound like a hysterical housemaid."

"But, Daddy, I can't bear it. I don't understand—"

He took the letter and glanced at it. "It seems to me his message is quite clear. He's fallen in love with someone else. For God's sake, Elizabeth, it happens!"

Elizabeth, her hands over her face, was sobbing. "I've never felt about anyone the way I felt about him. I thought he felt the same. I know he did."

"Be quiet!" Robert thundered, glancing down as a servant came out of the dining room. "Do you want everyone on the estate to hear?"

Elizabeth lowered her hands, furious. "That's all you care about, isn't it? That no one know! That appearances are kept up, no matter what the cost! You don't have any feelings, do you? You don't care about anything except how things look. You don't care about how your children feel. You never have. Not even when Mark was taken—you didn't care then—"

His hand cracked across her face. There was silence as they stared at each other. Then he said, "That is the traditional treatment for hysteria. Now go to your room and don't come out until you get hold of yourself."

CHAPTER

4

"I'm getting out, splitting," Elizabeth said to Caleb at breakfast.

He stared at her. "Where are you going to go?"

The word was on her tongue almost before she knew it was in her head. "England."

"Because of this jerk who threw you over?"

"No. Not because of him. A friend of mine from school is over there taking a course given by the University of London. She wrote about a month ago saying I could come and stay with her. I'm going to go."

"Maybe Dad won't let you."

Elizabeth turned. "I'm eighteen. I'm legally an adult. And I have the money from my last birthday. I'm going."

After a minute Caleb said, "Well, I guess we'll miss you. When are you going to tell Mom and Dad?"

"Not until I have everything in place—a passport, money, and so on. Then I'll tell them."

"If you're legally an adult and can do what you want, why are you being so cagey?"

"I don't trust Dad. He'll try to stop me somehow."

"So you want me to shut up about it."

Elizabeth turned. "Yes. At least back me to that degree."

Caleb stared at her, then down at his hands.

"What's the matter?" Elizabeth said sarcastically,

"Are you afraid Dad won't send you to a seminary to become a priest if you don't serve as his spy?"

Caleb looked back up at her. Both her cheeks were bright red now. With her auburn hair shimmering under the light and her clenched hands she looked like a painting of righteous indignation.

"Now you're sounding like Dad," Caleb said.

Elizabeth flushed. "I'm sorry. I'm upset. But that's no reason to take it out on you."

"I was thinking that it might be easier on Mom if she had some warning, if somebody talked to her about it." He paused. "And I guess the somebody would be me."

"You know she'd go blathering about it to Dad, especially if she was upset, or had a drink—or both."

"Let's not forget," Caleb went on. "She's lost one child."

"And whose fault—"

Caleb got up. "Yes, I know. She went back to the car to get a drink. And you were so preoccupied staring at your own riveting countenance in the mirror, you didn't even know when Mark left." He went to the door and turned. "Every argument in this family seems to go back to Mark, doesn't it?" Then he left, closing the door after him.

For the next week or so, Elizabeth stayed out of the house as much as possible. She applied for her passport and was told it would be mailed to her within a few weeks. She learned from a friend who had a summer job in a bank that she could, if she wanted, have a certified check made out to her for the full amount of her grandmother's birthday money, and when she got to England present it to a bank there. Quietly, hiding the bags in her closet, she packed. The day after her passport arrived, she went into Providence and made a reservation on a flight to London for two days hence. Then she went to the bank and requested a certified check.

She and her father had not spoken since their encounter on the stairs. She had not appeared at breakfast and had made a point of avoiding dinner as much as possible. When they met in the hall, neither spoke. Then he himself was away.

The morning after her father got back, Elizabeth appeared at breakfast. Her father and Caleb were there. Her flight from Boston left that evening. She had decided to rent a car and drive to Logan Airport.

She drank two cups of coffee, nibbled at her toast, then said quietly, "I'm flying to England today to visit Lucy Bayard."

Robbie first met Jenny at a private dance in Wellesley, about forty minutes from Boston. He had been dating Peg Lamprey, his hostess, since their first year at Harvard and Smith, and while he also saw other girls, he had more or less taken it for granted that when the right time came—when they were both through school and law school—he and Peggy would marry. They came from the same background. While Robbie himself would never have used the word "class," considering it outmoded and snobbish, he valued everything the term meant.

He'd been dancing with Peg when over her shoulder he saw Jenny talking to a classmate of his. At the same moment she turned and their eyes met. He felt as though an electric bolt had gone through him, yet afterward, thinking about it, he found himself unable to describe why. She was not outstandingly beautiful, being a little on the short side, and she did not have a perfect figure. Yet something about her expressive mouth and widely spaced amber eyes was magnetic, and altogether she proved unforgettable.

A minute later she started dancing with the boy she'd been talking to, and as soon as Peg was commandeered by someone else, he cut in.

"Do you go to Smith, too?" he asked.

"Yes. Although every vacation my family makes noises

about coming home. I don't think they've forgiven the North for the war yet."

Her pronunciation of north as "nauth" and something about the way she referred to "the wah" made him say, "I take if you're referring to the Civil War."

The amber eyes with their black lashes narrowed in laughter. "We prefer to call it the Wah between the States."

"I should have thought what with the civil rights movement, you'd have gotten past that by now."

"Oh, I have! But families are funny. Isn't yours in some way?"

"I guess so." He enjoyed her gentle teasing. There was something a little old-fashioned about it. The word flirting occurred to him, a word that somehow didn't go with the seventies and campus riots and the new freedom in sex.

"I ought to know, since this is a private party," he said, "but what is your name?"

"Jenny Taliaferro." She pronounced it Tolliver.

"T-o-l-l-i-v-e-r?" He spelled out the letters.

"No. T-a-l-i-a-f-e-r-r-o." They danced a step or two. Then, "You haven't told me your name, either."

He looked down at her. "Robert Beresford. You live in Peg's dorm at Smith?"

"Of course."

He took her out the following week and the week after that. Robbie, tall, lean, and good looking, with even, angular features and blue eyes, had had little trouble making it with girls since he was sixteen. That was the year he was introduced to sex after a hockey game with St. Paul's at which he had scored a pair of goals. Exalted with champagne and his celebrity status, he had joined a few of the players from both teams when they decided to treat themselves to an evening at Madame Wanda's, where one of the boys' father had made all the arrangements. "We don't even have to pay," one of them crowed. "My old man says every guy should learn about life this way."

"With your looks and talent, honey," Robbie's particular girl assured him as he struggled back into his clothes, "you shouldn't have any trouble with girls. You're a natural. Come on back next week."

And he had gone back occasionally, but then learned regular dates in the backseat of his car were often just as willing.

Jenny proved different. "No, hon," she said, removing his hand one night as it groped toward her crotch, "that's out of bounds."

Various dates had said something like that before, but he soon discovered that a little persistence and a few fervid kisses did the trick. Somehow, though, he knew that Jenny meant it, which didn't prevent him from trying again.

"I'm sorry, Robbie," she said, firmly holding his hand away from the danger zone. "I don't want that kind of thing before I'm married."

"That's pretty puritanical, isn't it?" Robbie said. "I thought we'd moved past the Victorian era."

"It's not a question of being Victorian," she replied after a moment. "It's a question of what—at least to me—is right."

"You sound like some kind of fundamentalist."

She looked at him. "I guess that's because I am. My family is. We're regular churchgoers and subscribe to all that stuff. If you feel you can't do without it, then maybe we'd better not see each other again."

"That's okay with me," he said, nettled.

He suspected not seeing her would be tough. But he was put out at how tough it was. Still angry, he called several of his old girlfriends and was able to make a gratifying number of dates, several of whose back-of-the-car protests were as flimsy as he thought they'd be.

Then one morning two months later, after a more or less sleepless night, and before he thought she'd be in her first class, he called Jenny.

"I'd like to see you," he said abruptly.

"I haven't changed, Robbie," she said.

He swallowed. "I'd still like to see you." There was a pause, then he asked, "When can I?"

"How about two weeks from Saturday?"

"Not till then?"

There was another silence. Then Jenny said, "How about this Saturday?"

Using all the self-control he had, he played it quite cool, not even trying to kiss her.

When they drew up outside the dorm and he started to get out of the car to take her to the door, Jenny said, "I didn't say you couldn't kiss me."

Robbie got back in. "All right, Miss Taliaferro"—he pronounced it as it was spelled—"you come on with your hot, sexy kisses—some of the hottest I've ever known and then, when I'm thoroughly aroused, you become Priscilla the Puritan. One thing leads to another, or didn't you know that?"

Jenny sat there for a moment. Then, "Sorry I brought it up." She started to get out of the car.

Robbie pulled her over and gave her a long, ardent kiss. Her lips, at first resistant, became soft, tender and lingering.

"Jesus," Robbie said, pushing her away and getting out of the car. Jenny jumped out her side.

"I hate your using that expression—taking the Lord's name in vain!"

"Oh for heaven's sake! Stop talking like a Bible thumper! All right, I apologize. Now let me take you to your door."

It was not a successful date.

Robbie went on a determined round of dates with other girls, just as pretty, he told himself, and much more willing. He thought about reactivating his relationship with Peggy Lamprey, whom he hadn't seen since the night of her party, but didn't. Then came midterms and he spent his evenings in study groups or working by himself. All the girls except Jenny disappeared from his mind. She kept cropping up, and he kept pushing her back. Several times he dreamed about her.

What was it about Jenny? he asked himself once when his efforts to banish her from his thoughts proved futile? She wasn't really beautiful. Plenty of the girls he knew were better looking. She was bright, but so were the others. Unable to arrive at an answer, he made a huge effort and returned to cracking books.

Then one night his father came to Boston on business and invited his son to dinner at his club.

Over lamp chops Robert Senior asked casually, "What about this southern girl I hear you're seeing so much of?"

Robbie grunted, a little annoyed. But he didn't bother asking his father where he'd got the information. The network of fathers, all old friends and fellow club members, whose sons were Robbie's classmates at prep school and at Harvard, was widespread and faster than the wire services.

Robbie didn't answer right away, and then was astonished to hear himself say, "I think I'm going to marry her."

His father didn't reply immediately, but sipped the wine he'd ordered with their steaks. Finally he said, "Southerners are different, you'll find."

You can say that again, Robbie thought. What he said was, "You mean their politics?"

"Not just that. They can sound as up-to-date as all get-out, and then you'll run up against an attitude that's out of the ark. They're still in many ways an agrarian society with all the inbred attitudes that such societies have."

"Such as?"

Robert Senior lit a cigarette. "They're more strict about things like family, sex, religion—that kind of thing. That way they're still in the nineteenth century."

"I don't know what you're talking about!" Robbie said, wondering how his father could have found out about Jenny's implacable virginity. "Anyway, our family's always been reasonably, er, behaved, sexually. Besides, that sounds like prejudice."

"I didn't mean it to be. It's more of an observation."

Robbie, disgruntled, muttered something about having to get back to his studies after dinner. Then, as an afterthought, said, "You didn't make much of an effort to stay with the tried and true WASPS when you married Mother, did you?" The words were no sooner out of his mouth than he realized he had given his father a splendid weapon in the point he was making.

Robert's eyes met his son's. "No. I didn't."

They were silent for a while. Then Robert said, "If you really want to marry this Jenny, I can't stop you. But I wouldn't be doing my job if I didn't tell you what I've found out the hard way: Differences in class, religion, and background may cause more problems than it's fashionable to admit right now. And as you just pointed out"—When Robbie started to object he held his hand—"Let me finish. As you pointed out, by now I should be an authority on the subject."

On their next date two nights later, they had dinner, went to a Broadway show playing up in Boston, and Robbie drove Jenny back to the dorm.

Without putting a hand on her, he said, "Jenny, I love you and I want to marry you. What about it?"

"I love you, too, and I'd love to," Jenny said.

Robbie laughed. Jenny might be a flirtatious southerner, but nobody could be more direct. "Wonderful!" he said, and took her in his arms. Far, far at the back of his mind his father's words echoed, but he pushed them away. That was then, he told himself. This is now.

A few months later, Robbie completed his first year of law school and Jenny graduated from Smith. When he learned she graduated cum laude, he was unflatteringly astonished.

"That's not what nice southern girls are supposed to do, is it, hon?" Jenny teased him.

"What do you mean?" Robbie countered, trying to recover.

"I saw your face," she said, and smiled.

And it was true. When he thought of brainy women he thought of Jess Allenby, or her friend, Sally Withers, with whom he would periodically enjoy intellectual discussions or even arguments. Had he ever had such with Jenny? None that made any impression. He always recalled so much more what she was and what effect she was having on him than anything she ever said.

The wedding took place in Memphis in October. Robbie, in the midst of his second year in law school, flew down with his best man the day before the wedding. Instead of the usual bachelor's dinner, which he had had before he left Cambridge, he was entertained by his future in-laws at a lavish dinner in their home. Jenny's mother, an attractive, lively woman, he found to be an older version of Jenny herself. Jenny's father was a handsome but severe-looking man who seemed to have little to say. When Robbie commented on this to Jenny, she said, "Daddy has two overriding interests in life—his job and his church. People are not his thing. If I hadn't threatened him before you arrived, he would have been questioning you all night about your theology and your morals."

"I'd have been happy to answer either one."

"Yes, but I don't think you'd have been at all happy with his reaction. Either you think, act, and believe like a rock-ribbed fundamentalist Presbyterian, or you're going straight to hell."

"My God! How did you survive?"

Jenny gave a sideways smile. "By going no'th to Smith."

After a moment Robbie asked curiously, "You said you threatened him. What did you threaten him with?"

Jenny grinned this time. "Eloping."

Robbie laughed.

For Robbie's Espicopal taste the ceremony itself, like the church, was rather stark. And there was no wine or champagne served at the reception afterward. Robbie found himself, more than once, thinking of what his father had said.

"Sorry there's no champagne," Jenny said as she caught him eyeing the (nonalcoholic) punch.

He smiled at her. "We can make up for it afterward." Jenny had always been abstemious on their dates, often taking a soda rather than wine or a drink. But being a moderate drinker himself, he had never been bothered by it. Now he was. Newlyweds should be toasted properly.

On the way to the airport, he said to Jenny, "Let's have some champagne while we're waiting for the plane."

"Lovely," she said.

And they did, at a bar in the airport and more on the plane back to Boston.

He and Jenny returned to his small flat in Cambridge, and he resumed his studies at law school. There was no time for a honeymoon, which had to be postponed till his next vacation in January, and even then, with all the work piling up, they could afford only a week. But the week in the Bahamas was all either could have asked. Robbie found himself astonished and delighted by Jenny's ardor in bed.

He had had some doubts as to how the rigors of law school would go with a new marriage. But, again to his surprise, Jenny proved an excellent aid in studying, and was often able to grasp certain aspects of a legal point that had not occurred to him.

One night, exhausted, he grumbled, "Sometimes I don't know how I'm going to get through all this stuff."

She smoothed the black hair off his forehead. "You'll make it, honey, don't ever doubt it."

He knew, of course, because she'd told him, that she had strong religious principles, but was still unhappy when he awoke on a Sunday morning a few weeks after they got back to find her dressed and on her way out.

"Where are you going?" he mumbled, having emerged from sleep with very different ideas of what they'd be doing on their morning of rest.

She smiled. "To church."

He sat up and glanced at the bedside clock. "At nine-thirty?"

"Well, to Sunday school."

"Where?"

"At Redeemer Presbyterian."

"Aren't you a little old for Sunday school?"

"I agreed to teach a class there, Robbie."

"When was this?"

"This week." She paused. "I went over there to transfer my membership."

"Oh." He lay back down.

"Are you angry about that, Robbie?"

"Hell, Jenny, I'm a great believer in everything the Constitution says about freedom of religion."

"That's your theory. What do you really feel?"

"What do you mean? I just told you what I felt."

She looked at him for a moment. "Robbie, haven't you ever found you can think one thing with your head and feel quite different in your middle—or wherever it is you feel?"

"No. I haven't," he said.

There was another pause. Then she murmured, "I have to go, honey."

But her question stayed in his mind, and when he was having lunch with his father in Boston a day or so later, he mentioned it.

"Jenny is very bright," Robert Senior said.

"Yes, I know," Robbie agreed proudly, and wondered why he felt vaguely disgruntled.

Robert Senior looked at his son who so strongly

resembled him and sent up a prayer that the kink that had so skewed his own life would not manifest itself in Robbie's. The boy doesn't have the capacity for deviousness that I've had to develop, he found himself thinking.

"Don't let it get you down," he said. "If I read Jenny right, she'd be happy to contribute those brains and that drive of hers to anything you want to do."

They drank their soup in companionable silence for a while then Robbie said, "Of course I knew she was pretty . . . well, puritanical."

"Wouldn't let you get very far before you took her to the altar, would she?"

Robbie stared at him. "How did you know?"

"A lifetime of observation." His father paused, trying to choose the right words for his next question. "I trust that your, er, marital relations are not, er, hampered by this puritanical tendency."

Robbie suddenly blushed. Then he laughed, "Not a bit. In fact, far from it." He glanced at his father. "How did you feel about Mother's being a Catholic?"

"Probably the way you do about Jenny's Presbyterianism. As much as possible I ignored it. I was in love, so what did denomination matter?"

"You didn't protest when we were all baptized as Catholics?"

"No. I didn't think it was important."

"But from what you said you do now."

"I didn't expect to be the father of an ardently Catholic son on his way to becoming a missionary priest burning to be sent to God knows what uncivilized outpost."

"But you didn't say boo when you learned Caleb was going to be ordained. Or at least not in my hearing."

"By then it was too late. I'd have had Matilda and the McGarrett clan all over me if I had. Besides," Robert Senior paused, "it's the one thing in a long while that seems to have ... well, cheered your mother. That and those wretched dachshunds."

Robbie grinned. "We always used to have retrievers. Mom liked them, didn't she?"

"Yes. But she did once say they were the canine version of WASPs."

Robbie laughed. "With a name like dachshund you could hardly call them WASP—or Irish. It was Caleb who gave her the first, wasn't it?"

"Yes. I think, maybe, to take her mind off Elizabeth's leaving."

Robbie turned his crab cakes around and then added some bernaise sauce. "Speaking of which, have you heard anything from Elizabeth?"

"You know your sister doesn't write to me. Have you?"

"Not since we got a wedding present. Jenny was asking me about it the other day. She seems to think that not to be in contact with siblings is worse than a sin against the Holy Ghost."

"Yes, southerners take the idea of family seriously."

"You'd think by this time she'd have gotten over Nigel's defection—Elizabeth, I mean. Granted, he was attractive. But I always thought there was something a little odd about him."

Robert Senior took a swallow of his burgundy. "How so?"

"Oh, I don't know. Maybe I mean just English."

"They do have a different manner—the educated ones, anyway." Robert Senior quickly changed the subject. "I'm thinking of selling Ransom, by the way. He was your mother's horse originally, but she doesn't go out much now and he's eating his head off. What do you think?"

Robbie, who kept his own mount at the family stables, entered eagerly into the discussion.

Tim knew from as easily as he could remember that the two people he called Ma and Pa were not his real parents. But even though he was aware—his father had let slip the information—that he hadn't been adopted until he was five, he had no memory of his biological mother and father. That didn't stop him from asking questions.

"Why didn't they want me?"

"Because you were bad."

That his real family hadn't wanted him ground like a knife in his guts.

"Rich people are like that," his father put in. "They don't care about ordinary folk—people who're hungry and don't have jobs."

He pounced on this tidbit of information. "Were they rich?"

"Yes. And like I said, they don't care about other people."

"Is that why they didn't care about me?"

"Stop asking questions," his mother said. "I told you everything you needed to know."

"What did I do?"

"I don't know, but they said you were bad and they didn't want you." She bent over and peered at him. He didn't like the way she smelled. In fact, he hated her. "Don't you remember?" she asked.

"Sure," he lied.

She leaned down farther and he recoiled. Putting out her hand, she grasped his shoulder. "What do you remember, son?"

He didn't say anything because he couldn't remember anything. He didn't even know why he wanted to pretend he did, except he somehow knew she didn't want him to.

She shook his shoulder. "What do you remember?"

"Leave the boy alone, Sarah," his father said.

"I'm just trying to see what—"

"I said leave him alone."

He didn't expect her to back off, but she did, still muttering she just wanted to make sure.

A while later, when she'd gone to the market, his father asked him, "What do you remember, son?"

He shrugged.

"Do you want me to bring your mother back to ask you?"

He stared at his feet.

"Well?"

He shook his head.

"Do you remember anything?"

"No."

And he didn't. There was some kind of barrier in his head, and he couldn't remember anything on the other side of it. His earliest recollection was sitting in the pickup between his mother and father as they drove from one place to another so his father could look for another job. But he had no memories before that, except whatever was in his nightmares. He had a lot of those. Night after night he woke up screaming—or was awakened by one or other of his parents. But after he was awake he could never remember what had frightened him.

CHAPTER
5

Elizabeth found London enchanting. Ginny, her convent friend taking courses at the University of London, had a tiny spare room in a flat in Barnes, south of the Thames. When she learned that Elizabeth had come over for an indefinite time and hoped to find a job, she said doubtfully, "The trouble is, my sister's coming over in September, and I promised her the spare bed."

"I'll find something by then," Elizabeth said.

To her surprise, she found a job in a publishing house fairly soon. The fact that an English cousin of Ginny's worked in the copy department there didn't hurt. The job itself was described by the woman who hired her as "an assistant to an assistant dogsbody. But you'll at least get a foot in, and I gather you can type." Elizabeth nodded. The convent back home had offered a typing course that she had rather snootily rejected until she learned it was that or an elective in philosophy.

Ginny congratulated her, and then said thoughtfully, "If I were you and wanted to improve my chances, I'd take a course or two at night—if you can afford it."

Elizabeth was hoarding her birthday money in case she lost her job or some other emergency arose, but she agreed it would be a good idea. So she enlisted for two classes in English literature and history and, a month after she arrived, found a bed-sitter in a somewhat dingy street in Nottinghill. In many ways she was sorry to leave Ginny, but in one respect she was relieved. Ginny was a stalwart Catholic, and every Sunday would casually ask Elizabeth if she cared to accompany her to mass, this despite the fact that Elizabeth had made a point of telling her she'd left the Church.

She enjoyed her job and her classes, and through the latter met some new friends, including a couple of boys with whom she went out from time to time. She was grateful for all this activity, because she was beginning to find life in a foreign city a little lonely. This surprised her. "After all," she said to Ginny when they were having dinner one night, "it's the same language. Same culture."

"Not really," Ginny said. "In many ways it's just as foreign as life in France or Germany or Italy would be. Only we'd expect them to be different, so it's more dismaying here, if you follow me. Not that I don't like it, I do. It's just that I didn't expect it to be as different as it is in lots of ways."

Elizabeth, who was enjoying her new freedom, didn't really know what she was talking about. Later, as she began to encounter her first experience with English anti-Americanism, she did.

"What do you mean we don't have any family life?" she asked indignantly of one of her bosses, a Miss Sedgewick, who ran the copy department. It was by no means the first such comment that Miss Sedgewick had made, but Elizabeth had let the others pass.

"I mean, Elizabeth, according to your own statistics, you have more divorces than all the rest of the western world put together. One of your papers said that. It was quoted yesterday in *The Observer*."

Elizabeth's immediate impulse was to say it was not true. But caution prevailed. Miss Sedgewick was known to be fanatically accurate.

As time passed, Elizabeth tried to avoid Miss Sedgewick as much as possible, but was not successful. Once she had been promoted to editorial assistant, she came into frequent contact with the dour-faced woman. Whenever the much-used opening—"Of course you in Ameddica"—was spoken, Elizabeth steeled herself. Without a job, and with dwindling money, she might well be deported. So she gritted her teeth and bore it.

"Of course she's a beast," Brenda, her best friend at work, said. "You're not the only one she's got her knife into. The trouble is, if you didn't care, she'd stop."

"How do you stop caring?" she asked Brenda.

Brenda sighed. "I suppose the trick is not to start."

Briefly, and on Brenda's recommendation, Elizabeth went to a psychiatrist. "Other people don't seem to care, or at least they've learned not to show it. Why can't I?"

"Because on some level you believe what they're saying." He hesitated. "There's a sort of Judas in you that says, 'Whatever they tell me, they're right.' "

One night when she came home late to her bed-sitter, she heard a meowing in the areaway down some steps. She saw a straggly looking cat that shrank back when she put her finger out. She wondered if it was a stray. But when she moved toward it, the cat recoiled and ran behind some of the bins at the bottom of the steps.

The next night it appeared again. This time, with little hesitation, Elizabeth went to a nearby market and bought a can of cat food. Then she took it back to the areaway, removed the lid, and put it down. The cat, torn between fear and hunger, hung back, but in a few moments hunger won out. It came over and started eating voraciously. Elizabeth climbed the three flights to her flat, filled a low dish with water, and brought it down.

The next night when she came home, much later, from a date, the cat was there meowing loudly.

She said guiltily, "I'm sorry, Cat, but the market is closed."

Her date stuck out a foot. "Shoo—she'll feed you tomorrow."

The cat fled.

"Why did you do that?" Elizabeth asked.

He ran his hand down her arm. "I thought we'd go upstairs."

Elizabeth, knowing he would suggest this, had half decided to invite him up. He was quite attractive, and they'd been out twice before without her inviting him in for a drink.

"No, not tonight. I'm going to look for the cat."

She turned and walked in the direction the cat had run. After some time she found it, meowing on the steps of another areaway.

"All right, Cat. I'll get you something."

She went back to her building. Her date and his car had gone. Up in her apartment she assembled the remains of some cold chicken and a little sliced ham on a dish and took it down. The cat was back at its old stand, obviously expecting her to come. She stood there with the dish, then went back up the front steps, still holding it, and held the front door open with one hand and the dish down near cat level with the other.

It took a half hour, but the cat slowly overcame its reluctance. When it approached her she put the dish down, and, as it swallowed hungrily, grabbed the cat with her other hand. Getting it upstairs was not easy, and required abandoning the dish and wrapping the cat's paws and mouth with her scarf. Eventually, she got it into her apartment and closed the door. Then she went down and retrieved the dish, managed to get into her flat again without letting the cat out, and put the dish down in her kitchen. Then she sat down, exhausted, and wondered why she'd got herself into this.

The cat had gone under her bed and refused to come out. Elizabeth tried to coax it, but to no avail.

After a while she filled a flat broiling pan with some torn-up newspaper and stuck it in the bathroom as a litter pan. Then she put the food dish and a water dish just beyond the bed and went to sleep. When she woke up the next morning, the food was gone, the water had obviously been drunk and the pan used, and the cat was under the bed.

She was telling Brenda about it the next day at the office when Miss Sedgewick came in.

"I'm so glad you took pity on that poor cat," Miss Sedgewick joined in without being asked. Elizabeth was feeling gratified and a little surprised when Miss Sedgewick continued, "I do hope you won't just turn it out when you move."

"Hardly! Why should I?"

"Because it's well known that Ameddicans always abandon their pets when they move on."

Elizabeth opened her mouth, but Brenda was faster. "That's a little unfair, isn't it? I can't believe that more than two hundred million people always do the same thing. And after all, we have shelters over here for abandoned animals, so some of us must do the same. Elizabeth, Mr. Soames wants to see you immediately."

Knowing she was being steered away from a fight, Elizabeth went out of the room, followed shortly by Brenda.

"If that lousy bitch—" Elizabeth started.

"She is a lousy bitch," Brenda agreed. "But she's also the sister-in-law of the chairman of the board, so if you want to stay you'd better put a zipper in it."

That night when Elizabeth went home, she found the cat sitting in the middle of the floor. It scampered immediately under the bed, but came out when Elizabeth, who had stopped at the market, set down some cat food. The cat ate it before going back under the bed. But in the middle of the night Elizabeth became sleepily aware that the cat had jumped up on the foot of the bed. After that they became friends.

Elizabeth named him George Washington, and for

reasons beyond logic, that made Miss Sedgewick easier to take. A week later, Elizabeth brought home a
carrier, and after inquiring around the office for a reli-
able vet, took George Washington there to have his
shots.

Letters from her mother and siblings arrived regu-
larly, often asking her when she planned to come
home. In each reply she stated flatly that she liked
London and planned to make her home there. Sometimes she added that when the money eased up she
might visit—a promise she had no intention of
keeping.

One day a letter from her father arrived in her mailbox. In it he expressed a stiff apology for the things
he had said in their stormy encounter on the stairs
and for striking her, although he restated his conviction that it was a perfectly acceptable treatment for
hysteria. He also wrote he had placed some money in
a bank account in London for her, which would more
than pay for any trip she took home.

Furious, she made sure she never touched it, even
in moments of financial desperation. After several
years she received a letter from the bank saying the
account had been closed and the money withdrawn to
the States.

"Good!" Elizabeth shouted at George Washington,
who had so far overcome his nervous fear as to sit
and continue licking his paw.

Her work and studying paid off. The loathed Miss
Sedgewick retired. One of the other editors left for
another house. Elizabeth, who had risen to being assistant editor, was promoted to full editor and inherited
three of the authors who had been with the departing editor.

One of them was Graham Paterson.

Caleb was sixteen when he knew he was going to
be a priest, and he could remember the exact moment
when it happened.

He was sitting late one Saturday afternoon in St. Mary's Church in the village near his boarding school—or Robbie's boarding school, as he often thought of it.

He had discovered St. Mary's almost by accident, having wandered in there one Saturday afternoon when he was playing hookey from soccer practice. After that he had gone back once or twice and made the discovery that the depression that seemed to envelop him almost constantly at school lifted when he was in the little church. Since his early enthusiasm for going to mass—very much a product of Grandfather McGarrett's influence—had waned since old Patrick had died, and Matilda had more or less given up on trying to keep her children true to the faith, no mention of Caleb's attending mass had been made to the prep school when he was first sent there. So, along with the rest of the student body on Sunday morning, he had gone to the service in the school chapel.

But after a few stolen visits to St. Mary's, he wrote his mother and asked her to get permission for him to attend mass at St. Mary's either later or earlier on Sunday morning and to go to confession there on Saturday afternoon. Then, until he heard from the headmaster, he worried that his mother's letter might not be quite as clear or the handwriting as legible as it might be.

But evidently it did the trick, because the headmaster sent for him and told him the permission was granted. Then he looked at Caleb and said, "I'm just curious as to why now?"

"I'm not sure what you mean, sir," Caleb said, being fairly certain as to what he meant, but fighting for time.

"I mean, Caleb, that you've been here two years, and this has never come up before."

"Well, sir, I've been thinking about it. As I'm sure you know, my mother is Catholic. As a matter of fact, we were all baptized in the Catholic church."

"Were you now! In all the years Robbie was here, I never knew that. He obviously considered himself an Anglican."

"Yes, sir, he did." Now that the headmaster had mentioned the name of his all-conquering brother, Caleb waited for what he was sure would come next. It came.

"You should be very proud of him," the headmaster said. "He left a truly splendid record here, both academically and athletically."

Caleb fought back the resentment that a comment like that always produced in him. Without enthusiasm he said, "Yes, sir, he did. We're all proud of him." And Caleb made up his mind that after a decent interval he'd get his mother to write another letter asking that he be excused from the school's service.

The decent interval came a few weeks later when Matilda, coached by Caleb, wrote that with the pressure of studying he didn't really have time to attend two services, so could he be excused Sunday morning in the school chapel?

Again Caleb was sent for by the headmaster and again granted the permission, and again the headmaster, chosen by the school board because he was an excellent administrator, not because of his penetrating insight, said, "I hear Robbie's headed for Harvard Law School. If he wants that, there's no doubt he'll get it. Harvard'll be lucky to get him."

"Yes, sir," Caleb said. He slowly ungritted his teeth as he left the headmaster's study.

After that he went late Saturday afternoon to confession and stayed for the vigil mass later.

"Of course," the coach commented when he explained why he was leaving practice early, "you'll miss valuable practice time. Time you could use."

"Yes, I know. I'm sorry. It's not exactly like I'm going to be picked for a team, though, is it?"

The coach sighed. "No."

Caleb waited. Robbie had been on both the soccer and the hockey teams.

"Guess you can't hit twice in one family," the coach said.

"That's right," Caleb agreed, and left.

He loved those Saturday afternoons sitting in the small Catholic church, which, from the outside, looked exactly like any plain white New England Congregational church. But the inside reminded Caleb of the church in New York that as a child he had gone to with his grandfather.

During those visits Patrick would take him to the children's zoo in Central Park, they'd ride around the park in a carriage, and afterward he'd have a sundae or a shake in one of the ritzy places south of the park. Most of all he enjoyed going to mass with his grandfather.

"Now remember, Caleb, you were christened a Catholic, and even though the rest of the children seem to have forgotten that they were, too, I don't want you to. You're much more a McGarrett, and McGarretts have always been loyal to Holy Mother Church."

Then they'd both go into the nearest church and light a candle and kneel in a pew while Grandfather McGarrett would say an Our Father or a Hail Mary for them both, or they'd say them together.

Grandfather died when Caleb was eleven, and the boy missed him sorely. Patrick McGarrett was the one person who made it clear he preferred Caleb to Robbie, to whom once he referred grumblingly as "our local C of E representative."

"What's C of E?" Caleb asked.

"Church of England." Patrick glanced at his grandson, taking in his McGarrett stockiness, gray-green eyes, and dark blond hair. He added, "C of E was a convenience invented by Henry VIII so he could divorce his perfectly good Catholic wife and still stay head of a so-called Catholic church."

Caleb absorbed that, then asked, "But what does Robbie have to do with Henry the Eighth?"

Grandfather McGarrett sighed. "Nothing, son. Forget I said it."

Once they spoke of Matilda. Caleb said suddenly, "Why does Mom drink?"

"I don't know, son. Maybe—but nobody ever knows why anyone drinks."

"Is it because she's unhappy?"

Grandfather sighed. "It's a bit like the chicken and the egg. I don't know which came first."

"What do you mean?"

"I mean, Caleb, that I don't know whether she drinks because she's unhappy or she's unhappy because she drinks. But I want you to be good to her, whatever she is. She's going to need it. Promise me."

"All right. I promise."

Sitting there in the little Catholic church, Caleb would think about Patrick and their conversations. His grandfather had been dead now for several years, but what he had meant to Caleb seemed clearer every time he came to the church.

One Saturday a former master, now teaching elsewhere, visited the school. He had been introduced to Caleb at lunch, and immediately recalled Robbie, whom he had taught.

"That's quite a brother you have!" he said to Caleb. "Where is he now?"

"At Harvard."

"Doing pretty well there, I'll bet."

"Yes."

The master looked at him. "It's probably hard to follow a brother like that. But I'm sure there are things you're good at, too!" Then he'd laughed. "The trouble is, Robbie was good at practically everything."

"Yes," Caleb said. "He was." Silently he added, Except being a Catholic.

It was on a Saturday afternoon sitting there, remembering Patrick and everything he'd said, that Caleb decided he would be a priest, and not a priest like so many of the newer kind since Vatican II. Patrick's scorn for and grief over what happened to the Church after the second Vatican council had remained vivid in his mind.

"Ach!" Patrick said. "It's not the Church anymore, Caleb. All this letting go of rules, eating what you like on Friday, not fasting before receiving communion! Do they think people will be better Catholics that way? They won't. I went into a church the other day—it was one I'd been in before but not for a few years—and there was the priest, swinging the rosary and inviting me to say confession with me head stuck in one end of a contraption that looked like an old-fashioned camera and his head in the other. No privacy, no nothing. Anybody coming in the church could hear everything, and there he was, looking at me so he could know me the next time he saw me and remember everything I'd confessed. 'What happened to the confessional that used to be against the wall there?' I asked. 'Oh this is the new church,' the idiot said. I don't have to tell you I didn't stay."

"How long did you used to fast before communion?" Caleb asked.

"From midnight on."

"Even if you went to the noon or the one o'clock mass?"

"Yes."

"Wasn't it hard?"

"Yes, it was. And that's what being a Catholic is about. Don't let them tell you anything else, now. It's about sacrifice and giving up. That's what made us different from the Protestants! No matter what, how hungry you were or anything, if it was Friday and you were at a dinner of some kind you didn't eat the meat and people knew you were a Catholic! Not like today when you might as well be a Methodist." He glanced at his grandson's horror-stricken face. "Well, almost."

He graduated reasonably well from school and went

home determined to go to a Catholic college and from there to a seminary. But at that point Robert Senior intervened. "I'd rather you'd go to Yale, which we talked about before you got this . . . this notion got in your head."

"About being a priest?"

"Yes."

"You don't much like the idea, do you, Dad?"

"What I don't like is the thought of you rushing around whipping up enthusiasm for—what do they call them?—novenas! Ten Our Fathers and ten Hail Marys and so many hours before the blessed sacrament. Why on earth does it always have to be the blessed sacrament?" His sarcastic tone underlined the word blessed. "We have sacraments in the Episcopal church, but they don't seem to be surrounded by so much paper lace and fakery."

Caleb felt a surge of anger start in him. "It's not fake."

"It's a peasant church, Caleb."

"Come on, Dad. You sound like some Boston Brahmin out of the Stone Age. They're not immigrant servants anymore."

There was a pause. Then Robert Senior said, "I don't like anything about the Catholic church, Caleb. And in the years since I married your mother I've come to know a bit more about it. Our forbears haven't been Catholic for four hundred years. And you may notice that countries that are mainly Catholic are frequently given to dictators. The Catholic church doesn't encourage the democratic approach. It's hierarchical and authoritarian."

"I didn't know you were such a Democrat, Dad."

"With a small d, Caleb. Only with a small d."

"Tell me, how on earth did you marry Mom? The McGarretts are Catholic of the Catholic." They even hate the changes of Vatican II."

Robert hesitated briefly. "I fell in love. People in the grip of that are quite rightly considered insane."

There was a pause, then Caleb said defiantly, "I'm going to be ordained, Dad. I'm sorry you don't like it, but that's the way it's going to be."

"Very well. I can't stop you. When you graduate from Yale you can do whatever you like. But since I'm paying for your college, I think I should have some say in that."

Caleb angrily went off to the local parish priest to confide his indignation and sense of unfairness. But he got little sympathy. The local priest, very much a convert to the new Church, was all for his going to Yale. He was also well aware of the prominence of the Beresfords. "All this separatism has to go, Caleb. I think the larger viewpoints you'd get at a prominent Ivy League college would be all to your—and the church's—advantage. You're lucky to be accepted."

So he went to Yale and after a while joined a small group of right-wing Catholics. They met frequently to discuss various aspects of the old Church, and he assisted once a week at the one Tridentine Latin mass permitted in the vicinity.

The second negative note about his intended vocation came from his spiritual adviser in New Haven, an older priest, Father Michael Donnelly, who knew his McGarrett uncles, the bishop and the priest, and to whom he confided his intention of studying for the priesthood and joining a missionary order.

One day Father Donnelly asked him what kind of relationship he had with his parents.

Caleb shrugged. "I have a mother who's a drunk and a father who's a WASP snob, who thinks the Church is good only for peasants. Does that answer your question?"

Father Donnelly hesitated. "I hope very much that isn't part of the reason you want to enter the priesthood—in other words, out of defiance."

Caleb said defensively, "Do you think it is?"

"Truthfully, I'm not sure. I know from your McGarrett uncles how fiercely your grandfather hoped you'd be a priest. He was a prominent man in the Church and didn't hesitate to let his views and wishes be known." Father Donnelly smiled. "And I have a fair idea of how much anger and defiance went into that."

"Yes, it's ironic, considering how eager he was for my parents to get married."

"Was he now? But you were quite young when he died. How do you know that?"

"Grandma McGarrett said so."

"She told you that? How old were you?"

Caleb hesitated. "She didn't exactly tell me. She and Grandfather were visiting. I was about eight, I guess, because she died just before I was nine. Anyway, Mom and Grandma were in the sitting room and I was in the library. The door in between was open and I could easily hear them talking. I don't remember anything that went before, but I remember clearly Grandma saying something like 'I never wanted the marriage, Mattie. Your father did. I think he thought of it as a sort of formal recognition by the WASP establishment. She'll be right up there with the Cabots and the Lodges, Mary, he said to me or something like it. But he was wrong, and now he knows it and it fills him with rage. He says your husband talks to him like he was the chauffeur.'"

Caleb paused. "I may not have all the words exactly right, but that's more or less the way I remember it."

What he never forgot was Father Donnelly's final comment: "For whatever it may be worth, I don't think you should be ordained. You're bright, Caleb. Brighter than you think you are—and that's one of your problems. Underneath everything else is an inferiority complex. But I think that's a poor reason for entering the priesthood."

"I want to serve people."

"You don't have to be a priest to do that. You can serve people in a dozen other professions—if that's your real motive!"

Caleb was furious. "And what do you think my real motive is?"

"Among Catholics, anyway, being a priest puts you on a higher level than other people. It won't help with your father's family. Becoming an outstanding lawyer or doctor would help you more with them." The priest paused. "But you won't take a shot at one of those, will you? It involves more of a risk, doesn't it?"

Caleb always remembered the fury that that comment provoked in him. "You watch! I know you're going to report what you think. But I'll become a priest without your help!"

"I don't doubt it."

Caleb was so outraged he got up and left the room and, his adviser or not, made a point of not consulting Father Donnelly about anything again.

CHAPTER

6

The first time Tim ran away he was seven. He had no idea where he was going to go, and no money to go with. But it didn't matter. He had to get away. He was walking along the highway when his father came after him in the pickup.

"Your mother sent me, son. Get in."

He bolted into the woods, but it wasn't any use. His father caught him easily. When they got back his mother didn't say anything, just marched him to the small closet and before he knew what she was going to do, pushed him in and closed and locked the door.

"You don't know how much I love you," she said through the door. "I couldn't stand it if you left me. So I'll have to keep you in there for a while."

He beat and pounded on the door, begging and pleading to be let out, promising he'd never do it again and then, when there was no response, he started screaming in rage and hatred.

"You just don't understand how much I love you," she repeated. Then he heard her footsteps going away.

He spent uncounted hours sobbing on the floor of the closet. He would never forget the horror and the sense of helplessness.

Eventually his father let him out. "Sorry I couldn't do it sooner, son. But she hung around before going into town."

He knew his father was weak and despised him for it. But he didn't hate him the way he hated his mother.

There were other times he tried to run away, but he was always found and brought back and locked in the closet. The terror was never any less, and he never stopped hating and fearing his mother. He also knew, because his father told him, that his mother was crazy. "She's not right in the head, son, never has been since our boy ... our first boy died. That's why she locks you in the closet. She's afraid you'll be lost, too."

He swore that one day he'd run away and neither of them would ever find him. Until then, he went to school when he could, although they moved constantly as his father got part-time work in mills or factories here and there, or worked in orchards at harvest time.

"Does everybody have this much trouble getting a job?" he asked his father once, when they were moving again. He'd finally settled into a school and stopped being the new boy.

"Not the rich, son. They have it easy. That's because they force people like us to work for them for slave wages. If things were the way they ought to be ..." and he'd be off on one of his political lectures.

As Tim got older he came to realize that his father, the blustering radical, had almost no education—less, as a matter of fact, than his mother—and that the only reading he'd ever done was books and pamphlets on the injustices of society.

"Pay no attention to him, son," his mother often said. "His head's always been stuffed with crazy ideas."

Then one day when she was particularly irritated, she made a fire in a barrel in the backyard and burned all his father's books. "I don't want you getting his nutty ideas," she said.

But Tim had learned that the old man wasn't wrong. The rich fattened themselves on the poor. And they were different, all right. He saw that in school where some of the kids had a lot more money than the others and never let them forget it.

One day a teacher said to him, "Look, you're bright. You write very well. You ought to go to college."

From that moment on, he made up his mind to do just that.

His father said, "I don't have any money to send you to college. The only way you'll get there is if you get a scholarship or some other help."

Tim decided that was what he was going to do.

Then his mother died. And for the first time he felt free.

Terry was eight years old when she understood—as angrily explained by her father—that her mother's drinking, at least on one notable occasion, was her fault.

It was the day near the end of school term when prizes were given out and speeches by valedictorians and other high achievers were given.

"Promise me you'll come," Terry pleaded with her mother. It was the only occasion on which she had a reasonable hope that she'd get some kind of a prize. There was no question of her father going. On that same day Robbie was going to preside at some law school shindig, and that, of course, took precedence.

"I don't know, Terry," her mother said vaguely. "Your father said something about dinner with Robbie after—"

"But Daddy's going to be at Robbie's thing," Terry said, desperate.

Her anxiety about being left out again must have penetrated the fog that her mother was in a large part of the time. "Is it that important to you, darling?" Matilda asked in such a normal voice that Terry almost didn't recognize it.

"Yes, it is, Mom. I just might get a prize in . . ."

Matilda was unable to hide her surprise. "In what, darling?"

"In poetry," Terry blurted out. She'd wanted it to be a secret until the moment it was announced. Nobody had ever suspected she liked poetry, and she'd never told anyone she wrote it. The kids at school, she was sure, would make fun of her. As for her mother, it somehow never seemed the right moment, and her father would consider it vaguely ridiculous and would say so in that elegant voice of his that could cut so cruelly. "But, Mom, you must promise, on your honor, that you won't tell anyone. I didn't tell anyone. I didn't tell anyone I'd written it and sent it in to the contest. Promise, Mom."

"Well, of course I'll promise, though I hate doing so. I think getting a prize for poetry is important. In fact, it's terrific. I didn't even know you wrote poems."

"You won't tell anyone?"

"No, if you insist. But I wish I could." She flashed a warm, loving smile. Running over to kiss her, she got a strong whiff of that smell she had come to know was alcohol. "You won't drink when you come to prize day, will you?"

Matilda visibly retreated. The smile faded. "Of course I won't. You didn't have to ask that."

"Mom, don't be angry. I'm sorry ... I'm sorry I said that."

"It doesn't matter."

Her mother got up and started doing various little bits of business around her study. The moment of intimacy had passed. Terry knew she had to go. She wanted to tell her mother what to wear to prize day, but she didn't dare, even though her mother had been known to be absentminded and one or two of Terry's classmates could be really gross about what some of the mothers wore.

"There comes that awful Mrs. Brennan," Jennifer, a class ring leader, had said, giggling, one parents' day. "Look at that loud suit and all that makeup. Anybody'd think she was here to act in a play." As Terry knew, and was quite sure Jennifer knew, Mrs. Brennan's daughter, Clara, was within distance of Jennifer's voice.

That was the problem with the day school Terry went to—everybody knew who everybody was. She'd started out in the larger private school that Elizabeth had first attended, but Matilda had not been happy with that. She wanted Terry to go to a new Catholic school not too far from the house. Terry had, at first, quite liked the new school. The classes were smaller and there was altogether a more cohesive atmosphere. But she discovered that the other side of that was far more gossip about family and parents, most of whom seemed to know one another. But she never really thought much about it until that terrible day when she talked her mother into coming to the prize giving.

The morning of the ceremony, Terry was seated on the stage along with the other prize recipients, listening to the headmistress talking to the audience about the aims of the school. The headmistress was followed by the main speaker, one of the more prominent priests in the diocese and a leader in Catholic education. Terry, scanning the faces in the audience, hardly heard what either of them said. After going over the rows twice, she had come to the crushing conclusion that her mother had not come.

The priest came to the end of his talk, and the bestowal of the prizes began. Finally Terry's name was announced. The priest, a book for her in his hand, had turned around and repeated her name when there was a disturbance at the back of the audience. Someone was at the door and insisting in a loud voice on coming in. Terry, recognizing the voice, froze. All the heads on the platform were directed toward the back of the hall.

"Of course I know it's prizing-giving day!" The slurred words penetrated the entire room. "My daughter is going to get a prize for her poetry!"

The girls occupying the front rows were half standing and craning their heads back to see what was going on.

"It's Terry's mother. She's drunk!" Jennifer's voice, followed by her unmistakable giggle, echoed in the silence following Matilda's entrance.

Terry, half on her feet to receive her prize, shrank down again. Then she jumped up and ran off the stage back into the corridor leading to the main part of the school. The classrooms were dark, of course, but Terry went into one of them and sat at the back, her head down on her arms on the desk. All she could think was that she wanted to die.

A long time later, the door opened and steps approached where she was sitting.

"Terry." A hand touched her arm. "Terry, look at me!" It was Sister Agnes, an older nun who served as assistant headmistress.

Finally Terry looked up. The nun's gray eyes were kind. Terry started crying and found she couldn't stop. Sister Agnes let her cry for a while. Then she said, "I know. It was hard for you. Here's a tissue. Now dry your eyes. I have your prize here."

"I don't want it!"

"Yes, you do. It's a beautiful poetry anthology."

"I'll never write poetry again!"

"Of course you will. Now dry your eyes."

Terry complied, blew her nose and took the gift-wrapped book.

"Open it and look at it," Sister Agnes said.

Without much enthusiasm Terry did as she was told. It was, as the nun said, an anthology. "Thanks."

"Try not to feel too bad about ... about your mother."

Without raising her head Terry said, "She was drunk!"

"We mustn't pass judgment on people too easily, Terry. For one thing, people have different capacities. Perhaps your mother has a small capacity for liquor, in which case she might get ... well, intoxicated after only one or two drinks."

"She drinks a lot—most of the time." Terry almost wondered if God would strike her for saying that, because family loyalty was always stressed as so important.

The nun, who well knew Matilda Beresford's reputation, decided she'd done her bit for minimizing the matter. "Then you'll have to be particularly brave and responsible, won't you? Running away won't help."

"No."

They both sat there for a while, then the nun said, "Your father is here to pick you up. I'll take you to him."

"But what about Mom?" Terry asked.

"She went home in a taxi."

There was another bout of silence. Then, "I guess somebody told Daddy."

"Yes. Mrs. Beresford's car was here. Sister Mary Magdalen, she thought it would be better if Mrs. Beresford took a taxi home, but then she had to call your father about her car."

When Terry was brought into the reception room, her father had that aloof, closed-down look on his face that she associated with royal displeasure. She wanted to shout out, it wasn't my fault, but knew she couldn't—at least not in front of Sister Agnes.

"Thank you, Sister," Robert said. He turned to his daughter abruptly. "Are you ready? Where is your coat?"

"Her coat is here, Mr. Beresford," the nun said. "I had it brought from the school cloakroom."

Robert took his daughter's hand as they walked out of the school. She thought his hand felt angry.

In the small parking circle in front of the school, only two cars remained, and even Terry could tell neither was theirs. She heard her father mutter, "Now where the hell did she put it?"

They walked beyond the school grounds and finally

located the sloppily parked car, its rear sticking into the street. "I suppose," Robert said in his icy voice, "we must be grateful no one has run into it."

Terry sat beside him in the front seat as they drove home. Her father's expression was stony. Finally she burst out, "Are you mad at me?"

"It certainly would have been far better if you hadn't talked your mother into going to the prize giving or whatever it was. It just made things that were already bad, worse."

"You mean it's my fault?"

"To the extent that the whole thing could have been avoided, yes."

Terry never again asked her mother to attend a school function.

She dreaded going back to the school the following fall, but for the first week no one referred to what had happened at the prize giving. Still, she knew that everyone knew, that they remembered. Early in the second week Jennifer, surrounded in the school yard by several of her cronies, called out as Terry passed, "Written any more poetry lately?"

"That's mean, Jennifer," one of the girls said.

Jennifer shrugged, "So. It's mean. She'd better get used to it, hadn't she?"

That weekend, down at Summerstoke, Terry said to her father at the breakfast table, "I want to go back to my other school."

Her father looked at her over his morning paper. "Running away doesn't help."

"I don't care. I don't want to stay there."

"What happened?"

Reluctantly, Terry told him. She was afraid that he'd look upon it as an opportunity to be brave, and he did. "No," he said, his eyes on her seeming very blue, "you can't run away from things like that. You have to stand and confront them."

Her mother found her in her room. "What's wrong, Terry? You ought to be out with the others, riding."

"I don't like riding."

Her mother sat beside her on the bed. "Are you afraid?"

"No." She was, of course. She couldn't understand how people could enjoy sitting on top of a huge animal that was so much stronger and obviously controlled the situation. What was even odder was that her mother actually liked doing it and was good at it.

"You know," Matilda said, "the more you ride the less you'll be afraid."

"I didn't say I was afraid, I just don't like it."

Her mother didn't say anything for a moment. Then, "Your father said you wanted to go back to Brockhurst School."

Another lecture on being brave, Terry thought resentfully. "Yes," she said.

"I don't blame you. It was my fault. I think ... I think things are going to be better. I'm seeing a doctor. I'm very sorry over what happened. I guess I was thinking of Mark that day."

Always Mark, Terry thought. What had happened to him was, of course, horrible. But she sometimes thought they'd rather have him back than her. There was no reply she could think of, so she didn't say anything.

"I'll see what I can do about persuading your father."

Terry was quite sure she couldn't do anything, but she said grudgingly, "Thanks."

To her surprise her mother succeeded. "You'll be going back to Brockhurst."

For a moment Terry couldn't believe it. Then, "Mom!" she yelled. "That's terrific! You did it!" She leaned forward and hugged her mother and, distracted as she was, registered the fact that her mother's breath did not smell of alcohol. It'll be different now, she thought. "When? When can I go to Brockhurst?"

Her mother hesitated a minute. "I know—I can sympathize—that you want to leave right away. But your father was adamant. You have to stick out this term. He said it mustn't look like you're running away. Then you can go."

"Oh." Terry sat back. If she was going to have to stay until the end of the term, she might as well stay forever at St. Catherine's. "Okay."

"I know you feel like it's as bad as having to stay permanently at St. Catherine's, but it isn't really. Any time . . . any time things get difficult, just think that in a few weeks you won't have to be there."

"All right," Terry said. She looked up. "Mom, have you stopped drinking?"

"Yes, darling. At last! This doctor is wonderful."

Terry never forgot that term at St. Catherine's. Jennifer was the only one who would periodically make snide comments, but she'd succeeded in raising giggles and knowing looks and the humiliation remained constant. Terry stopped seeing any of the other girls after school.

"You don't see any of your friends anymore, dear," Matilda said to her one Saturday afternoon after lunch.

Terry shrugged. "I have homework to do."

"It's because of what happened, isn't it?"

"Mom, it's okay. You're not drinking now. And I'm going back to Brockhurst in two and a half months." She could have actually told her mother the number of days, but she didn't.

"Come on, I'll take you out for a milk shake," Caleb said. He was home for the weekend from Yale.

Terry was thrilled. She loved going out with her brothers.

Then Robbie with his new wife came for Sunday dinner. Terry waited to see if the subject of her changing schools would come up. Finally, Matilda mentioned that Terry would be returning to Brockhurst in the winter term. Terry held her breath, glancing under her eyelashes at her father and oldest brother and his wife. Jenny wasn't a Catholic, of course, but in some ways Terry found her worse. She was always talking about giving herself to Jesus. Terry found it embarrassing.

"Why does Jenny talk about Jesus that way?" Terry asked her mother after breakfast the next morning when she thought the two of them were alone.

"Because she's a southern fundamentalist," Matilda said. "It's pretty dire, isn't it?"

"I'm not sure it's any worse than a lot of loose talk about the Blessed Sacrament or the Holy Virgin Mary," Robert Senior said, coming into the dining room to collect his mail.

Terry giggled and, to her astonishment, saw her father wink at her.

Elizabeth called the first two authors she had inherited upon her promotion, announcing to them that she would have the pleasure of editing their books. When she tried to call Graham Paterson, however, he was away, she was told by his office, and no one was quite sure when he'd be back. He was the most distinguished of her new authors, and she had been warned by Sam Butterworth, the managing editor, that if Graham Paterson wanted one of the more experienced house editors, he would certainly be given his choice. "His last book on economics sold extremely well, which, considering the subject, was miraculous, and this one promises to do even better. So your working with him is only temporary until he gets back."

Having read the first book and, despite her aversion to the subject, found it absorbing, she then started the manuscript of the second. That, too, made a difficult subject interesting and accessible, and her desire to work with the author increased. She made several more efforts to reach him to get his go-ahead, before she finally had to admit to the managing editor that she'd been unsuccessful.

"Umm," Sam said. "I wonder if he heard that his editor had left."

"Why would that make him duck my calls?"

"Who knows? But we don't want to lose him. I'll give him a ring."

Later that day Sam called her. "Well, I reached him. Said he'd just come back from the States. Didn't sound too happy about the change, but said he'd expect to hear from you. Do try not to lose him. We have this book, of course, but we don't want him to go anywhere else for his next efforts."

"Why would I want to lose him?" Elizabeth muttered to herself, and dialed his number.

She was surprised when he picked up. "Graham Paterson," he said. He had the average educated English voice, but she thought she detected a tinge of something else.

"Mr. Paterson, I'm Elizabeth Beresford of Houghton and Lord. As I'm sure you know by now, Daphne Ellis has left and I've been given the pleasure of working with you on your new book."

"Yes, so I've been told. Is there something you specifically want to talk to me about?"

The faint burr in his voice, Elizabeth decided, was Scottish. "Well, I thought it'd be nice if we met for lunch."

"It would be, if I weren't so pushed in the few days I have back here before going off again. Is there anything specific—about the book, I mean—that you wanted to bring up?"

"A few nit-picking things. It's a wonderful book, I've enjoyed reading it."

"Good. Well, collect the nitpicks, as you call them, and perhaps when I return from India we can go over them. As I'm sure you know, I allow no changes without giving my permission."

Elizabeth had nearly decided he had all the marks of an egotistical bully. Most authors she'd worked with were much nicer. "Yes, of course I know that. I'll send the list to you." And she hung up without waiting for any more instructions.

Brenda, who shared her office, glanced at her. "Temper, temper," she said.

Elizabeth didn't reply. A week later, she sent Paterson three pages of queries accompanied by an extremely polite letter.

To her shock he called her. "I've read the queries and admire your thoroughness. What about that lunch you mentioned?"

She met him at an Italian place in Soho and realized as she entered that she had no idea what he looked like. The book jacket of his previous book had not sported a photograph, and there were none in the files.

A man bustled forward. "A table, madam?"

"I'm supposed to meet a Mr. Paterson."

"Miss Beresford?"

"Yes."

"Sir Graham is waiting for you. This way, please."

How on earth had she missed the fact that he had a sir in front of his name, making him at least a knight, possibly a baronet? She had read through much of his biographical material, and either it wasn't there or she missed it. Elizabeth felt her cheeks burn at such a gaucherie on her part.

As they approached a table looking out on a courtyard at the back, a stocky man of medium height folded his paper and stood up. Elizabeth saw an angular face, short dark hair, and light gray eyes.

"Miss Beresford?"

"Yes, Sir Graham. Sorry about addressing you in the wrong way—" When he looked bewildered, she added, "As Mr. Paterson."

"Oh, that. Don't let it worry you. I've only just become a sir. I'm not used to it myself." That certainly explained, Elizabeth thought, why none of the biographical material had mentioned his title. He smiled and she dropped some of her guard. The warmth of that smile made up for the stiffness on the phone.

"Actually," he said as they sat down, "I'm the one who owes you an apology. I didn't sound very friendly the day you called. I was in the middle of a muddle at the office. In any case, your queries were good, even though I didn't agree with all of your suggestions. Here"—he drew folded papers out of his pocket— "I've tried to answer most of them. In the meantime, what would you like to drink?"

While he ordered, she scanned his replies to her queries. His answers were to the point, occasionally a bit acerbic, sometimes even funny. "Oh, come now!" he had written against one of them.

She smiled as she read it.

"That's better," he said.

She enjoyed the lunch more than she would have believed possible. At one point, as she groped in her handbag for a pencil, she flipped out some snapshots that she had picked up at the photo store on her way to the office.

"Snaps?" He inquired.

"Of my cat," she said, a little abashed. She had become absurdly fond of George Washington.

"May I see?"

Feeling rather foolish, she passed them over. He looked through each one. "A male?" he finally said.

"Yes. How did you know?"

"I didn't. Just something about him. What's his name?"

She hesitated. "George Washington."

He gave a shout of laughter. "Is that pure patriotism or some other reason?"

Feeling a great deal more relaxed, she told him about Miss Sedgewick.

"Yes," he said. "I know the type well. They can be almost as disdainful about the non-English parts of Great Britain. "Oh yes," he said in an exaggeratedly affected voice, "the Scots are rather well known for their frugality, or is it their drunkenness, or their dreadful churches. . . ."

"I thought it was just Yanks she didn't like."

"She might not even have known she was being

offensive. Sometimes the Miss Sedgewicks of the
world look on it as a sort of missionary effort to bring
the savages up to scratch—for their own good, of
course."

"You're Scotch, yourself, I take it."

"Tut. Scottish. Scotch is reserved for our national
drink."

"But you had a bourbon."

"My tastes have been hopelessly vitiated by being
in—what did your Miss Sedgewick call it?—Ameddica."

By the end of lunch, Elizabeth decided that though
she didn't find him particularly attractive, she liked
him.

She was barely back in her office when Sam Butterworth strolled by. "How did it go?" he asked, and she
realized that he had been almost as anxious as she.

"Very well. He's rather nice. Only ...."

"Only what?"

"I'd been calling him Mr. Paterson on the phone.
When I got there and the headwaiter referred to him
as Sir Graham, I felt a complete fool. But I'd swear
there was nothing about it in the bio."

"Good heavens! And nobody thought to tell you, I
suppose. It's very recent. He was on the honors list, of
course, which appeared in the paper and I'm surprised
Daphne or somebody didn't put it in his file. Did he
seem put out?"

"Not a bit. He went through the queries I sent him.
The manuscript's ready to go."

"Good show! Well, that's fine. Keep him happy!"

"By the way," Elizabeth said, "he insisted on picking up the tab."

Sam raised his brows. "Unheard of in an author.
Hang on to him!" He grinned and went off down
the hall.

In the general line of keeping Sir Graham happy,
Elizabeth made a note to call him as soon as the
proofs were ready and arrange to have them sent to

wherever he wanted. But long before that happened, he called her.

"Oh, hello," she said when he announced himself on the phone, wondering frantically if he had suddenly discovered something she had failed to do.

With surprise she heard him say, "I was wondering if we could have dinner sometime this week. I find I'm going to be here a few days before I have to go off again to Hong Kong. What about Thursday?"

On the calendar page for Thursday was the name of a man she'd met at a recent book convention. But without a qualm she said, "I'd love to," and told herself that keeping an important author happy was worth any sacrifice.

"May I pick you up?"

Thinking of her bed-sitter in its squalid surroundings, Elizabeth said, "That's very kind, but why don't we meet at the restaurant?"

They met at a quiet, elegant place not far from where they'd had lunch. Elizabeth had managed to get home and bathe and change and was wearing a patterned silk dress with patches of green, which she'd been told matched her eyes.

She knew from the office files he was a widower. He was, also, she discovered, an easy person to talk to, interested in a wide variety of things and with a pleasantly dry sense of humor.

"I've never been to Rhode Island," he said at one point, after questioning her about her home.

"It's easy to miss. It's the smallest state in the union."

"Why did you come over here?"

"Oh," Elizabeth said, twisting her wineglass. "A friend from school was attending London University and invited me to come and stay with her, and one thing led to another."

"Do you intend to go back?"

No one had asked her that question, nor had she asked herself. In fact, she discovered, sitting there, thinking about it, she had studiously avoided it. "I don't know."

"With a cat named George Washington that must indicate a reason for staying away."

She suddenly found herself thinking of Nigel, someone she had carefully kept out of her mind for all these years—how many was it? About nine. An old pain stirred.

"Obviously I've intruded. Forgive me."

She looked up to find the gray eyes on her. They were kind and intelligent, she found herself thinking, and in their kindness, totally unlike her father's.

"It's all right. My exit from the States did come about rather dramatically. I-I fell in love with somebody—English, as a matter of fact—who dropped me flat for reasons I still don't know. And for other reasons I still don't understand, that precipitated a fight with my father that ..." To her horror she found herself near tears. "I'm sorry," she muttered, flung down her napkin and made for the ladies' room at the back of the restaurant.

What got into me? she wondered as she splashed cold water on her eyes. She had managed—she thought—to exorcize Nigel from her mind. Until now. Oh God! she thought, how awful! But there was nothing for it but to go back. She repaired her makeup as well as she could and returned to the table.

He got up as she returned.

"I'm sorry," they both said at once. And then smiled.

"Elizabeth," he said—"may I call you that? I really am sorry for prying. Please forgive me."

"It's all right." She sat down and pulled her seat forward. "I don't know what got into me. Let's forget about it."

He looked at her gravely, then smiled. "The desserts here are particularly delicious. Do have one." And he handed her the menu.

When they left, he hailed a taxi and, getting in beside her, asked for her address. Plainly he was going to take her home.

"It's a rather crummy part of London," Elizabeth said a little defensively.

"I know. I used to live there."

"You did?"

"Yes. Right after Oxford when I was on my first job and determined to be independent."

When they reached her address, he paid the taxi and got out with her. At the front door she turned to say good night.

"Thank you," she said. "I really enjoyed dinner."

"I don't think that's totally true," he said, "but thank you for saying it. You know, I was—" He stopped.

She looked at him in the lamplight. "You were what?"

"I was hoping to meet George Washington."

Somehow she hadn't thought he'd make a pass—certainly not on their first evening together. But she was amused at the device he used. "I take it you're an admirer of cats."

"I am. I don't have any right now because my son dosen't share my taste, and I'm away so much of the time. But until then I've always had one."

"All right. But the stairs are steep." As they climbed she tried to plan how she'd manage to evade the advances of an important author whom she did not want to offend.

Three flights later she opened her door and found George Washington eager to greet her.

"George," she said, "this is Graham."

George backed, visibly alarmed.

Graham came forward a few steps, then leaned over, holding out his finger. George Washington regarded it, but didn't move an inch.

Elizabeth closed the door behind them. "A life on the streets has not made George particularly trusting," she said.

"I can see that, and I certainly can't blame him." He straightened. "Perhaps he'll come around eventually."

"Can I offer you something?" Elizabeth asked formally, intensely aware of the smallness of the bed-sitter and its inevitable untidiness.

"No. I'll be running along. I must say, though, you manage to keep your flat a lot tidier than I did mine. Good night. I'll give you a ring."

He had gone out the door before Elizabeth could think of anything to reply. "Well," she said, looking down at George Washington, "apparently he did want to meet you."

Two weeks later, Graham called again and they went to dinner at a restaurant in Mayfair and after that to the theater. He took her home but left her at the front door. "I'm sorry about George's unfriendliness last time," she said.

"As you said, life as a stray does not engender easy trust."

They went out again and then again, each time when he was back in London. Elizabeth found herself thinking of him as more attractive than she had. More important, she realized how much she liked him. With that realization came another: Friendship was not an attribute she had thought of in connection with men who might become her lovers. The chemistry of their mutual physical attraction had always bypassed simple liking. It had also left untouched that area that, after Nigel, had closed down.

She found she was able to talk to Graham as she had never talked to any man, to discuss things with him—thoughts, ideas, opinions—that she'd normally keep for her friends, both male and female, and her colleagues. She was not, as she always had been in the past when interested in a man, constantly worried as to whether or not he found her attractive.

One night she woke up and found herself thinking how different Graham was from her father. No, she thought, that's not quite right. It was something else.

She went back to sleep, but the next day she knew what she'd been trying to define: Because of all those years of failing to win her father's affection, men, not just those that attracted her but all men, became a sort of pass-fail test for her. That was probably why she was never totally at ease around them. Except for Graham. Was it because she wasn't in love with him?

He was gone a month the next time. When he came back he called her and took her to dinner the following night. At dinner he proposed. "I've been sure now for weeks that I'm in love with you and want to marry you. Elizabeth, will you marry me?"

She heard herself say yes and knew she was making the right choice. At the same time it all seemed so surprising.

Graham asked her where she'd like to be married, and she quickly replied, "A registry office."

"Sure?" he said, smiling.

"Of course. Why?"

"No reason, really."

Plainly she had surprised him, but she decided she didn't want to pursue the matter. To do so would bring up such subjects as church, which church, and, sooner or later, lead to a discussion of which church she had been brought up in. And she wasn't ready to cope with that.

Their attendants at the ceremony were his lawyer and Brenda from her office. Graham put a plain gold ring on her finger at the appropriate moment. Afterward, they all went to an elaborate and festive lunch. That night, when Graham and Elizabeth were alone together, he also placed on her finger a beautiful emerald set in gold. "It matches your eyes," he said.

Elizabeth was moved almost to tears, not because it was so obviously a magnificent and expensive ring, but because he had plainly taken thought about it. His rather austere face when he gave it to her was gentle, and he pulled her to him and kissed her.

Although she was by no means a virgin, she had

not slept with him yet, and she felt almost as odd about that as a woman of another generation might have felt at no longer being a virgin.

"You never even made a serious pass at me," she said at breakfast after a tender, passionate night.

"No."

She gave him a quizzical look. "Why not?"

"I knew almost immediately that I wanted to marry you, and I saw no reason to, er, push intimacy before that. Besides ..." He paused and made a slightly wry face. "If you want to know the aboslute truth, I was afraid you'd turn me down."

"If I was going to turn you down, why would I marry you?"

"Well ... marriage is different."

He was right, of course, but the statement had all sorts of resonances that she knew she didn't want to probe further. At least, not now.

They had no honeymoon because he had to leave for Buenos Aires almost immediately, but he stayed long enough to help her move into the narrow, graceful house in Belgravia that he had occupied since his first marriage. And that first weekend he drove her to the mellow stone house in the Cotswolds that he had owned since before he had married Fiona Palfrey.

She found him a shy but ardent lover, and their nights of lovemaking made up for the first months in the Belgravia house which, until she grew used to its size and the formality of a staff, was rather inhibiting.

The supreme irony, she often thought later, was that she married Graham without being in love with him, and then, as though fate or whatever ruled her life were thumbing its nose at her, she woke up early one morning a few months after the wedding, looked over at Graham asleep beside her, and was stunned to realize she had fallen in love with him after all. It was not the exalted, blinding adoration that she had felt for Nigel, and she was grateful. She leaned over and rubbed her cheek against his until he woke up.

"Good heavens," he said, shocked. "You're awake!"

"For once." Always before she had awakened to find Graham gone—on his way to the office in London or Germany or New York or Tokyo. "Don't leave," she said, and kissed him passionately.

Surprised, gratified, he held her to him, and their bodies moved and blended and reached a climax together in a way that had never happened before.

Two amazingly happy years followed. Considering his age and sophistication, forty-two—fourteen years older than her twenty-eight—when they married, plus the fact that he had been previously married, Graham was surprisingly shy in their lovemaking.

"You know," Elizabeth said one night when they were lying, sated and happy, beside one another, "You may go to the Church of England, but I think you're really a puritanical Scot, a true spiritual descendant of John Knox."

He sighed. "That's what Fiona always said." Then, as the silence stretched, he leaned up on his elbow. "That wasn't very tactful of me, was it?"

"Because you mentioned your first wife? It didn't bother me." She knew right away that wasn't true, not since she had fallen in love with him. "Did you love her very much?"

"It sounds strange to say, but Fiona and I weren't really friends. We had Ian in common, and she enjoyed having money. I don't say that to be critical. So do I. But after a while it was almost as though I talked in one language and she answered in another."

She was about to reply lightly. *And I did not marry you for your money,* when she stopped, appalled. She may not have been fully conscious of it at the time, but she was suddenly aware that Graham's evident wealth had indeed figured in her decision to accept his proposal.

A wave of guilt surged through her. For a moment she knew she would give almost anything if that aspect of his attractiveness for her could be denied. She opened her mouth, but closed it again. His money had been a factor and she was pretty sure he had known it from the beginning.

She closed her eyes. "I do love you," she said.

He took her hand and pulled her over. "Yes," he whispered, his hand on her breast, "I know, my darling."

CHAPTER

7

As everyone expected, Robbie graduated with honors
from law school, and he and Jenny moved back to
Providence, taking an apartment on the East Side, not
far from College Hill. Shortly after that, to no one's
surprise, he was asked to join a firm of lawyers with
offices in the Fleet Building.

. One Sunday morning after they'd been back in
Providence for a month, Robbie surprised himself by
saying to Jenny, "How about coming to Saint Matthew's with me? It's been the family church for
some time."

Jenny looked across at him. "I can't this morning.
I'm supposed to meet Sue Fraser at Redeemer Presbyterian." He knew that was where she had transferred
her membership. "But if you want me to, I'll go next
Sunday with you."

Robbie went by himself that morning, something he
had not done since before his marriage. He'd taken
St. Matthew's for granted the way he'd taken his family. It was there. It belonged to them. Now suddenly
he felt less sure.

The rector, the Reverend James Mallory, greeted
him with warmth after the service. "Good to see you,
Robbie. Wish you'd come more often."

"I might do that, Rector."

He'd enjoyed the service. He'd got up and knelt

and got up again, and for the first time in his life he was conscious of the stately passage of the liturgy. He remembered the shorter, far less formal service at Jenny's church and decided he didn't like it.

The next Sunday, Jenny went with him. He was proud to show her off. "I liked having you along," he told her.

After that he went almost every Sunday to St. Matthew's. About once every three or four weeks Jenny would go with him, but made it a point never to go on Holy Eucharest Sunday.

"Why not?" Robbie asked, when she had canceled her visit with him for the second time.

"I really don't like the wine."

"I don't know what your objection is. It's what Christ himself used."

Jenny didn't say anything.

Then the rector asked him to serve on the vestry. He was more pleased than he would have thought.

"That's because two of your law partners are on the vestry," Jenny said, teasing him.

"No, it isn't. But I guess it doesn't hurt."

One night a few months afterward, there was a dinner for the vestrymen and their wives. Jenny went, of course, but felt a little out of it. The other wives all did various things for St. Matthew's.

A week later, Jenny announced that she'd decided to attend St. Matthew's with him for the time being. She immediately became active in church functions— serving the weekly lunch for senior citizens and contributing to meals cooked and taken by church members to shut-ins. Six months after that she was confirmed by the Bishop of Rhode Island.

"What made you change your mind—about church, I mean?" Robbie, more gratified than he could have believed, asked that night when they were on their way to bed.

"Oh, we're both working toward the same goal, and I like being there with you."

*   *   *

Jenny was, if anything, more interested in his family than he was, an interest all the greater since she was soon well along in her first pregnancy. So she was particularly pleased when, at the start of their second summer in Providence, she and Robbie were invited to a family dinner by the senior Beresfords at Summerstoke, their country house on Narragansett Bay.

When they arrived, they stood for a moment looking up at the contour of the house against the western sky. The old buccaneer, Peter Beresford, who had built the house, had been taken with some of the French chateaux he had seen when off on a European tour while his own place was being built. When he returned, he had insisted on two small turreted towers being put on either side of the main front of the house.

"That's not the style of the house at all, Mr. Beresford," the architect had protested.

"I don't care whether it is or not. Just put them there."

The architect debated within himself about saying something like it would make his handiwork look ludicrous, but decided not to.

"That's a good lad," Peter said.

The turrets went up.

Jenny, looking at them now, said, "They're really quite romantic."

"Stylistically, they're atrocious," Robbie said. "But I like them."

The dinner was served in the larger dining room, a high-ceilinged chamber with oak paneling in the English fashion that Peter admired, and a huge portrait of Peter himself over the mantelpiece. Seated in an armchair, he gazed sternly out at his descendants from blue eyes set deeply under an overhanging brow. His hair was gray and full. Will and unstoppable drive showed in the curved nose and the wide, thin mouth.

On either side of the mantel were smaller portraits, one of Peter's wife, Bessie, and of his oldest son, Robert, known now as Robert the First, father of Robert the Second, who, on his father's death, had become Robert Senior. The other walls had smaller paintings and some photographs. Two paintings in particular caught Jennie's eye. One was of Robert Senior when he was about ten, and another of his son, Robbie, astride a pony, when he was approximately the same age. Jenny gazed at the painting of her husband as she stood behind her chair waiting to sit down. She was placed at her father-in-law's right hand.

"That's a wonderful painting of you, Dad-in-Law," she said as they all sat down. "You look so much like Robbie."

"D'you think so?" Robert Senior said. He glanced over. "I guess you're right."

But the older Robert did look somehow different, she thought. The ten-year-old was seated on a small chair with his arms on the back. His face was a little thinner than his son's at the same age, but the difference wasn't just that. There was something else, but Jenny couldn't figure out what it was. After a while she gave up. Then she spotted a photograph on another wall that she hadn't noticed before.

"Who is the little boy in the picture above the small table there?"

There was a few seconds' silence at the table. Then Robert Senior said, "That's Mark."

"Oh."

Conversation broke out all around on a variety of other subjects. They don't talk about it, Jenny thought. And pondered how different it would be with her family back home in Memphis. There they would talk and talk and talk, some of them through tears. Not this stifled, rigid New England silence.

She had observed this when the subject of Mark first had come up between her and Robbie, not long after they had met and were discussing their siblings.

"So, there were four of you," she'd said to Robbie when, following her detailed descriptions of her own family, he had given her the rundown with thumbnail portraits of his brothers and sisters.

"Actually, there were five," he said, "but Mark ... Mark disappeared when he was five."

"Disappeared?" For a moment she thought he must be making a bad joke. Then she saw he was serious, and she waited for him to explain. It was the first time she encountered the silence that always followed Mark's name.

"What happened—that is, if you don't mind talking about it."

Reluctantly, Robbie told her.

"How ... how awful! I'm so sorry," she said. She looked at his face. "You don't like to talk about it, do you?"

"No."

Robert Beresford III was born shortly after the dinner at Summerstoke. It was on one of Robbie's visits to the hospital to see his son that he was shocked to discover that along with being bright and charming and a great help, Jenny was also ambitious. He was sitting beside her bed, delighting in a scene of mother and child that would, he thought, have inspired a Renaissance painter: Jenny, her light chestnut hair falling over her shoulders, his son, the third Robert and fourth Beresford since the founding buccaneer, in her arms, sated after a long, full lunch at her breast.

"Robbie," she said softly, her face tender with love as she gazed down at their son, "have you ever thought of running for political office in Rhode Island—maybe for governor?"

The words, taken in conjunction with her expression of maternal adoration, were so incongruous he'd shouted with laughter.

Jenny, taken aback, looked up, her eyes narrowed. "What's so funny?"

It was at that minute that Robbie first realized his adored wife did not have much of a sense of humor—a quality he would have put at the top of any list of requirements for friend, relative, or coworker. "Nothing," he said quickly. And then, to forestall any further question, "this is a very Democratic state."

"I've thought of that," she said. And he knew instantly she had. "A liberal Republican is often more Democratic than a conservative Democrat. Look at the South!"

Sometimes it was hard to remember that she was a Smith graduate. On impulse he said, "I often wonder why your family didn't send you to Sweetbriar or Newcomb."

"They wanted to," Jenny had said, her eyes still on the baby. "But I wanted to come up here."

"Why?"

She looked up then and smiled, and he forgot his irritation at her lack of a sense of humor, because it was the same smile that had brought him to her across a crowded dance floor in Cambridge three years before. "I wanted to see what northern men were like. Somehow I suspected they were more sophisticated, more attractive, than the boys I'd known." Her smile widened. "And I was right."

Immediately after graduating from Yale, Caleb, to his mother's joy and his father's utter lack of interest, applied to join a well-known order noted for its worldwide missionary endeavors. In this, of course, he was enthusiastically supported by the McGarrett side of the family, several of whom were more than willing to pull strings within the Church on his behalf. No one was surprised when the order accepted him.

After a year's novitiate he started attending the order's seminary, and four years later was ordained a priest. For five years following that he served in a parish in New York City, during which time he was able to see a great deal of his mother's family and in many respects was under the immediate eye of his uncle, a bishop in a Brooklyn diocese.

When his uncle died, he applied to his superior to be sent abroad. "After all," he said when he broached the subject, "that's what made me join the order."

"I thought it was simply to serve God," his superior, a friend of the family, said.

"I could have served God as a diocesan priest," Caleb pointed out. "It was to carry God's work abroad that I joined this particular order."

"Very well, I'll take it up with the Provincial."

A few months later, Caleb was summoned and told that he was being sent to a parish in the mountains of Guatemala. Delighted, he read everything he could about the country while he was taking a crash course in Spanish and getting a wide variety of shots.

Guatemala, a tropical country with some of the more spectacular mountains of Central America, impressed Caleb with its beauty, and shocked him with the dire poverty of the Indians who lived up in the hills near the small religious community he joined. He had never seen such poverty, and it shook him badly.

He'd been in the country only a few weeks when he was sent down to the capital, Guatemala City, to pick up some supplies being held for them at a church. "And you might as well have these parish bulletins printed and copied," Father Matthew, his superior, said. "Not that most of our parishioners can read. But some can. And they need encouragement. Besides, it's a good thing to send back to the States for mission Sunday."

"You can take them to the print and copy shop in that export building near the church," added Brother Paul Carpenter.

So Caleb went into the copy shop near the church and, while he waited, found himself staring at a pamphlet that had fallen on the floor.

He stooped to pick it up and was shocked to find himself perusing an article in which the Church, along with the U.S.-backed government, was accused of a

9

FA3

FAM333

cynical disregard for the welfare of the people and an abdication of duty before the brutality of the army.

"This is a bunch of lies!" he said to the blond head bent over one of the copy machines.

The woman's head shot up. "What is?"

"This—this garbage!" He shook the pamphlet at her.

There was a moment of silence in the office, then heads turned back and a typewriter somewhere started clacking.

"Let me see." She held out her hand.

He gave it to her. She scanned it for a moment and shrugged. "Someone must have dropped it here. I've never seen it before." And she tossed it in the wastebasket.

As she handed back the parish bulletin and its copies, she asked, "Anything else we can do for you, Father?"

For all her beauty, she irritated him and he didn't for one moment believe her. "You can tell the truth, for one thing."

The blue eyes under the lifted brows regarded him coolly. "What truth?"

"That the Church cares for the people."

"I told you. Someone must have dropped the leaflet. By the way, how long have you been here?"

"A month," he said after a moment.

She smiled, a very sweet smile. "I hope you have a happy stay. Are you in the capital?"

"No. Up near Chichicastenango."

"Ah yes, with Father Matthew."

"You know him?"

"His work among the mestizos is known everywhere."

Since Caleb had asked to be sent to Father Matthew, he was somewhat mollified. "How long have you been here?"

"Three years, off and on. Why did you come to this shop in particular?"

"One of our brothers suggested I come here."

"Ah, Brother Paul. A very sound man, even though he is a priest."

"Brother, not priest."

"Sorry, I didn't mean to offend your hierarchy." The sarcasm was muted but still obvious.

Caleb pegged her as a left-winger foe of the Church. He had come across plenty of those in ivy-covered Yale.

"You couldn't," he said agreeably, and left the print office.

A few weeks later, a hunger riot erupted in the capital. Then soldiers descended on the village ransacking homes and raping several women in their supposed search for revolutionaries. When added to the Indians' desperate poverty, Caleb soon was seeing that the leggy blonde had been right.

When he mentioned something of the sort to Father Matthew, the latter said, "With you there's no such thing as the moderate approach, is there?"

"How can there be?" Caleb replied heatedly. "Look at the misery, the money pouring into the fincas. And the army seems to regard human life less than the zopaloties—the buzzards—feeding off carion."

"*Zopaloties* serve a purpose," Father Matthew said mildly. "They're nature's sanitation disposal."

"How can you talk like that! You of all people!"

Father Matthew, a tall, craggy man in his sixties, regarded him silently for a moment. "You asked to come down here and I took you, partly because you pulled some powerful strings in the Church back home and partly because of the respect everyone seemed to feel for your ardent Catholicism—a rarer quality than one would believe in the Church today," he added dryly. "I could have all the hotheaded young social activists, indifferent to theology and dogma, I wanted. But that's what I didn't want! So I agreed to take you. And now less than a year after you've come to Guatemala, all you want to do is join the revolution.

else after the unexpected visit of some soldiers and their officer a few weeks after his last conversation with Julie.

They had arrived, suddenly, as they always did, late one afternoon. He and Brother Carpenter had just returned from visiting three of their sick parishioners, two of whom were almost certain to die.

"If José were anywhere near a decent hospital he'd get some antibiotics and pull through this!" Caleb said angrily to Brother Paul.

"Yes, but he isn't. And at this point if we were to take him to the capital he'd die on the way. That's a day's trip through mountains and baroncas, and the chances are we'd be stopped, anyway."

That, Caleb knew, was more than likely. There'd been an upsurge in guerrilla activity, and soldiers seemed to spring from the lowlands as though warned of their impending arrival.

Nevertheless, he exploded, "What I can't understand is how come you're so calm. I've seen you with these people. You care for them."

"You make your decision as to what you're going to do. You can call on the sick, administer the sacraments, teach the children, do everything you can to help them, or you can decide to tear everything down in the name of the revolution. Paul turned and eyed Caleb solemnly. "Why did you become a priest?" he asked.

"Because I—" Not since he had been asked this question in seminary had Caleb tried to put it into words. "Because I felt a calling."

"To do what?"

"To visit the sick and those in jail and help the broken and the lonely hearted—if you want a direct quote."

"How about 'Go ye into the world and preach the gospel baptizing in the name of the Father, the Son, and the Holy Ghost,'—to throw in another quote?"

*   *   *

The final incident that drove him from the mission occurred a year and eight months after that. Soldiers suddenly arrived in one of the villages, having heard, they said, of guerrillas there and village sympathizers. Men and women were dragged out of their huts and lined up and questioned. As the soldiers left, one of them, hooting drunkenly, sprayed shots from his automatic rifle in an arc. A man and a woman toppled to the ground, both shot in the legs. Then a three-year-old boy, bellowing for his mother, darted across the street. The soldier, alarmed, fired a spray of shots in his direction. Screaming, the child toppled in agony. In moments he was dead. The soldier laughed carelessly as the jeep drove out.

That night Caleb did not return to the mission. He stayed with the family of the child, reading, praying, saying the rosary. But inside he was churning in rage. How could he sit by and allow such atrocities to happen?

The next morning Brother Paul came to the family's hut. "Father Matthew says I am to relieve you," he said. "He wants you back at the mission."

"I can't go back. That child was shot down in cold blood by a drunken soldier."

"Before you walk out on your job here, on what you came to do, at least have the guts to tell Father Matthew yourself. You owe him that much."

So Caleb drove back to the mission and found his superior in the garden and delivered his statement.

"Yes," Father Matthew said, "I've been expecting something of the sort." He straightened, his gardening tool in his hand. "Are you sure this is what you want to do?"

"Absolutely!"

"Very well. There are some papers you must sign, some formalities to go through."

"I don't have time for formalities. I have work I must do." His words sounded childish in his own ears, echoing another occasion, years in the past. "I'm not going to talk to the headmaster, I want to leave right now!" How old was he when he had shouted back at his father? Eleven? Twelve? The memory came at him like an arrow and made him ashamed. "All right," he said. "Where'll I find the papers?"

In the end Father Matthew drove him back to the village, his worldly possessions and a few books in his carryall.

"I'll leave you here," Father Matthew said. "You'll have to find your own way to wherever you want to go." He added, *"Vaya con Dios."*

One day a school official, sorting through the school's meager information about Tim, asked if it were true he had been adopted. When he said he had, the official said he'd like to see the adoption papers for the school records.

Tim went home and asked his father. When the latter didn't answer right away, Tim was pretty sure he was thinking up a lie.

"They got lost, son, in one of our moves."

"You never had any, did you?"

His father didn't say anything.

"How come I landed up with you?" he asked. Then, jokingly, because it was such a wild idea, "What did you do, kidnap me?"

His father's head swung around. In his eyes was fear, and Tim felt a jolt go through him. "It's true," he said after a moment. "You did kidnap me, didn't you?"

"No. Like your mother told you, you'd been bad so your family didn't want you."

"For chrissake, how bad can you be at five?"

"It was like I told you."

But Tim could see his father was scared. In a minute the latter grabbed his jacket and left the rundown rooms they were occupying at the time.

Once or twice more he tried to get an answer out of his father, but the old man stuck to his story like glue.

Finding a dead end that way, Tim asked a teacher, "If you wanted to find out about something that happened maybe ten or eleven years ago, how would you go about it?"

"What kind of thing?" the teacher asked.

Tim was as leery of telling anybody about it as his father—quite why he didn't know, except maybe because he had been so imbued with his father's conviction that anybody in authority is the enemy.

"Oh, some kind of event"—Tim saw the skeptical look in the teacher's eyes—"like a crime."

The teacher shrugged. "You can always check the back issues of newspapers. Where did it happen?"

He lied. "Somewhere out west." He knew that within his memory they'd never been west of the Mississippi, although that didn't mean anything. Before that, they could have been anywhere. "Where'd I find these old newspapers? At the local rag?"

The town they were in was so small it only had a weekly paper.

The teacher said, "The public library, and probably not the one here. You'd do better in Bangor for that."

Tim took some money he'd saved from working after school in a local diner and got on a bus and went to Bangor, the nearest big town. That was where he learned about microfilms.

They opened up a whole new world. He didn't know where he'd been when he was kidnapped and wasn't sure when and could only go to the library once a week. But he kept at it.

"Where're you going, son?" his father asked him once as he set off for the bus.

Instinctively, Tim lied. "I've got this job in town once a week," he said.

"Oh."

CHAPTER

8

Elizabeth often found herself thinking that if not for her stepson, Ian, her marriage to Graham would have been a success. Of course he was home only during school holidays, and not all of them, because he also liked staying with his maternal grandparents, Lord and Lady Palfrey, in their house in Cheshire.

She didn't actually meet Ian until after she and Graham were married. But as her relationship—such as it was—with Ian developed, she had more than one occasion to remember an exchange she had with Graham prior to the marriage.

He had mentioned Ian's name in passing, and she had quickly interjected, "Does Ian know that we plan to be married?"

"Of course. I told him."

Elizabeth waited, but when Graham said nothing further, she asked, "How did he react?"

Graham reached for his coat preparatory to their leaving the restaurant where they were having dinner. "Oh, you know how boys that age are—they're only really interested in their own affairs."

Elizabeth asked slowly, "Was he very close to his mother?"

"Yes, very close, and to his mother's family."

The actual meeting took place two weeks after the wedding when Ian came home for the summer holidays.

"Elizabeth," Graham said, "I'd like to present my son, Ian." Graham was an undemonstrative man, but she could hear the love and pride in his voice. "Ian, this is Elizabeth, my wife."

Elizabeth found herself looking across at a slightly built adolescent with thick, waving light hair, blue eyes, and a triangular face that at the moment showed absolutely no expression.

Elizabeth gave her warmest smile and held out her hand. "I'm so glad to meet you at long last, Ian. I-I hope we'll be good friends."

"How do you do," Ian said politely. And then to his father, "Am I in my usual room?"

"Of course. It's your bedroom."

Ian, Elizabeth discovered, was a master of muted, undeclared hostility, which, however, was never on display when his father was present, only when he and Elizabeth were alone either in their town house or the country.

"Couldn't you at least go to the Cartwrights' party for a while?" she asked Ian one morning, trying not to show her exasperation over the ruin of a carefully planned occasion with close friends of hers.

Ian pushed away his half-eaten breakfast plate. "I'd really rather not." He poured himself some more tea. "I know they're pals of yours and all that, but I really don't find them frightfully interesting. Anyway, I half agreed I'd meet David and look in on that play his friend Tony's in."

Elizabeth said as calmly as she could, "But the Cartwrights made a special point of inviting you so you could meet their son who's new over here. And you knew about the party because I asked you a week ago if you'd be free."

Ian took a large swallow of tea. "Did you? I must have forgotten."

Elizabeth got up. "I realize this is part of your baiting technique to be indulged in whenever your father isn't here, and it shouldn't surprise or ... or upset me ..."

She had almost used the word wound and hastily rejected it in favor of upset. To use wound would be to acknowledge that Ian had, indeed, made a hit, and that, for him, would make everything worthwhile. She had also learned to her cost that in any argument or fight between them she always came out the loser, and now regretted saying anything.

"You Americans are always so concerned about your feelings," he drawled. "Perhaps that's why half America seems to be in therapy and the other half searching wildly for—what do you call them—support groups?"

But he went too far that time and she was able to smile. "Come, come, Ian. You're breaking your own rules. Verbal barbs, but not outright rudeness. Didn't you describe that as common?" She had the pleasure of seeing him flush with anger as she walked out of the dining room.

During the summer hols, as Ian called them, the problem surfaced again. Graham was home the first two weeks of the holiday, but then took off for Germany. Once he was gone the note in Ian's voice that Elizabeth had come to dread—sarcastic, contemptuous, elaborately polite—reappeared. But she kept on trying.

"Would you like to go out riding this morning, Ian?" she asked one day at breakfast when they were still in the country house, following the weekend. "I can easily get Davis to saddle Prince and Brandy."

"I thought you were going to go to your office in London," Ian said. Elizabeth now had a working arrangement with Houghton and Lord whereby she went in three or four days a week and took home much of her editing. "Anyway," Ian went on, finishing his tea, "I was thinking of meeting James at the club for lunch and going to Lord's afterward."

"I thought you didn't much like cricket."

"Well, I'm not one of the hearties about it. But it

is the national game and one must rally round." And he got up and left the table.

Shortly afterward, Elizabeth said rather nervously to Graham, "I'm afraid Ian doesn't like me."

"Nonsense!" Graham replied, his eyes still on the financial reports that his assistant had hand delivered on his return from one of his trips. "Give him time."

"The thing is," Elizabeth said to Brenda, "he never talks to me like that when Graham is home."

"I don't want to incur your wrath, Liz, but Graham may be right. I don't mean Ian isn't being a snob and a bore, but you have to take his age into consideration. Adolescent boys can be the end, and you are, of course, taking his mother's place. Also—now don't bite me!—you are quite touchy and sensitive."

Elizabeth sighed. "I suppose so. You're not the only one to say that."

Without bringing Ian into it she tried to talk the matter over with Graham. "Do you think I'm too touchy?"

"Yes, darling, I think you're inclined to be." He smiled and her heart gave a little thunk. The warmth of his smile in his rather austere face always got to her. "Not everybody is anti-American," he went on, "but I think you see a spirit of 'bash the yank' in every comment about the States or Americans that isn't openly admiring."

Perhaps he's right, she thought. What was it her father back in Rhode Island had said all those years ago? "Unless somebody's actually telling you he loves you, you seem unable to assume that love is there. It makes it hard to give you any guidance or even to talk to you." And the thirteen-year-old Elizabeth, hungry as always for her father's praise, had felt instead the lash of his contempt.

She had never heard that note with Graham, which was perhaps the reason above all that she had married him.

*   *   *

"Well," Terry's father said at dinner one night shortly after her graduation from Brockhurst, "What now?"

"I want to go to Boston Academy," Terry said.

Robert Senior stared at her. "Never heard of it. Why there?"

"I know it's not Smith or Harvard," Terry said defiantly. Her mediocre academic record was a slightly sore subject. "But I couldn't get into them anyway."

"But you can get into this Boston Academy?"

"Yes. I wrote to them awhile back. They'll take me."

"What's the point, darling?" Matilda asked. "Why don't you let us give you a coming-out party, then you can go to art school or something here in Providence."

"You mean that's all I'm good for?"

"Wouldn't you rather have a coming-out party?" Robert asked.

"No." She was surprised at how strongly she felt.

Robert put down his cup. "All right. I'll send you to this academy, whatever it is. I really don't see you getting any decent kind of a degree. But then you don't seem to have any notion of what you want to do with your life."

For the first few months at Boston Academy, she performed more or less as she had at her various schools. But she found she liked being in Boston. She liked the ordinary people in the street, the coffee shops, the little stores, "Those dreary little people in their dreary houses on their dreary streets," she'd heard one of her mother's horsey friends say once.

"Why are they dreary?" she'd asked.

"Well, look at them?" the friend said. "All fat and polyester. Common!"

Thirteen-year-old Terry had looked down at her thin body. "Is being fat common?"

"Yes. Haven't you noticed? Most of our friends are reasonably thin. But when you go to Boston, people

look square and the women positively wobble like
Jell-O." She gave a slight shudder.

"Maybe they can't help it."

"My dear child, anyone can help it if they want
to. Anyway, why are you concerned about it? You're
thin enough."

She had never really known what her mother's
friend was talking about until she got to school in
Boston. The academy was in the South End, one of
the less affluent parts of the city, and for the first time
she saw the dreary little shops and the dreary people
the friend was talking about.

"All fat and polyester," she said happily to David
Stein, whom she had just met the previous week at a
student party. The two of them were having dinner at
a pizza parlor.

"What are you talking about?"

Terry told him.

"What a lousy bunch of snobs! I bet she'd say that
all Jews are hairy and have hooked noses!"

Matilda had said something very like that once
when she was slightly in her cups. Terry looked now
at David, whose nose was, if anything, tilted. As far
as she could tell he was no hairier than her father or
any of his friends. "Are you hairy?" she asked.

He shoved the last piece of pizza in his mouth.
"Why don't you come back to my room and see for
yourself?"

Terry could feel the blush start almost at her feet.
Sex was one of those subjects that had never been
talked about at home, and discussions about sex at
school were discouraged. Her heart started to beat.
"All right."

As it turned out, David wasn't particularly hairy.
He had only a modest sprinkling of dark hair on his
chest and of course in his pubic area, which fasci-
nated Terry.

What surprised her was the surge of desire that
went through her when he kissed her, put his hand on

her breast and then between her legs. His fingers gently stroked her genital area and slid into her vagina.

"Aahh!" she whispered.

"Let's take these off," David said, his voice hoarse. He ripped off her panties and panty hose and his own clothes.

She'd seen pictures, of course, on her various school visits to art museums and in art books. But nothing had prepared her for the reality. He came almost immediately. When he came again, so did she.

They lay together on his bed in his tiny studio room.

"So that's what it's all about," Terry said. She thought of all the classics that had often struck her as dreary or exaggerated and that now made sense.

He leaned up on an elbow. "You haven't done this before, have you?"

"No."

He slid his hand over her breasts. "Do you like it?" He knew he didn't need to ask, but he wanted to hear her say so.

"Yes. I do. A lot."

"We can do it again. But—"

She looked up at him. "But what?"

"But we're going to have to be more careful. I can wear a condom, or you can wear a diaphragm or get the pill. The pill would be easiest."

"What's a condom?"

"Jesus, I didn't know there were any families left like yours. Didn't they tell you anything?"

"Not about sex."

"Don't you have brothers or sisters—or both?"

"They were practically grown when I was born. I've seen them on their vacations and so on, but I don't really know them. Certainly not enough to talk to about sex. And Elizabeth, my sister, left home when I was four. She hasn't been back since."

"Why?"

"I don't really know. Mother says she quarreled with Daddy. Daddy won't talk about it."

"Nice, close, loving family."

"You mean it's better to be poor."

He lay on his back. "Maybe. On the other hand, if people who live jammed together have fights, they can't retreat to distant bedrooms. Either they make up or kill each other."

They lay there in silence while she thought about it. Then she repeated, "What's a condom?"

He told her about condoms, adding, "Like I said, the pill would be better."

"Why?"

"We'd both enjoy it more, especially me."

That was one of the things she grew to love about David. He was implacably honest, totally lacking in what she had heard somebody in class describe as well-bred pretensions.

"All right. Where should I get the pill?"

"You could try Planned Parenthood."

Matilda slid into her mind. "My mother always called them Planned Butchery."

"That's right. Your family's Catholic. I'm glad to see it didn't have a permanent effect."

She looked into his gray eyes, also slightly tilted up at the outer corners, "So'm I!" Reaching up, she pulled his face down and kissed him. After a second or two he opened his mouth and gently pushed his tongue between her lips. She opened her mouth wider. A little later everything started all over again.

The fateful dinner with David and her father occurred three months later.

Robert Senior, visiting Boston on an unexpected business trip, decided on impulse to take his daughter out to dinner. Somehow he assumed it would be a great treat for her. But when he drove up to the academy dormitory, he met Terry and a strange young man coming out.

"Daddy!" Terry said, confused and a little frightened. She hadn't planned to introduce David to her family so soon.

He bent down to kiss her. "I came to take you out to dinner."

Terry's confusion increased. "Daddy, this is David Stein. We were on our way out to get a pizza."

Robert looked down from his six-foot-three height to David's five foot eleven. "I'm sure you could rearrange it some other time."

David took in the tone and all it implied. "Why don't you join us, sir?"

"Oh, I think not." Robert smiled. "I'm sure the two of you would rather have dinner alone."

A spurt of indignation rose above Terry's muddle of feelings. She, too, recognized her father's tone, which she had dubbed in her mind as suitable for the fat-and-polyester crowd. "No, we'd love you to join us. Please do!" Then she wondered where on earth they'd take him. The pizza place and the fried fish diner were out.

"There's a nice pub not far from here," David said.

Terry knew the pub and also knew it was beyond David's rigidly maintained budget. "Of course that's—"

"Just the place," David put in, staring hard at her.

By this time Robert had become aware that the relationship between his daughter and this Jewish young man was more than a casual dinner would imply. "Very well, but please let me pick the place."

The evening got off to a bad start when Robert pointedly addressed Terry and asked her about her studies. She stumbled through her answer. Her grades were pretty much as they had been at school.

Robert said impatiently, "I still don't understand why you bothered with college instead of the coming-out party we promised you."

"Maybe Terry felt she had already come out on her own," David said.

Robert turned to him. "A coming-out party is a custom—"

"I've heard the term before," David said, ostentatiously pushing the remains of his soup around the plate with a piece of roll and then shoving it in his mouth, something Terry had never seen him do before. "It sounds to me like a bunch of snobbish, er, nonsense." At the last minute he lost his courage and changed crap, the word he had been going to use. "Girls don't need to do that anymore. It's really just a high-toned auction block for eligible females, anyway, isn't it?"

Terry giggled. No one to her knowledge had ever talked like that before to her father. She was both frightened and exhilarated.

Robert, far from stupid, was aware that David was baiting him by being deliberately outrageous, and he rather liked him for it. Despite his regrettable background, Robert thought, David was an attractive boy. "You have some prejudices of your own, don't you, Mr. Stein?"

David glared at him. "Such as?"

"All WASPs are stupid snobs."

David blushed a little. "Not all. Terry isn't."

Robert smiled. "But then Terry is redeemed by her Irish mother."

Two months later, she found out she was pregnant. She had delayed getting the pill and had depended on a diaphragm that didn't fit too well. When she told David he made no bones about what she had to do. "Terry, I can't take on any more! You have to get rid of it!"

"David—no! Can't we—?"

"I've a full-time job as an accountant during the day and law school at night, and to help pay for everything I coach accounting students in what is laughingly called my free time. I just can't! You have to have an abortion!"

Afterward she often reflected on the irony that at least in this respect her father and David thought as one.

Perhaps because deep down she hoped her mother,

the Catholic matriarch, Matilda Beresford, would rouse herself to refuse even to consider letting her have an abortion, Terry made a sudden decision to go home to Providence the next weekend.

When her mother said in her slightly vague, disoriented way, "How are you, dear?" Terry blurted out, "I'm pregnant." She heard the door to the living room open and looked up. Her father and her older brother, Robbie, were standing there.

Her father stared at her. "Did I hear you right?"

"Yes. I'm pregnant." She almost flung it at him, frightened but taking pleasure in it nevertheless.

"That young man I met?"

"Yes. David Stein."

"Who in God's name is David Stein?" Robbie asked.

"Not that young man you met when you were in Boston?" Matilda asked her husband. "That Jewish young man?"

"Yes," Terry almost shouted.

"I assume you're planning to have an abortion," Robert said.

"Can't have a half-Jewish grandchild, can you?" Terry said, near tears.

"I don't think I've ever given you reason to think I was bigoted or anti-Semitic," Robert remarked coldly.

"Or me, for that matter," Robbie put in.

"Lots of Jewish voters in the state, aren't there," Terry sneered. "And you plan to run, don't you?" As the angry words snapped out of her mouth, she kept glancing at her mother.

Matilda, sitting there with a Scotch in her hand and a frown on her face, obliged. "He's not the kind of boy we hoped you'd become engaged to," she said, a little thickly.

Robert snorted. "That kind of comment, Mat, is just going to feed Terry's conviction that we're all a bunch of bigots."

"It's not that at all, Terry," Robbie said as Jenny

walked in. "But it'd be a disaster for you to have this baby now. What about your college career? What about anything you want to do after that?"

"I want to marry David and have his baby." She glared at her family and added defiantly, "I want to be Mrs. David Stein."

"I can't help but think—" Matilda mumbled.

Terry whirled on her. "You're the devout Catholic! You're the one who insisted that we all be baptized in the faith, who sent Elizabeth and me to convents! I thought you'd be horrified at even the thought of me having an abortion. I thought you'd be the one person I could count on to back me up in having this baby!"

"Well . . ." Her mother's voice trailed off. Her face looked stricken. She seemed to grasp her whiskey glass more tightly. Terry, easily reading her mother's bewilderment, knew she was caught between her Catholic disapproval of abortion and her snobbish disapproval of David.

"And what does Mr. Stein feel about all this?" Robert asked dryly.

"As if you cared!" she stormed back at him.

"I take it," he responded, "that the proud father is no more eager for you to have this baby than we are."

"He's putting himself through night law school, has a full-time job during the day, and is even coaching extra hours for extra money. He can't . . . he can't—"

"He can't take on a wife and child at this point even though the child is his. That's a fine, loyal lover, and you have one hell of a nerve to criticize us for not giving you support," Robbie said.

At that point Jenny spoke up. She'd been sitting a little apart from the family circle, saying nothing. "If you're interested in what I think," she said, "I don't agree with either Robbie or Mother Beresford. I think abortions are wrong and that you ought to have the baby and give it up for adoption. There are plenty of

families out there who are standing in line to get a
healthy white baby."

"Of course it's only white babies they're in line for,"
Terry sneered.

"I'm stating a fact, not a political theory," Jenny
replied calmly. "Are you trying to tell us that Mr.
Stein is black as well as Jewish?"

"No, of course not. But I'm sick of all this bigotry."

"When did you become such a raving liberal?"
Robbie asked. "You used not to know a political attitude from the square on the hypotenuse."

Terry sprang out of her chair. "All right, all right,"
she screamed. "I'll have the damned abortion. And
you can all go to hell!"

"Terry," Matilda said, and then didn't go on.

"Does that include the proud father?" Robert Senior asked ironically.

Terry ran from the room.

She stayed upstairs for the rest of the evening. Both
her mother and father, separately, knocked on her
door, but she shouted for them to go away.

Early next morning, she went to her father's study.
As she knew he would be, he was there in his dressing
gown, seated in an armchair reading his paper, with a
pot of coffee and a cup on a small table beside him.

"If I'm going to have the abortion you want me to
have, then I'll need some money. I refuse to go to
some agency and pretend to come from an impover-
ished family just to save you the expense."

Without a word her father opened a desk drawer
and started writing a check. "I think you'll find that
this is the right thing to do."

She hated him for saying that. But she took the
check. "Thanks." And walked out of the room.

When she got back to Boston, there was a message
from David to call him. Angrily she tore it up, but
later, when her phone rang and she was reasonably
sure it was David, she picked up the receiver.

"Hi!" David said. "You were away."

"Yes," Terry almost bit off the word. "You'll be glad to hear that my family, well, almost all my family, agrees with you."

"Look, I know how you feel, but I don't want you to think it's because I don't love you. I—"

"You can relax. I'm going to—" Just in time she remembered that the phone was operated by a central system and the dorm operator could easily be listening in. "I'm going to do as you want me to," she said quickly, and before he could reply, "And I don't want to talk about it now."

There was a short silence. Then, "I'm supposed to coach tonight, but I can cancel it and we could meet for dinner."

"No, don't cancel it. I'll see you over the weekend," and she hung up. When the phone rang again, she didn't answer it.

Arranging for the abortion was easier than she had thought. She went to a well-known agency and lied about her name and her financial status. The operation was over fairly quickly and cost her nothing. She was given a number to call in case of any postoperative problems, but she didn't have any. She'd heard one girl say "it's no worse than a D and C." And though she'd never had a D and C and wasn't sure what it was, she guessed the girl was right.

"Will I be able to have children in the future?" she asked the doctor.

"No reason why on earth not," the woman replied.

The doctor had come to see her after the anesthetic had worn off and was offering various bits of advice on what to do if the bleeding went on. She was kind and Terry liked her.

"Do you think what I've done is wrong?"

"No, or I wouldn't be working here. But the only person who can really answer that is you."

Suddenly she remembered the picture of a fetus from an anti-abortion leaflet.

"What's ... what happens ... to ... to the baby?"

"That shouldn't concern you. It's only a piece of tissue."

"Yes, it is, isn't it?"

She went back to the dorm and followed the various instructions the clinic and the doctor had given. There were no complications.

When David called again and suggested dinner on the weekend, she found words she hadn't thought about ahead of time coming out of her mouth: "David, I don't think we ought to see each other for a while."

He argued, of course, and tried to make her agree to one more date, but she found it oddly easy to shut him out of her life.

CHAPTER
9

Tim remembered the day—the hour—when he was sure that he was Mark Beresford. He had spent months of looking through archives, newspaper back-issue files, and endless tolls of microfilm in the Hartford public library. And then, at seven-thirty-four on Tuesday evening, November 8, when the library was almost empty because everybody was at dinner, he saw the words in a two-page headline in a 1968 news magazine: MARK BERESFORD DISAPPEARED IN PROVIDENCE DECEMBER 17. And he knew.

It was the date, December 17, that did it.

That was the date his mother had picked when he asked her when his birthday was. He was fairly sure she was lying, although, at the time, he thought she'd hit on that day because it was near Christmas, and, as every kid knew, if your birthday is too near Christmas you only get one set of presents. Angry and doubting and hating her, he persisted.

"That was the day I was born?"

"Much more important, son, it was the day we adopted you."

As he left the room he heard his father's whisper, "What the hell did you tell him that for?"

He slowed down, listening for her reply.

"What difference does it make? He's only seven. He'll never know anything else."

Tim got a scholarship and went off to U. Mass. It was not exactly Ivy League, but it brought home to him as nothing else had how skimpy his education had been. He still had to have a job, so between that and the schoolwork he was lucky to average five hours sleep a night. As a result, his search through the back issues of newspapers came to a halt. He wasn't too upset. He hadn't gotten anywhere. The whole thing about his being kidnapped was beginning to seem more and more outlandish, particularly when carried out by two such ineffectual people as his parents. There were hundreds of cases of kids disappearing. Some seemed to have wandered off and were never seen again. Others were undoubtedly kidnapped. Still others could be ruled out: The children—or their bodies—had been found.

But the search had done something positive. It had shown him what he wanted to be: a journalist. Journalists had power. They interviewed and wrote stories about the rich and mighty and exposed them. Watergate had been uncovered by a couple of newspapermen and they had brought down a president. Leading families had had their dirt dug up and put on front pages. Some of them had landed in jail. That appealed to him. It would also, he knew, appeal to his father—his adoptive father. Not that the latter could do anything to help. He was always on the move and could never seem to hang onto a job for more than a few months. But when he learned what his son wanted to do, he was happy.

"That's great, boy! You go after them! You're a chip off the old block!"

Yeah, he thought. Right.

The whole college-graduate school process took longer than he'd planned. Sometimes the scholarship was enough to keep him in school full time. Other times he had to find additional jobs and that delayed his education.

"When you think of all the rich kids who don't have to work and who spend their time on campus getting drunk at fraternity parties and dropping out," his father said when he grumbled to him at one of their increasingly rare meetings, "it's enough to make you want to bring the whole system down."

Basically, Tim agreed with his father, but he didn't want to give him that much satisfaction. "Well, good for them. If they weren't rich they'd be competing for the scholarships and financial aid I want."

"If things were as they ought to be, everybody would be equal and college would be paid for by society."

He thought his father right about that, too, but again, wouldn't say so.

Graduating took a year and a half more than Tim had counted on, but he was willing to take the extra time because by this time he was determined to get into the best journalism school that would give him a scholarship. So he stuck it out with his additional jobs—waiting on tables in diners and hamburger joints and bars near the school. The bars were the best. For one thing, the tips were bigger, and he could get drinks there for nothing, or next to nothing. He'd never drunk before college. His parents were pretty much teetotalers, although he knew his father would have the occasional beer after work. But they both disapproved of drinkers, his mother because she believed drinking was wicked, his father because he considered it the workingman's curse—and all the greater abomination because it enriched giants like Budweiser and the whiskey distillers.

Tim remembered the first drink he ever had. It was in a bar near college where he'd gotten a job. One of the other kids working there told him he was going to have a drink on the house and invited him to join in.

He never forgot that first drink. A wave of ease and confidence he'd never had surged through him as the liquor slid down his throat. After that, he always had two or three in the course of an evening's work in the bar. One night, as he was throwing back a Scotch, the owner said, "How many's that? And don't tell me it's your first free drink of the evening. I've been watching you. You've had at least two more."

Much as he resented what the owner was saying, he was in too good a mood from the drinks to make a big deal out of it. Besides, he didn't want to lose this job. "That's it, Mr. Bellows."

"See that it is."

Tim knew after that he was being watched, so he was careful never to go over three. But he really looked forward to those three. They made the grind bearable.

The journalism school Tim finally got into wasn't one of the top ones, but it was okay and he was glad he was there. By that time he'd learned how to use a word processor and had bought a secondhand one, so some of the outside work he did was writing of one kind or another. It wasn't only easier on his feet, it paid better. He wrote well and he knew it, and a couple of the professors told him so, too.

"You're pretty good," one of them said as he handed back an assignment—a profile of an imaginary local politician. "But go easy on the sarcasm. Remember, less is more."

After three years he graduated and got a job as a beat reporter in nearby Springfield.

For the first time in as long as he could remember he started enjoying his life. He liked writing articles. He liked the weird hours involved in following the police and their suspects and writing up the cases. And he enjoyed hanging out with other reporters after work.

In a couple of years he had a chance to move on to Hartford and he'd been there a year when he got a call from a hospital in Lawrence, where his father was then working as a handyman in a factory. There'd

been an accident and his father was badly hurt. "I'm
not sure how long he's going to be able to hang on,"
the doctor who called said.

Tim caught a bus and made his way to the hospital.
His father was lying on his back, absolutely still, and
Tim's first thought was that he was dead. Something
queer happened to him inside. That wasn't his real
father. He still didn't really know how he had come
to be with the couple he thought of (sometimes) as
his parents, and he had never trusted either of them.
But they were the only mother and father he could
remember—and the only link to whoever he really
was. When his mother died he had felt nothing but
relief. Seeing his father like this was like having something cut off without really knowing what it was.

He bent over the dying man. "Dad, it's me."

He wasn't expecting a response, but he saw his father's eyes half open. "Son?"

"Yes, Pa. What happened?"

"Machinery collapsed." His father fought for
breath, then "I was under it."

"Dad, let me—"

"No. Listen."

Tim leaned closer. After another struggle for breath
his father gasped. "We took you." That brought on
more fighting for air. A glaze was forming over his
father's eyes. At that moment a doctor walked in and
came over to the bed.

"I'm not sure how much more he can talk," the
doctor warned.

He leaned closer. "Where, Dad? Where?"

"Rhode ..." The old man's voice, barely audible,
faded. "You were standing there, crying," he wheezed.

"Where? What road?" Tim just barely managed not
to shake him.

"The store." The dying man took two long, shaking
breaths. "In front of the store ... crying ... your ma
said ... nobody wanted you ..."

Tim ignored the presence of the doctor and the

nurse who had also come in. "What road?" He almost shouted.

"I don't think he can—" the doctor started. But Tim was already asking another question. "What's my name?" He knew how crazy that must have sounded to the doctor and nurse, but he didn't care.

"Mor ..." It was a blurred sound and could have been Mar or Moor.

At that point there was a queer-sounding rattle, and his father's face fell to the side.

Tim looked up to see the doctor and the nurse staring at him.

"You wouldn't understand," he said to them, and walked out.

There was nothing in the dreary single room his father lived in except a few clothes, one or two paperback copies of books he thought had been in the pile that had been burned, and a beaten-up trunk that he vaguely remembered from the back of the pickup. He looked in the drawers. There were no letters, no papers, nothing.

He flipped open the top of the trunk. At first he thought there was nothing in it. Then he saw at the bottom a small bundle wrapped in brown paper. He reached in and took it out. There was something hard at the center. He unwrapped the paper. Inside, folded, was a little boy's brown corduroy pants. Underneath that was a child's beige sweater. Inside the sweater was a toy train engine, now rusted and scratched. Once it might have been black and red.

He held it and waited for something, some fragment of memory, to come back. But nothing did. As far as he knew, he'd never seen either the clothes or the engine. They could, of course, have belonged to Mickey, the son who had died. There was no way of knowing. Rewrapping the small bundle, Tim put it under his arm.

Everything else of his father's he threw out, and he made arrangements to have his body cremated the following day. Then, on his way back to Hartford, he got out of the bus at one of its stops and scattered the ashes in a nearby field. He didn't think he owed his father anything more than that, and every dollar he owned had an allotted place.

"Goodbye, Pa," he said as he emptied the container. He threw the container away, then got back onto the bus and went on with his life.

Inspired by his father's dying words, Tim went back to the library and the microfilmed back issues of newspapers. A check with the library's atlas indicated no U.S. town's name beginning with "Road." That didn't mean there wasn't any. But they weren't large enough or significant enough to be listed in an atlas of this size.

More sophisticated than he had been the last time he did this, he checked in the public library under "kidnapping" and started tracking the cases they listed. There were a lot of them. He wasn't sure when he would have been—in his father's words—taken. According to the dates his parents had given him, he would now be around twenty-five or -six. His earliest memory was being told he was five. So he checked the larger newspapers and weekly news magazines of twenty to twenty-one years before, keeping alert for any little boy named Martin or Moore or Moreland, aware as he did so that his father could have been referring to either the surname or the Christian name—or to something else altogether, and he could have misheard—in fact probably did mishear—his father's strangled sounds.

There were a lot of cases of children who had walked out or "been taken," but none of them had either a surname or Christian name that remotely fitted Martin or Moore or Moreland.

Then finally, in *The Providence Journal,* he saw the headline, MARK BERESFORD KIDNAPPED DECEMBER 17. Plainly, what he'd heard as "road" was Rhode Island.

And it all came together.

After that, Tim read everything he could about the Beresfords.

But no account mentioned the toy engine he'd found in his father's trunk. However, as a police reporter he knew enough about kidnapping and crime as a whole to know that the police usually held back some detail with which to floor any false claimant or pretender and apparently no news hawk had nosed that out.

The two main targets of his anger were Matilda, the woman he now believed to be his real mother, and Elizabeth, his sister. He conceded—sometimes—that a thirteen-year-old girl was not an adult and could not rightfully be held responsible as an adult. But what possible excuse could there be for a woman who'd leave both her children in a crowded department store during the Christmas season while she went back to her car for the purpose—according to the more sensational press—of drinking from a flask she kept in the glove compartment? That she was an alcoholic? The rage that had been the engine driving him as far back as he could remember made his heart pound. Why couldn't she have controlled herself enough to keep an eye on her children? While she was having that slug from her flask and sister Elizabeth was buying herself a forbidden lipstick, Mark had wandered off and—in the words of the man he came to call Pa—was crying outside the store. Holding the toy engine?

He swore to himself he would make them pay dearly for having ruined his life.

All the time he was reading every account of this he could find, he kept waiting for his own memory to come back—to recall the department store, the toy department, being picked up. But it was like reading about somebody else. There was nothing back there in his memory. Nothing—not even when he'd get the engine out of his bottom drawer and hold it. But he told himself that didn't mean he wasn't Mark. It didn't mean he wasn't part of a rich and powerful family, and that some of their wealth—denied him all these years—wasn't his.

As he took the last microfilm back to the desk in the library he knew his next step. He was going to Providence and somehow, by some method, get a newspaper job there.

The eight months after Caleb left the mission were filled with secret meetings and trips and—after it was discovered he could write quite well—the writing of pamphlets and letters, which were to be smuggled out of the country to the outside world. He was hidden by the guerrillas in various houses and warehouses and storerooms and offices in the capital and in shelters and lofts and barns outside. He had been bitten by, he was convinced, at least half of the country's incredible assortment of insects. Then one day when he didn't know there were soldiers or police or any of their informers within miles, he was struck in the back by a bullet.

When he recovered consciousness, he had no idea where he was and no one would tell him. But he was in a house where a man who was obviously medically knowledgeable had removed the bullet and dressed his wound and visited him until he was ready to convalesce. After that he was taken care of by a man and woman who appeared to speak neither Spanish nor English—either that, or they had been forbidden to say anything.

"All right, don't talk," he grumbled once. "What do you think I'm going to do? Run to the police or the army?"

"You can't blame anyone for thinking you might," Julie said from the next room. In the past weeks she had become a frequent visitor. "I'm not the only one who saw you as the exemplar of Holy Mother Church at its most reactionary."

"By this time you should know I've changed."

"Yes, I really think you have. Every line we put out came back affirming that."

He felt he should not give in so easily to the arrogant young woman, but his heart leaped up whenever he saw her. He reminded himself that he was still a priest, sworn to celibacy. But the triple vow—celibacy, poverty, and obedience that he had once taken so willingly and passionately—now seemed hollow. Or at least two-thirds of it—celibacy and obedience—did. To break his oath on poverty didn't appear much of a likelihood.

"It's nice to know you trust me," he said.

"The work is too important not to make sure of those we can trust."

Looking at her slightly tilted nose, the wide curving mouth, the long slim body in jeans and shirt, the fall of waving blond hair, he found he was having a hard time breathing. He had felt arousal before, but nothing like this.

"Where do you hail from originally?" he asked her abruptly.

"San Francisco."

"Why are you here doing this?"

Her brows shot up. "What a sexist you are, Father. Something tells me if I were short and dark and fat, you wouldn't question it for a moment."

She was right on target, of course. Priest or no priest, somewhere deep within him he assumed that the only purpose of such a beautiful woman would be to arouse and then satisfy a man. So he said nothing.

When he was well enough, he was set to writing reports, news artciles, and pamphlets on an ancient typewriter. He saw Julie at least once a day and knew that there were others in the house, although he rarely glimpsed them. The wound had taken a toll of his strength, but he forced himself to work until the pain in his back and shoulder became unbearable. At which point Julie would give him a mild painkiller to enable him to sleep.

Then one night, while he was lying in the dark, he heard the door open and expected the light to go on. When it didn't, he was pushing himself up on one elbow when he felt the cover pulled away and someone slid in beside him. He knew, even before he touched the long hair, that it was Julie, and whispered her name.

"Hush," she whispered, and then covered his mouth with her own. He was not a virgin, but he felt as though he were.

"Julie," he whispered. "Julie!"

Somewhere in the back of his mind, a part of him sensed that at least some of the attraction for Julie was that he was a priest. Seducing a priest would have a special lure for her. But he didn't care. In sex, as possibly in other aspects of life, she was a superb coach. She knew when to speed things up and when to slow them down. Under her careful handling he came and came and came again, finally falling back exhausted, dripping with sweat and happy beyond anything he had known.

"I love you," he said, not really knowing whether it was true. But it was the only statement that seemed exalted enough for the occasion. Then he went to sleep. When he awoke, the sun was fairly high in the sky and she had gone.

He didn't see Julie for a while, then she reappeared and they slept together again.

"Tell me how you got started in this," he said once. "You must have had a very different upbringing from any girls I ever knew."

She laughed. "You don't know a lot about people, do you?"

Despite the power she had over his emotions, he was nettled. "What do you mean?" And then, "You sometimes make me feel like the most incredible fool. Is that the way you think of me?"

She laughed. "Caleb, if I thought of you that way, I wouldn't be in your bed doing what I'm doing. I don't go to bed with people I consider stupid, foolish, or unattractive." She glanced at him. "And the fact that you think I do doesn't make me think you have a high opinion of me."

"I'm sorry. You know what kind of opinion I have of you."

She sat up a little, leaning her head on her hand. "I'm not a sex maniac, nor do I do it for a feeling of power. Whatever you're feeling about me, I'm feeling about you."

"But I told you, I love you. Didn't you believe me?"

She pulled the tips of her fingers across his chest. "I wasn't sure you weren't . . . well, carried away."

"I am carried away. But another name for that is love."

After a while he said, "Will you marry me?"

"Not now. We still have work to do, and for us, two foreigners, even without the technicality of your having been a priest, it wouldn't be a good idea. Let's wait until we get back to the States, and then we'll see."

"Thou art a priest forever," the bishop had recited at his ordination. "I can get laicized," Caleb said. "By the way, what religion were you brought up in?"

"Episcopalian," she said carelessly. "I told you. You're not the only rebel."

Then the letter from his father came.

When was Elizabeth first aware of the shadow that lay between them? She wasn't sure. When she tried to think through what that something was, she always emerged baffled. There was Ian, of course, but at least in the first year, his barbs had not penetrated to that degree. There was Graham's eternal traveling. Somehow there never seemed a moment when he was not on his way somewhere and three-quarters of his mind was not already at the destination.

When Duncan was born, it was different for a while. Graham stayed home for the birth and for a short period immediately afterward. Elizabeth had an easy time with Duncan, who arrived promptly, exactly when he was supposed to, and inherited from somewhere a sunny disposition that didn't even seem to be particularly rumpled by an occasional dig from Ian. Although Ian saved most of his hostility for Elizabeth, he made it clear he included her children in his general condemnation of everything belonging to her.

"Of course they won't really know what being truly English means," he said once to a pal from Oxford who was staying with them.

"Oh, come on," his pal said, and then laughed. "You do have your knife into your stepmother, don't you?"

"Don't call her that," Ian said sharply.

"Don't be an ass. That's what she is!"

"The word mother applied to her in conjunction with me, even with step in front of it, is repellent."

"Why do you hate her so much?"

"I don't hate her. I simply don't like Americans!"

"Some of them are often tiresome and vulgar, I grant you. Still, I have to point out, Winston Churchill's mother was American."

"Does that excuse the entire race?"

Elizabeth, overhearing this conversation, as she knew she was meant to, was tempted to walk in and demand, like Ian's friend, why he loathed Americans with such fanatic fervor. Instead, she asked Graham.

"I'm sure he doesn't," Graham said. "You know, we've talked about your ... your sensitivity on the subject."

"Graham, I'm repeating a conversation—word for word—that I overheard. I didn't make it up. Ian said what he did. I've passed beyond feeling hurt by it. I think its pathological."

"I'm sure it isn't," Graham said sharply. "Ian's a perfectly normal boy who undoubtedly misses his mother. They were very close. He's also at an awkward age."

"He may have been at an awkward age when we married. Sixteen can be difficult. But he's now twenty-one, doing very well at Oxford, and there's nothing awkward about it."

Graham made an impatient sound. "I can't help feeling that all this boils down to being my fault. And I suppose you're right. I haven't been a good father. I've been away too much. But if I'm to keep the family firm going, I have to take care of its business in addition to teaching and writing."

"I wasn't even implying that it was your fault! But if you really think that—that your being away has something to do with Ian's problems and his hostility to me and my children—then maybe you ought to consider Ian and his attitudes more important than the family firm."

"Would you like that? If the family company declined and our money along with it, we'd be living at a far different standard from the one we—all of us—enjoy now."

There it was again. "Are you saying I married you for your money?"

Graham turned and faced her in their bedroom where they were going to bed. "That had something to do with it, didn't it?"

She didn't answer. When they got into bed they turned their backs to one another. Elizabeth switched off the light beside her bed.

Lying there, she finally acknowledged to herself that the swift flare-up was not a cause, but the result of a barrier that had come between her and Graham. Or perhaps the barrier hadn't just appeared. Perhaps it had always been there, and she had simply been unaware of it—or deliberately ignored it.

The next day she had lunch with an American friend who worked in England, and found herself telling Judy about Ian's conversation and the ensuing argument with Graham.

"I am probably being oversensitive. Any English person I mention this to thinks I am."

"The English are tougher than we are," Judy, also married to an Englishman, said. "Somebody, I think it was Barbara Tuchman in her book on Vinegar Joe Stilwell in China, said something about the greatest English achievement not being the British Empire, but the English self-image, which was undentable. I've noticed, in the years I've been married to Colin, the English often pride themselves on being shy, but the chronic self-doubt that seems to afflict us is unknown to them and they don't have much patience with it."

"I know what you say is true, but I continue to think there's something more than just British undentable self-image in Ian's hostility. Brenda at the office says it's because he knows he can get to me. And I think it's at least partly true. But why? Why is it necessary to him? Why does he bother?"

Judy shrugged. "The real question is, is it worth breaking up your marriage about?"

After a minute Elizabeth asked, "Do you think I'm doing that?"

"From what you tell me, every time you criticize Ian to Graham, Graham goes on the defensive. You're putting him in an impossible position. He's torn between his wife and his son. Whose side is he going to take?"

Elizabeth blinked back tears. "I thought when I presented him with incontrovertible evidence, he'd be forced to take mine."

"And then what?"

"Well, he'd make Ian ..." Her voice trailed off as she really understood what she was saying.

"And lose Ian? More fool you! And if you're wise you won't try to force him anymore."

After that Elizabeth never again complained to Graham about Ian. But that didn't mean the matter didn't rankle within her.

Then Ailsa was born, different in every way from

Duncan, but, increasingly through the years, a haunting reminder of Mark, with her noisy demands, her easily triggered temper, and her growing physical resemblance to him.

It had been a difficult pregnancy and was a premature birth culminating in a Caesarian section. Graham, who had carefully planned his trip to South Africa to occur before Ailsa's arrival, had been in the hospital the actual night Elizabeth was operated on, but he had left for Cape Town the next morning, and a series of upsets and mishaps when he was in South Africa prevented him from getting back for a month. He called her almost daily, but something in Elizabeth had closed off. Often she wasn't even there when his call came in, and though he usually left a number, she only occasionally called back.

Ailsa turned out to be as full of problems as Duncan was easy. Elizabeth desperately tried to be there for her daughter whenever Ailsa was upset, which was often. But the results were not happy for either.

On her own, and without consulting Graham, Elizabeth hired a specially trained nanny, who seemed to be able to handle the volatile little girl far better than Elizabeth could.

Discovering this, both in relief and guilt, Elizabeth went back to working part time at Hougton and Lord, but she stayed longer hours in her office in London than she had since her marriage.

The increased hours were, ironically, the reason she learned that Graham was having an affair.

Afterward, she realized that for some time she had been growingly aware that this was a possibility. For one thing, their sexual encounters had become first infrequent, then rare, then stopped altogether for at least a month.

One day when she was in London, having lunch with an author in a Soho restaurant, she glanced out the window and saw Graham and a tall, lovely young woman walking past. Her hand was on his arm. On his face was a look that left her in no doubt as to their relationship.

Her first thought was, of course: it was so obvious, why hadn't that occurred to her before? Her second was angry amusement that he should stroll with his girlfriend in Soho. He must know, she thought, that she always took her authors there. It was near Houghton and Lord, and Soho was filled with small, good restaurants. The third thought was that he probably didn't care. Somehow that was the most devastating of all.

She confronted Graham that evening in the sitting room after dinner. Having served them coffee, Parker, the butler, had just left. As she stirred her coffee she said in a calm voice, "I saw you today when I was having lunch on Greek Street. Who was the lovely you were with?"

Deception didn't come naturally to Graham. A flush stained his whole face. "I don't ... I don't know—"

"Graham, it's no use lying. I saw you, and I saw your face. You're having an affair, aren't you?"

He put his cup down on the table beside him. "Yes, I am."

"When did it start?"

"About a month ago."

"What happened? Did you just see her and fall in love?"

"Yes. At least—I suppose that's what happened." He sounded desperately unhappy, but she assumed it was less any lingering love he might have for her than guilt from the strong puritan streak that ran in him.

"Do you want a divorce?" The words came out of her mouth without any previous thought.

"No. Elizabeth, I'm sorry. We have to talk about this, but not tonight. I'm off early tomorrow for Johannesburg. Can we talk when I get back?"

She shrugged. "As you wish."

He went to bed soon afterward, and she sat there in the elegant town house that had been her home for ten years and finally came to grips with how angry she was.

The next day after breakfast, after the continuation of their argument of the night before and on her way to work, she read her father's letter concerning the trust.

Despite what Graham said, she might well be facing a divorce, and she knew that no matter what the settlement, she would need her own money—and the independence it would bring.

THE
TRUST

CHAPTER
10

Tim had never been able to make any friends, partly because when growing up he had moved too much. And partly because the only way he could endure life with the woman he called his mother was to pretend—pretend when he was locked in the closet that he was not there: that his body might be there, but he was somewhere else. As a survival technique it worked, but at the price of his being unable to break through his own isolation—even when he wanted to. Once he was old enough to go to bars, alcohol and the undemanding camaraderie there helped. But even with the aid of alcohol he found it almost impossible to confide or trust.

The other reporters with whom he drank after the paper closed were cohorts, buddies, colleagues. They all stood around the bar or sat in a booth and traded gossip and stories about work. At some point the others eventually went home to wives, husbands, girlfriends or boyfriends. That was when he headed for another type of bar, usually in a seamier part of town. There was less laughing, fewer stories exchanged. These bars were retreats for loners of both sexes. From time to time he went home with some girl he met there. If whoever she was started showing more serious interest, he switched for a while to another of his haunts. Occasionally he picked up tidbits he could use as background in some of his stories. He came to be known as a reporter and one who sometimes exchanged a twenty for a good lead or tip.

After he was hired on the *Providence Times* and to get his foot in the Beresfords' door he suggested to Jock Holcomb, the managing editor, a series on Providence's leading families. Holcomb was less than enthusiastic. A similar series had been done sometime previously on the other newspaper. But Tim was persuasive, proposing different angles, and Holcomb gave a guarded go-ahead.

To deflect suspicion, Tim started with two of the other prominent families and was about to embark on the Beresfords when news of the Beresford trust filtered into the office, and Robbie made things easier for him by running for the Republican nomination for governor.

Elizabeth strode into the British Airways reception area at Logan Airport. She could have booked a short connecting flight to Providence, but decided instead to take a taxi or a limousine from Boston to Summerstoke. It would, she thought, give her a closer view of her native land, which she hadn't seen for twenty years. But just as she was headed for the baggage claim and cab stand, she saw a familiar figure coming toward her.

"Robbie!" she cried. She had written the time and flight of her arrival to her mother, but she hadn't really expected to be met.

He smiled and kissed her cheek. "The same. In person."

"You haven't changed at all," she said. And he hadn't. He still had the tall, lean Beresford build, and his hairline had receded only a little at the corners of his forehead. If anything, he looked better.

"You have," Robbie said bluntly. "You were a pretty girl. Now you're a knockout! Marriage must agree with you." He bent and picked up her bag. "I assume you have more baggage."

Elizabeth grinned, reminding Robbie suddenly of the feisty younger sister of long ago. "Why do you assume there's more baggage? I might have just come for two nights, gotten my share of the trust, and then gone back again."

"After twenty years? I don't think so."

"All right. Two more pieces."

"Then we'd better get over to the baggage claim."

Forty-five minutes later, they'd left the airport and were headed toward Rhode Island and Summerstoke.

Elizabeth looked out at the suburban houses and trees and patches of green. In many ways, the passing view was not that different from the outskirts of London, but it felt different, probably, she supposed, because of the muddle of emotions—old homesickness, anticipation, fear, and a sudden new homesickness for England—that seemed to be roiling inside her. Part of her would like nothing better at this moment than to turn around and get back on the plane and return to London. To distract herself she glanced at her brother.

"How are Jenny and the children?"

"Fine. Jenny's anxious to meet you. How are Graham and Duncan and Ailsa?"

Robbie the diplomat, she thought. He had never met her children, but he knew them by name. Temporarily—she devoutly hoped—any recollection of his children's names had vanished.

"Fine, thanks. Duncan's getting ready to go off to boarding school next term."

"He's pretty young for that, isn't he? Although I guess the English have always done that with their boys. Seems sort of barbarous to me."

"Yes, it did to me, too. But Duncan can hardly wait. All his friends have gone off to school." She sighed. "He's a very healthy, well-adjusted boy."

Robbie laughed. "I should think that'd make you happy. Instead you sound resigned."

"I guess because Ailsa is anything but." Elizabeth almost said, She remains me of Mark, but changed her mind. Twenty-six years of silence on the subject had had its effect. At that moment her memory clicked into place. "And how are Robert Three and Deirdre?"

"We call him Three," Robbie said. "Both fine. Three's in prep school and Deirdre has just started at boarding school."

"Mom wrote me you're running for governor. Is that right?"

"Yes. I am."

Elizabeth glanced at him and smiled. "And what's your platform?"

"More jobs for more people, less waste in government, both local and national, less government interference, getting rid of the mob and corruption in the state and city government, and stabilizing the banks."

"Who's your main competition?"

"A guy named Pennell."

"Mob connected?"

"There's not a shred of evidence that he is."

"But you think he is?"

"He's cousin to one of the leading mob figures. His father, by the way, changed the name from Pennelli, but that, of course, does not mean he's mob. In these days one has to be very careful not to make that connection without a lot of solid backup." He glanced sideways. "Do you have the same thing in London?"

"No. At least, nowhere near as much. The English are very busy assimilating members of the former empire, but they're a small percent. The bulk are still homogeneous, with all the confidence and xenophobia that usually implies."

"You don't sound as though you are in love with the place. In which case, why didn't you at least come back and visit? I think it would have made a big difference to Mom."

"Is she sober enough to have anything make that big a difference? Mom's drinking is Mom's responsibility, just as it was when ..." Her words were followed by the feeling of depression that always came when she was reminded of the day Mark disappeared.

"Just as it was when what?"

"Nothing. Never mind." Then she laughed. "I'm away twenty years and within ten minutes of being back we're quarreling. *Plus ça change,* et cetera."

"I don't think we're quarreling," Robbie said.

After a few minutes' driving in silence, Elizabeth said, "I was a little surprised when I got Dad's command performance letter, that we were all going to meet in Summerstoke instead of College Hill."

"I think that was a concession to Mom. She doesn't much like the College Hill house, although I'm not sure why. She says her dogs have more room in the country."

"How many does she have now?"

"Three or four, all children or grandchildren of the original Honey that Caleb gave her."

"Is Caleb back?"

"Yes. He arrived yesterday and called me from town. He'll be there tonight."

"Tell me about Terry. Last I heard she was going to some little college in Boston."

"She's done some kind of turnaround since then," and Robbie told Elizabeth about David Stein and Terry's pregnancy and abortion. "She always struck me as a sort of meek little thing, poor grades, no good at athletics, not really interested in anything. I think she expected Mom to back her up in having the baby, anyway ..."

"And Matilda, the Catholic, didn't?"

Robbie didn't say anything for a moment. Then, "Maybe if it had been somebody we all knew, one of our own kind, Mom's feeling might have been different. But—"

"Abortion was less horrifying than a Jewish son-in-law, I gather."

"Come off it, Liz. I know you and Mom never got along, but do you have to hammer at her all the time? Maybe she just felt that having an illegitimate baby at seventeen was not the best possible start in life for Terry."

"But I thought Catholics—particularly the McGarrett kind—were strong prolifers, or has Beresford snobbery overcome McGarrett Catholic orthodoxy?" She saw her brother's jaw harden. "Sorry. I guess I shouldn't criticize her the way I do."

"Why are you so tough on her—apart from her share in Mark's disappearance?"

At the words Elizabeth experienced the odd, closing-down feeling that she often had when she thought of her mother—or tried not to think about her. She struggled against it. "You forget. You're older than me and probably have some memory of what she was like before she drank so much. I don't."

"That'd have more credence if you were a lot younger, Liz. But you're only two years younger than me. Is there something else?"

"I don't think so. After all, girls notoriously have problems with their mothers and mothers with their daughters. Doesn't Jenny get along better with Three than with Deirdre?"

Robbie gave a short laugh. Elizabeth wondered if she had inadvertently trodden on a sensitive spot. "Don't answer if you'd rather not."

"Oh, I don't mind. As a matter of fact, it's the opposite with us. Deirdre is her mother's greatest ally and advocate. Has the same approach to—well, all kind of things. But Three is the rebel."

"I see. Is it just all-purpose adolescent rebellion, or is there something specific he's rebelling against?"

"I'm not sure what started it. Right now it takes

the form of being violently antichurch. Won't go. Has refused to go to chapel at his prep school and when the headmaster threatened him with punishment, he said he'd appeal to the civil liberties people on some kind of grounds of separation of church and state."

Elizabeth laughed. "Robbie, I don't mean to sound unsympathetic. I know what you're talking about. I'm bound to tell you, though, Three sounds interesting."

They drove for a while in silence, interspersed with desultory questions and answers about friends and relatives. Then Elizabeth said, "The actual election is a year away. What are you going to do between now and then to get yourself before the public eye? Of course, the name doesn't hurt."

"No. At least not with most people in College Hill. But there're an awful lot of people not in College Hill. Anyway, I have to start somewhere, so I'm being interviewed tomorrow by a guy from the local paper."

"At Summerstoke?"

"Yes. He wanted the interview to be against the family background."

"Is this at your instigation or his? If that's a stupid question, I'm sorry. But I don't know how these things go."

"A little of both. Actually, it was the idea of my new political aide, a gal named Kate Malloy. This news guy has done pieces on various well-known families in Providence. When I announced that I was going to run, Kate, who knows him, suggested the idea to him, and he called me. I wasn't that enthusiastic, but since I hired her for her political savvy, I guess I should do what she suggests."

"Why weren't you that enthusiastic? As a candidate you're obviously going to need all the exposure you can get."

"Because his pieces on some of the other notable families, while not antagonistic, seemed—to me, at least—to have an anti-rich, anti-establishment note. I suppose that's the atmosphere today, but I don't have to like it."

"Then why did this Kate suggest it?"

"She thought it was the best way to spike his guns. If I welcome the idea, instead of holding off, he might be nicer to the Beresfords than to the others. Anyway, it's set up now, so I can't back out."

At that moment the turrets of Summerstoke, rising above the rest of the roof, came into sight through the trees on the right.

Elizabeth felt a tightening of her stomach. For a moment she wished again she were back in England. England was at least a known quantity. But England contained Graham, and Graham, dependable Graham, was no longer a known quantity.

"Well, here we are," Robbie said, turning in at the gates. "Welcome home and all that." He went around the half circle of the drive and drew the car up behind another car parked to the right of the front door. Elizabeth got out. Staring up at the sprawling red brick house with its absurd turrets, she felt a strange pang that could have been nostalgia or regret or even bittersweet pleasure at being back at her own home.

The front door opened, and Robert Senior came down the steps, followed immediately by Matilda.

"Elizabeth," her father said, walking over to her. He took her hands in his and bent and kissed her cheek. "Welcome back. It's good to see you."

Elizabeth stared up into his face. She didn't know what she expected to see in her father after twenty years' absence. He was now in his late sixties. The thick, waving hair that his son had inherited had barely receded. Nor was it completely gray, and his figure had remained lean. The blue eyes stared down at her. She felt suddenly as though she didn't know him at all.

"How are you?" he asked.

"Fine, thank you, Dad. How are you?"

"Well."

Matilda came up to his side. "Elizabeth, my dear. It's so good to see you at last. It's been such a long time." After a second's hesitation she came forward, her arms out as though to put them around Elizabeth's neck. As she did so Elizabeth understood her hesitation. As the older woman leaned nearer, Elizabeth smelled the alcohol on her breath. A jolt of irritation went through her, followed immediately by guilt at being so judgmental. Emerging from her mother's embrace, she looked into the older woman's greenish eyes, so like her own, and was suddenly overwhelmed by how unhappy Matilda seemed.

"Hi, Mom. It's good to see you again."

"You look lovely," Matilda said almost wonderingly.

Through the open door came a stocky, elderly dachshund followed by a much younger version of herself. The older dog went straight to Matilda, but the young one flung herself against Elizabeth's skirt.

"Oh dear, I'm afraid her paws are dirty," Matilda said. "Down, Honey," she said and was ignored by the golden long-haired little dog.

"Down!" Robert Senior said. The little dog immediately withdrew and sat down, looking up at Elizabeth.

"You're very pretty," Elizabeth said to Honey, "and I guess you know who's boss."

At that moment Caleb's car turned into the gates and drove up, parking behind Robbie's.

"Here's Caleb," Matilda said happily.

Caleb got out of the car to greet his parents and then turned toward Elizabeth. "Liz! It's good to see you." And he hugged her.

The sight of Caleb proved more of a shock to Elizabeth than any of the others. Somehow she'd expected to see him in a round collar. Instead, he wore jeans, a blue shirt without a tie, and a plaid jacket. His tawny hair looked oddly long for a priest—at least any priest she ever remembered. But more than any of that, there was a quality about him that was different from what she remembered. Her parents and Robbie were older but substantially the same. Caleb was not.

"We'll have cocktails in the library around five," her mother said. "The whole family's coming. And then an early dinner." She looked at Elizabeth. "I realize it's much later for you. You must be suffering from jet lag."

"I am," Elizabeth said. "But I expect I'll get a second wind. All this is in preparation for the big day tomorrow, I take it—like something out of an English mystery." As her mother stared without commenting, Elizabeth, trying not to feel annoyance at her parents' slow perceptions, went on, "The reading of the trust."

"Yes," Matilda replied. "I know your father wants to say something about it at dinner." Then she rushed on, "Why don't you go on up and unpack? Maureen would normally be here to help you, but unfortunately, her mother's sick, so she is away at the moment. We're a bit shorthanded."

"It's all right. I'm happy to do it. I'll see you in the library at five."

Up in her old room, from which she could see the long lawn sloping down to Narragansett Bay, Elizabeth put away her clothes, hanging the dresses and suits in the roomy closet and placing her underwear in bureau drawers that had been freshly lined. She took a long shower, graduating the water from hot to warm and briskly toweled her body dry. It was not a substitute for a nap, but she felt somewhat revived. Then she slid into a straight silk dress in patterns of blue and green. Combing out her thick auburn hair, she wondered what her father was going to say about the trust at dinner. Well, she thought, it didn't matter. The main thing was the money that would be coming to her. She had spent most of the flight struggling to block out thoughts of Graham and all that had gone wrong between them. Since he had taken the step of being unfaithful, she wanted to have her independence assured.

Elizabeth walked into the library a little afer five and glanced around. It seemed full of people. She recognized her father's cousin, James, and his wife, Sally. Among the half dozen or so adolescents standing around were, she assumed, their children, Joan, Barbara and Ted, along with Robbie's two, Three and Deirdre. Also, of course, their mother, Jenny. Suddenly she found herself wishing that Duncan and Ailsa were there, Duncan who looked more like his father every day, and Ailsa who could pass for a younger version of the slender, dark-haired young woman talking to Caleb. Who was she? Joan or Barbara?

"Dad wants to know if you'd like a drink."

The boy who stood in front of her was about fifteen. Straight light brown hair fell over his face and covered his collar. "I'm Three," he said. "Robert Three. I guess you can't tell us younger ones apart, can you?"

"No," she admitted and smiled. So this was the rebel. "I think I'd like a wh—Scotch and water."

She went with him to the table that was serving as a bar and watched him make the drink. When he handed it to her she said, "Maybe you can help me. Who is the dark girl talking to Caleb?"

Three turned and looked. "That's Terry, my aunt, your younger sister." He sounded surprised at her question. "How old was she when you left?"

So that's the girl who had the abortion, Elizabeth thought. She said, "About four. Suddenly twenty years seems a long time."

"Well, if you left as an act of rebellion, more power to you."

"I did, I guess. Althugh maybe it felt like something else at the time. Your father told me you were this generation's rebel."

"Yeah." The boy stared moodily into his glass. The liquid inside looked as though it were some sort of cola drink. Elizabeth found herself wondering if there were anything in it but ice. The stories about drinking and drug taking among American adolescents of all classes filled English tabloids and gossip columns.

She knew she ought to move on to some of the others, but she said, "What especially are you rebelling against, or is that too long a subject?"

"You sound a bit English. I guess it's natural after living over there for so long—gosh, since before I was born."

"I suppose I do."

He looked up quickly. His eyes, Elizabeth noticed, were an amber shade. "It's nice. I didn't mean it wasn't."

She smiled at him. "It's all right." She waited to see if he'd answer her question. A little to her surprise he did.

"What am I against? Religion and social hogwash."

"By social hogwash you mean all this?" And she waved her glass around the room.

"I don't mind family gatherings. It's just how important class is—the right school, the right friends, that kind of thing." He looked up. "Of course, you've got a title. Mom's always talking about it."

"What do you mean, talking about it?"

"Oh, dropping it when she's talking. 'My sister-in-law, Lady Paterson.'"

"And religion?"

But at that moment a woman in her late thirties came up behind Three. Elizabeth took in the well-cut dress, fashionably styled light brown hair and amber eyes and put out her hand. "You must be Jenny."

"And you're Elizabeth." Jenny had taken her hand and was beginning to lean forward as though to kiss her. Then she stopped. "I take it you've met Three." And she put her hand on her son's shoulder. "We're all very proud of him. He just won the class writing prize at his school."

"Mom, for chrissake." And he moved from under her hand.

The amber eyes seemed to flash. "You know I don't like to hear you say that."

"It's only an expression," Elizabeth said as peaceably as she could—then noted that Three had already disappeared.

"I know. And I also know he does it to annoy me." She made a face. "The bad part is I let myself be annoyed."

"I know what you mean because my daughter, Ailsa, manages to annoy me even when she's not trying."

"We must try to be patient," Jenny said. Elizabeth could hardly quarrel with the sentiment, but there was something in Jenny's voice that made Elizabeth understand why Three was rebelling.

Caleb strolled up with Terry. He said with a smile, "I know you've met Terry, but not for quite a while."

The girl put out her hand. "It's nice to see you, Elizabeth."

Elizabeth grasped her hand, then leaned forward, kissed her cheek and gave her a brief hug. "And it's wonderful to see you. You're at school in Boston, aren't you? Mom wrote me."

"Yes, well, I was at Boston Academy. I'm now at Boston University, teaching and working on my doctorate."

"I'm not sure I knew that. What's your field?"

"Women's Studies." Her tone was defiant.

"I see."

Terry seemed about to say something, then appeared to change her mind. Instead, she turned her head one way and then another. "I don't see Mom; isn't she down yet?"

"No," Jenny said briefly. "The maid said she'd be down for dinner but was resting until then."

Elizabeth glanced at Jenny. Had she become the daughter in charge? Well, she thought, why not? She herself had abdicated any such position and Terry lived in Boston. They were surrounded by people now, but at some point she intended to talk to Jenny about Matilda.

It seemed a long time before Parker came in and said something to Robert Senior. He glanced at his watch and at the clock on the mantelpiece, then said something back to Parker. After the butler left, Robert raised his voice above the cocktail clamor. "All right, folks. Dinner is ready. Let's go on in."

"I thought Jon Treadwell was going to join us," Jenny said.

"Something's probably held him up. We won't wait any longer."

They were seated before Elizabeth noticed that there were two empty places, one on the side of the long oval table, the other at the opposite end from her father.

"Is Mom not coming down?" Terry asked her father.

"No, I think all the excitement has tired her out. We'll go ahead."

They were halfway through dinner when Parker came in and said something to Robert Senior in such a low voice that Elizabeth only caught the name "Treadwell."

Her father's reaction was instantaneous. He stood up. "Excuse me," he said to the table at large, then followed the butler out. A few minutes later he came back into the room. He walked slowly to the table and stood there for a moment. All talk stopped.

"I'm sorry," he said slowly, "to have to tell you that Jon Treadwell had a heart attack an hour ago." There was a murmur of voices.

"Where is he now?" Robbie asked.

"In the hospital. I'm afraid he's dead."

Everyone seemed stunned for a moment, then Robbie said, "That's terrible."

"I'm so sorry," Jenny said.

She sounds as though she really is, Elizabeth thought. She herself had barely known Jon Treadwell when she was growing up, so though she knew it seemed lacking in feeling, she asked the question that was on her mind. "What does that do to the reading of the trust tomorrow?"

"It certainly won't be read tomorrow," Robert Senior said. His face looked almost drawn. "Jon was a loner and pretty much handled everything in his office."

"But didn't he—wasn't he part of one of those law firms with lots of names?"

"Yes," her father said. "But most of them were old and have retired or died. Anyway, each partner handled his own stuff. Jon inherited the Beresford portfolio from his father."

"So who will handle it?" Elizabeth asked. All she could think of was how long she'd be kept here, away from England and her children and job and home. And then wondered: In that order?

Robbie said, "His son, Andrew, is a lawyer, but lives in Seattle, and anyway, he's—"

"I don't see what that has to do with anything," Caleb broke in angrily.

"No. Of course not." Robert Senior made a visible effort to compose himself. "According to the man who called me—one of the partners—Andrew is coming east. Apparently he's the one who has kept up with his father's work and was simply running the firm's western branch. He'll be here in a few days, but it may take him awhile to catch up enough to do the reading. We'll just have to postpone it."

CHAPTER

11

As the plane taxied to the airport terminal, Andrew Treadwell pulled himself up using the back of the seat in front of him and reached for the cane that he had stashed in the overhead baggage rack. Then he leaned down for his briefcase. He'd spent all the hours from Seattle going over some of the papers that his father's secretary had faxed from Providence. At this point he figured it would take him at least two or three weeks to know what action to take on various pending matters. His father should have retired a couple of years back and Andrew knew it, but his fondness for the old man plus his distance out in the Seattle office had kept him from pushing the matter.

Andrew looked around him as he limped through the corridor to the terminal. He had told Josh Emory, his father's oldest partner, what flight he'd be coming on, but that didn't mean that Josh would take it upon himself to meet him. Andrew remembered Josh as aloof and rather forbidding. He had shown up at Andrew's graduation from Yale Law School, but his sole comment was that they had done things somewhat differently at Harvard Law School, where he himself had gone.

But Josh was at the gate, neat and trim, with gray hair and gray mustache. "Hello, Andrew. Sad occasion, but always good to see you. I'm sorry about your father. He was a good man and a good lawyer."

Andrew was astonished and embarrassed to feel the beginning of tears in his eyes. "Yes, he was, wasn't he?"

"The car's outside. I'll take you to the house. The funeral's at three. I thought we might go together. Unless, of course, you'd rather go alone. Your father's car is in the garage, so you can certainly use that if you want. I'll understand."

"Do you mind if I do, Josh? Although I'm grateful for your suggestion, and I'll certainly need to lean on you in the work that I know has to be done."

"Not a bit. Just call if you need me."

Andrew stared out the window as they rode, not inclined to talk and grateful for Josh's silence. They passed through the outskirts of Providence, then into the city through one of the Italian neighborhoods.

"I used to get pizza there," Andrew said once, pointing to a one-story pizza place.

"I always liked that place, too, though your father claimed you could get better pizza across the street."

Finally Josh said in a casual voice, "Everything okay with you these days? Your father wasn't a talker about other people's affairs, but I gathered that the divorce was . . . well, difficult."

Andrew looked over warily. "It could certainly be described that way. Althea took everything she could get her hands on."

"Did you have to let her?"

"It was something of a trade-off. I could have dragged it through the courts for a few more rounds, but it was tough on Jonathon and Desmond because I gather they got the backlash every time Althea lost a point. And she made it quite clear that she'd be as difficult as she could over custody if I was—as she put it—stingy over the property settlement."

"I'm sorry," Josh said.

"So'm I. Except for having had the children, who are great, the marriage was something of a disaster."

The car approached the bridge, and Andrew looked down at the river and then at College Hill rising above it. Until that moment he hadn't realized how greatly he'd missed Providence. His house in Seattle overlooked Puget Sound from the front and had a magnificent view of the Olympic Mountains from the back. He liked the softer, mistier climate, and he liked the people. But on his visits to Providence he was overcome with the realization of how much of an easterner he had remained.

The Treadwell house was on one of the shorter roads in College Hill, slanting steeply uphill. It rose between two brick houses with a small garden at the back and two narrow strips of green on each side. Three very old trees rose up on either side and in front of the house.

"Here we are," Josh said, and pulled up outside the iron gate. He reached in his jacket pocket and produced a handful of keys. "Here are the house keys and the keys to the garage and the car. If you change your mind about going to the funeral alone, you can still get me at the office."

"All right, thanks."

Andrew was an only child. His mother had died after he had returned from Vietnam but while he was still in an army hospital being patched up after a Vietcong grenade had almost finished him off. Except for a slightly shorter right leg, which forced him to use a cane when he walked, he had fully recovered. It had been five years since he had returned to the house in which he had grown up, although he and his father had managed to meet somewhere—either in Seattle or in the cabin they frequently rented in Wyoming— each year. But with his father now dead, the house he entered was empty and would remain so. I'll have to think what to do with it, he thought, and knew as he did so that he had not yet made up his mind as to whether he would return to Providence or stay in Seattle. His children were with his ex-wife in Portland. He had buit up a practice in Seattle and had a number of friends there. Yet—

He closed the front door behind him and stared at the hall and the curving staircase. He had an hour before he had to leave for the funeral, and he was pretty certain that the Beresfords, gathered in Providence and full of expectation about the reading of the living trust, would attend. He had gone to boarding school with Robbie, and he'd seen Elizabeth at parties and dances during those years. He had liked Robbie well enough, considering him a chip off the old WASP block, like many of the other guys in his class. And just as boring, he'd often add to himself.

Jon Treadwell, a product of a puritan background, had never told Andrew what was in the trust, but he had stipulated in his will that should anything happen to him, Andrew was to take over the administration of it. Jon had followed his own father into the firm of Treadwell, Emory, Hives and Barker and had sent Andrew out to their office in Seattle, where Hives and Barker had started. Andrew, still embittered over the war and the way the veterans were treated, sometimes rubbed people the wrong way, particularly those whose sons had managed not to get drafted or whose draft status had been deferred. Seven years of college and law school had not smoothed this down much, so Jon dispatched Andrew west to calm down a bit. Meeting Althea and getting married out there had made Andrew's stay permanent.

Now he was back. He glanced at his watch. He had to get his bag to his old bedroom and wash up. After that it would be time to leave for the funeral.

Elizabeth, sitting across the church from Andrew in a pew filled with Beresfords (except for Matilda), decided that time and distance had not changed the boy she remembered. He had been a gawky, silent kid, and she had wondered what had made the popular Robbie pay much attention to him. Robbie, captain of the football team and star pitcher in baseball, usually hung out with other jocks. Once she had asked him what he saw in Andrew.

"Oh, he's not half bad. He's sorta bright."

At that moment Andrew turned and looked toward the back of the church. The closed coffin was at the front, resting on a catafalque, so, Elizabeth thought, he must be waiting for someone. The minister? His wife? But it turned out to be a man whom Elizabeth recognized from the past as one of Jon Treadwell's partners.

In turning back, Andrew's eyes met Elizabeth's and he smiled suddenly.

Startled, he thought to himself, She's become a beauty. At sixteen she had abandoned the heavy glasses that had covered her face like a mask and (he assumed) had substituted contact lenses. But she must have been twenty pounds heavier than she was now and for all her memorable green eyes and dark red hair had been only mildly attractive. Now— He became aware that a black-robed minister had emerged into the church from a side door and was waiting to get Andrew's attention so he could begin. Guilty because his mind had strayed from his father, whose body lay a few feet away, Andrew focused his eyes on the minister. The latter opened up a book and started.

"I'm sorry about your father, Andrew," Elizabeth said outside the church as the coffin was being lifted into the hearse.

"Yes. So'm I. But he once said to me that he had enjoyed his life thoroughly, so I'm concentrating on that." He had an impulse to ask Elizabeth if she would have dinner with him afterward, but instantly became ashamed. What's the matter with me? he reproached himself. And then felt the beginning of tears in the back of his eyes when he suddenly was sure what his father would have said, "What's wrong with that, Andy? Life goes on."

But he decided to ask her at some later point.

Elizabeth was also experiencing a sense of shame over her impulse to ask Andrew if he knew how much each Beresford would receive under the living trust. How mercenary can I be? she wondered, and backed away from Andrew just as Josh Emory and Robert Senior came up.

Her father, Robbie, and Jenny joined Andrew and the partners in their journey to the cemetery. Muttering something about meeting a friend, Caleb slid away and got into his hired car. Terry turned toward the family car, chauffeured by Carter, in which the other Beresfords had arrived. "Coming?" she asked Elizabeth.

Elizabeth was in a quandary. She did not have a car of her own here, which meant that if she didn't go with Terry she'd be stuck with no means of transport. Nevertheless, she found herself balking at the idea of returning immediately to Summerstoke. Stuck twenty miles out in the country without a car she'd feel trapped. When she had thought the trust would be read the day after she arrived, the matter of transportation had not seemed that important.

"Elizabeth, are you or are you not coming?" Terry asked in an exasperated voice.

"Just a minute, Terry," Elizabeth said, then walked quickly toward Caleb in his car. "Caleb," she called. She saw several heads turn in her direction. It couldn't be helped, she thought. "Caleb," she called again.

He stuck his head out the car window. She went over to him. "Take me into Providence," she said. "I need to rent a car, too."

"I wondered what you were going to do without one. Okay, I'll take you into the city to where I got this car."

"All right. Just let me tell Terry."

When she returned, he thrust open the door of the passenger seat and she got in.

As they turned away from the curb she asked, "How long do you think it'll be—before the trust will be read?"

"I haven't the faintest idea. But if that firm of shysters holds us up too long, I'm going to another lawyer to sue."

Elizabeth turned her head and stared at him. "Why on earth do you call them shysters? They haven't stolen anything from us."

"How do you know?"

"Look, Father Caleb, the burden of proof is on you. You can't just throw that kind of accusation around unless you have something with which to back it up. Now what do you have?"

"Don't you find it suspicious that one of the other lawyers doesn't read the trust tomorrow? What's holding it up?"

"That just could be that Jon did his own thing. Why, what's your hurry?"

His hurry, Caleb thought, was that Julie, stowed at an inexpensive hotel in town, was getting impatient. "Come on, Caleb," she'd said over the phone when he'd managed to call her the day after his father's announcement, "the guerrillas can't wait forever. The dry season is about to start and we need to pour money in now, to get the different groups in place, to lay in medical supplies and food. Isn't there anything you can do to speed things up?"

"I don't know what I can do, Julie, but I'll sure see if there is."

"Can you get into the city tonight?"

"I'll be there," he promised.

He hadn't thought of an acceptable excuse to Robert Senior and the others, but he'd call them and make up something.

"You are in a hurry, aren't you?" Elizabeth asked now, her eyes still on him as he drove.

"For reasons I don't want to go into, Liz, I really need that money now, not a month from now." As he reached out to the floor shift of his car, a spasm of pain crossed his face, twisting his mouth.

Elizabeth, who was looking at him, said, "What's the matter?"

"Nothing."

"Doesn't look like nothing."

"I hurt my shoulder."

"How? What happened?"

Caleb didn't answer right away. Then, "If you must know, I got shot in the back."

"What?" she asked, astounded.

Caleb said hastily, "I'm fine now, but every now and then it gives me a twinge."

"Who shot you?"

"A soldier from the great, peace-maintaining Guatemalan army."

"Good heavens, Caleb! Do they just go around shooting priests?"

"It was in the good Catholic country of Nicaragua that those six Jesuits were murdered, or didn't you read about it over there?"

"Yes, I guess so. I didn't pay much attention. That was before Mom wrote you were in Central America as a missionary, or I would have taken more notice."

Before he could stop himself Caleb snapped out, "Is that the only thing you notice—what has directly to do with you or your family? Isn't the fight for justice and democracy in a dictatorship worth noticing?"

Elizabeth, astonisheed, turned her head. Then she laughed. "All right, Father Caleb. Climb down from your platform! And you'll have to forgive me if I find this tack of yours a little surprising. When I left you were an ardent right-wing Catholic. Now you sound more like Che Guevara. What happened?"

Caleb wished now he'd kept his mouth shut. But he'd been so long with Julie and other members of the movement that his reaction had been automatic.

"Well?" Elizabeth said, after they'd driven for a few minutes in silence. "Did all this metamorphosis happen in Guatemala? Wasn't being a missionary priest what you expected?"

"It wasn't so much what I expected or didn't expect," Caleb answered, annoyed. "It's just that things down there are radically different from what I thought they'd be."

"In what way? Didn't you talk to priests who'd been there? Didn't they give any hint of all that liberation theology stuff. It's not exactly a secret."

"No, it's not exactly a secret, but I wasn't exactly listening." He paused. "You're right, of course. I was the guy who was going to save the Church from its own left-wingers. You mentioned Che. Well, I came to see that what people like him are doing is a lot nearer to what Christ talked about in the gospels than the reactionary crap the Vatican is handing out these days." He glanced sideways at his sister. "You seem to be in shock. I don't remember you as one of Catholicism's greatest advocates. You were the one who sneered at me as a good little Catholic when I became an altar boy."

"Yes," Elizabeth said dryly, "I remember."

They drove in silence for a while. Then Caleb said, "There's something I particularly want to talk to you about."

As he hesitated, she said, "What is it?"

"Have you ever heard of an outfit called All Americas Import and Export Exchange?"

"No. Should I have?"

"When the trust money is distributed, most of what we'll be getting is from the family investments in that company."

"So?"

"How much damage do you think it'd do to Robbie's campaign for governor for the voters to learn that the bulk of the family income is derived from a company that props up most of the fascist regimes in Central and South America?"

Elizabeth was confused. "What are you talking about?"

"You've heard of United Fruit? Even in England you must have read about how it's been accused of supporting all the right-wing governments down there. All Americas is even bigger and into more payoffs to the government goons that oppress the people." He glanced at her. "You know how it became a political disaster for any company to have anything to do with South Africa? Well, a few well-placed stories about the family relationship to All Americas and what it props up in Guatemala—illustrated by some pictures of the starving Indians and a rundown of the wealthy coffee fincas held together with Beresford investments and banks—would be a gift to anybody who runs against Robbie."

Elizabeth's shock and revulsion showed on her face. "You'd do that to your own brother?"

Caleb, carried away for a moment, was caught short. He reminded himself that he was not talking to Julie, who would have been every step of the way with him.

"Let's say I'd offer not to do it in exchange for ... for some of Robbie's trust money."

"That same tainted money, of course," Elizabeth commented sarcastically.

"At least it'd be going back to the starving people of Guatemala and the guerrilla and freedom groups helping them!"

"So it's the ends justifying the means, even if the means require blackmailing your own brother. What in God's name has he ever done to you?"

"It's not a question of what he's done to me," Caleb said angrily. "It's a question of priorities—serving something more important than the governorship of one small state!"

"Caleb, not that long ago people burned each other at the stake—all in a higher cause. God! I'd forgotten how long I've been away. I'll say this for the English. They don't run things by theory, however noble. They're pragmatic to a fault, which is probably why they've indulged in less high-minded slaughter than most other Europeans—or their descendants over here, for that matter."

"You're forgetting the Irish," Caleb said grimly. "The English kept their filthy heels in the face of the Irish for eight hundred years."

Elizabeth sighed. "True. But I don't think even they thought it was for a noble reason. They just wanted Ireland and to keep the Irish subjugated."

"And that was okay?"

"No, it was not okay, but at least they didn't talk a lot of blather about how high-minded their purpose was."

"No? Have you ever read any of the things that some of the men in that noble institution, the House of Commons, said when the subject of Irish home rule came up? Grandfather McGarrett used to quote some of them. Did you know that Catholics in England couldn't even vote until well into the last century? Don't tell me that wasn't all in the higher cause of the Church of England!"

Elizabeth found herself wondering what Graham would make of this conversation, and knew immediately he'd probably find a reason to make himself scarce. "I'm not a philosopher," he had once said. At the time she had thought it was an admission of weakness. Now she wasn't so sure.

"Aren't we all, including you, Caleb, going to get money?"

"I want more than my share. There are a lot of hungry and oppressed people down there." For a moment he saw Julie in his mind. She was so vivid he almost found himself wondering if Elizabeth could see her, too. He looked at his sister for a second. "It'd help if you'd side with me."

"You mean help you in getting some of Robbie's money? What about mine, or Terry's?"

"Neither of you is running for office."

"You mean we can't be blackmailed. Is that your idea of justice?"

"What's so wonderful and just about our family being filthy rich when people are starving, and starving because of our support—our family's support—of the regime that keeps them that way. Or have you become so rich you don't care?"

"Come off your high horse, Caleb. I'm not the enemy!"

Caleb took a breath. "Sorry. I didn't mean to imply you were."

They drove for a while. Elizabeth stared at the road and thought about Caleb. She glanced at his profile. Twenty years was a long time. She hardly knew him—or any of her siblings. "Are you still a priest, Caleb?"

He didn't answer right away. "According to the ordination liturgy," he said, "I am a priest forever. Nothing can change that."

"But priests get laicized. Plenty have. They get married and go into other professions. Is that what you have in mind?"

She was so on target that Caleb was unnerved and didn't answer.

He was so changed, Elizabeth thought, from the fanatically Catholic boy she remembered. Somewhat appalled, she said nothing until they pulled up outside the car rental place in Providence.

"You can get a car here, Liz. If you have your license and so on."

"I have an English license, I suppose that'll do."

"I really don't know. But I'll wait to see if you have any trouble."

His solicitude, Elizabeth thought as they got out of the car, came oddly from someone who was so calmly planning to blackmail his brother.

They walked in together and she went through all

the formalities, choosing a Toyota with a floor shift. "Okay, Caleb. Thanks for bringing me. I can manage from here."

Caleb drove quickly to the hotel where he had ensconced Julie. It had not been his idea for her to come to Providence with him. When he had first made arrangements to return to the States, he'd been taken aback when she asked, "Do you want me to go with you?"

"No," he said quickly. Too quickly, he realized almost immediately.

"Why not?"

"Look, I left home a missionary priest—and a very conservative one at that. You know that better than anyone. They—the family—don't really know what's happened to me since."

Julie stared. "They don't know you left the Church more than a year ago?"

He immediately became uncomfortable. "I'm the world's worst letter writer. There never seemed the right moment to make sense of it—in their terms, anyway. And of course I never knew when I might be taken and any letters I was carrying read."

"Jesus, Caleb! Don't you think your family's heard from your former superior or somebody in the order about your leaving?"

At moments like that she made him feel a naive fool. "They don't seem to," he said stubbornly.

In the end, and over his doubts, she had come with him, and he had installed her in the hotel in downtown Providence. "This is not cheap," he had pointed out as he helped her check into a room. "And it's using movement money. Are you sure you ought to be here?"

"It's only for a couple of days, for heaven's sake." She smiled and slipped her arms around him, and for an hour he forgot about everything else. When he finally got into his clothes she said, "If you're right and your family doesn't know, you'd better tread carefully about how—and how much—you tell them. Just keep your eyes on the prize! Your own money from the trust plus any your political brother will give you to keep you from ruining his campaign."

And now they were going to have to wait a month. It made nothing between him and Julie, or between him and the family, easier.

The house on College Hill looked the same from the outside. Elizabeth was halfway up the path before it occurred to her she didn't have a key. "Now what?" she said aloud and stood still, staring at the big porch. After a minute she walked around the house into the garden at the back and went toward a small shed. She stood there for a moment as memory assailed her.

It was here, near the shed, that she and Mark had had one of their fights. What was it about this time? She couldn't recall. What she remembered clearly was losing patience and pushing him and then being only partly horrified to see him fall backward, his hands out. That was when his left hand was punctured by a nail projecting from a board left carelessly there by the carpenter who was fixing something in the house. An almighty fuss followed, not helped when the cut became infected. Standing there, more than twenty years later, the memory was so clear she could almost see it happen all over again. Elizabeth sighed. When was that? The spring before Mark disappeared.

Going into the shed, she reached up and felt along the main overhead beam. The key was there. Dusting off her hands, she went to the back door and slid the key in. It still fit.

Inside, the house looked much the way it had, and an overwhelming ache took hold of her. This was where, as a small child, she had returned day after day from her local school, dropping her satchel of books and sitting and talking to her mother. Her mother, Elizabeth thought now, standing there.

While she was still very young, in kindergarten or

first grade, her mother would come to school and pick her up and bring her back here and they'd have milk and cookies and her mother would read aloud from whatever book Elizabeth was reading at the time. Macdougal, that last of the retrievers, would snooze on the hearth rug immediately in front of the fireplace while Matilda was reading aloud. Curious, Elizabeth reflected now, whenever she thought about her mother, which wasn't often, she never recollected that period. A sadness added to her ache. It was as though Matilda and the relationship between them had been born on that terrible day when Mark disappeared, because nothing that had ever happened between them prior to that ever came into her memory. Until now. What was her mother like then? She had no cohesive portrait, but was aware of flashes of dark gold hair, eyes that were sometimes green and sometimes hazel, and a slight figure in a coat and skirt and blouse or shirt. Someone who laughed and hugged her. Did she drink then? Elizabeth didn't know. But the moment the word drink entered her mind the feeling in her changed to something dark and angry.

And her father?

The magic of early, undamaged recollection didn't extend to him. This house, this living room, was where one terrible day when she was sixteen, out of her constant never satisfied need for his good opinion and conscious of having on a new and more sophisticated dress, she had asked him how she looked.

He had been standing in front of the mantel, his eyes on the open newspaper he was reading.

"Don't—" her mother, holding her predinner drink had said. But it was too late.

Her father glanced at her over the lowered newspaper. "Too fat and too made up, which makes you look common. With that hair you should dress down, not up. As I've told you before, no man will look at you unless you do something about your appearance." Then he'd raised the newspaper again. . . .

I shouldn't have come here, Elizabeth thought. Summerstoke was not as full of painful memories.

"How on earth did you get in here?"

Elizabeth swung around to find Robbie standing in the doorway. "I didn't hear you come in."

"I have keys. But how did you get in?"

"I remembered the key above the beam in the gardening shed."

He grinned. "I'll be damned. It was still there?"

"Yes."

"Why didn't you go back to the country with Terry?"

"Because I wanted to rent a car of my own. I'd expected to be here three days at most—just long enough to hear the Trust read—"

"And to collect the check," Robbie said dryly.

"Yes. Aren't you interested in the money? Or are you too high-minded?"

His brows went up. He looked mildly irritated. "Of course I'm interested in the money. Whether I run for the governorship depends on it."

At that moment Jenny came into the room. "Hello, Elizabeth. I thought it was a nice service, didn't you?"

"Yes, it was." Elizabeth glanced at her brother. "What's Andrew like these days? Do you know?"

Robbie shrugged. "I haven't seen him since he left Providence right after law school. He ought to be good. He was always bright. What happened to Caleb?"

"I don't know. He dropped me off at the rental place and left." She paused, wondering whether she should give Robbie any hint of Caleb's blackmailing scheme. But horrified as she was by his plan, the old loyalty between them held. She'd wait until Caleb actually did something first. She was still inwardly debating this when Jenny appeared in the doorway.

"Robbie, are you coming?" she asked. "I have to get to that meeting."

"Yes, I'm coming. Elizabeth, I guess I won't have

to offer you a lift if you have a car of your own. By
the way, do you have any idea what Caleb's hurry is?
He seems to want the money urgently?"

"No. But you're right. He does."

"And there's something else going on. He's the
most restless, driven priest I've ever come across." As
he spoke, Elizabeth knew that what he said was true.
Caleb never had been good at hiding how he felt.

"It's such a surprise to see him in civilian clothes,"
Jenny commented, going over to the window and raising it. "This place could do with an airing out."

"Yes. But let's not forget and leave the windows
open when we go," Robbie said. "We don't want the
place robbed."

"Priests don't always have to dress in their clerical
garb, do they?"

"No," Robbie said. "I don't think so. Especially in
recent years. But from the moment Caleb was ordained, when he did come home, he was rabid about
wearing the round collar. I used to tease him about
it. He was obsessed about being a priest."

"Thou art a priest forever, in the order of Mel-
chizedek," Jenny said.

Robbie laughed. "Good heavens, fancy you knowing that!"

The reporter, Tim Laughlin, was shown into the living room at Summerstoke for his interview with Robbie, postponed because of Jon Treadwell's death.

Robbie, who had been reading the newspaper while
he waited, looked up and felt a jolt of surprise. He
didn't quite know what he had expected, but the tall,
dark-haired young man facing him did not somehow
fit his picture of a muckraking journalist.

"Sit down. Can I offer you anything?"

"No, thanks." The reporter ignored the invitation
to sit and wandered around the room. "I suppose a
statement such as this is quite a place you have here
would be a cliché. Nevertheless, this is quite a place."

He stopped in front of the mantelpiece arrayed with photographs. "Family pictures?" he said.

Robbie got up. "That's right." He came over and stood beside Tim and indicated a picture on the left. "That's of my parents taken shortly after they were married. The rest are of us children—all at various stages."

Tim stood for a minute, then reached out and picked up a picture of a boy of about five standing beside a girl of twelve or thirteen. The boy was wearing a dark T-shirt, but since it was a black-and-white photograph it was impossible to know the actual color. Tim stared at it for several seconds. "This was the boy who was kidnapped?"

Robbie was surprised. "Yes. How did you know?"

Tim replied without taking his eyes off the photograph. "Oh, I looked up previous stories on your family, and there were pictures of Mark in the ones about the kidnapping." He paused. "Have you heard anything since?"

"Not for a long time."

The reporter turned, the picture in his hand. "But I gather from some of the news accounts that you did hear after the kidnapping itself."

"A few inquiries."

"From people who might be Mark or others who thought they knew something?"

"Yes. But they didn't turn out to be anything." With each answer Robbie's tone grew brusquer, his reluctance plain. Like the rest of the Beresfords he disliked discussing the kidnapping.

The reporter glanced up from the picture, then turned and put it back on the shelf. "Just one more question on that subject. I believe that even after the federal agents more or less gave up you—your father and mother—had private detectives on the case. But they were taken off after a relatively short period, six months, I think." Tim paused, then said without expression, "Couldn't that be interpreted as giving up too easily?"

Robbie took a breath. "In the professional judgment of the detectives there were no further leads to explore, and the constant ... anxiety ... of waiting to hear was having a ... a deleterious effect on the rest of the family. There were the other children, you know, and their needs." He paused. "Now can we discuss something else—such as the campaign?"

"Of course." Tim strolled over to the window and looked out. "You go right down to the bay here, don't you?"

"Would you like to walk down there?"

"Sure, why not?"

They left the living room, crossed the hall and went out onto the big back porch. From the hall the wings of the house stretched in both directions.

Along with his irritation over the reporter's questions about the kidnapping—no newspaper interviewer had ever had the tactlessness to bring it up—Robbie had a strong suspicion that to the reporter the house with its lawn that sloped down to the bay must represent everything he disapproved of. He wished now he'd insisted on seeing him at his office.

When they were halfway to the water, Tim turned and stared at the house. "Architecturally speaking," he said, "it's a bit of everything, isn't it?"

Robbie grinned. "Especially the turrets." And he told him the story of Peter Beresford and the turrets.

The reporter laughed, then added, "But don't you—as an aspiring politician—think that in the world of today, with its poverty and suffering, such places are pretty outmoded?"

There was a satirical gleam in the young reporter's eye, and Robbie was well aware he was being baited.

"To me it's home, containing many of my boyhood memories. And anyway, where are you going to draw the line? The suburban home or country cottage, containing, perhaps, your own parents—anything more than the poorest dwelling—would then be considered ostentatious."

Repressing a familiar thrust of anger, Tim leaned down and dabbled his fingers in the water of the bay. "They'd certainly be getting to the lowest level if they reached any of the houses I grew up in. We didn't even have indoor plumbing for a while there."

"And is that the origin of the satirical, somewhat iconoclastic, note I've detected in your pieces on other Providence families?"

Tim straightened and looked at Robbie. "You mean poor boy strikes back?"

With his blue eyes and angular features, Robbie found himself thinking, he'd be a good-looking kid, if it weren't for an angry and faintly dissolute quality about his face.

"Something like that," Robbie replied.

Tim turned and started to walk back toward the house. "Well, what is your platform, beyond the all-purpose and vague 'a better way of life for everybody'?"

Robbie hung onto his temper. "I believe my plan has more bite to it than that." He had some very specific ideas, which he outlined one by one, aware as he did so that by the time they reached print through this young man's typewriter—or these days, computer—they would probably sound different.

When they got back to the house, Tim took a notebook and started jotting down Robbie's replies. At the end of an hour he put it away.

"All right, I think that about does it."

"Care for a drink?" Robbie said, not thinking he'd accept, and was therefore surprised when the reporter nodded. "A Scotch on the rocks if you have one."

They were sitting there with their drinks when Elizabeth came in. Seeing the newcomer, she stopped at the door. The men got up.

Here, Tim thought, was one of the two people responsible for the disaster of his life. He had seen pictures of her, of course. But in the flesh, beautiful, well dressed, assured, she typified the different paths their lives had taken, and he felt his anger burn inside him.

"Come in, Liz," Robbie said. He turned to the reporter. "This is Elizabeth Paterson, my sister."

Elizabeth held out her hand. "How do you do? Did you have a good interview?"

Tim forced a smile. "I believe so, Lady Paterson. Will you be over here long?"

"At the moment, it looks like it—at least a month, anyway." She turned to Robbie. "Do you know if Mother's around?"

"I think she's in the study with Father."

"Nice to meet you," Elizabeth said. For a second her eyes studied the reporter's face. Then she turned abruptly and left.

"Any opportunity of meeting your parents?" the reporter asked.

"Of course." Ever the politician, Robbie put down his glass. "And I think my wife is with them at the moment. Come with me."

The rest of the family were gathered in the study. As the two walked in, Sweetpea ran over, sniffed at the reporter's shoes, then jumped up on him.

"Down, Sweetpea!" Robert Senior said.

Sweetpea sat.

"That's all right," the reporter said. He bent over and reached out a hand. Sweetpea got up and licked it. He patted her.

"Golden long-haired dachshund?" he asked Matilda, eyeing her closely. This was the other one—the main culprit—who had allowed his life to be ruined. The anger in him stirred more strongly. He felt his heartbeat increase.

"Yes."

He's as bad as Mom, Robbie thought with amusement.

"You like dogs?" Matilda asked.

The reporter straightened. "Yes."

"We used to have retrievers," Robbie said.

"Wasn't one named Macdougal?" The question was out of Tim's mouth before he was even aware he'd thought of it.

Matilda looked at him, her face showing astonishment. "How did you know that?"

Tim paused, then smiled a little. "Knowing I was coming here for the interview, I read up on the Beresfords."

"You've just met my mother," Robbie said. "And this is my father."

Robert Senior, crisp and courteous, held out his hand.

They could all have been cut from the same New England block, Jenny thought. And then reflected this was one of her days of feeling like the perpetual outsider. She turned to the reporter.

"Do you come from around here?"

"More or less. Massachusetts, Vermont, New Hampshire. We moved a lot."

"Boston? You don't sound like it."

"Oh no, the rural slum area south of North Adams."

"And this is my wife," Robbie said.

"Yes, I know. I've seen your picture, Mrs. Beresford. You've been pretty active in the Right to Life movement, I believe."

She seemed to withdraw a little. "Yes, but not recently. I've directed my work more toward shelters for the homeless."

The satiric smile was back. "Politically safer?"

"Now, just—" Robbie said.

Jenny made a gesture. "Are you trying to say that one isn't as important as the other?"

"Depends on your politics, Mrs. Beresford. But the antiabortion groups are usually considered pretty right-wing, and your husband seems to consider himself a centrist."

"He is. And so am I."

Tim acknowledged her statement with a slight nod. A few minutes later he took his leave. Just as he got to the door, Matilda said abruptly, "Don't be too hard on him."

As though drawn against his will, he turned. There was something about her face. He had seen pictures of her, of course, in his research. But the woman in person had shaken him. The word vulnerable went through his mind. He was surprised by a sense of pity and reminded himself of how much she had done to destroy his life. A strained smile touched his rather severe mouth.

"That's a promise no reporter can make, Mrs. Beresford, but I'll remember you asked."

CHAPTER

12

Something else nagged at him: He couldn't remember exactly where he'd read about Macdougal, their last retriever. He sifted through his notes and couldn't find any reference to him or any other dog. Well, he thought, why should their dogs be featured? But Macdougal must have been—where else would he have gotten his name and the information about him?

Unless, of course, he remembered it. . . .

Again he got out the engine and the child's clothes and stared at them as though by some ESP magic they could produce some other shreds of memory. But nothing came.

Then why Macdougal?

He didn't know.

Skip it, he told himself. He had more important things to think about. But off and on during the day it would occur to him. Finally he went to one of the older reporters and asked him if he'd ever read anything about the dogs—retrievers first and then dachshunds—owned by the Beresfords.

"No," he said. "Should I have? Is there something special about them?"

Tim shook his head, went back to his desk and closed his computer. Then he went to his usual bar.

He got home finally around eleven, threw his clothes off and went to bed. This time he remembered a recurrent dream. It was all about a large golden retriever whose back was almost taller than his head and whom he kept running after, yelling, "Macdougal! Macdougal! Wait for me!"

When he woke up, he was wet with sweat and his heart was pounding.

Proof?

The next day, he went back to the older reporter and asked, as casually as he could, where he could maybe find some account of the Beresfords' pets of some years ago.

The reporter gave him a strange look. "You're really obsessing about them, aren't you? The Beresfords, I mean."

"Well, no more so than the other families I did," he protested.

"If you say so," the reporter said. "About when—how long ago—would this be?"

"Maybe twenty-five years ago."

"Jesus! What are you going to do, write a family biography?"

"For God's sake, no! I'm just checking details. Forget it." He started to walk away.

"You might check some of those cozy women's magazines of the period. 'Daily life with a prominent Providence family' kind of things."

"Thanks."

He went to the newspaper morgue and the city library and checked in microfilm all possible magazines. And there, in one of them, was something about the Beresford children romping with their retriever, Macdougal, with accompanying picture, including the two-year-old Mark.

Had he seen that story before?

Not that he could remember. He was sure he hadn't. But there had been so many stories. And that story could be used as proof that it wasn't memory.

*   *   *

Elizabeth picked up the receiver and dialed her home in London. It was Duncan who answered. "Darling," Elizabeth said. "How are you?"

"Mummy? Is that you? Are you calling from America?"

"Yes. I am, indeed. Tell me how you are."

"All right. But I think it's too bad that you and Daddy are away at the same time. Nanny's a beast about letting us have fun. She's horribly strict, and anyway, she's supposed to watch over Ailsa, not me."

Guilt, like a glass splinter, pricked Elizabeth's conscience. She reminded herself that she was here because her husband was having an affair, which could easily lead to a divorce, and then how would she support herself and the children?

"What are you saying, darling?"

"I do wish you'd listen, Mummy. I said that Ailsa's been behaving very funny lately."

"What do you mean?"

"She won't say anything to anybody. Just sits and stares."

If her conscience smote her before, it really bore down now. Not that strange behavior with Ailsa was unusual. "Is she ill in any way, Duncan?"

"No, just sits and stares, like I said." There was a distinct grievance in his voice.

Poor little boy, Elizabeth thought. Both parents had deserted him during the sacred summer hols, as the children over there called them, his sister's nanny was paying little attention to him, and he obviously didn't have enough to do. This was her one extended trip in twenty years, and her husband, who was away all the time, couldn't even arrange to be there in her absence!

"Duncan," she said now, "I'm really sorry that I'm not home." She paused, then justice and a desire not to let her children suffer from the differences between their parents made her say, "And I know that Daddy is, too. Neither of us could help it, and before too long one of us will be home. I promise you that. Now are you sure you're all right?"

"Yes." This time the voice was grudging.

"Tell me exactly what you've been doing for the past three days."

Pulled out of him like that, Duncan admitted that he had been to a cricket party given by one of their neighbors, Philip Reardon, who lived not far away, and gone bicycling with Philip in a nearby park.

"But not in the road, Duncan, except just to get there. You didn't go through the streets, did you?"

"No, Mummy. I told you. We just went on that path by the canal, and Jessie Cartwright came with us." Jessie, the daughter of the local vicar and his wife, was a plump, strong-minded girl who made it obvious she adored Duncan. "Mummy, when are you coming home?"

"I'm not entirely sure, Duncan. I came here for the reading of something like a will. But there's been a delay. The lawyer who was supposed to do the reading died suddenly, and I think we're going to have to wait until his son can take over."

"Couldn't you come back here until then? I bet England's much nicer to wait in than America."

Shades of the xenophobic English! And now from her own son!

"If it is," Elizabeth said, "it's because England has you and Ailsa and I miss you both horribly. Now be a good boy and let me talk to her."

After what seemed like a long wait a small voice said, "Hello, Mummy."

"Hello, darling. How are you?"

"All right."

Elizabeth waited a second or two, hoping against all experience that her daughter would volunteer something. "Darling," she said finally, "tell me what you've been doing for the last three days. I've missed you so much!" Had she? the hated voice that lived in her head asked.

"Nothing."

"Haven't you done anything? I'm sure Nanny wouldn't let you spend three days doing nothing."

"Oh, well. I went to a party."

"Whose party?"

"Marjory's." .

"Did you have a good time?"

"Not much. I don't think she likes me very much."

Elizabeth choked back the impulse to say something like, I can understand why. "What else did you do, darling, besides the party?"

There was another long silence. Elizabeth was about to try to prod some response when Ailsa said grudgingly, "Nanny and I went to the zoo in London."

Full marks to Nanny, Elizabeth thought. "I'm glad, darling. Did you enjoy it?"

"They had a huge elephant and a tiger that glared at me." Unexpectedly, Ailsa giggled. "Nanny said it was probably thinking what a nice meal I'd make!"

"Quite probably. Darling, is Nanny there? I'd like to speak to her."

"All right. When are you coming home?"

"As soon as I possibly can."

"Will you bring me a present?" At that point her voice became dimmer, as though she were speaking to somebody there. Elizabeth was sure she caught the words, "But she always does!"

Another, adult voice came on the telephone. "This is Pam Fletcher, Lady Paterson."

"Hello, Pam. I'm afraid there's been a hitch over here. The lawyer who was involved in the reading of the trust died suddenly, and we have to wait for his son to sort things out and do the reading himself. How is Ailsa? She sounded rather sullen and grumpy on the phone just now."

"I think she was angry that Sir Graham rang up from South Africa when she was at Marjory Butler's party, so Duncan got to talk to him and she didn't."

"Oh dear! Did he leave a number where he could

be reached? Because you could let her put in a call to him."

"I did ask him that, Lady Paterson, but he said he'd be traveling almost all the time and would ring again."

So what else was new?

Caleb woke up and sat up in bed, rubbing his eyes. He hadn't meant to nap, but he hadn't slept well the night before, and one of Julie's greatest gifts to him during their sexual encounters was her ability to make him relax.

"Awake?" she said now, smiling. She was standing at the window of her hotel room staring out. The afternoon sun streamed into the room making her hair, normally a Saxon straw color, honey gold.

Caleb stared. "I haven't seen that robe before. In fact"—he put his head on one side—"I've never seen you in anything but jeans and a shirt"—he grinned suddenly—"and nothing. That robe looks, well, sort of feminine."

"Not the kind of thing we associate with the movement," she said dryly.

"I'm not putting the movement down. Whatever you wear—or don't wear—is fine with me." There was a brief silence. "Come on," he said. "I'll buy you lunch."

They went to a coffee shop near the hotel.

"Isn't there anything you can do to speed things up?" Julie asked. "Carlos is frantic to get some money for supplies and guns."

"Julie, I'm sorry. Really sorry. But Jon's dying really screwed things up."

"Why will it take a month for what's-his-name to read the bloody trust? It's not as though there were some work he'd have to do on it."

"I don't know the answer to that, either. I haven't had a chance for any private conversation with him. I'm sorry, Julie, that's the reality." He reached his hand across the table and she, after a short pause, briefly put her own hand in it. "Will you marry me?" he asked.

She made a funny face. "Isn't there some slight impediment to doing that immediately, something to do with being laicized? Is that the right word?"

"Yes, darling. That's the perfect word." He squeezed her fingers. "I'm not in particularly good odor at the moment with the order, but I do have a date to see Father Gilbert next week." He paused. "It's not a date I'm looking forward to."

"What do you think this Father Gilbert will say?"

"There's not an awful lot to say," Caleb answered. "There's nothing legal he can do to me. If he wants to hold up the laicization, then he can. But he can't stop me from going down to city hall and getting a license."

"How do you think your family will feel about it?"

Caleb shrugged. "Mom might be a bit upset—that is, if she's in any condition to take it in. But I can't see my father getting upset."

"You still don't have any idea of how much money is involved?"

"No. 'Fraid not. How long can you stay?"

"That depends," she said vaguely.

"Depends on what?"

"On what I hear from Guatemala. There is a war going on, Caleb. We have to remember that."

"Yes. Okay. You haven't told me if you'll marry me."

She smiled, then leaned across the narrow table and kissed him lightly. "Ask me again when you're free."

"I wish I could ask you to come and stay at the family place," Caleb said passionately. "It'd be wonderful to have you around!"

"But I think it's much safer for me to be here, under a nice false name. Your family may not be superreligious, but what would they think—and you a monk!" She wrinkled her nose at him—her lovely straight nose that along with her blond hair and long straight legs gave her such a California look.

"As soon as we're married I'll take you home."

"Summerstoke?"

"Yes. Or maybe College Hill, or both."

There was a silence as he went on holding her across the table.

"By the way, you've been careful, haven't you?" Julie asked. "You haven't told anybody about all those Beresford investments in the All Americas Imperial Robbery, have you?

Caleb grinned at the term. "Only Elizabeth," he said a little defensively.

"And how did she take it?"

He shrugged. "She was less than sympathetic."

Julie was watching him. "Don't mention it to anyone else, darling. I think the shock value itself will be helpful—once you know how much money is involved. Couldn't you go and see Andrew and find out? Could there be anything more important than what we're planning?"

"I won't mention it to anyone else. And yes, I could try and see Andrew at his office. If you think I should." His hand tightened on hers. "You'll be stayinbg for a few days, anyway, won't you?"

"Of course, darling."

Elizabeth was walking downstairs at Summerstoke when she saw Andrew Treadwell being ushered in the front door by Carter.

"Andrew," she said, coming down the rest of the stairs, "I'm really sorry about your father."

"Yes, so'm I." He limped in. "Your father asked me to come and see him."

How like him! Elizabeth thought. Summoning Andrew, fresh from his father's funeral. "I don't know why he couldn't have gone to see you in your office."

"To be fair, he offered to, but things are in such a state there that I thought it would be easier to drive out here after the interment."

"Oh. Well, you must be tired. Can I offer you anything?"

"Actually, a cup of coffee would be welcome. I

know jet lag goes the other way, from east to west, but I'm beginning to feel that seven hours of travel."

"Come in here," Elizabeth said, leading the way into the library.

After ordering coffee from the maid, who appeared after she rang, Elizabeth said, "I should know all this, I suppose, but how long have you lived in Seattle?"

"Since a year after law school. I worked here for the year after I graduated, then Dad decided I'd learn more out from under his wing."

At that moment the coffee arrived, along with a couple of toasted and buttered English muffin halves. "Umm," Andrew said, biting into one of them after taking a swallow of coffee. "I'm also hungrier than I realized."

"Law school came after Vietnam, I seem to remember."

"Right. That's probably another reason Dad sent me to Seattle. At that point I was inclined to get huffy with people whose sons got deferred while I was being shot at, and after offending two of Dad's biggest clients, the idea of getting me somewhere else developed appeal."

"Do you still get huffy?" Elizabeth asked.

"Depends. Sometimes yes, sometimes no."

"Depends on what?"

Andrew grinned. "Often on how much my leg bothers me."

"Does it bother you a lot?"

Andrew turned his cup around. "It's stiff, and walking with a cane sometimes irritates me. Particularly when some peacenik contemporary implies that if I'd had the brains of an ant I'd have stayed home."

"Are you sorry you didn't?"

Andrew blinked in surprise, then smiled again. "I'd forgotten how much you favored the direct approach, even as a fifteen-year-old."

"With braces and glasses."

"Yes, but you've gotten rid of both and become"—

he grinned—"a knockout." He saw the blood rush up into her cheeks and hurriedly went on, "In answer to your question, given the way I thought at the time, if I had stayed home I think I'd have spent the rest of my life defending that. Which at least I don't have to do now. Certainly not to anybody I have any respect for. Tell me about your life. You have a title, don't you?"

"Yes. But Graham's family is not one of the grand ones with bloodlines going back to the War of the Roses. His grandfather was a Clydeside dock worker with a knack for invention."

"Children?"

"Two, Duncan seven and Ailsa five. And you?"

"Also two. But two boys, Jonathon and Desmond. They live with my former wife. We were divorced four years ago." He paused. "One reason I have stayed out there, though, is that the boys live in Oregon and it's a lot easier to commute there than if I were here."

"True."

They had come to the end of casual conversation. Elizabeth was intensely aware of two things: one, that she had invited Andrew to get some hint of the size of the trust, and two, that she was finding him more attractive than she'd bargained for.

Then he surprised her. "What is it you wanted to ask me, Elizabeth?"

She made a wry face. "Not only direct but obvious."

"It's all right. I understand. You probably want to know how much money is coming to you in the trust. And the answer is, I don't know. Dad was a rock of propriety when it came to keeping confidential those legal things that had been entrusted to him."

"I see. All right, next question. Do you know how long before you'll be able to read the trust and let us know?"

"I can't tell you exactly, but I'd say a safe guess would be about a month."

"Do you mind telling me why so long? Was there some mistake, I mean," she amended hastily, "a muddle involved that has to be sorted out? I always thought of your father as Mr. Meticulous."

"That's a fair name for him. He was. But I'm the executor of Dad's estate, and I'm also the successor trustee to the trust, which means I have to order a final accounting of everything in the trust."

"Oh."

"I take it you're in something of a hurry to get back to England."

"Yes. I feel a bit guilty being away so long."

"There's nothing to prevent you going back. I could promise to call you over there and let you know when the trust is going to be read and you could hop on a plane and come back."

This was so obviously a reasonable solution that she was puzzled as to why she felt opposed to it. "I know you could, but for reasons I'm not entirely sure of, I'd rather stay. Maybe because I think it would be easier on the children than to go back, get them into the habit of having me there and then leaving again—to say nothing of the travel expense."

Andrew stared down at his empty cup. "I may be entirely wrong, but I seem to recall hearing somewhere that your husband is quite a wealthy man."

"Yes, he is. But things aren't quite—" She paused, not sure how to go on.

"You certainly don't have to explain," Andrew said hastily.

They both heard Robert Senior's voice in the hall. "If you decide to stay," Andrew said quickly, "would you consider having dinner with me tonight?"

Elizabeth looked at him. Her father's steps were just outside the sitting room. "I'd love to," she said.

As Robbie drove down out of College Hill, he thought about Tony Belmonte—lawyer, one time councilman, effective advocate for certain important unions—whom he was about to meet for lunch. This was at the urging of his new chief political advisor,

Kate Malloy, who had said the previous week when they were having a snack deep within the Italian section, "If you don't get Tony Belmonte on your side, Robbie, you don't have a prayer."

"I thought he was a Democrat." The moment Robbie had uttered the words he had revealed more ignorance than he would have liked. "Well, at least some of the time," he amended.

"Tony is for whatever supports the interests closest to his heart."

"And those are?"

"Himself, his pocket and the pockets and interests of those who usually make up his constituency—i.e., his unions, political buddies, and his ethnic cohorts."

"That's pretty cynical, isn't it?"

She put down her hero sandwich. "Robbie, even fortified as you are by your distinguished family history and wealth, you must know that our beloved state has a national reputation for its total corruption."

He did know it. He knew it well. He just hated to think about it. "It'd be nice if we could turn that around, wouldn't it?"

"You mean if you ran a successful campaign and got elected you could restore honor to the fair name of Rhode Island?"

"Anything wrong with that?"

"If everything were on the up and up, laid out fair and square, how often do you think a rich WASP would get elected?"

"That's not exactly the point." Hearing a familiar huffy note in his own voice, Robbie tried for a smoother approach. "Surely it's what the candidate represents, not what his particular group is, that counts."

"Get real, Robbie! It's who he pays off and how and how much trickles down to the people. Remember that oceanfront boon doggle? Remember the bank fiascos?"

This was one of the moments, sitting there in the greasy diner across from her, that Robbie had wondered what on earth had made him select Kate as his personal adviser. Then he was unnerved when, looking at him, she said, "Maybe you ought to get a higher type on your payroll. I can think of at least two who'd be happy to jump in." She grinned at him. "And probably at less pay."

When she had agreed to be his political adviser, Kate had taken a sabbatical from the newspaper, where she had her own column, and she had not come cheap.

He suddenly found himself thinking about one of Jenny's southern expressions: "Them as lies down with dogs gets up with fleas." There was another one, a verse about a drunk who lay down in the gutter with a pig, the last line of which went something like, And the pig got up and slowly walked away.

"Well?" Kate asked, watching him.

"Well what, Kate? So far you've been right in everything you've said."

"It's just that from time to time the whole thing gives you angst in your WASP puritan conscience."

"I'll admit to that."

Abruptly she asked, "Why do you want to be governor?"

"Incredible as it may seem, because I think I can do some good."

"For whom?"

"For everybody—for the whole damn state and everybody in it. Now can you put a sock in it for a while?"

She stopped. They ate in silence. Despite the rather brassy hair Kate was a good-looking woman in a somewhat tough way. Thin, hard edged, she always wore a well-tailored suit—at least whenever Robbie saw her.

And, as he reminded himself now, she knew he had to have a meeting with Tony Belmonte. "If you wave the right carrot in front of his nose," she'd said, "he can deliver a lot of votes, a whole lot of them."

He'd met Tony before, of course. No one around the State House could avoid it, but to the Beresfords and those like them Tony represented the mob. Robbie had resisted Kate's suggestion for about a week, but then disastrous polls had come out, showing him trailing the other candidates in many of the Italian sections. So after a night in which he'd slept only sporadically, he'd put in a call to Tony's office, which was above the city's best Italian restaurant.

If Tony had made one faintly smartass comment about the mountain coming to Mohammed or anything remotely comparable, Robbie would have made some acceptable excuse and rung off.

But Tony turned out to be receptive. He suggested that they have lunch at Piccolo's, the restaurant below his headquaters.

Robbie parked the car and walked into the restaurant at exactly twelve-thirty.

"Mr. Beresford?" the maître d' said, without a moment's hesitation.

"Yes. I'm meeting Mr. Belmonte."

"Over here, sir."

Tony Belmonte was sitting at a table for four in one corner of the room. He got up as Robbie approached and they shook hands. Shorter than Robbie by several inches, Belmonte was strong looking without being stocky.

An hour and a half later, Robbie knew exactly which votes from what district Belmonte would deliver, if certain concessions were made regarding some city union contracts that were about to come up, and if other laws, stiffening the regulations governing trucking across the state, were allowed to die in the assembly.

"But those trucks can cause one hell of a lot of damage if they crash," Robbie protested. "Several already have. These regulations would increase the number of inspections required for the licensing."

"And would drive at least two of the smaller trucking concerns out of business," Belmonte said calmly.

"But these rules exist in neighboring states."

"That's why produce people come here; they're

cheaper. More regulations to fulfill means more expensive to run."

Robbie wondered what Jenny would think. "That's going to be hard to explain to the families of the people who died because the trucks hadn't been recently inspected."

"There are more of us than there are of them." A plain statement. No covering appeal to a higher cause.

"Let me think about these matters, Tony."

"Sure. Take your time. When do you plan to make your formal announcement?"

"Next month."

"Well, I guess that's how much time you have."

Elizabeth was in the hall on her way out to meet Andrew for dinner when she was stopped by Terry, who said, "At some point I'd like to talk to you about Mother."

"What particularly about Mother?"

At that moment Robert Senior opened the library door and came out.

Terry continued, "I'm trying to find some member of the family who cares enough about Mom to help her do something about her drinking."

Elizabeth, watching her father's face tighten, felt a certain dour satisfaction. He was now reacting to Terry the way he always had to her.

"The only person who can do something about her drinking, Terry, is herself. No——" He forestalled her attempt to speak. "That's not just hardness of heart, male or otherwise. I am quoting the doctors themselves—at least two of them female—and I've talked to a friend of mine who's been in AA for some twenty-two years. I've also taken her to meetings."

"Then why?" Terry asked angrily. "Why doesn't it work for Mother?"

"I just told——"

"I don't accept that," Terry said. "It's a cop-out!"

"People die, Terry," her father said, "from illnesses from which others, no better off, recover. That's life."

"Why are you so exercised?" Elizabeth asked, nettled by this sudden crusade. "You say you come down here frequently to visit. What's different now?"

"Because after I came home from the funeral yesterday, I went upstairs to see her and I found her—I can't describe what condition she was in! She'd fallen, and she was soaking wet because she hadn't made it to the bathroom. That's the second time it's happened since I've been here. The only creatures that care are her dogs who were around her, whimpering!"

There was a silence. Then Robert said, "I'll call her doctor and see what he recommends."

"Give the problem to somebody else, as usual," Terry said.

"What do you suggest?" Elizabeth asked. "What's your solution?"

"To make her feel loved."

"I take it," Robert said, "that according to your diagnosis all the streets and shelters are filled with addicts and drunks who were simply not loved enough. From everything I've read, alcoholism is considered a disease and recognized as such by employers and the medical profession."

He went back into the library and shut the door.

The sisters stared at each other for a few seconds, then Elizabeth continued toward the front door. Before she shut it behind her she looked back and said to Terry, "I'm sorry. I can't think of anything else to do for Mom but what Dad says. And I really don't think that reassuring her how much she's loved is going to stop her from drinking."

Terry was still standing in the hall when her father came out of the library again. They looked at each other for a moment. Then her father said, "I don't think we're quite as hard-hearted as you seem to believe."

But vivid in Terry's memory was her mother's heavy

body lying on the floor, her eyes glazed, her face flushed red, her clothes soiled. In that moment she became to Terry a symbol of women rejected or ignored by those who had used them and should now care for them.

"What do you know about feelings, Daddy?" Terry asked angrily. "You've never really approved of them, have you?" And she stormed upstairs.

A short while later, she sat in her mother's study trying to interest the latter in playing a game of double solitaire.

"Come on, Mom. We can play for money. If I win you can pay me huge sums."

There was no use asking if her mother had been drinking. No bottle was visible, but Terry could smell the older woman's breath. What she wanted to do was to divert her mother enough so that Matilda, involved in a game, would taper off drinking—at least for a while. When she was a little more alert, a little less sodden, Terry hoped to talk to her about ... about ... about what?

"Come on, Mom," she said now. "I'll deal the cards."

Her mother looked at her. There was a dazed, not quite focused expression in her eye. "You'd help me more if you'd take the Honeys and Sweetpea out for a few minutes. They haven't been out since early this morning."

And when I'm gone, Terry thought, she'll have another swig. "Okay, Mom. But before I do that, I want to talk to you."

Matilda's green eyes rested on her daughter. "I suppose you want me to stop drinking."

Terry, who had prepared a few careful paragraphs in her mind, was taken aback. "Yes. We all do. We love you so much we want you to be healthy. And drinking is destroying you."

"But not fast enough," Matlida said quietly.

"What? What are you talking about?"

A heavy shoulder shrugged.

"Mom, what did you mean by that?"

At that moment Honey I, wheezing and whimpering, waddled over to Matilda. "I told you, she has to go out," she said. She leaned down as much as her bulk would allow and rubbed the golden dachshund between the ears. "Good dog," she said in a tone of voice Terry hadn't heard for years. "Very good dog! Go out with Terry now."

Terry got up. "All right. But, Mom, please don't drink until I get back." She paused. "Remember how much I love you."

Her mother looked at her. "Love like that is a chain."

Elizabeth had remembered Le Marmiton as an ornate, slightly overdecorated restaurant in downtown Providence. Looking at it now as she entered, she could see it had been vastly improved. The decor was smoother, subtler and visibly more expensive.

Andrew was sitting at a table that looked out over the river.

"Don't get up," she said as he struggled to his feet.

He smiled a little. "It doesn't do to get lazy."

She sat down and shook out her napkin. "This place has changed since I was last here. It's a lot—well, more understated."

"I think the original owner's son has taken over and ungilted it some."

After they'd ordered, he said easily, "So, how do you like living in England? Or, considering you married there and have lived there twenty years, is that a stupid question?"

"No. The answer is, I do like it there—most of the time. It's funny, since coming back here all the homesickness I squashed down came back with a rush. I miss my home, of course, and my children. And my cat," she added.

"That's funny. I have a cat out in Seattle."

For some reason that surprised her.

"You look surprised," he said.

"I am. I'm not sure why. Maybe because I've always associated cats with women and crusty old bachelors."

"Well ..."

"And you're neither old nor crusty."

He laughed. "I got Crackers by accident. In fact, I almost killed her by walking over her one day when I was coming from my garage to the apartment. She was the size of a large mouse. I had no idea what to do with her, but I couldn't leave her, so I took her home to my apartment."

"How old is Crackers now?"

"Two." He paused. "I put up notices around the neighborhood, but nobody claimed her. In my mind I'd always thought I'd take her to a shelter if I couldn't find her owner, but I found I didn't want to."

"Who's looking after her now?"

"I've bribed a kid who works in my office to stay in the apartment till I get back. What about your cat?"

Elizabeth told Andrew about George Washington. "He's really quite old now, but he still sleeps at the foot of the bed, and while he accepts Graham—just—he manages to act as though everyone else except himself and me doesn't exist."

They were in the middle of dessert when Andrew said abruptly, "You know, Caleb has changed a lot, hasn't he?"

Elizabeth was a little startled, since, as far as she knew, Andrew had only seen Caleb at his father's funeral. But she also remembered her own conversation with her brother in the car after the service.

"Yes, he has—a lot. But since you only saw him at the funeral, your intuition gets full marks."

"No, he came to see me early this morning in the office."

"Oh. About the trust? How much we'd get?"

"Yes. When I said I couldn't tell him, he was pretty put out. I explained why as carefully as I could, but he didn't seem much mollified. Since he's a priest, I couldn't help wondering what his hurry was."

Elizabeth sighed. "When I left home he was your basic right-wing pre-Vatican Two Catholic. Guatemala changed him. He's now practically a revolutionary."

"There's something else going on with Caleb. I don't know what it is, but I'm pretty sure it's there."

Elizabeth stared at him for a moment, then said slowly, "I hadn't put it like that to myself, but I think you're right. It's more than just switching sides in the Church."

They lingered over coffee and liqueur. Finally Elizabeth said, "I suppose I ought to be getting back. I meant to call the house when I got here and tell them I'd be out for dinner. But I forgot. I hope they haven't sent out a search party." She glanced up. "Are you staying at your old home?"

"Yes."

"I guess it's yours now."

"Yes." He rolled his brandy glass around, looking into the bottom of it. "Half of me would like to stay there and take up where Dad left off. You can take a boy out of the East, etcetera . . . A pity I can't drive you back. We'd have that much longer." Suddenly he glanced up and looked at her.

Above his thin, intelligent face, his hair was straight and thick, his eyes light gray with black lashes. My God he's attractive! Elizabeth thought.

"I don't suppose," Andrew said, "that you'd consider coming back to the house with me?"

It was out of the question, of course. Leaving aside her tangled relationship with Graham, she was the mother of two children. Graham had obviously had his flings, but she hadn't. It wasn't the kind of thing she ever thought about herself doing.

"Yes," Elizabeth, astonished, heard her own voice saying. "I would."

CHAPTER
13

Tim's feature articles on the Pells and the Browns had almost written themselves, but the Beresfords turned out to be far more difficult than he had imagined, even with the added interest of Robbie's run for nomination for governor. Finally Tim managed to produce something and took it over to the managing editor's desk.

"Put it down," Jock said. "I'll read it in a minute."

A while later he summoned Tim over. "This is pretty rough stuff," he said. "And did you have to beat up on the mother?"

"All I said was she'd been in and out of rehabs for years. Anyway, she was the one who was too drunk to look after the kid."

"Yeah, I know she went out to get a drink from the car when the kid disappeared." Jock stared at the piece for a moment. "But it happened years and years ago. So soften it. This makes it sound as though the paper were attacking the family. And we're not. Or maybe that's what you want to do—for whatever reason." He stared at the reporter for a moment. "What is your reason?"

Tim shrugged. "I just don't like rich families getting their profits off the backs of the ordinary people."

"That's a whole class, not just the Beresfords. Your politics are your own. But for this piece stick to the relevant facts with emphasis on Robbie. You'd better rewrite it."

The managing editor watched Tim as he walked back across the floor.

Malilda, alone with Honeys I and II and Sweetpea, drank more slowly but steadily. Fantasies drifted in and out of her head: Robert, her husband, coming at last to understand how much his neglect and chilly indifference had brought about her present state; Robbie, her son, winning the governorship and delivering his inaugural speech in which he gave, for the first time in his life, full credit to his mother for her help and influence; and her daughters, Elizabeth and Terry ... But the script here became confused and less compelling. Much clearer was another scene: a young man, now thirty, arriving at the door and demanding to see her, a young man named Mark. . . .

I wish I was dead, Matilda thought. I wish it was over. She looked down as Honey II started pushing her leg and raising her front paws to Matilda's lap. "And if I were dead, Honey, what would happen to you and your mother and your great-granddaughter, Sweetpea?"

At the sound of her name Sweetpea woke up, ran over to Matilda and jumped in her lap. Matilda put her arms around her. Honey II also jumped up and pushed her nose under Matilda's arm. Tears filled Matilda's eyes and started to run down her cheeks. "What would happen to you if I was dead? Who'd look after you? They'd send you to be put down soon enough."

Matilda sat there, her arms around her dogs, rocking back and forth. "Who'd look after you?" she muttered again. Certainly not that chilly block of nonfeeling, her husband.

Twenty-four years ago, when she was forty, he had made his last visit to her bedroom. She was never sure why he had come, since it had been some time since his previous visit. But she came to believe it might have been an attempt at reassurance—either for himself or for her or for both—a few weeks after Mark's disappearance. But that visit, which had produced Terry's birth, ended more than just their physical relationship. After that it became as though she and Robert occupied the same house but had no other contact. Her memory drifted to the letters from people who thought they had sighted Mark, or psychics who were sure they knew where he was hidden, or, in the past few years, one or two young men who claimed to be Mark. The latter were the most painful of all, raising hopes that were dashed when their claims, examined by police and lawyers, proved to be fraudulent.

"My drinking picked up then," Matilda said aloud, her voice slurred. "Oh God! What did they do to Mark?" Clear, unhampered by the alcoholic fog that almost constantly surrounded her, came the memory of every parent reported by the news media whose child had been taken and who lived to learn some particular horror. There was a parent whose child had been found in a ravine, her body hideously abused and mutilated. The worst was the father whose little boy had been kidnapped, only to have the child's severed head found later by the searching police.

"No, no, no!" she cried now, rocking back and forth.

"Mom!"

It was Terry, standing at the open door.

"Go away!" Matilda screamed. "Go away. Please go away!"

Terry came into the room, tears in her own eyes. "I don't know why you won't let me comfort you." She hesitated. "I suppose I'd better talk to you tomorrow morning before you've had time to drink so much." Reluctantly, she withdrew.

Matilda poured the last of the whiskey into her glass. She knew that before she was interrupted, there was something she wanted to think about: Caleb. "I may be drunk and old and stupid and useless, but

there's something funny going on with him," she muttered aloud. Quite why she was so sure she didn't
know. He had come to see her in the morning, before
she had drunk much. She had, of course, as she always
had, a ferocious hangover, but an Alka-Seltzer taken
with two aspirin and a modest amount of liquor had
left her feeling relatively clear and pain free—for a
while. He had talked about the sorry state of the Indians in Guatemala and, with increasing passion, of the
fascist iniquity of the government and its state police.

When he was through, Matilda looked at her son.
Just as Caleb had made a right turn in the past that
had freed him from competing with his brother—as
her husband had once pointed out—he'd now made a
left turn. Had he, seeing the terrible suffering around
him, suffered a political conversion as he had once a
religious one?

In a minute she got up, bent down toward Honey
II's bed, almost fell over, but balanced herself by putting a hand on the guard around the fireplace. Her
head spun. A wave of nausea surged up in her. When
she felt a little less dizzy she pushed her hand under
the cushion and retrieved the bottle. Somehow she
would have to get out and buy some more. It was no
use ordering from the store to be delivered, it would
be intercepted. But for now this would do.

She made her way back to her chair, twisted off the
top of the bottle and drank.

For a moment the horror of what she was doing to
herself hit her. I'm committing suicide, she thought.
And then, I have to find a faster way. Drinking was
one degrading step down after another. It was because
of drinking that Mark had been taken. If she hadn't
gone back to the car for the bottle from the glove
compartment . . . If Elizabeth . . . She felt the sting of
an old, deep anger. If only Elizabeth would go back
to England. Here, she was a constant reminder. . . .
Matilda pushed that thought down as she always had.
It wasn't Elizabeth's fault. It was hers, hers, hers. She

had nothing to live for. But life without liquor was unthinkable.

Elizabeth stepped out of the shower. There was something about the almost prissy neatness of the bathroom in Andrew's house that made her think of a rectory in Oxfordshire in which she had once stayed as the guest of an author. The soap had been flower scented, the soap dish polished, the towels folded in neat squares. But at least at the rectory she had been an expected guest. She couldn't suppose that Andrew, assuming she'd accept his invitation to come back with him, had effected such household perfection. As she went back into the room he was coming through the other door.

"I'm still sorry I can't drive you home," he said. Somehow, in his shirtsleeves, with his thick hair falling over his face, he looked vulnerable. "I'm also sorry you can't stay the night. But I think that might give you more trouble than you'd want once you got back."

"Yes. I may be nearly forty, married, and the mother of two, and have lived abroad for twenty years, but that won't prevent either of my parents from wondering aloud where I was."

Elizabeth smiled wryly, picked up her handbag and turned to look at Andrew. Even though she had known what accepting Andrew's invitation meant, what actually happened was a total surprise. She was unprepared for his tenderness and skill and for the hunger they both felt. His mouth and hands were gentle, yet there was an urgency that she had not experienced for what seemed like years. She had been prepared to feel guilty. She had not been prepared to be so near tears so much of the time.

"Andrew," she said now.

He got up and came over and put his arms around her. She felt his lean, hard body and the slow swelling that was pressed against her. "I can't stay any longer," she said desperately.

He stepped back. "I know. I mustn't try to make you stay. Elizabeth, I don't pretend to have been a monk or a celibate since my marriage broke up, but I've never experienced anything remotely like this. Truly."

She knew that he was telling the truth. She also knew that it was the same for her.

As they walked downstairs, she tried for a lighter note. "Have I told you that I've only once before stayed anywhere where the bathroom was so neat? Is that you or your father?"

"Neither, I'm afraid, although Dad was always something of an old maid. But our cleaning lady came today, and she'd wash the street in front of the house if we gave her any encouragement."

As they reached her car, Andrew said, "This has to happen again. I have to see you. When can we meet?"

She stared ahead into the darkness. "I have no idea what the family plans are, but I'm going to say day after tomorrow. Caution tells me not to be absent for dinner two days in a row."

"All right. Let's meet at another restaurant—say the Chateaubriand—at seven. We'll have dinner and . . ." He looked at her and smiled.

She smiled back. "Yes. And . . ."

The guilt came, as she knew it would, as soon as she drove off, staining like a taint the remembered joy and tenderness with Andrew. Even as she relived the feel of his mouth and lips and hands, Graham's face kept getting in the way. His was nowhere near as handsome as Andrew's. Yet there was something about it that pleaded silently with her as she kept trying, unsuccessfully, to push it from her mind.

"You started it, Graham," she finally shouted, horrified, into the empty car. "You were having the affair. You've got no reason to make me feel this way!" What was that line she used to like to quote? Love is not love that alters when it alteration finds . . .

Maybe not, she thought angrily. But equally maybe she wasn't up to such a pure level of devotion.

Julie opened the Sunday paper and glanced at the headlines. Two more banks were threatened with closure by state financial authorities. Three councilmen from the two main parties were flinging accusations at each other. A prominent city official, still in his fifties, had managed to secure not one but two city pensions for himself, starting almost immediately.

"In other words," Julie said aloud to herself, "business as usual."

After staring out the window for a few minutes, she went to the phone and dialed a New York City number. When a voice answered at the other end she said, "Johnny? Julie."

"Aren't you in Providence?" Johnny—whose real name was Juan Mendoza—said.

"I am."

"When can we get our hands on the money and how much?"

"There's been a delay. I don't know when and I don't know how much. That's what I called to say."

There was a silence at the other end. Then, "Damn it to hell, things are just beginning to break for us. Isn't there anything you can do to speed things up? At least find out how much Caleb is getting?"

"I've tried. But so far, no good. Caleb's talked to the lawyer who's handling it now and gotten nowhere."

"Why don't you have a whack at this lawyer yourself? You're a hot-looking chick."

"Yes," Julie said thoughtfully. "That did occur to me."

"Didn't you tell me Caleb's brother is running for office?"

"Yes. Caleb and I've talked about blackmailing him—and the rest of the family—so they'll hand over more than just Caleb's piece. But there's no use in

jumping the gun on that. It'd just give away everything." She paused. "Don't worry, Johnny. I'll get it."

"In time?"

"Yes. In time."

She was putting down the phone when she heard a
knock on the door. Making no sound replacing the
receiver, she gave herself a passing check in the bureau mirror and opened the door to admit Caleb. He
rushed to embrace her the moment the door was
closed, and they spent a passionate two hours in bed.

Later, as they were lying there, she asked casually,
"Have you seen the head of your order yet?"

"I'm to see him tomorrow afternoon. He's been
away. And then I have to go and see the bishop's
secretary."

"Do you think they'll make trouble?"

"They won't be happy, but there's nothing they can
do to stop me, and as a whole there's less scandal to
the Church if I get properly laicized than if I don't."

"You still haven't told anyone in your family
about us."

"No. All that would do is cause trouble."

"What about your mother?"

Curiously, Matilda had asked him last night if he
would take her to mass in the morning. Caleb hadn't
been to mass in months and he hadn't wanted to go.
But he couldn't bring himself to refuse. They had
driven into Providence to the church she always attended. He had sat through the mass, going through
the motions of getting up and kneeling down. He had
expected to be left cold by the whole affair, but he
had been more upset than he had bargained for. Neither he nor his mother had taken communion. Unlike
Caleb, she had sat throughout the mass staring straight
ahead, not attempting to lower herself to the kneeler
in the rather narrow space within the pews, nor standing, except during the reading of the gospel. But at
one point Caleb had had a severe shock. Turning to
look at her, he was appalled and rather embarrassed

to see tears coming down her cheeks. Leaning over, he had touched her hand and said, "Mom, are you okay?" When she didn't answer he had clapsed her hand. "Mom?"

"As okay as I can be."

Lying now in bed with Julie, Caleb found the memory disturbing. "No, I didn't say anything to her. As I told you, she has a problem." He added, almost unwillingly, "She and I went to mass this morning."

Julie lay there, looking relaxed, almost sleepy. But she was thinking furiously. She had discovered that Caleb back home was not the same man as in Guatemala. That meant if she could do anything—anything at all—to speed things up, she would have to do it.

"I don't suppose you've seen the lawyer since we talked." She knew she was risking his disapproval, but it was a chance she was going to have to take.

"No, I haven't." Then, because he realized it sounded abrupt, "I made a date to see him in his office tomorrow at eleven. He wasn't too keen to make it. I guess he thought that it would be about the trust. But I told him it was about something else."

"What is it about?"

"I just want to be sure where I stand legally with the Church. All the papers I signed. That kind of thing."

"Oh. Well, that's a good idea." She paused. "Will you be anywhere near here?" She grinned at him, deliberately provocative. "So you can drop in?"

"Actually, his office is only two blocks away, in that big office building over there."

There was a brief silence. Then Caleb slid to the edge of the bed. "I'm sorry I wasn't able to find out anything about the trust from Andrew. It wasn't for lack of trying. He may have lived on the West Coast for the past twelve years, but he can get very New England and prickly on the subject of honor and integrity and all that jazz."

"Funny, isn't it," Julie said. "Thousands of people can be suffering every kind of outrage—being shot, tortured, killed—but as long as it isn't up here, then your New Englander can get stuffy about his honor."

Caleb got up and wrapped the sheet around him. "Look, I know what you're saying, but to be fair, if his own family—maybe his own children—were the ones involved, knowing Andrew, he'd still be worrying about integrity and so on."

Julie didn't reply immediately. Then she said, "How's your brother's campaign going? I see his name in the paper about something almost every day. Whoever's doing his public relations is doing a good job."

"Yeah."

She turned and said gently, "You aren't weakening, are you, Caleb?"

He paused on his way to the bathroom. "What do you mean?"

"We need a lot of money—the movement does. Here, with your family, will you be able to blackmail him?"

His face hardened. "Why are you doubting me? Because I couldn't wring information out of Andrew?"

She moved over to him quickly and stood in front of him, her arms on his shoulders, her body touching his. "Of course I'm not doubting you."

"Then why did you ask me that?"

She smiled and gently took his head between her hands. "Just to jerk you back to reality. While we're up here in the land of the lotus eaters, lolling around in bed in a luxurious hotel room, people are dying. The money that may or may not make your brother governor will buy lives and health among the desperate people of Guatemala."

Suddenly, from nowhere, a quotation an old Jesuit had once spoken to him came back. He said it aloud. "I will restore unto you the years that the locusts hath eaten."

"What?" Julie asked.

"Nothing," he said, going into the bathroom.

*   *   *

Tomorrow night, Elizabeth thought at dinner, I'll be with him. She hadn't felt this way since ... since Nigel. And that in itself was upsetting. It reminded her that for all the passion that had once marked the relationship between herself and Graham, it was a different kind. She and Graham had been married when that happened between them, and somehow that fact changed the nature of the passion itself. One was forbidden and one was not. And perhaps being forbidden added an extra element of mystery and suspense. But as she thought that, Graham's face seemed to slide in front of Andrew's.

At that moment she could hear the phone ringing from the hall. She glanced at her watch. Seven. In England it would be midnight, so the call wouldn't be from Duncan or Ailsa. Unless something had happened to one of them. Fear darted up inside her followed by guilt. Please God ... she thought.

Carter appeared behind her. "Sir Graham is on the phone from England, Miss Elizabeth. He'd like to speak to you."

CHAPTER
14

Well before ten-thirty the next morning Julie had
scouted the area, located the office building and discovered that Treadwell, Emory, Hives, and Barker
were on the twenty-third floor. She'd then bought a
newspaper, located a coffee shop opposite, taken a
table at the window and ordered enough of a breakfast to secure her place. She had no particular plan
other than hoping that, however unlikely, Caleb and
Andrew would leave the building together so that she
could spot Andrew and estimate her best approach
to him.

Her wish was granted. She saw Caleb go into the
building and three-quarters of an hour later come out
with a thin, taller man with light hair who limped as
he walked with the aid of a cane.

Without even stopping to think, Julie flung more
than enough money onto the table and left the coffee
shop. She didn't want Caleb to see her until she had
crossed the street and could appear to be meeting
them by accident. It took fast walking and a little ma-
neuvering, part of the way with the newspaper held
up against her face, until she could slow down and
appear to meet them casually.

The meeting was all she had hoped. Caleb's surprise
was obvious. It was also obvious to Julie that he wasn't
too pleased.

"Andrew," he said, "this is an old friend of mine from Guatemala, Julie Manners. Julie, this is Andrew Treadwell. What are you doing here, Julie?"

This question, more than anything that had gone before in the last two weeks they'd been in Providence, showed Julie how far Caleb had traveled from the man she had known in Guatemala. That man might not have announced, This is my mistress, Julie, but he would have altered nothing in his tone or voice or words to hide the nature of their relationship. Now Caleb's worry that Andrew might catch on was fairly obvious. So be it, Julie thought. It made her way clearer. She smiled and held out her hand. "Hello, Caleb has spoken of you."

Andrew shook her hand. "Do you live in Guatemala, or were you just visiting?"

"No, I've been there a couple of years, working with some of the clinics in the poorer areas."

"That must be rewarding—or is it? Are you a doctor?"

Julie and Caleb spoke at the same time. "Julie's a very fine administrator," Caleb said. "Oh no," Julie said at the same moment. "I just help out."

"Nice to see you," Caleb said, taking a step in the direction in which they had been going.

He so obviously wanted to get rid of her that Andrew said politely, "We are just on our way to lunch. Would you care to join us?"

Julie, a cool estimator of the effect of her good looks on men, was pretty sure that the lawyer was reacting more to what seemed like Caleb's rudeness than to any personal desire to have her join them. But she was not going miss the opportunity. "I'd love to," she said.

The lunch, at a small Chinese restaurant near Andrew's office, was for Julie both enlightening and frustrating. Enlightening because she saw the pleasant but unbreachable barricade Andrew had put up around any discussion of the trust; frustrating because, with Caleb there, Julie did not feel free to go to work on Andrew.

However, she didn't allow this to impede her, so she played the role of a girl to whom the whole subject was brand-new and fascinating. "Caleb mentioned the trust," she said, smiling. "But except that it's going to be read, he doesn't know a thing about it. Why are they all so secretive?"

"Because that's the way it was drawn up by Caleb's grandfather," Andrew said.

"But if knowing how much each family member is going to get may have a . . . a crucial effect on their plans, surely it's being terribly rock-ribbed not to tell them something."

"Sorry, I can't talk about it," Andrew said, also smiling. "Why don't you tell me about Guatemala instead?"

Julie realized that to press for more information would only damage her cause. So she did as Andrew asked and talked about Guatemala, its beauty, its poverty, and the needs of the indigenous peoples there, always being careful not to go into her political feelings.

"It's so hard to know why the government doesn't do more," she said mildly, careful to avoid Caleb's eye.

Andrew simply replied, "Umm" and summoned the waiter. "May we have the bill?" he asked. "I'm sorry, Julie and Caleb, I'm afraid I have to get back. The pile on my desk is not to be believed."

He brushed aside Caleb's halfhearted attempt to split the check and left almost immediately, collecting his cane and limping out.

"I don't think that was very smart," Caleb said when he and Julie were alone.

She shrugged. "Anything's worth a try. What did he tell you in the office?"

"Nothing about the trust."

As they were leaving the restaurant, Caleb said, "Why don't I come back to the hotel with you?"

"Wonderful!"

She left nothing to chance. Their months of love-making had made her an expert on what most aroused and pleased Caleb, and she used it all, with cunning and passion—which she did not have to simulate.

"My God!" he said finally. "What you do to me, Julie!"

Her hand ran over his body lightly and gently, her fingers barely touching. "Was it good?"

"You must know it was."

Yet this time she was aware of some part of Caleb that had remained uninvolved. Every other time he had lost himself. This time he didn't—quite. How she knew that she wasn't sure. His lovemaking was as violent and ardent as ever. But there was a difference ...

"By the way," Julie said, suddenly sitting up, "weren't you supposed to see the head of your order this afternoon?"

"It was postponed again. Father Gilbert had to be in New York for something. I'm to see him Thursday." He pushed himself off the bed. "I'd better be getting back."

When he was dressed, he went over to Julie, took her face in his hands and kissed her. "I'll call you tomorrow."

Driving back, he found himself almost praying that the reading of the trust would come sooner than Andrew seemed to think possible. Although he hadn't told Julie, he had brought it up when he was in Andrew's office.

"Why the urgency?" Andrew had asked. And then, echoing Elizabeth, "Are you in any kind of trouble?"

Caleb had denied it. Yet he knew that he was in trouble, but not the kind he'd ever imagined. The trouble was not in the money or getting it or his family or even in his relationship with Julie. It was in his head.

*   *   *

Robbie had put off until the last moment calling Jenny to say he might be home late.

"That's too bad," she said. "Did you forget that we were supposed to go out to Summerstoke?"

Robbie had, not that he would have changed his plans. "Yes, I'm afraid so. But it doesn't change anything from this end. It's stuff to do with the campaign."

"I see. Well, I guess I'll see you when I see you."

Jenny hung up and stood for a few minutes by the phone in the empty hallway. Both children were away at school. She wished now they weren't, then reproached herself as selfish. She knew she had several letters to write in the hour before she left for Summerstoke, and, repressing a sigh, went off to attend to them.

An hour later, after finishing the last of the letters, she was passing through the hall on her way out when she saw the mail that Robbie had retrieved from the mailbox and put on the hall table. Evidently he had done this just before he left for the office, and until now she hadn't noticed. She went to the pile and sifted through it rapidly. Any that were for him she'd put back on the table. Mostly it was junk mail. There was one letter and one postcard for her from Memphis. The last letter, addressed to Mr. and Mrs. Robert Beresford, Jr., carried the engraved return address, St. John's School, an Episcopal boarding school usually mentioned in the same category as Andover and Exeter. Three was a student there.

Her heart beginning to beat more rapidly, Jenny slit open the envelope. Three was an atrocious correspondent, and when he did write he used cheap lined paper and dime-store envelopes. A formal letter like this very likely spelled trouble.

The letter, which was from the headmaster, said simply that after due consideration he and the faculty had agreed that Robert Beresford the Third would be happier at another school.

"He's not a bad boy, and certainly not a stupid one," she read. "But it is obvious to me and the rest of the teachers he comes in contact with that he hates the school and everything it stands for. And from the school's point of view he is a thoroughly unsettling and disruptive influence. A certain amount of rebellion is normal at that age. But Robert stirs up revolt even among those who are not particularly rebellious, and with his constant protests and sit-ins and challenges in and out of the classroom, he keeps his dormitory as well as his class in a state of turmoil. I am sure he will appeal his dismissal to the Civil Liberties people, as he has on many occasions, undeterred by their reply to him that a private school, by the very nature of being a private school, has a right to establish rules.

"If it were a question of our being flexible and making adjustments to make things easier for him, we would be willing—to a point. But it's become obvious that Robert enjoys rebellion for the sake of rebellion and thrives on agitation. But others who fall under his influence would be happier if left simply to their studies and/or their athletics.

"I'm afraid we're the wrong school for him—too traditional and conventional. There are several I can think of—good schools all—where he'd be happier, and I'd be glad to write a letter or put in a word for him. We would like you to pick him up no later than Wednesday the twelfth."

Jenny read the letter standing in the hall, then she took it into the sitting room where she sat at her desk and read it again.

Her first feeling was one of total dismay. To be expelled from a school like St. John's was a disgrace for the entire family, and, considering his father and grandfather had gone there, a testament to how much they wanted to get rid of him. Her next feeling was one of anger that Robbie wasn't there. Obviously he hadn't looked through the mail but just pulled it out of the box and plunked it down on the table. Surely, if he'd seen that the letter came from St. John's he would have forgotten everything else and opened it. Unless, of course, something overpowering was filling his mind at the time.

Suddenly Jenny remembered that he wasn't coming home until much later. What was the reason he had given? Campaign work. She glanced at her watch: five-thirty. Would anybody be in his office? She went quickly to the phone and punched the number. A little to her surprise, the phone was picked up. "Mr. Beresford's office."

"Marianne?" Jenny said.

"Yes, Mrs. Beresford. You caught me on the way out."

"I'm sorry to hold you up, but do you know where I might find my husband? Something's just come up and I need to talk to him."

"I think he's working with one of his campaign advisers, Mrs. Beresford."

"Yes, he called me less than a half hour ago and said he'd be late because he'd be doing campaign work. Where I can reach him?"

Marianne was thrown off balance. She was planning to meet a friend for dinner and an early movie in fifteen minutes. Forgetting her usual instinct, developed over years working as a secretary in prominent offices, that told her not to be too forthcoming, she said, "He said he was going to meet some of the campaign people at Piscatore's."

"Thanks, Marianne."

Kate had chosen a fish restaurant in the Italian section of Providence. Robbie had expected some kind of superfish diner, but when he got there he found it quiet and rather elegant, with the tables commendably far apart. Kate was already at a table for four in the far corner.

"For somebody with a name like Kate Malloy, you seem to have strong affiliations with the Italians," Robbie commented as he sat down at the table.

"That's probably because my mother's maiden name was Maria Gratziano."

Robbie wondered why when he had asked around about Kate and looked up her credentials he hadn't been told that. "Nobody mentioned that," he said.

She grinned. "My name doesn't exactly stand high with much of the Italian community."

"Why?"

She took a sip of the red wine at her place. "My mother's people were from Boston, which in some ways might as well be L.A. as far as the Italianos here are concerned. And then I didn't stay with a lot of the family traditions."

"Such as?"

She raised her eyes from her glass. They were, Robbie found himself thinking, a peculiarly Irish gray— not the light gray eyes of his friends and relatives, but a dark gray with touches of deep blue that he had seen only among the Irish. As gray as the mountains of Mourne, he thought. And then, where on earth did that come from? "Your eyes are a very Irish gray," he said. "My grandfather, who was Irish, once talked of somebody's eyes being as gray as the mountains of Mourne."

"Which flow down to the sea."

He smiled. "Yes. Granny McGarrett used to sing that song when I was a boy."

"It's hard for me to remember that half your family tree is Irish. I've never met a Waspier WASP."

"Why do I feel vaguely insulted?"

"I don't know. You shouldn't. You're still the power structure."

"Do you always think of everything in terms of politics and power?"

"If you're Irish it's hard not to." She tore off a piece of Italian bread and started to butter it. "We're brought up to it. Particularly if the parents or grand-parents were recent immigrants. Your folks back in England ruled Ireland for hundreds of years. And then when my folks finally made it over here, guess who was sitting in the catbird seat?"

Robbie poured himself some more wine. "The only people I know who think in long, historic terms like that are the southerners."

They were both silent. Neither mentioned Jenny.

Kate said, "It's always the defeated who sing the songs and tell the stories and hang onto the traditions for dear life. That's one reason why I got out from under." She glanced up. "I decided to declare my own independence from the defeated and join the winners."

"And what Italian traditions did you flout?"

"I got divorced."

"Is that more of a flouting of the Italian side than of the Irish? They're both pretty Catholic."

"Yes, but they deal with it in different ways. Italian women are frequently aware that Italian men often have a little something going on the side. They don't like it, and some of them express themselves on the subject quite violently—with rolling pins on the head, that kind of thing. But divorce—especially among the older generation—is not even considered."

"And what do the Irish do when faced with marital woe?" Robbie asked, amused.

"Get drunk."

"Oh." An image of his mother flashed across his mind. He pushed it away and picked up a menu. "What's good? What do you suggest?"

Kate, who missed little, said, "I like the broiled shrimp. But the filet of sole is also good."

"Maybe I'll try that."

When they had ordered, Kate said, "Why did you

look like that a few seconds ago? When I said the
Irish solved their problems by getting drunk?"

He sighed. "My mother ... has a problem. She ...
she drinks."

"Yes," Kate said. "I'd heart that."

Robbie was jarred. "I didn't know it was such common knowledge."

"You looked me up pretty thoroughly, Robbie,
didn't you?"

"When I was thinking of talking to you about ...
well, the campaign. Of course." Her hair, Robbie
thought, was somehow softer, less brassy than he'd
remembered it. With those gray eyes and white skin
she was really good looking. And the tough manner
that had so put him off he'd come to find attractive.
Horrified, he found himself wondering what she
looked like without any clothes on, what the color of
her pubic hair was. He could feel himself blushing.

She was smiling. "What's on your mind, Robbie,
and why are you looking so embarrassed?"

"Am I?" he said off handedly, torn between wanting to go where his thinking was leading him and the
need to put on the brakes.

"Yes. By the way, how did the interview with Tim
Laughlin go? What do you think of him?"

Glad to have something to latch on to, Robbie said
easily, "It was fine."

"He's a good writer and reporter." Kate said.
"Something of a loner. Funny thing is ..."

"What?" Robbie asked.

"When I first saw him, he reminded me of you.
How you might have looked at that age."

Robbie was startled, yet the moment her words
were out he knew he had thought something of the
same sort—that the young reporter could have been
a Beresford. "Yes, I know what you mean."

"But let's talk about the campaign," she said,
"That's what you wanted to discuss, isn't it?"

"Yes, of course. The campaign."

The waiter appeared suddenly and said to Robbie, "Sir, your wife is on the phone."

Robbie stared. "My wife?" An absurd feeling of guilt filled him. "Where? I mean, where is the phone?"

"Over here, sir."

Robbie followed him to a corner where there was a telephone and took the receiver. "What's the problem, Jenny?"

"You and I got a letter from St. John's. I'll read it to you."

After she'd finished, he said irritatedly, "That damn boy, why doesn't he straighten up?"

Jenny paused. "You don't sound as upset as I feel."

"Jenny, he's been headed this way for a couple of years. Remember that brouhaha at the day school two years ago when he organized the sit-in? Anyway, the headmaster is only repeating what he's said over the phone and in person."

"When did you talk to him in person about this?"

"Several months ago. He was in Providence for something or other, and we met at the club. Once I went up there."

Surprise and anger were in her voice. "You didn't tell me."

Robbie hesitated. He had feared that sooner or later this would happen, but because he kept hoping that Three would calm down, he'd ducked talking to Jenny. "I guess I was hoping Three would straighten up. "Well, there's nothing I can do right now. I'll call the headmaster in the morning. When is the twelfth?"

"A week from Saturday." Her voice had suddenly taken on a sharp edge. "Robbie, I can't believe you're taking the whole thing this calmly."

"What would you suggest I do?"

"Go right now to St. John's and talk to Three. He just might listen to you."

"He might. But I doubt very much if any promise of good behavior I can wring out of him will last to

the end of the year. And short of an ironclad oath
that he'd do nothing rebellious till then, the school
won't even begin to listen to me."

"So you'll just let him ruin his life!"

Robbie felt a thrust of irritation. "It won't ruin his
life, Jenny. Anyway, nothing on earth is going to make
him change. He's going to do things his way. I'll talk
to him tomorrow." And Robbie hung up.

When he went back to the table, Kate took one
look at him and said, "Trouble?"

"Yes." He told her about the phone call and the
letter.

"You don't seem in a state over it."

"That's what Jenny just said. Kate, Three's been
headed for this kind of trouble since he was nine. For
God's sake, he organized sit-ins in the third grade and
declared himself an anarchist in the sixth. If he doesn't
become a full-blown revolutionary in another year or
so, I'll be astounded." He paused. "We probably
shouldn't have sent him to St. John's. But it's been a
family tradition, and anyway, Jenny was very much in
favor of it."

Kate didn't say anything, but she wondered how
Jenny had known where Robbie was.

"Robbie," she said now.

"Yes."

"Does Jenny know that you hired me?"

"No."

"Somehow I didn't think she did."

Graham's phone call had upset Elizabeth. When he
got home he had learned about the delay in the reading of the trust. "If it's going to take as long as the
lawyer seems to think, then why on earth not come
home and fly back for the reading later?" he
protested.

"The trouble is, nobody's sure exactly when the
trust will be ready."

"There are such things as trans atlantic phones,

Elizabeth. Your children need you." He paused, then added, his voice gruff, "And I need you."

There was no way to deny outright such an appeal, even though she resented it. "I'll see what I can do," she said coldly. "Please give my love to Duncan and Ailsa." And she hung up.

She continued sitting by the phone for a while, appalled at her response to Graham, not so much for his sake as for her children's. Sighing, she got up, collected her coat and left the house to drive into Providence, where she was meeting Andrew.

She had expected Chateaubriand, whose address she had looked up in the phone book, to be large and elegant and was surprised when it turned out to be small, intimate, and obviously expensive. It was also somewhat off the beaten track.

Andrew was sitting at a table in the far corner, apparently perusing the menu.

"Sorry to be late," Elizabeth said.

He glanced at his watch. "Ten minutes. That's not a lot. He smiled. "Except for the fact that my heart was going ninety miles an hour because I was afraid you'd decided not to come."

"I'd have called you, Andrew, if I'd done that."

"But you wouldn't have got me, probably. I was out of the office seeing some of the clients Dad had. This isn't a reproach," he said quickly. "Give or take ten minutes when you have a long drive is nothing, but it made me realize how much seeing you meant."

"You want to talk about anxiety over seeing you? How about my changing my dress three times because I was so anxiety-ridden as to how I'd look?"

He reached out and clasped her hand lying on the table. After a moment he said, "I wonder what hit us! Nothing like this has happened to me before. Yes, I was in love with Althea when we got married. But it wasn't like this, so I wonder now if I was." He looked at her. "Has this—this feeling ever happened to you before?" He added quickly. "Don't answer it if you don't want to."

"Yes. Once, when I was eighteen, with an English classmate of Robbie's at Harvard named Nigel. But that's the only time. I . . . I came to love Graham after we were married. But it's different from this."

Andrew looked a little surprised, "Nigel Conway?"

"Yes. Do you know him?"

"At Harvard, when I knew Robbie." Andrew paused. "I always thought he was gay."

"Gay? Nigel?" After a minute she said, "I find it hard to believe anybody'd think he was gay. And yet—"

"I'm sorry. I didn't mean to be . . . well, tactless."

"No. It's not that. What—what made you think that?"

"Well, for one thing, he was rumored, maybe wrongly, to be having some kind of relationship with an older man."

"I see. He was sort of . . . different. But then, he was English. And I'd never met any before."

"True. What happened with him?"

Elizabeth shrugged. "He wrote saying he couldn't see me again because of someone else. I tried to get in touch with him, but he was unreachable. After that I went to England."

"And you never found out who?"

"No. Sometimes I've wondered if it was somebody he met at the party. But with what you've said—"

"Do you remember him meeting anybody in particular?"

She shrugged. "Only my father."

Andrew looked quickly at her, opened his mouth but then, seeing she was looking down, closed it again.

After a minute she glanced up, saw his eyes on her and smiled. "Andrew," she said, "I'm very glad to be here."

Neither of them ate much of the steaks they'd ordered. They refused dessert and hurried through coffee. Without asking, Andrew drove to his house. She could barely wait for him to pull her clothes off, which he did hungrily as she tugged at his. He was more than ready by the time they were naked and so was she. He moved his mouth and his tongue down her body, then, catching his breath, he entered her. Their mutual climax came in a rush.

After a while they started again, this time more slowly, less urgently, with lingering tenderness. But the urgency returned and the climax was as shattering.

By the time she'd showered and dressed, Andrew had put on his trousers and shirt. As he held her to him, she realized with astonishment that it was more than possible for them to start all over again. She pushed him gently away. "I really have to go."

"I know. I wish you didn't."

In silence Andrew drove her to where her car was parked near the restaurant. Without further word or gesture she got out and got into her car. Andrew waited until she had started her engine and then driven off.

She felt numb as she drove the miles back to Summerstoke. She was almost home when she found herself thinking of the fact that, as though by mutual, if unstated, agreement she and Andrew hadn't discussed the future. And then the words formed in her head, what future? She saw Graham's face and was surprised at the pain it brought. But whether the pain stemmed from her anger at him or because she was betraying him, she couldn't decide. And considering his own affair, she thought indignantly, whose betrayal was the greater?

CHAPTER
15

Robbie sat in the headmaster's office at St. John's School. The chair, on the other side of the desk from Martin Bayard, the headmaster, felt at first odd to his big, mature body. He'd sat in the same chair as a boy of fourteen and then once a year through eighteen in the annual "talk" that the headmaster always had with each student. As a result, he felt curiously as though he had been summoned to explain himself.

Martin Bayard was not a graduate of St. John's, but he and Robbie had attended Harvard at the same time and belonged to a couple of the same clubs.

"I told you, Robbie," Martin Bayard said, "it's not that I don't like him. I do. But this is the wrong school for him, much too traditional and conventional."

"But expelled!" Robbie protested. "You must know what that'll do to his record when he tries to get into any halfway decent college."

"I'd be highly surprised if he even applies to what either you or I would call a halfway decent one. I'd fully expect him to want to go to some way-out school in some way-out place."

Robbie didn't say anything, largely because what Martin said was true.

The headmaster said, "Somebody, I don't know who, once said that we choose our enemies when we're very young for entirely emotional reasons. And then we spend the following years building up all the rationalizations to support our choice. Taking that, for the moment, as true, what started Three on his role as radical and/or anarchist? Do you have any idea?"

"His mother, I'm afraid," Robbie said. "Of course she didn't mean to, and I think she'd die of grief and humiliation if anyone pointed this out. But she's— well, she's very religious and from the time he was four, Jenny started taking him to Sunday school and later on church and cramming the Bible down his throat." Robbie paused. "She'd resent my putting it that way, and, of course, I'm to blame, too. If I'd paid enough attention, I might have seen what was happening sooner and put a stop to it. But I was busy establishing my law practice and building up the beginnings of a political career ..." He sighed. "By the time I did see what was happening with Three, the pattern was set."

"I see."

"Look, Martin, can't you give him another chance? I'll talk to him as soon as I leave you. If he goes home now, he wouldn't have a prayer of getting into anything but the local public and/or parochial school. That would mean his living at home, and given what I've told you, it could be a disaster."

Martin got up and walked to the window, where he stood staring out for a minute. Then he turned, "You know, Robbie, I'd do anything I could for you, but I could face a real rebellion in the ranks among the teachers. There isn't a rule Robert hasn't flouted at some point, and with the outlook about things as they are today, more than a few teachers would be happy to point out that Robert's still here because of who you are and because his father and grandfather came here."

Robbie didn't reply or comment. He sat quietly, hoping Martin would talk himself into giving Three one more chance, which he looked like he might be doing.

Finally Martin said, "All right, I'll give him one more chance, but that's it. Either he toes the line or he gets the boot. Now I'm going to send for him so you can talk to him."

"Don't you want to talk to him, too?" Robbie asked.

"Not with you here."

Martin pulled out a class plan, then pushed a button. When a young woman came in he said, "Please go to Mr. Edwards's class in room 210 and tell Robert Beresford that his father is here in my office and would like to speak to him."

Robbie rose, "I can't thank you—"

"Don't thank me. I don't think it will last a week. Now I'm going to go. Unless you want to, you don't have to write or call. Whatever results there are will be enough."

When Martin had left, Robbie went over to the window and was staring out when he heard a knock on the door. "Come in," he said, and turned.

His son stood in the door, his light brown hair falling over his face.

"Come in," Robbie said.

Three came in.

"First," Robbie said, drawing the headmaster's letter from his pocket, "I want you to read this."

Three took it and skimmed it quickly. "So?" he said. "Have you come to pick me up?"

"No. After a lot of begging and pleading I've managed to secure one more chance for you."

The boy scowled fiercely. "Thanks a lot. What if I don't want another chance?"

"Then the alternative is to come back home and to go to either public or parochial school At this point I can't get you into a private one and I don't greatly feel like trying."

"I've always wanted to go to public school. I hate these ... these prisons of eliteness."

Robbie stared at his son. Where had all this started?

Had Jenny's born-again enthusiasm really set him on this path?

"Sit down, Three."

"I don't need to—"

"But I do. I'm a lot older than you."

Three sat in one of the chairs. "Okay. I'm sitting."

"I know I haven't paid enough attention to you or taken the time to talk to you enough, but when did all this rebellion, radicalism, or however you think of it, start?"

Three's boyish, rather sensitive mouth hardened. "Do we really have to go into this? I mean it wasn't like you were off at war or something. You were around . . ."

"Yes, I accept the reproach. I was around and should have noticed, and didn't. But I'd appreciate an answer."

Three stared at his sneakers for a moment. "I guess the . . . the first thing I remember was when Mom told me I shouldn't play with Mozie Burrell because he wasn't up to our people."

"Mozie Burrell? Who—? Oh yes. I remember his name, but that's about all. That was at the Country Day school, wasn't it?"

"Yeah. Before St. John's. He was half black and Mom didn't like that."

"Are you sure that's the reason? Couldn't Mozie— quite apart from being black—have done something that she didn't particularly like?"

"Sure. He used the word fuck."

Robbie sighed. "And how old were you both?"

"About seven."

"Can't you make any allowances for your mother's upbringing? She didn't grow up here. People are different in different parts of the country."

"Yeah, like in the South blacks have to eat in the back of the room and go to a different toilet."

"You're a little behind the times. That's one of the things the civil rights movement changed."

"I guess Mom never caught up with that."

Robbie sighed, then surprised himself by asking, "Why do you hate your mother so much?"

"Because she's a hypocrite! All this guff about the love of God and her personal relationship with Jesus, but she doesn't want me to play with lower-class kids. I like lower-class kids. I like them better than the upper-class ones."

"Did it ever occur to you that that might be because you can feel superior to them?"

"That's a fucking lie!"

"Is it? Think about it. And now I'm going to go. If you want that badly to leave, you have my permission to do so—not that you'd probably feel the need to wait around for it! And you'll certainly make the headmaster happy. But it's up to you. I'm sorry you feel the way you do about your mother. Most of us are hypocrites about something. I know it's useless to tell you she loves you, but she does." Robbie put his hand inside his coat and brought out his wallet. "Here is a hundred dollars. If you decide to come home you can use this. Or if you want me to come and get you, then I'll do that. But you'll have to call me. You're almost sixteen, which means you're almost an adult, so on your way to saving the world you'll have to take on some responsibility."

Robbie put the money on the headmaster's desk and left.

Matilda made sure she was alone, then she went into the bathroom, ran her hand to the back of one of the shelves in the linen closet and found the pill bottle she was looking for. She'd managed to collect about fifteen tranquilizers by skipping her daily dose from time to time. If she skipped too many days the doctor would, she was sure, suspect something, so she could only slowly add to her hoard. Would fifteen be enough to do the job? The doctor had gone on and on about how strong they were and how they were never, ever to be taken in conjunction with alcohol, but she wasn't sure she believed him. He knew perfectly well she was a drunk and was, she was fairly certain, deliberately exaggerating. However, she didn't want to take the pills and then wake up still alive with tubes running in and out of her and probably brain damaged—that is, if her brain wasn't already damaged from the alcohol.

But more than her worry about that was her concern about Honeys I and II and Sweetpea. There was really nobody she completely trusted to make sure the dogs were found a good home.

Clutching the pill bottle, she came back to her chair and looked down at the sleeping Honey I. "Honey," she said, and leaned down awkwardly to stroke her.

At her voice the dog awoke, turned its head toward her and tried to lick her hand. Honey II, hearing this, also woke up and came over, also licking any part of Matilda's hand or arm she could reach. And then, of course, Sweetpea bounded over and leaped up, her tongue reaching for Matilda's face.

Straightening, Matilda sat down in her chair and patted her lap. All three of the dogs tried to jump up. She helped up Honey I and Sweetpea, and tried to lean over them to stroke Honey II by way of compensation. "You can come up next," she said.

Honey II sat down on her feet.

Matilda sat there with the two dogs in her lap and the pill bottle in her hand. She hadn't actually had a drink for about an hour, because she was trying to clear her head to face what she knew she had to do.

If only she could have seen Mark first. She closed her eyes. To think of Mark was disastrous. She would then drink and after that everything would stop until she could pull herself together and plan again.

But she couldn't not think about Mark. He had been on her mind and in her consciousness more than anyone else the past months. Almost as though he were near and on some level she knew it.

Don't go into that again, she told herself. There'd been a time when she had gone out seeking psychics and mediums, indifferent to the warnings of the Church on the subject. The only statement from any of them that she had not finally dismissed as ridiculous was a woman who didn't have much else to say, but who did tell her, "Mark is alive. When he comes near you will know it."

She'd clung to that, and lately had begun to realize that Mark filled her mind far more than at any other time except right after he disappeared.

Maybe you're putting it in your mind so you can bring it about, she told herself. It's the kind of thing her husband or any of her children or her confessor in the Church would say, but she didn't think she was bringing it about.

"Mark," she said now.

There was a knock on the door. Quickly she thrust the pill container into her pocket and turned almost defensively. "Who is it?"

"Caleb."

"All right. Come in."

"Hi, Mom," he said, closing the door behind him. Then, as Sweetpea bounded off Matilda's lap and toward him, "Hi, puppy! Which one is this?"

"Sweetpea. She's not a year yet. She's Honey Two's granddaughter—I think. Maybe great-granddaughter. Sometimes I get muddled with the generations, along with a few other things."

Caleb rubbed Sweetpea's head, then walked toward Matilda. "How are you, Mom?"

Most of the time she just said "Fine," because it saved a lot of trouble. For some reason she said now, "I've been better."

He sat down in the chair opposite, and when Sweetpea jumped on his lap he adjusted his knees so she'd be comfortable and stroked her.

"You should be flattered," Matilda said. "She doesn't do that to many people. In fact, I can't think of anybody she's jumped up on like that for a long time."

"I like dogs. I particularly like these long-haired dachshunds."

"You brought me the first Honey, grandmother of the current Honey One. That's one reason why I love them. Your father's never liked them. He much preferred the retrievers."

"I have to admit, I loved Macdougal. He was a great dog. But I like these, too."

"These made me feel less lower class. They're not as WASP as the retrievers."

Caleb put back his head and laughed. "I never thought of dogs that way. But you may have a point." And then, before he could think about it, "That's the kind of comment Julie would"—he saw his mistake, but also saw that leaving it unfinished was worse—"would like," he said.

"Who's Julie?"

"She's a friend of mine from Guatemala. Somebody who works to change things."

"You mean a radical, like you."

"Yes. Like me." He felt relief in naming her. "Mom, I'm thinking of leaving the order, the priesthood." When he had imagined making that statement to the family, it had never been to his mother, the only practicing Catholic. Yet here he was, telling Matilda what the previous day he had stated vehemently to Julie must not be even hinted at until the right moment.

Matilda didn't answer for a moment. She went on stroking Honey I. Finally she said, "I'm sorry." Then, after a brief silence, "Are you sure?"

He was about to say yes when he found the word wouldn't come out of his mouth. What he finally said was, "Oh, Mom, I don't know. I thought I was. I was sure that was what I wanted to do and then marry Julie, but—somehow, it doesn't seem so much the absolutely right thing anymore."

They sat there for a while in silence, then Caleb said, "What about you, Mom? You know you're killing yourself, don't you?"

Once again the words, but not fast enough, were in her mouth, but this time she didn't say them. "I can't stop, Caleb. I guess I don't want to."

Caleb sat there staring down at the dog in his lap. "Mom, what does it do for you?"

"Sometimes it makes me feel wonderful—powerful, able to do everything I ever wanted to do—at least it used to. Now it just blots out things."

"What kind of things?"

"Mark." She paused. "And my other failures."

"I can't comment about Mark, Mom. I know it's a horrible tragedy that affected you more than it did the rest of us. But what other failures?"

"Any relationship I had with your father. Elizabeth's leaving . . ."

"But that wasn't your fault. She had a row with Dad."

"If only I hadn't gone back to the car."

Tears were pouring down Matilda's cheeks. She put up her hands and covered her face and started to cry. Honey I licked her arm, then jumped off her lap. Matilda started to rock back and forward. "It was my fault. My fault." She looked up and around. She'd forgotten that she had no drink handy. Caleb was there, which normally might have been some kind of a brake. But, unlike everybody else, he did not make her feel guilty. She tried to get up and started to sway.

"Mom!" Caleb said and stood up, unseating Sweetpea, who fell off and to the ground. "What do you want?"

"There's a bottle in the desk drawer over there, Caleb. Please get it for me."

"Mom, do you think—"

"Get it, Caleb. Do you think not giving it to me will make any difference? I'll just ask you to leave and then get it myself."

Caleb went over to the desk and started opening drawers.

"Bottom drawer," Matilda said, hanging onto her chair.

He found the bottle, glanced over to the table beside his mother's chair, did not see a glass, and started to the bathroom to get one.

"Bring it here now!" Matilda said. "You can get the glass later."

Caleb took the bottle to her. Matilda twisted off the top and drank from it. After a moment she lowered it, saw her son still watching her, and said, "You can bring me a glass now, if you want."

"Mom, what's the end of all this?"

"Death," she said. She looked at him. "Caleb, I don't want to go on living."

"Will you try a rehab just once more—for me?"

"That's dirty pool, Caleb. What difference do you think it can make?"

"I don't know. But maybe it'll give me time to pray about it."

The second phone call from Graham came two nights later when Robert Senior and Caleb were alone at dinner. Matilda had not come down. Terry had left for Boston more than a week previously, Robbie and Jenny were at their own home in College Hill, and Elizabeth had left in her rental car at around six saying she would be back later.

For the first time Robert Senior had said, "May one ask where you're going?"

Elizabeth, standing in the door of the sitting room where, unexpectedly, she found her father, felt an old familiar prod of anger. But she said evenly enough, "To see some old friends." And she'd left before he or Caleb, who was also there, could say anything else.

She and Andrew had dinner at a French restaurant on the outskirts of Providence. For the first hour or so, as though by mutual consent, they did not discuss her husband or her marriage or her children. They talked about his two sons, about whether or not he would return to Seattle, about Seattle and the West Coast.

They were sipping their coffee when Andrew said, "Elizabeth, we have to talk. Nothing has changed. I feel exactly the same way as I did the first time we ... we were together. Let me get it out into the open. Will you divorce Graham and marry me?" He hesitated. "I don't think I'm that overwhelmingly moral, but I never thought I'd be asking a woman to do that. I guess I never thought I'd fall so damn heavily in love with a woman who was already married."

"Neither did I," Elizabeth said. "I mean ... you know what I mean."

He stirred his coffee, waiting for her to answer. "Well, my darling, will you?"

There in the restaurant, she started to cry and felt humiliated because she wasn't able to stop.

"I'm sorry, I shouldn't have asked that here. Let's go. You don't have to answer that now, anyway."

"Andrew, I don't know. I just can't think! They're the children ... and ... and Graham."

"Do you still love him?"

"How can I love two men at the same time?"

"I don't know, but I think in some way you do."

Back at his house, their lovemaking was, if anything, more urgent than it had been before. At one point she looked at his naked body beside her and decided that, bad leg and all, it was one of the most beautiful things she had ever seen.

"Have you ever seen Michelangelo's 'David'?" she said idly, touching his thigh.

"Yes, when I was at college I spent a summer vacation in Italy. That was when I thought I was going to be an artist."

"I didn't know that about you. You didn't say a word. Painter? Sculptor?"

"Painter. Not that I was that good."

"You were probably better than you thought."

"No, I wasn't. I wasn't bad, but I was far from being good enough to spend a life at it. I knew Dad was waiting in the wings for me to come to my senses, which, of course, kept me on the painting track an extra year or so. But one day I took a look at all my canvases, and I knew that whatever it was that makes a true artist, I didn't have."

"Was that before or after your year in Italy?"

"After. I take it you've been to Florence?"

"Yes, but I'm afraid that of all the arts, painting seems to make the least impression on me. I'm ashamed to say that when I was in Florence I went zip through the Pitti and zip through the Uffizi, but I did sit two hours in the Academy looking at 'David.' It's the most gorgeous piece of sculpture in the world."

"I'll agree to that, although I also liked the Bernini 'David' in the Borghese Museum in Rome."

After she was dressed and driving home she confronted Andrew's question which, either out of fear or generosity, he had not brought up again: Would she divorce Graham and marry him?

"I don't know, I don't know, I don't know," she said aloud, and felt once more the tears. "Oh God, I don't know."

When she got home, it was later than she had realized. But her father was still up. He had obviously been listening for her because he appeared in his study doorway when she walked through the front door.

"Graham called and wants you to call him back, no matter what hour you get in. Ailsa is all right, but she has had some kind of an accident."

CHAPTER
16

Elizabeth waited impatiently for her call to go through. Finally she heard Graham's voice, "Elizabeth?"

"What happened to Ailsa?"

"She fell off her pony. The doctor says she's perfectly all right, but she did seem to knock herself out for a brief period."

"What pony?"

"I got a pony for the children a week ago. Most of their friends seem to have ponies and take part in the gymkhana coming up, so I went to an auction and got one."

"If you wanted them to ride, Graham, why couldn't you wait until they could take riding lessons? This mightn't have happened if they'd been taught properly." She heard the accusatory note in her voice and knew it came from her own guilt.

"May I point out that people who've been taught properly and ridden all their lives fall off occasionally? I have myself many times."

"I didn't even know you rode. But I still think to get them a pony without having someone show them how to ride—"

"But I did. Barbara Hinsley came and schooled them a couple of times. It was very nice of her because of course she did it without fee. But she was at the auction when I got Peterkin—the pony—and offered to do it.''

"Another of your lady friends, Graham?" The moment the words were out of her mouth she regretted them, not only because they sounded spiteful but because of her own relationship with Andrew, which seemed to rear in front of her on a giant screen. "Graham—"

"No, she is not what you call my lady friend. I do not have any at this time. And obviously your desire to pick a fight is greater than your interest in either Ailsa or me. Goodbye." And he hung up.

Elizabeth called back again, of course. But the phone was not picked up. After six rings she put the receiver down. She had called from the phone in her father's study and became aware of him still sitting there. As she looked up she saw him watching her. "That wasn't a great success," she said lightly. "But at least Ailsa seems to be all right."

When he didn't reply, she said, "I think I'll go upstairs." And started to get up.

"You're having an affair with Andrew Treadwell, aren't you?"

Pushed again by her own guilt, she swung around at him. "What right have you to say that?"

"I don't know what right I have. You're certainly an adult and in charge of your own affairs—"

"Then let's leave it at that."

He went on as though she hadn't spoken. "But I do have some concern as your father."

"Concern? For me?" Hearing the sharp, sarcastic note in her voice she stopped. Thus far she'd avoided a confrontation with her father, but the memory of the scene that had driven her across an ocean was never far, especially when she was in his presence. At that moment she remembered her conversation with Andrew about Nigel. She said now evenly, "Andrew and I were talking. I mentioned Nigel." She glanced at her father. "You do remember him, I take it."

"I remember him."

Her father's face, Elizabeth thought, seemed set and grim. She took a breath. "He—Andrew—said he knew Nigel slightly when they were at Harvard. He said he'd always thought Nigel was gay." She looked at her father. "Did you know that? Did it have anything to do with why you told me not ... not to run after him?"

After a pause Robert said, "I did know it. And yes, it had a great deal to do with ... with our conversation."

Elizabeth took a breath. "Is that what you call it? I remember it as a vicious harangue, ending with a slap across my face. Wasn't there another way you could have warned me off him—instead of abusing me?" She eyed him steadily. "Of course, you'd always put me down, made me feel ugly! There was certainly nothing different about that. I've spent twenty years trying to overcome it. It's affected my relationship with every man I've ever known—the men I knew before Graham, with Graham ... and now in some way with Andrew. And you have the gall to question me about my relationship with him!" A small voice within her was saying, "Don't do this. You'll be sorry!" But a long-festering rage, made worse by guilt, threatened to engulf her.

Robert Senior's face was as white as the curtain behind him. Yet he seemed ... Elizabeth groped for the right word. Surprised? Even relieved? Finally he said, "I didn't mean to abuse you, make you feel ugly."

"Are you denying it?"

"No. Matilda accused me of the same."

"You always hated me!"

"No, Elizabeth, I didn't hate you. For God's sake, you were my daughter. What I didn't like—" He paused.

"Well?"

"I didn't like being begged for approval and affection. You were a needy, sometimes hysterical child and it brought out the worst in me. Your mother made that eminently clear when you fled to England."

"I don't remember your saying any of this in your letters."

"I wrote you an apology."

"It wasn't what I call a mea culpa. It was a haughty acknowledgment that you might have been wrong."

Robert got up. "What do you want of me now, Elizabeth? I'm sorry about the past. I'm sorry if I ruined your life, although I can't see how I can be held responsible for whatever is happening between you and Graham or between you and Andrew. But you must surely know that to talk to a man the way you just did to Graham is no way to preserve a marriage. If, that is, you want to preserve it."

Three threw his things in his bag.

"What about your hockey stick?" Jeddie Bloom said. He had bravely cut class to be with Three while he was packing to take his final leave from St. John's.

"Screw the hockey stick. If things go the way I want, I won't have to play that lousy game again as long as I live."

"But you're good at it."

"It's still a lousy game."

Three shoved in the last of his shoes and closed the suitcase. Then he started loading his shoulder carry all with books.

The final breach of rules that had sent him first to the headmaster's office and then to his dormitory to pack had been to set free all the animals in the science lab. He'd been planning that for some time and managed to get into the lab at six in the morning, before anyone was around. The whole thing took only a few minutes. The frogs and mice he had simply taken outside and set free and stood there watching them hop and run to liberty. The rats he had taken into the woods beyond the school grounds, figuring they'd be more likely to find food there. Then he'd left a hand-printed, unsigned note saying: "They deserve to live in freedom as much as we do."

He had expected the first discovery to be made about nine o'clock. It was eight-thirty when, sitting in his history class, he had heard the distant banging of doors and knew that somebody had discovered the open cages in the lab. Twenty minutes later the head-master's secretary appeared in the door and asked him to come to the headmaster's office. When he got there he found not only the headmaster but the science master.

"Robert," the headmaster said. "Some idiot has opened all the cages in the science lab and let the animals out. Was that you?"

"Yes, sir."

"Do you realize the harm you've done?" Ted Thornton, the science master asked. "Some of those animals have been injected with things that will make them sick if we can't give them antidotes, which of course now we can't. Also the experiements that some of the seniors have been working on for months have been destroyed. Are you out of your mind?"

"I don't think we ought to experiment on animals. After all, we wouldn't like it if they experimented on us. They're no different. They feel pain just the way we do. But I guess you think if it's to our interest to torture them, then it's okay."

"Of all the brainless—"

"Yes, Dr. Thornton, I agree with you," the head-master said. "But what's done is done. Perhaps you'd better start on getting some new animals. I have to talk to Robert here."

When the science master had left, the headmaster said to Robert, "You know, of course, that that's the end. Do you want me to call your father?"

"No, sir. He gave me money before he left." Three looked at the headmaster's skeptical face. "You can call him if you don't believe me. I'll pack and call a cab and take the ten of six train to Providence."

"All right."

As Three walked to the door the headmaster said, "Just to satisfy my curiosity, was this an act of principle, or were you deliberately doing it to make sure you'd be asked to leave?"

Three grinned suddenly and the headmaster struggled against grinning back. The boy was so damn likable, he thought.

"Both, sir. I meant what I said about animals deserving the same rights as people—but I knew it would also do the trick."

"How do you think your father will feel about it?"

Three looked down at his sneakers. "Oh, he'll get used to the idea. He's pretty good."

"And your mother?"

As the headmaster saw Three's face harden, he remembered what Robbie had said.

"I'm looking forward to her reaction, sir."

"Robert, why do you . . . why do you dislike her so much? Is it the religion thing?"

Three came back into the room a couple of feet. "Do you know what she did when I was six? I had a dog, a mutt named Buster, that I'd got from the shelter with my birthday money. Once when I wouldn't do what she wanted me to—something to do with her rotten church or Sunday school—she waited until I was in school, then she took my dog back and told them to destroy it. I went and begged, but because she was my mother, they couldn't do anything. So Buster died because of her and her . . . her lousy stinking fundamentalism!"

"But you got another dog—your father told me about him."

"Yes. Patches." Three paused. "Mom got him for me for my eighth birthday. He's a spaniel. Natch, Mom likes a pedigreed dog better than a mutt."

"Do you like him?"

"Yes, he's okay. But he's not Buster."

"She must have been sorry for what she did to Buster. I mean, her getting another dog would indicate that."

"Yeah. She's said she was sorry—a lot of times."

"But you haven't forgiven her."

Three's face hardened. "No."

"Well, Three, I don't want to incur your wrath, but I think that you'll be happier if and when you do."

"Screw that—sorry, sir. I think I'd better be getting packed."

"All right."

Three was almost at the door when the headmaster said, "You're very like her, you know." When Three swung around, the headmaster went on. "Where do you think you get your passion from? Not your even-tempered father. Think about it!"

At the last moment Three changed his mind. He decided to get himself and his bags to the main highway not too far from the school and hitch a ride home. Then he could keep the hundred dollars.

"I can just see the headlines," Jeddi said. "School allows expelled boy to hitchhike home."

"Why the hell would the papers care?"

"They'd care all right if something happened to you—like you were murdered for your money by some nut who picks you up."

"You have a gross imagination. Here, you carry the bags, I'll lug the books."

Three and Jeddi managed to get through the gates without being noticed.

"Here you are," Jeddi said, dropping the bag on the side of the highway. "Give a guy a ring. Keep in touch!"

Robbie was in his office when the phone rang. Mari-anne buzzed him and said, "It's the headmaster at

Saint. John's. He sounds quite angry, or maybe just anxious."

Robbie picked up the phone. "Martin?"

"I wish to God I hadn't listened to you, Robbie. That freakish son of yours really pulled a lulu! He let the animals in the science lab out of their cages and then freed them outside. And I don't have to tell you how the school prides itself on its strong biology department. The science master is out of his mind. No— I haven't finished," he went on as Robbie started to interrupt. "I guess Three wanted to keep whatever money you gave him, so with the aid of a buddy, he got his stuff to the highway and is hitchhiking back to Providence. Somebody saw Jeddie Bloom, his friend, sneaking back in and wanted to know where he'd been. Jeddy's loyal to Three, but he's not fast on his feet, so he blurted out the truth."

"Oh God!" Robbie said tiredly. "Jenny'll have a fit. She thinks every driver who picks somebody up is a potential rapist and murderer."

"I take it you don't."

Robbie thought for a moment. "What time did Three set out to hitch?"

"About half an hour ago."

"Thanks." Robbie hung up. If Three walked in now, Robbie felt he'd have no hesitation in flaying his beloved son alive. But he knew he'd have to be patient and bide his time.

Robbie then considered calling Jenny and telling her, but decided against it almost immediately. Left to herself, Jenny, he was sure, would have the state police patrolling the roads.

A small, nasty voice in the back of his mind murmured that if anything happened to his son, he would profoundly regret that he hadn't let Jenny follow her instincts. But he ignored it. He'd hitched himself the summer he was a sophomore. It was something any boy liked to do. He'd just bide his time.

*   *   *

Three thanked the kind, elderly man who'd given him the last lap of his ride into the city. The trip had taken more than three hours because he'd had to hitch with four different cars on various legs of the journey. The first time he was picked up was by a man driving his pickup truck. Unfortunately that didn't last long. When the man got out to put newspaper down in the back of the truck so Three could put his bags there, Three had smelled a strong unpleasant odor. When they were in the truck and on their way Three led the conversation to where he could inquire about the smell.

"Oh, that's just the pigs I take to market. The poor things are so scared they just let go all over the place. I've scrubbed the back of the truck I don't know how many times, but I can't get the smell out."

Three, who had become a vegetarian the year before, forgot that the man was doing him a favor. "Don't you think it's horrible cruelty to raise animals only to kill them? That's why I don't eat meat. I don't think we have any right to."

"Well," the man said, "you're entitled to what you think, but so'm I. And I have to make a living on my farm. This is the only way I can do it."

"Don't you feel like a murderer knowing what you plan for them when you go out to feed the pigs and they flock around you?"

The man stopped the truck. "Son, if the thought of all the pigs dying is too much for you, maybe you'd better get another ride." The driver leaned across Three, opened the door and said, "I'll give you one minute to get out before I push you out. And I'll give you another two minutes to get your stuff out of the back of the truck."

Three jumped to the ground and ran to get his bags. He yanked them from the back just as the man drove off. "Murderer!" Three yelled. As he stood there, he wondered if, even with the protection of the newspaper, the bags would ever lose the repellent smell they seemed to have acquired in their brief sojourn on the truck floor.

The second ride was from a businessman who was only going to a town fifty miles away, and the third, ironically, was from two women schoolteachers who ignored him and chattered all the way. The fourth ride was from a polite elderly man who hadn't even planned to drive in to the center of Providence, but veered from his route past the city to bring Three in. Three thanked him sincerely and tried hard not to focus on the fact that when he asked the man what he did, the man had told him he was a retired Methodist minister.

When the man drove off, Three stood irresolute for a few minutes, pondering his next step. In front, up on the hill, was the State House. To his right was College Hill and home. He could flag down a cab, of course, but that would take some of his money. If he didn't, he'd have to lug his suitcases and his book bag up College Hill's steep slopes. The trouble was, at the end of the journey would be his mother. He glanced at his watch. It was still too early in the afternoon for his father to be home. Suddenly Three felt he couldn't confront his mother right away. He should have asked to be let out at the train station. He glanced over his shoulder. The station was a lot nearer than his house would be. He could check his bags there and then make up his mind what to do after that.

By the time he got to the station he was puffing and his arms ached, but he checked the suitcase and the bag and then considered his options. Finally he called his father from a phone booth.

For the past hour Robbie had only pretended to be working. He had canceled his lunch date with someone in the municipal government recommended by Kate, had had Marianne order him in a sandwich and had let it sit there unopened.

He was not quite at the point where he wished to God he'd let Jenny know about Three's thumbing a ride home, but he was close. Further, the man he had stood up was not happy to have the lunch canceled. "Robbie," Kate had said when she had told Robbie to call Joe, "Joe Muncio needs you a lot more than you need him. You're not going to be out on the street if your opponent gets in—Joe is. He can spill a lot of municipal dirt for you to use."

He would have to make it up to Joe in some other way, soon, Robbie was thinking when his phone rang.

Marianne buzzed. "Your son, Mr. Beresford."

Robbie snatched up the receiver. "Where are you?"

"In the train station."

"I thought you were hitching a ride."

"I did. But I lugged my stuff here to check it until you were ready to go home. I didn't want to ... I didn't think ... I, er ..."

"You didn't want to face your mother, did you?"

There was a silence. Three didn't like being backed into a corner.

"Did you, Three?"

"No."

Robbie drew a breath and managed not to say, I don't really blame you. "For your punishment I ought to send you back to St. John's to find all those animals you loosed."

"You wouldn't do that, Dad."

"No," Robbie acknowledged, "I wouldn't. But I'm no vegetarian."

"No, sir. Can you come and get me?"

"No, I can't. I stood up a very important man in my campaign so I could be here when you called. I'm now going to invite him out for a drink and dinner."

"But, Dad, you know what Mother'll be like. Does she know I've been canned?"

"No. She knew you were going to be because she read the headmaster's letter, and she also knows I got you a reprieve. But she doesn't know that you let the animals out and blew it. You know, there are moments I could brain you for doing anything so dumb."

"It's not dumb. Aren't you always saying in your speeches that you're proud to be part of a country where people can express their beliefs, no matter what they are?"

Robbie was pulled up short by that. "It's nice to know you read my speeches."

"Sure I do. But I think you ought to stick by what you said. Don't I have a right to think using animals for experiments is wrong?"

"Yes, you do, nutty as it is. I won't even talk to you about the desperately sick people who need the medical research that might come out of such experiments. But destroying property is not the same as expressing an opinion."

"Oh, when it comes to property, of course—" Three said sarcastically before he remembered it was his father he was talking to and his father who had stuck up for him.

"Don't take that tone to me, Three," Robert said evenly.

"Okay, sorry, Dad. I guess ... I guess I just get carried away."

"So does your mother," Robbie said.

This was the second time in one day someone had implied this, and it did not make Three happy. However, he said grudgingly, "The headmaster said something like that."

"Is that right?" Robbie was not that interested in what Martin Bayard thought. "Now listen. I was talking on the phone to your uncle Caleb a few minutes ago. He's home. I want you—no, I'll call him and ask him to pick you up at the station. Stay there. Promise?"

"Okay. I promise."

When Robbie called, Caleb was just about to leave to pick up Julie and take her to the station for an overnight trip to New York—ostensibly (as she claimed) to meet her sister who happened to be visiting there from California.

Quickly Robbie explained the situation to Caleb. "Could you just take Three to College Hill and keep him in our parents' house until I can pick him up? Or drive around with him, or take him out for some kind of treat—a movie or pizza or something. I should be able to get away no later than seven-thirty, and I'll call you there when I can come and collect him."

Caleb would have given anything to refuse, but he knew he couldn't. Over the time he and the others had been there, waiting for the trust to be opened and read, it had become harder and harder to contemplate the blackmail he and Julie had planned. For one thing, and against his will, he kept remembering occasions when Robbie had stuck up for him. "Okay," he said. "I'll be there."

Driving into Providence as fast as he could, Caleb realized there was no way he could get Julie at her hotel and bundle her onto the train without running into Three. The terminal at Providence was not Grand Central Station, where armies could move in and out at opposite ends and not run into one another.

"Look," he said to Julie when he collected her at the hotel, "I have to do this for Robbie. Three, his son, is a nice enough kid. I thought I'd explain you as the sister of a priest I worked with in Guatemala."

"That sounds virginal enough," Julie said with light sarcasm. She would do much for the movement, but she knew from her growing tendency to make biting comments that the situation was beginning to get her down.

Three was standing at the entrance to the train station when they approached. Julie saw a slender boy of medium height with amber eyes and light brown hair falling over his forehead and part of his face. "He doesn't look anything like you," she said to Caleb. "Not that there's any reason why he should."

"He looks like his mother," Caleb said.

"The Bible-thumping southerner you told me about?"

"Yes."

At that point they drew even with Three, who leaned toward the window. "Hi," he said to Caleb.

Caleb got out. "Three, I'd like you to meet Julie Manners. Her brother is one of the priests I served with in Guatemala, and she wanted to catch up on the latest news about him and his work. She's here to catch the train to New York. Julie," he turned toward her, "I'll get your ticket for you."

Julie and Three stood near the entrance while Caleb waited his turn at the ticket window.

"Were you in Guatemala?" Three asked.

"Yes, I've been there."

"Is it as awful as people in outfits like Freedom International and other ones say it is—with killings and torturing of the people?"

Julie looked with awakened interest at her young companion. "How do you know all that?"

"Well, I'm the family radical." Three spoke with a certain pride. "My father even calls me an anarchist. I've just been expelled from my school."

"What did you do to get expelled?"

"I freed all the animals they were experimenting on in the lab."

Julie's interest in animals was zero. But she recognized a fellow activist when she saw one.

"I think that's terrific. We need more people like you."

As Three's face lit up in surprise and pleasure, she said, "In Guatemala people see Americans, unfortunately, as the owners and operators of an outfit like the All Americas Import and Export Exchange. Have you heard of it?"

"Yeah, I think so. Sort of like another United Fruit?"

"Very much like. In fact, we call it 'All Americas Imperial Robbery Inc.'" She watched his face for a moment and wondered whether she should take the next step. She decided to. "You know, your uncle Caleb came up here to confront the family—your family—with their holdings in such a piratical fascist outfit. It practically owns the government down there. If something happened to it, the whole establishment would fall, and maybe the people would be able to have true democracy. Oh, here comes Caleb with my ticket. It was nice to meet you." Quickly, she leaned forward and kissed Three on the cheek and then on the mouth.

"What did you and Julie talk about?" Caleb asked Three later when they were at a pizza joint to give the ravenous Three some long delayed lunch.

"About how awful it is in Guatemala and how our family money is invested in some big greedy American company that's practically running their government."

A wave of anger started up in Caleb, directed this time not at rich North American gringos but at Julie. By dropping this information in Three's ear, Julie was showing where her first loyalty lay. He had wanted to marry her. A thought that at the moment seemed bizarre. But he now doubted that she ever intended to marry him.

He did know he was desperately unhappy. All he could think of now to say to Three was, "For God's sake, keep that to yourself. What with the trust coming up, you could blow your father's campaign to kingdom come."

When he'd delivered Three to his parents, Caleb finally returned to Summerstoke and went up to see his mother.

As he expected, she was sitting in her chair. "Mom," he said.

He had expected her to be drunk. But since she seemed to be sitting there in a fairly—for her—normal fashion, he had expected some kind of a response. There was none. He came closer. The light over her chair was off. There was an odd stillness about Matilda's posture, but as he drew near he could hear her breathing, slow and labored.

"Mom," he said again. When she didn't reply, he reached up and switched on the light. "Mom!" He saw her face then: gray, her eyes closed. Then he saw the glass on the table and next to it the empty pill bottle. "Oh, my God!" he said. "Oh, no!"

Putting his hand to her neck, he felt for the carotid artery. The pulse was faint and abnormally slow. But at least she was still alive. Running out the door to the stairwell, he shouted, "Dad!"

His father appeared in his study door downstairs. "What is it?"

"It looks like Mom's taken a load of pills. Call the doctor. I think she's tried to commit suicide!"

CHAPTER
17

The call from Robert Senior came while Andrew and Elizabeth were lying in bed, relaxed and sated after their lovemaking.

Andrew reached across Elizabeth to pick up the receiver. "What? Oh. Yes." He listened for a while, his face growing tense. "All right, I'll tell her."

He put the receiver down and turned to Elizabeth. "That was your father. Your mother tried to commit suicide tonight. She's now in St. Catherine's. They don't know whether she's going to make it or not." He eyed Elizabeth's stunned expression and added, "I'll drive you there."

The ride was silent. When they arrived at the hospital, Andrew got out but at the door he said, "This is a family thing, Elizabeth. I'll wait for you here in the reception area."

Elizabeth nodded and went over to the desk. Directed to the twelfth floor, she got in the elevator and went up. Once on the floor, it was easy to find her mother's room. Her father, Robbie, and Caleb were sitting on chairs in the hall.

"How is Mom?" she asked as she joined them.

"Alive—still," Robbie said. "They're working on her, pumping her stomach, giving her stuff to counteract the tranquilzers."

"Why—?" Elizabeth started and then stopped. It was a useless question.

Nevertheless, her father answered, "A lethal combination of alcoholism, depression, and hopelessness." He looked up at his daughter as he said it.

A nurse came up with another chair. "You're a member of the family?"

"Yes, I'm Elizabeth Paterson. Mrs. Beresford is my mother."

"I'm sorry," the nurse said. "We're doing everything we can."

"Do you think she'll come through?"

"We can't say for sure yet. There are complications brought on by her drinking."

After a minute Elizabeth asked, "Has anybody told Terry about this? About Mom, I mean?"

"I'll called her tonight," Robert Senior said. "She'll be here tomorrow."

The three sat there in silence. After a while a doctor, clad in white with a stethescope around his neck, approached. "Mr. Beresford I think your wife's going to make it. If you'd found her any later, it would be have been too late, but we were able to get most of the sedatives out of her stomach."

Robert Senior stood up. "Can we see her?"

"In a while. Needless to say, she's feeling pretty terrible, both mentally and physically." The doctor hesitated. "From her condition and from what she said, I gather she's been drinking alcoholically for some time."

"Yes." As she's probably told you, no rehab has been able to get her to stop. Each time she came out and started drinking again."

"We have one here that we think's pretty good."

"If she'll go to it, I'd certainly be happy. But she's refused to go to any for some time now."

Caleb, listening, remembered what he'd said to her: if she did go, at least it would give him time to pray.

"Well," the doctor said, "let's get her past this. I've

given her a sedative. She may sound a little vague or disoriented when you talk to her. Give her another few minutes and then you can go in—briefly. I'm sure she'll be glad to see her family rallying around. But don't keep her talking too long, please."

When they went in, they stood around the bed and looked at Matilda, whose eyes were closed.

Somehow, Elizabeth thought, she looked not only a lot paler, but smaller. "Mom," she said and took her mother's hand lying on the white sheet. "We love you and we're glad you're going to be okay."

Matilda's eyes opened and stared up first at her daughter's face and then at the faces of her husband and her two sons. "I'm sorry," she whispered.

"It's all right, Mom," Robbie said. His somewhat austere face softened. "We understand and we'll help. It's going to be all right."

"No," Matilda said. "I meant I'm sorry you didn't let me go." The others looked stunned, but she ignored them as she went on. "The only thing that's better about stopping me is that Honey and the others'll be okay. It bothered me so much who would take care of them."

"Your dogs?" Robert Senior asked. He sounded as though he couldn't believe his words.

His wife looked at him. "They're the only creatures that really need me and who love me without qualification. You don't." She paused, but Robert Senior didn't say anyting. I didn't mean that as a reproach," she said tiredly. "I've really messed up my life—our lives, I guess I mean."

"Mom," Robbie said, "we were told not to talk to you too long. We'll be back tomorrow. But we'll be thinking about you every minute. I know Jenny would say the same. She's sleeping at the shelter tonight, otherwise she'd be here with me."

Robert Senior, Robbie, and Elizabeth moved away.

"Caleb," Matilda said.

He took her hand. "Hang in there, Mom. I need a little more praying time."

She didn't say anything for a minute. "I can't ask you to stop trying to leave the priesthood. After all, I didn't stop trying to kill myself, which is a mortal sin."

Caleb paused. "I think they're more aware of alleviating circumstances now."

"Alleviating circumstances, is it? Maybe it's just cowardice and giving up."

"No, Mom, it isn't. We have to talk. But first you have to sleep. Do you want to see a priest?"

"I'm looking at one now. That's enough."

Caleb leaned down and kissed her cheek. "I'll see you tomorrow."

They all went down to the first floor. Andrew, scanning a magazine in the reception area, stood up.

"Hello, Andrew," Robbie said.

"Hello." He hesitated. "How is Mrs. Beresford?"

"She'll be all right," Robert Senior said. "Good night," and he walked out of the hospital.

Andrew glanced at Elizabeth. "I'll drive you back to where you can get your car."

She nodded. "Thanks." She glanced at her brothers. "Good night. I'll probably see you here tomorrow."

After she and Andrew had left, Caleb looked at Robbie. "I thought you wanted me to pick up Three because he didn't want to be alone with his mother."

"I'm sorry," Robbie said. "I'd forgotten that tonight she was helping with the feeding and then sleeping in the shelter." He hesitated. "Thanks anyway for collecting him. Like I said when you brought him home, I hope it wasn't too much trouble."

Jenny got back from the shelter around eight in the morning. When she walked into the dining room she expected to see her husband having breakfast. What she did not expect was to see Three sitting there as well. For a second, mother and son stared at each other.

"Three!" Jenny cried and went over and kissed him, which he grudgingly submitted to. "Three, darling, why aren't you in school? Anything wrong?"

"I got expelled," Three said baldly.

She stared. "But I thought—" she started and then looked at Robbie. "Didn't you—"

"Yes," he said. "I told you I got Martin to give Three one more chance. But he blew it. Listen, Jenny, Mother tried—"

"What do you mean he blew it?" She looked at Three. "What did you do?"

"I let the animals out of cages in the science lab." He took a breath. "So they expelled me."

Jenny glanced across at her husband. "You knew about this yesterday." It was a statement, not a question. "Our son gets himself expelled for some idiotic act at his school, and you don't even let me know."

"It wasn't an idiotic act," Three said defiantly. "You like to help the homeless, I like to help animals."

"Animals are not human beings."

"They're a lot nicer."

"I will not have you—"

"Yeah, I know. It's not a Christian thing, is it? That's why you killed Buster."

"Easy does it," Robbie said.

"I've apologized again and again for that. I gave you Patches, whom you ignore. Why punish him?" Jenny's voice was shaking.

"I do not ignore him!" Three shouted. "You have no right to say that!"

Jenny suddenly stood up. "You really hate me, don't you? Sometimes I think you both do." And she left the room.

After a moment Robbie said, "She never let me tell her about Mother."

"Granny loves her dogs. Is she going to be okay?"

"She does indeed love them. And yes, she's going to be all right." He looked up at his son. "I think you owe your mother an apology." He sighed. "I guess we both do. And she's right. You do ignore Patches. Whatever problem there is between you and your mother is not Patches's fault."

Three pushed his cereal around the bowl. "I know. But every time I look at him, I think of Buster."

"In other words, your resentment toward your mother is more important to you than the dog's happiness."

"That's not fair!"

"If Patches could talk, you should ask him if he thinks it's fair."

"I thought you were on my side."

"I'm on your side all the time, as you should know. But when it's you and your mother going at each other, then I'm on your side only when I think you're right."

Robbie got up and started to leave the room. When he was at the door, Three asked suddenly, "Do we own a lot of stock in something called the All Americas Import and Export Exchange?"

Robbie stopped. "Yes. Why? How do you know about that?"

"The sister of Uncle Caleb's priest friend told me. She knows a lot about what's going on in Guatemala—the torturings, the killings, and how that company practically runs the government."

Robbie came back in the room. "Where did you meet this woman?"

"She was with Uncle Caleb when he came to the station yesterday. She was going to New York."

Robbie looked at his son for a moment. "And she told you this with your uncle there?"

"No. He went to get her ticket. That's when she told me. What difference does it make?"

Robbie paused. "I don't know."

Three at that moment was remembering that Uncle Caleb had cautioned him about not mentioning it to anyone because it could blow his father's campaign sky high. He knew it was better not to repeat that, but he said, "Don't you think you ought to take our money out of that company? It's a gross outfit."

Robbie was beginning to feel beset on all sides. "In the first place, I don't have command of the family money. Your grandfather and his cousins do. In the second place, that's one person's opinion and she could be wrong. In the third place, your grandmother's suicide attempt is something that, as a family, we have to pay attention to and my mind is on that. In the fourth place, your getting yourself expelled and then fighting with your mother hasn't been any help, and I wish to God you'd forget your radical posturing and try to be a little help within the family. And finally, running a campaign while all this is going on is more than I need right now. Why don't you see if you can't—just for a change—lend a hand instead of being such a headache!"

Going upstairs, Robbie knew he ought to stop by his and Jenny's bedroom both to tell her about Matilda's suicide attempt and to try to make some kind of peace before he left. But then he reflected that she usually went straight to bed for a few hours after staying overnight at the shelter. For a moment he hesitated. Would she be sleeping after the row with Three? Then he decided she probably would—it wasn't as though their fight were anything new—and went off to his own dressing room. He'd call her from the office.

Lying on her bed, Jenny heard her husband come upstairs and waited, hoping he would come in. When she heard him walk down the hall to his dressing room, the hope sudsided, and the tears that had started after she left the dining room came back. As usual, she'd handled Three in exactly the wrong way. And she'd had no right to include her husband. It was his nature to be a politician, a compromiser.

"Don't compromise with sin," her father had always said.

Then her mother would add, "But deal gently with the sinner."

"Not if it means he considers it permission to go on sinning. After all, what's at stake is the immortal soul."

How often when she was growing up had she heard that argument in some form or other?

"Who was it," her mother had once countered, "who said 'let him who is without sin among you cast the first stone.' I think it was the same person who also said, 'Judge not that ye be not judged.'"

Jenny could see her father's intense dark eyes when he replied, "And when you see young people Jenny's age, drinking and living promiscuously and aborting unwanted babies, doesn't it ever occur to you that yours are the arguments that led them there—one excuse after another?"

And what would he say now to Three?

The first thing he'd say, Jenny knew, would be "your mother was right about Buster. Animals have no place in the house." The second thing he'd say would be "honor thy father and thy mother."

Why was it that discipline had worked with her but did nothing but drive a widening chasm between her and her son?

She was tired. The night at the shelter had been disrupted a couple of times by a street crazy's nightmares. He'd shouted and awaken a couple of the others. What she ought to do, Jenny thought, is go downstairs and make peace with Three. But memories of other times when she had tried marched through her head. She would make the effort, then something she would say would invariably start Three off again. She would respond and the peace would again be destroyed. Why had it been so easy with Deirdre, now in her first year at boarding school? Was it something to do with the difference in sex? She herself had been an only child, so she had no way of knowing. She ought to go down ...

Suddenly she was aware of her bedroom door opening slightly. She sat up, saw nothing, then glanced down. Patches, a King Charles cavalier spaniel, poked his white and reddish brown head into the room. He gave a desperate whimper.

"Hasn't anybody taken you out this morning?" Jenny asked. So much for the great animal lover downstairs, she thought bitterly.

"Sorry, Patches, your cause is hopelessly tainted by being associated with me. Come along!"

Jenny pulled herself up and, following Patches's speeding form, went downstairs. The leash was on the hall table, but Jenny was only going to let Patches out in the garden, which had a wall and a gate. Once she'd let him out, she could have gone back upstairs. But something made her stay and watch as Patches lifted his leg and examined plants and trees and pushed his nose against a ball embedded in the grass somewhere.

Why had her father been so unrelenting about animals being kept outside the house? Did it have to do with his need to control everything and everyone within his household? She hadn't even questioned his absolute authority until she had come north to college and had learned phrases like "the controlling parent" in her psychology course. But she had stayed north to marry Robbie instead of going back home to marry a nice southern boy. Why had she? Partly it was Robbie. Could part of it be that, underneath everything, she had rebelled against her father the way Three showed every sign of rebelling against her?

A great longing for her daughter, loving, affectionate, and admiring, filled Jenny. She wished now she had insisted that Deirdre continue at her day school for another year or two. But all Robbie's cousins and their wives seemed to think it was more in the family tradition to go off to Hazelcroft.

At that moment, Patches, who had been pretending to chew the ball, came and put it at Jenny's feet. As she looked down at him, a great affection for the little dog filled Jenny. Contrary to what her son thought, she had not bought Patches because he was pedigreed—although she did have an impressive list of papers for him. She had bought him at a local dog show both because she had fallen in love with the bustling round puppy and because she so bitterly regretted what, in a moment of anger, she had done to Buster. As the years went by, Three had usually been good about walking him and watched over his feeding, but he had never let him sleep where Buster had slept— on his bed. So poor Patches had been banished to the kitchen.

Jenny played ball with him for a while, tossing it into the air and across the garden. Then she said, "I'm wiped out, Patches. I'm going to bed."

Patches watched her as she went into the side door, then sped in after her and climbed the stairs with her. Jenny paused at the top, wondering if Robbie was still in his dressing room or if he had gone off, wondering if Three were still in the dining room or had repaired to his own room. Then she shrugged and went into her bedroom. Just as she was going to close the door, Patches pushed inside. Jenny looked down at him. Then she said, "Come on, Patches, nobody else wants to be with me. Let's take a nap."

Downstairs, Three had decided to start on his new campaign of paying more attention to Patches. With this in mind he went to the kitchen looking for him. Patches wasn't there, so Three went outside to see if he'd been left in the garden, something usually not done, because Patches could jump over parts of the wall and down to the street level. But Patches was nowhere in the yard. Three then went upstairs to look in his own room and in all the other rooms except his parents' bedroom. He didn't go there both because he knew his mother would be sleeping and because having the dog in the bedroom with her was something she wouldn't permit.

Three stood still in the upstairs hall. Patches was

nowhere. Could he be locked in some closet? Could he have been left in the yard and run away? Could he have been run over? Three's imagination, propelled by guilt, leapfrogged ahead. The thought of waking up his mother was unacceptable. Then Three found himself walking slowly to her door. For a few minutes he stood outside, then he put his hand up preparatory to knocking. But he dropped it. A fierce anger shook him, a recoil of everything she stood for: her religion, her rigidity, her moralism, her attitude toward animals—at that point he remembered Patches and why he was there.

"If Patches could talk, you should ask him if he thinks the way you act toward him is fair." It wasn't exactly what his father said, but it was close enough, and the reproach still stung.

Three put his hand on the doorknob and turned it as silently as he could. If his mother were asleep—But Patches was missing, he reminded himself. He couldn't just walk out of the house and leave it like that.

Three got the door open about a foot. His mother was sound asleep under a quilt on the bed. Patches, curled next to her, had been asleep but woke up and stared at Three. Then he put his head down again and burrowed into Jenny's side. Only his eyes remained open, staring at Three, as though daring Three to come over and throw him out.

Three, a little taken aback, closed the door again as quietly as he could.

The managing editor walked over to Tim's desk. "How's the piece on the Beresfords going?"

"Fine," Tim replied briefly, though it wasn't.

"Have you heard about Mrs. Robert Senior?"

Tim looked up. "What?"

"She tried to commit suicide. She's in the hospital now."

As though on a screen Tim saw again the bloated,

despairing face and heard her words: Don't be too hard on him.

"Anybody know why?"

"As we all know, she's a drunk. Maybe she had a moment of clarity. Anyway, another facet of the fascinating Beresfords."

Tim stared at his computer for a while, then shut it off and left. He got into his car and drove to the hospital. At the information desk he got the number of Matilda Beresford's room. Then he took the stairs and started walking along the floor glancing at the cards in their slots beside the rooms. In a few minutes he found himself looking into a room with a single bed. The woman in the bed looked considerably smaller than the one he had met at Summerstoke, and the once flushed face seemed almost yellow. Her eyes were closed, and he wondered if she was unconscious or merely asleep. He went in and stopped uncertainly by her bed.

Her eyes opened. She stared up at him. "Mark," she said groggily.

A shiver went down his back. Suddenly he became aware of his heart beating. Sweat broke out on his forehead.

"I—" he started.

At that moment there were steps behind him. He turned. Elizabeth came in, saw him and stopped.

"You're the reporter who interviewed my brother, aren't you?"

He was still shaking, but the tone in her voice jolted him back to reality. "Yes."

"What are you doing here? Can't you see my mother is ill?"

He glanced down at the woman in bed, whose eyes were still on him and, as though something outside of him directed his hand, he touched her shoulder. Then he heard himself say, "Hang in there, Mrs. Beresford." He walked past Elizabeth into the hall and turned. "Lady Paterson," he said, "can I speak to you out here?"

When Elizabeth joined him in the hall, he said, "We got news that your mother had attempted suicide."

"So you came to inverview her? While she's still on a suicide watch? That's fairly despicable, isn't it?"

Her arrogance grated on his nerves. "News is news. The paper wants a story on all the Beresfords—the whole family, not just your brother, running for governor."

"And this will form part of it?"

His anger mounted. "You know, Lady Paterson, your brother's PR sidekick called me to do a story on him, not the other way around. With rich people like you the press is something to use. When it suits your purposes you're nice as can be and full of cooperation. If it's a story that strikes us as news but you want to keep under wraps, then you suddenly remember you're the aristocrat talking down to the peasant. I'm sorry about your mother. She must be an unhappy lady." He paused. "And of course her role in the disappearance of your brother Mark is well documented. I've read everything I could find about your family, so I know—"

Elizabeth, so angry herself she could hardly speak, interrupted him. "I was responsible, too. I'm sure you also read that."

"Yes, Lady Paterson, I'm well aware of it." The reporter and the woman he believed was his sister glared at each other. He asked, "What was he wearing, that little five-year-old boy who was found by himself in front of the store, crying?" The words seemed to tumble out of their own accord.

"If you've read everything, you know he was wearing a camel hair stadium coat, a wool cap, corduroy pants—"

"And a beige turtleneck and a belt." He hadn't meant to reveal so much of what he knew so soon. He had to make his announcement at the right time.

But it was said before he could stop himself. "Good afternoon." And he walked away down the hospital corridor to the elevator.

Elizabeth went slowly back into her mother's hospital room. She was furious at the young reporter, but, belatedly, she remembered that Robbie was indeed running for office and as his sister she should not alienate the press.

"I suppose he's going to write a story about me," Matilda said tiredly.

"I hope not, Mom. It may be naive of me, but I keep hoping decency will win out."

"A bad news story about me won't help Robbie, I'm afraid."

"Did he say anything to you?"

"No. I was dozing, thinking about Mark. When I opened my eyes and saw him— I know it sounds crazy, but I thought for a minute it was Mark."

"Did you say anything to him?"

"No, except just Mark's name, I think."

No wonder he seemed so hung up about Mark's disappearance, Elizabeth thought grimly.

She sat down on a chair beside the bed. Various members of the family had come to visit. Since she had no job or anything else to do while here, and since family members had decided that Matilda should not be left alone, she had offered to sit with her mother between visitors.

Glancing over at her mother, she noted the latter's eyes were now closed again. Yawning, Elizabeth opened the newspaper she'd stepped down the hall to get and let her eyes range over the headlines.

After a minute or so, she realized she hadn't really taken in one of them. Something was bothering her. That thought had barely presented itself in her mind when she knew what it was: the interview with that young reporter, which had upset her more than she wanted to acknowledge. Granted he was pushy, arrogant and rude. And she had remembered too late about Robbie's campaign. But there was something beyond that which clawed at her mind.

Robbie sat in his club lounge and waited for Caleb. He had called Caleb at Summerstoke on reaching the office and suggested they have lunch.

"Sure," Caleb said. "What's up?"

"Let's wait till lunch," Robbie said.

He had arrived at the club early so Caleb, if also early, would not be forced to cool his heels in the reception room. Since Three had dropped his information about the All Americas Import and Export Exchange, Robbie had found himself beset with all kinds of questions.

When Caleb had arrived in Providence, he had been more than willing to talk about the terrible conditions he had left behind, and Robbie remembered feeling profoundly grateful that Three was not there to hear his uncle. Robbie's own attitude had been that the conditions in Guatemala, though undoubtedly regrettable, were not his fault and did not affect him or the United States or his immediate nomination. So when the subject had come up one night at dinner, he had listened politely. But more recently Caleb had been rather quiet about his passion for Guatemalan politics.

Glancing up, he saw one of the doormen usher Caleb to the door. Caleb had been here often, since Robert Senior was a member, and could undoubtedly have joined himself, but had always made a point of calling the club "the hideout of the elite." Robbie would not have invited him to the club, except that they could have far greater privacy there.

After the drinks had arrived, Caleb said, "Okay, Robbie, what's up?"

Robbie had hoped that he'd be able to lead into the subject a little less abruptly, but he reflected he should have known better.

"This morning Three said he'd met the sister of a priest friend of yours in Guatemala. Apparently she was ranting and raving about the iniquity of the All Americas Import and Export Exchange, of which the family owns a considerable share."

None of this was news to Caleb. But all he said when Robbie stopped was "So?"

"So is this woman really a sister of a priest friend down there, or is she something else in your life?"

"What business of that is yours?"

"First, you're my brother and I'm concerned about you." Robbie paused for a minute, hoping that his perfectly sincere statement didn't sound as phony to Caleb as it did to him.

"And second?" Caleb asked challengingly.

"And second, since I'm running for governor, I like to know about as many glitches or dropped stitches in my or my family's background as possible. There's nothing like standing at a press conference and having a hostile reporter fling at you an embarrassing question based on information he has but you don't."

Caleb said sarcastically, "Such as how can a candidate running on a liberal, albeit Republican, ticket own stock in a company that is ruining the lives of millions of people in a country no better than South Africa? Can you explain that, Mr. Candidate, and why haven't you got rid of that stock?"

Robbie looked at him. "Why didn't you tell me this when you arrived? Why do I hear about it now, and not from you?"

I should have known he'd ask me that, Caleb thought. He couldn't think of any answer but the truth. He glanced down at his lap. "I was hoping to use it to get some more money from the trust for needs in Guatemala."

Robbie said harshly, "Since the trust is to be liquidated, and you'll get your share along with everyone else, I assume you mean you wanted to use it to blackmail me into giving you some of mine."

When Julie had said it, it sounded brave and idealistic. In Robbie's mouth, it sounded immoral, even criminal.

The decades-old anger at his handsomer, more popular, more successful brother surged up. "Do you realize how it feels to know that back home we sit on top of our moneybags in our fine houses with our bank accounts and our lawn service and other luxuries while two thousand miles to the south of us live people who don't make ten dollars in a year, who live off cornmeal, without any protein, without running water, without medicine?"

"And that's our fault?"

Caleb suddenly stood up. "Do you know what Christ said? Do they teach that in your genteel church? 'Thou shalt love thy neighbor as thyself.' Is that the way we love our neighbors?"

"Sit down, Caleb. That's a chair, not a pulpit, and this is a club, not church."

But Caleb slammed his drink down onto the table. "Go to hell, Robbie. I'm leaving."

"And is Julie your mistress?" Robbie said as Caleb approached the door. His words carried across the elegant room.

But Caleb ignored him, staiking out into the reception area, snatching his raincoat from the attendant as he passed the cloakroom, and then through the door and out into the street.

CHAPTER
18

Elizabeth, returning from a quick snack in the hospital cafeteria, returned to her mother's room and found Caleb there, sitting beside the sleeping Matilda.

"Hello," she said in a low voice, tiptoeing into the room. "Has she been asleep since you've been here?"

"Yes. Want to talk outside?"

They walked out and sat in some chairs that were outside against the wall opposite.

"Elizabeth," Caleb said, "have you told Robbie or anybody what I said I wanted money for—I mean family money, not just what's coming to me in the trust?"

"No. Why?"

"Well, Robbie and I had a ... a disagreement." He paused.

"If you carried on with him the way you did with me in the car, I can see where you would. Was that what it was about?"

Caleb took a breath and told her about the lunch and Robbie's accusation that Julie was his mistress.

"Is she?" Elizabeth asked.

"Yes. I came back to leave the Church, Liz. I wanted to marry her. She lives down there and works with one of the liberation groups and came up here with me so we could take the money I told her we could get."

Elizabeth absorbed this. "Why did she tell Three? Just to make trouble?"

"Because she's mad at me for not being able to talk Andrew into telling me how much money is involved." He sounded desolate.

"I'm sorry, Caleb." It was obvious to Elizabeth that Caleb had been wounded. He was certainly different from the high-minded, cause-obsessed man who'd talked of blackmailing his own brother. "Maybe she's one of those people to whom the cause, whatever it is, means more than anything else."

"Maybe. And maybe she was just using me."

"Where does that leave you?"

"Nowhere."

"If you've been having an affair with her, how does that affect your relationship with the Church?"

"I don't know. I came here not only because of the trust money, but to get myself laicized. That was when I thought I'd marry Julie. I had a couple of appointments lined up with the provincial head of my order. But he broke one because he had to go to New York, and I broke the other."

"Maybe you don't want to be laicized."

Caleb put his hands over his face and didn't say anything. Elizabeth looked up and saw a familiar figure walking purposefully toward them. "Jenny's here," she said quietly.

Caleb quickly got up, his back to his approaching sister-in-law, and walked toward the window at the end of the corridor. Just before he turned, Elizabeth was sure she saw tears on his cheeks and felt both sympathy and sadness for him.

"Hello, Elizabeth," Jenny said. "How is Matilda?"

"Right now she's sleeping. They give her a sedative every four hours. I hope to heaven it doesn't get her addicted to those as well as alcohol. On the other hand, from everything I've heard, withdrawal can be pretty horrible—and dangerous." Elizabeth sighed.

"It's a terrible pity, but nobody seems to know what to do about Mom's drinking."

Jenny sat down. Because of Elizabeth's European manners and her English clothes, she felt a little ill at ease with her. "I wonder if anybody has made any real attempt to get her to AA."

"Didn't she have to attend meetings in the rehabs she went to?"

"Yes. But from what I know, it's the transition from the meetings in the rahab to going to meetings back at home that's the crucial point. And even if somebody takes her, it doesn't always work."

At that point Caleb strolled back. "Hello, Jenny."

"Hello, Caleb, thank you for picking Three up yesterday."

Caleb, looking at the handkerchief he was folding to put back in his pocket, said half jokingly, "Did he also tell you about our acrimonious lunch?"

"No. I'm sorry it was acrimonious." She paused. "Why was it acrimonious?"

"Oh, well ..." Since Robbie hadn't mentioned the subject to his wife, Caleb seemed sorry he'd brought up the subject. "We, er, disagreed about ... family investments." When Jenny didn't say anything, he went on, "In case no one has told you, money can be a very emotional subject, particularly among family members. Our ideas—Robbie's and mine—on what to do with the money from the trust didn't altogether, er, agree."

"I see."

At that point they heard the bed creak in the room. Jenny got up and went in. "Mother Matilda? How are you. I only just heard today. I'm so sorry." She leaned down and kissed Matilda's cheek.

"Yes, thank you," Matilda said.

Elizabeth and Caleb joined them. Matilda's eyes went immediately to her son. He moved along the other side of the bed and took her hand. "How goes it?"

She didn't answer, but squeezed his hand a little.

"I thought I'd like to sit with you for a while," Jenny said.

"That's nice of you, Jenny. But I'm tired and I think I'm going to take another nap. Another time, maybe." And Matilda gave a faint smile.

"All right," Jenny said. She didn't move for a moment. "I'll be in touch later or tomorrow. Please, please let me know if there's anything I can do."

Elizabeth leaned down and kissed her mother's cheek. "I have to get on home. Graham is going to call, and I ought to be there."

Elizabeth and Jenny left together.

"Do you want me to go?" Caleb asked, still holding Matilda's hand.

"No," she said. "Stay with me awhile."

As Elizabeth and Jenny headed toward the elevator, Elizabeth said, "I heard about Three." When Jenny didn't say anything, she added tentatively, "I'm sorry. But it's not the end of the world."

"I suppose not. It just feels that way."

"I met Three only that one time, but he certainly strikes me as bright and attractive." Elizabeth paused. "Hearing about his rebelliousness made me think of a joke someone once told me. Two Irishmen were shipwrecked and washed up on a desert island where there was nothing and no one in sight. One turned to the other and said, 'Name yer giverment and I'm agin it!' It was an Irishman, by the way, who told me."

Jenny gave a strained smile. "Yes, that fits Three very well." As they were walking toward the front door, she said suddenly, "It doesn't make it any easier to realize that I was probably the one who inspired it. Robbie says I should stop sounding moralistic. But when I see what so many young people get into— children of good families—I wonder what principles they grow up with. How can they grow up without being told what's right and wrong?"

Elizabeth hesitated as they came out the lobby door.

"I think it was easier at an earlier time. Family discipline was unquestioned, the whole *zeitgeist* was different."

The use of the German word irritated Jenny. It made her feel uneducated. She asked bluntly, "What's *zeitgeist*? I heard the word when I was in college, but I never understood it."

"The general trend and thought of an era."

"Well, I didn't grow up before World War I. We had television, movies, radio."

Elizabeth said, "I think I've irritated you. I didn't mean to. I'm sorry."

"No, I should apologize." Jenny rubbed her hand across her forehead. "I wish I knew what to do now, but I don't."

"Maybe stop worrying about it. Let it go for the time being. Three will have to go to another school, but I'm sure you and Robbie can work that out."

"Yes. Thanks." Jenny walked off quickly, her high heels clicking across the asphalt of the parking lot.

Arriving back at Summerstoke, Elizabeth found a cablegram from Graham. It said simply, "Arrive Tuesday," followed by a time and a flight number.

Stunned, Elizabeth sat with the cablegram on her lap in her bedroom. Tuesday was four days away. Her first reaction was shock. Then she started feeling an unpleasant mixture of anxiety and anger. Why was Graham coming? She'd been able to dismiss her first fear—that something had gone wrong with one of the children—immediately. If that were true, Graham would certainly have called her. So why was he coming?

The most pedestrian explanation was that he had business in the States, as he occasionally did. Somehow, though, Elizabeth didn't think so. Her thoughts went to Andrew. Could Graham have heard about her affair with him? No, that was too implausible.

She found herself staring at the telephone in her

bedroom, then lifted the receiver and dialed. When the receptionist answered, she asked for Andrew.

"I'm sorry, he was called away on business unexpectedly and won't be back until tomorrow. Who is calling?"

"It doesn't matter," Elizabeth said. "I'll call back."

She hung up, feeling absurdly let down. He hadn't told her he was going, and now she had no opportunity to tell him about Graham's expected arrival. Everything suddenly seemed jammed up, condensed. All this meant less time for her to decide what decision, what choice to make. Sitting there, she could feel her heartbeat speed up a little.

"Damn!" she said aloud. "Damn!"

As good as his word, Robert Senior had tried to call Terry in Boston that morning at the apartment she shared with a couple of other students. But instead of his daughter, he got an answering tape. Not wanting to go into the details of Matilda's suicide attempt on a phone message, he simply asked his daughter to call him back as soon as possible. Then he wondered gloomily if she'd start up again on Matilda's alcoholism being caused by lack of love.

Because Terry was working on her dissertation in the library, she didn't get the message until midafternoon, when one of her roommates, running into her outside the cafeteria, said, "By the way, your dad wants you to call him A.S.A.P."

Terry, on her way back to the library, paused. "Did he say why?"

"No. I just got it from the answering tape when I went back after lunch. He'd obviously called this morning after we'd all left."

"Thanks. It's probably nothing serious," Terry said, only half believing it.

"Don't forget about the committee meeting at five," the roommate said.

"No. Okay." Terry's mind was still on her father.

"The group needs all the support we can get, and we have living proof of what we're talking about in that memo sent out today from the president's office."

"Yeah, I guess." Although a feminist, Terry sometimes found herself less than enthusiastic about the multitude of small committees that sprang up to discuss the nitty-gritty of the ways in which women found themselves oppressed. But because she didn't want to seem tepid about her roommate's favorite cause, she added, "Of course. See you later," and headed back to her apartment to call Robert Senior.

Briefly, he told her about Matilda's suicide attempt, adding quickly, "She's all right, Terry. Caleb found her in time. We got her to the hospital, and they were able to pump everything out of her stomach."

"Oh, my God!" Terry said. "Are you sure?"

"Yes. Because of drinking over a long period her health isn't that great, but she's recovering. The doctor suggested that when she's physically able, she should be moved to the rehab attached to the hospital. It's new and apparently rather good. I can't make her go. But I'm hoping she will."

"If she just felt that anybody truly cared—" Terry started.

"Terry, you're my daughter and I love you. But God defend me from an enthusiast with a bee in his—or her—bonnet. Despite what you may think, I care greatly. So do her two sons and both her daughters. She hasn't been alone once during the day, and she has private nurses at night. Now, if you want to see her, I can meet you at the station and take you there. Or if you want to drive, I can meet you at the hospital. Or you can go by yourself." And he hung up.

She still believed that her mother didn't feel truly cared for. But she had done what she had said she would: she had looked up alcoholism in the library, consulted various books and queried colleagues who had had any experience in the field. From them she had learned that what Elizabeth and her father had

said on the subject—that alcoholics drank because
they were alcoholics rather than from any direct
cause—was more or less the case.

It was while she was consulting the books and papers in the library that she came across the name Arnold Stein, one of the medical authorities quoted. She
had paused at the name, a curious pain going through
her. David had had an Unce Arnold who was, indeed,
a doctor specializing in the field of addiction, and who
had worked in some of the poorer parts of Boston
with the homeless, many of them alcoholics and/or
drug addicts. When she finished with the books, she
sat in the library for a while, thinking.

It had been seven years since she had seen David.
After she had told him she didn't want to see him
again, he had tried calling her several times, but, angry
at him and outraged at his refusal to support her desire to have their child, she had not returned his calls.
After a few months he gave up. Still, she dreamed
about him often and found herself scanning legal news
and names in the newspapers. By now he should be a
practicing lawyer. He was also married. She knew that
because once, two years before, after a particularly
vivid dream, she had called the old number where he
had lived. A woman had answered.

"Who is this?" Terry asked abruptly.

"This is Mrs. Stein," the woman said.

Terry simply hung up. She was surprised at how
wounded and betrayed she felt. What had she expected? she asked herself. After all, she was the one
who had broken off the relationship. But it didn't
help.

After she finished talking to her father, Terry sat
there for a moment, thinking about her mother and
what she'd done. On impulse she picked up the telephone directory and looked up the name Arnold
Stein, not expecting to find it. But it was there, and
she dialed it. A man answered.

"I'd like to speak to Dr. Stein, please."

"This is Dr. Stein. What can I do for you?"

Caught short, Terry said baldly, "My name is Terry Beresford, and I've been reading your book on alcoholism in the library. I've just learned that my mother, who is an active alcoholic, has tried to commit suicide. She was found almost immediately, so my father and brother got her to the hospital and she's all right. I'm about to drive there now. But I don't know what to do or to suggest. She's been to I don't know how many rehabs and has always started drinking again."

"If that's so, I don't really know what to suggest, either." There was a pause, then he went on, "If you've read my book, then you know that trying to save her from the consequences of her drinking is less than no good. In the field it's called enabling the drunk. I'm glad your mother was found in time, but only she and God can decide to do something about her drinking. Basically, a drunk stops drinking when he or she, in AA lingo, gets sick and tired of being sick and tired. Why this happens with some and not others is still a mystery to us all. Sometimes what's called an intervention works, when the drinker is threatened with the loss of something he or she values—the job, the spouse, the family."

"Does money, or lack of money, have much to do with it?"

"Speaking only for myself, I'd say that having money is a greater disadvantage than not having it. I'm not talking about poverty as in being homeless. But somebody who has to work to pay the rent, to support the family and/or keep himself—or herself— off the street is better off, I think, than someone who doesn't have to do anything to pay for the cushions— the servants, baby-sitters, schools, nannies, et cetera. In the latter case there's less incentive to do something about the drinking."

"I see." Terry hesitated, then, "Is there anything to support the theory that women become alcoholics because they live in a male-dominated society and are oppressed by it?"

"No. There were once far more male alcoholics than women. Their pattern was also very different. Males were more liable to be bar drunks and women solitary drinkers at home. But women are catching up in this, as in other things—like lung cancer from smoking. Equality is bringing the same advantages to everyone."

Terry heard the irony in his voice but decided not to comment on it. What he said backed up what all the other experts said. And while most of them were men, it didn't mean they were wrong—necessarily.

"By the way," the doctor said, "are you by any chance the Terry Beresford my nephew David Stein used to go out with?"

Terry took a breath. She hadn't expected this. "Yes," she said. And then, "How is David?"

"Fine. He's now with a good law firm."

The words popped out of her mouth. "He's married, isn't he?"

"No, he isn't. Why did you think he was?"

Her heart gave a queer surge. She said slowly, "I called his apartment once and a woman who said she was Mrs. Stein answered. And she didn't sound old enough to be his mother."

"That could have been my own wife. We used to live in a suburb, but when we came into Boston to a play or a concert or some other event, we'd stay with David. She is, incidentally, my second wife and much younger than me. Which is probably why you thought she was David's wife. By the way, are you married?"

"No. No, I'm not."

"I know you said you were Terry Beresford, but you can never tell with you feminists whether or not you retain your own name when you marry."

"Why shouldn't we?" Terry said cheerfully.

"No reason at all. May I tell David you called?"

Her heart flipped again. "Yes, why not?"

Terry threw some clothes in a bag, got into her car parked on the street and was at the hospital less than two hours later.

Caleb waited in the official reception room of the provincial's house in Boston. After what seemed a long while the brother who had let him in reappeared in the doorway. "Father Gilbert will see you now."

Caleb had known that the provincial he was to meet was not the one who had interviewed him twelve years before when he had sought to enter the order. The old provincial, friend of many McGarretts, had died. This was a new man, sent from Rome.

"Come in, Father Caleb." the provincial said.

Caleb found himself almost stopped by the English accent. Even though he had—in his own mind—left the priesthood, he was aware that the new provincial was an Englishman, a Cambridge graduate. Yet obviously it had not sunk in. He found himself facing a tall, fair-haired man only a few years older than himself.

He came around the desk and held out his hand. "I'm Father Gilbert. Thank you for coming."

"Thank you for seeing me," Caleb said automatically.

"Do sit down." Father Gilbert indicated one of the two chairs in front of the desk. Then he walked to his own chair behind the desk.

"Now," he said, "I take it from your letter—" he tapped Caleb's letter, open on the desk in front of him—"that you wish to be laicized."

"Yes."

"Why?"

"As I said in the letter, I feel I can no longer carry out the function of a priest and a religious."

"Why do you feel that?"

Caleb found the provincial's gray eyes uncomfortably penetrating. "You must know—you must have heard from Father Matthew in Guatemala—that I left the mission and all work as a priest and missionary almost two years ago. Since then I've rarely been to mass. I did go recently with my mother, but other than that, I've left the Church." Caleb took a breath. "Further, I've been living with a young woman I met in Guatemala who is very involved in political liberation there and with whom I've been working."

"Yes, I see. Some of that I did know. Do you intend to marry this young woman?"

The words "of course" were on Caleb's tongue. For some reason he didn't say them. The silence stretched. He started thinking about his mother, about her saying, "I can't ask you to stop trying to leave the priesthood, Caleb ..." But she so obviously had wanted to ask him that. He looked up. The provincial's eyes were on him. They struck him as singularly nonjudgmental.

"I thought I did," Caleb said. "I'm not sure now."

"I see." He paused. "Would you like some tea or coffee?"

"Coffee would be nice. The stuff at the roadside cafe was about the worst I've ever had."

Father Gilbert pressed a bell and lifted the phone. "Brother Mitchell, could you bring us some coffee?"

When the brother returned with a tray carrying two cups, a pot, cream and sugar, Father Gilbert indicated two armchairs facing each other on the other side of the room, with a table between. "Why don't we sit over here? I think it might make conversation easier." He poured coffee for them both. "What do you want me to do, Father Caleb?"

Caleb passed his hands over his face. His mind felt numb, nonfunctioning. He knew he was here to start the process of his laicization, but he couldn't seem to focus on it. "Did I tell you my mother tried to commit suicide? That she's an alcoholic who blames herself for my brother being kidnapped, for my sister having an abortion? She lay there in the hospital bed telling me that she couldn't ask me to stop leaving the priesthood because she herself had committed a mortal sin.

And I couldn't help her." To his horror and humilation Caleb found he was crying.

The first time Terry visited the hospital, Matilda had been too somnolent or tranquilized or both to do much more than acknowledge her presence with a tired smile. But Terry stayed until the end of the visiting hours. Then, instead of going to Summerstoke or staying alone in the empty family house on College Hill, she'd begged a bed from an old school friend in Providence. "It's easier for me to get from your apartment to the hospital," she said, knowing as she did so it was only partly true. She didn't feel quite ready to cope with the family, although, of course, they would know that she had come.

The next morning, she showed up at the hospital fairly early. Matilda seemed more alert.

"How are you, Ma?" Terry asked, bending down and kissing her mother's cheek. She pulled a chair beside the bed.

"All right, considering," Matilda replied. "It's nice to see you." Before Terry could reply, she went on, "Tell me what you've been doing."

"Oh, just more of my women's studies. I've also been working on my dissertation."

"You'll be the first person in the family to get a doctorate," Matilda said proudly.

Terry reached out and took her mother's hand. "Tell me how you are—truly."

"You know how I am, Terry. I tried to comitt suicide and got rescued. I'm still not sure how happy I am about that."

"Oh, Ma, we all love you so much! I wish you believed that."

"I do." Matilda looked at her daughter's face and decided that Terry looked prettier than she ever had before. Her coloring was rather neutral—light brown hair and eyes and pale, colorless skin—but her features were well shaped and she had an intelligent, lively expression. "You're looking well, Terry, and very pretty."

Terry colored slightly, which irritated her. She resented the assumption that for a woman looks remained all important. "Thanks. Listen, I've reached a point in my dissertation where I could use a break. Why don't you and I go to Narragansett or Newport for a week or so? The ocean air would do you good."

Matilda didn't reply for a moment, then she said, "The doctor here thinks as soon as I can get out of this hospital bed, I should transfer over to their rehab they've just built. People seem to think it's very good."

"Well, we could go to the shore for a week and then you could come back to the rehab."

"Terry, I haven't had anything to drink now for several days. I realize they're using a certain amount of drugs to taper me off. But if I go to the shore I'll drink again, and then I won't want to come back to the rehab. It's better that I go from here—before I pick up another drink."

"What makes you think this will work when the others didn't?"

"I don't know whether it will or not, but I think—I think I owe it to the family to give it a try."

"I don't know why. The family hasn't done that much for you."

"Listen to me, Terry." Matilda put out a hand and with surprising strength clasped her daughter's wrist. "I'll admit it's a faint chance, but ... well, something in me thinks this time it's worth a shot. Don't try to talk me out of it."

"I'm not. I wouldn't do that! I just wanted you to go in after a week we'd have together, just the two of us, knowing how much you mean to me."

"During which you'd be directing my every minute, wouldn't you, Terry my dear? Hovering over me. I told you, love like that is a chain."

Terry didn't say anything for a moment. Then, "All right, Ma. You've got to do what seems right to you."

There was a silence between them. Why am I here? Terry thought. She doesn't need me. "Funny thing," she said after a minute. "Do you remember David Stein? His uncle is one of the experts on alcoholism that I looked up in the library. In fact, I called him just before I came here." When her mother didn't say anything, she went on, "He asked me if I was the girl David used to go with."

Matilda, who'd been vaguely looking out the window, looked directly at Terry. "Why don't you call David?"

"Why all of a sudden, Ma, do you find him acceptable? Is it because I'm older and my chances are getting fewer? That really burns me up! Getting married is not the only possible career for a woman, for God's sake!"

Matilda took her hand. "Don't be cross, Terry. Please. And now I'm tired and want to go to sleep."

When Jenny got home, she found on the answering machine a message to call Deirdre's school. Frightened that her daughter might be ill or hurt, she dialed. At least, she thought, listening to the phone ringing, it wouldn't be anything Deirdre had done. When the school operator answered, she identified herself and asked to speak to the headmistress.

"Yes, Mrs. Beresford, I know she's been waiting for your call."

When Mrs. Stevens, the headmistress came on, she said quietly, "Mrs. Beresford, we found, to our distress, that we had reason to look for drugs in some of the girls' rooms. I'm sorry to have to tell you that one of the rooms in which we found some cocaine was Deirdre's. When we questioned her, she broke down and admitted it almost immediately."

"But—" Jenny cried.

The headmistress went straight on as though Jenny

hadn't spoken, "We'd like you to come and pick up Deirdre as soon as possible. And we can talk further then."

Jenny put down the phone. Then she lifted the receiver again, preparatory to dialing Robbie's number. But before she'd punched out three numbers she replaced it. Robbie hadn't told her about Three's expulsion and his hitchhiking home. She would deal with whatever had happened to Deirdre. Patches, delighted to see her home, flung himself at her. Plainly he needed to go out. With an exclamation, she let him into the garden and stood impatiently at the door while he relieved himself and played with a stick he found.

"No, come on back in, Patches. I have to go."

But Patches had other ideas. Finally Jenny said, "All right, stay out here if you have to. I can't wait any longer."

Then she backed the car out onto Benevolent Road and headed toward Hazelcroft.

The school was an hour's drive north and west of Providence. Jenny made it in fifty minutes. Set just outside a town, the school occupied a large frame building, with additional buildings erected in the same style forming dormitories and classrooms. The mansion had originally belonged to a well-known and wealthy New England family whose last girl had attended the school. In gratitude, she had left the building, the grounds, and a sum of money to the school, which had almost, if not quite, paid for the additions and renovations.

Jenny turned into the half circle drive and parked. Then she got out, walked up to the porch and rang the bell. A maid answered.

Jenny wasn't kept waiting long. Mrs. Stevens, a tall, somewhat angular, good-looking woman came out of her office. "Mrs. Beresford, thank you for coming." She paused. "I take it you're alone. Mr. Beresford couldn't come?"

"No," Jenny said, and hoped she'd be forgiven for the lie. "Where is Deirdre?"

"She's in her room—packed and ready to go."

"You're surely not expelling her without even finding out if the cocaine or whatever it was had been put there by someone else?" Jenny asked indignantly.

"Give us credit for a little sense, Mrs. Bereford. When we found out that some of the girls were using drugs, we sent for all the ones involved and then searched their rooms. When it was Deirdre's turn she didn't even make much effort to pretend what was there wasn't hers."

"Did you ask her why? Why on earth she'd ever have anything to do with cocaine?"

"Of course. By the way, I'd prefer it if we could finish this conversation in my office, and I'm sure you would, too."

As the headmistress closed the door behind Jenny, she said, "Things are quieter in here."

"I was asking you—" Jenny started.

"You were asking me why Deirdre had started dabbling in cocaine. I asked her that, of course. Apparently she did it because others were doing it. Unfortunately, that's so often true. And in her case it's a tragedy. I don't regret losing the hard core few who introduced the wretched stuff into the school and got girls like Deirdre involved. But I do regret Deirdre and one or two others. They went along to be considered cool."

"I don't even recognize the Deirdre you're describing," Jenny said. "She left home one of the best-behaved children I've ever known—and that is not a mother's bias. She was outstanding in church and in her Sunday school. She was taught to love and obey the commandments and her parents. I wish . . ." Jenny's voice faltered, "I wish I could say the same of her brother. I can't. But Deirdre and I've always been close and shared the same view of everything."

"Yes . . . she was very, well, good, when she came

here. I guess I mean she talked a lot about right and wrong."

"You sound as though that were some kind of a disadvantage," Jenny said.

"With many of today's young people, it is. It becomes a ... well, a sort of target they can aim clever remarks at. The girls who come here are for the most part pretty sophisticated—or at least they think they are. Deirdre isn't. She got left out. Children can be cruel, you know, and from everything I've heard it was made clear to her that she was far too much ..." The headmistress hesitated and looked at Jenny before she went on.

"Too much what?" Jenny asked angrily.

"Too much of a goody-two-shoes. Adolescents don't like that, you know."

"And knowing that, you did nothing to protect her?"

"Mrs. Beresford, there was nothing I, or any of the teachers, could do. Do you think it helps a teenager to be known to be under the particular protection of the faculty and/or headmistress? That would just make her the target of more cruelty."

"Why didn't she let us—let me—know?" Jenny said, almost to herself. "I'd have come and got her immediately and put her back in her day school. She was doing so well."

Mrs. Stevens didn't say anything for a moment. Then, "I gathered from her, and now from you, that she is very much under your influence."

"You gather right," Jenny snapped.

"And what will happen when she finally goes to college, or gets a job out in the real world? You can't protect her forever. She has to learn to be her own guide, to set her own standards and boundaries."

"I can see she's done an outstanding job of that here."

"She wanted to be liked. That's one of the most

deadly needs there is. Responsible for more foolish and destructive behavior than almost anything else."

"If you had just—" Jenny suddenly realized she wasn't sure how she was going to finish the sentence.

"If I had just what? I could turn the same implication toward you. Among the things she came out with when we questioned her was the fact that she had never been popular in her day school either. Everyone there had considered her some kind of holier-than-thou. It didn't start here."

"She had friends there," Jenny said. "Plenty of friends."

"Did she?"

"She went to lots of parties, and when we gave them we could barely pack them in."

When Mrs. Stevens didn't reply, Jenny said, "Before she left home, Deirdre wouldn't have touched a drug." She hesitated. "The girls who brought drugs into the school and . . . introduced others to them ought to be expelled. But why an innocent like Deirdre?"

"I can't make that distinction, Mrs. Beresford. You must be able to see that. The only way I can make sure drugs are out of the school and will stay out is make it abundantly clear that to touch them means automatic expulsion." As Jenny continued to stare, Mrs. Stevens said gently, "After all, Deirdre did have a choice. No one held her down and forced the wretched powder up her nose. She could have refused."

Jenny didn't say anything for a moment. Then she took a breath. "I want to talk to Deirdre."

"I'll get Lisa to take you to her room."

Jenny followed the young woman named Lisa who took her upstairs two flights, and stopped outside a door with Deirdre's name in the slot.

"Thank you." Jenny said. "I'll take it from here."

After Lisa had left, Jenny opened the door and walked in. Deirdre was sitting on her bed, staring out the window.

"Deirdre," Jenny said gently.

The girl didn't turn around. She just said, "Have they told you?"

"Yes."

"They're going to expel me."

"Yes, I know. I've just been talking to Mrs. Stevens."

When Deirdre continued to stare out the window, Jenny walked toward the bed and said, "Deirdre, darling, why did you—" That was as far as she got.

Deirdre's head swung around. "It's your fault, Mom. You filled me with all that stuff about sin and always doing right, and everybody here hated me and made fun of me for it. When the drugs happened, when Sally brought some in and told me to try it, I thought maybe they'd like me, maybe they'd think I was okay. That's why I did it, and now they're going to expel me and everybody in the world is going to know!" Deirdre put her head down and started sobbing. "It's all so awful!"

Jenny was shocked by Deirdre's attack, but she put her arms around her daughter. "Deirdre, darling, you'll come back home to Country Day where everybody loved you."

"No, they didn't. I don't want to go back to that school I want to stay here. And I don't want to go back home to have you feed me with all that religion stuff again. I don't want to hear about it ever again!"

Jenny's arms dropped. Of all the things she had expected from Deirdre, this total rejection was not one. "The devil's really—"

Deirdre gave a cry and pushed her away. "Don't talk to me about the devil. I came here talking like that. And you know what they called me? Angel Puke. That was my nickname because I was always saying the things you said to me!"

With a curious sense of apology to Mrs. Stevens, Jenny said slowly, "You didn't have to accept the drug, Deirdre. You could have refused. Maybe some of the others did refuse."

"But they weren't brought up like me to sound ho-lier-than-thou—you know that's what they called me at Country Day? H.T.T.—for Holier-Than-Thou."

"If you were so unhappy there, why didn't you tell your father and me? We could have sent you some-where else."

"To that fundamentalist school you wrote to down South?"

"But you didn't hate the things I tried to teach you until you came here, did you? You always told me you and I thought alike. What happened to change you? Just the way the girls treated you here?"

Deirdre didn't answer immediately. Then she raised her head and said, "Being holier-than-thou wasn't so bad in Providence. I always made myself believe the kids who laughed at me there were wrong. Now I know they weren't. It's you that's wrong!"

"I'm not wrong, Deirdre! Jenny said, losing her temper. You're the one that used that foul cocaine. How could you do such a thing?"

"Go away!" Deirdre screamed. "Just go away and leave me alone!"

Jenny was suddenly aware of other people walking back and forth in the house, of doors opening and closing. This wasn't the place to make a scene. She said, "I'm afraid there's no choice. You have been expelled. They want me to take you home. I'm sorry you're so upset. I'd like to comfort you, but you won't let me. Let's go now and we can talk later." With that Jenny reached out and lifted one of the packed bags on the floor.

Deirdre stared as Jenny reached toward the other. Then in an incredibly swift move she ran toward the window, jumped up on the ledge and before the horri-fied Jenny could stop her, leaped out.

CHAPTER
19

Tim stared at the screen of his computer. His story on the Beresfords was becoming increasingly difficult to write. It had, in fact, come to a halt. Temporarily, he hoped. Filling his mind, pushing out all other aspects of Beresford history, gossip, and highlights to go into the story, was the kidnapping.

He had meant to assemble, slowly and methodically, all the evidence to prove beyond doubt his identity as Mark so that he could use it where and when it would have the most impact. Instead, he had found himself rapping out questions to Robbie that if the latter bothered to think at all, gave him proof of Tim's real aim—and more than enough time to build a defense: a denial that Tim had any claim to call himself Mark Beresford.

A small, persistent voice within him kept asking why they would want to deny any such thing. So many of the kidnapping stories quoted both Robert and Matilda Beresford stating, again and again, that they would give anything they owned to find out where their son was; that his loss had been a horrifying tragedy. A picture of Matilda's face slid in front of his mind. He found himself thinking words that a short time before would have been inconceivable: Her face seemed a mask of living pain.

But he had never believed them. He told himself it

was the kind of thing they'd give out to a compliant and sympathetic press. People who loved their children looked after them. They didn't allow a five-year-old little boy to wander through a crowded department store a week before Christmas. And they'd make a more sustained effort to find him. It therefore stood to reason the Beresfords wouldn't be overjoyed at his return because it would show up how little they had cared.

Just as he had hated the people who had abducted him, he had always nursed a profound grudge at whoever had been his real family. Now he was also furious at himself because he felt his control slipping. Always, or at least since the death of the madwoman who claimed she was his mother, he had been in control. His plans, brick by brick, had been laid carefully. He had been master of what happened.

But it was as though some maddened spirit within him had decided to blow it all apart.

Jenny sat beside Deirdre's bed in the hospital in Providence. It was eleven o'clock that night. Deirdre, back from surgery, where rods had been placed in her back, had been given a painkiller and a sleeping pill and was dozing. Robbie, who had been with Jenny in the hospital for the past two hours, had gone down to the cafeteria to get a sandwich and to bring her back one with some coffee. He had urged her to go first, but she had flatly refused.

"The best thing for Deirdre is sleep," Robbie had argued. "If she's asleep she won't know whether you're there or not. And you must be exhausted."

"I don't want to leave just yet," Jenny said flatly. "You go."

"All right."

Sitting there, looking at Deirdre, Jenny caught sight of her watch and realized with a sense of shock that it was only five hours since Deirdre had jumped out of the dormitory's second-floor window. It seemed more like eighteen, with events like islands between long, agonizing waits.

She remembered screaming as she saw Deirdre go through the window. She remembered seeing her daughter's body lying on the lawn below. There were voices and figures pouring out of the house. There was her own frantic rush downstairs and out the front door with other voices behind, calling her name. Then she was bending over Deirdre, who was moaning, "My back, my back!"

"Don't move," said an authoritative voice behind Jenny as she knelt beside Deirdre.

"Deirdre, darling," Jenny said, "Deirdre, darling," she repeated, and put out her hand.

"I wouldn't touch her, Mrs. Beresford," Mrs. Stevens said. She moved to where Jenny could see her and went on in a kind but firm voice, "Deirdre might try to move or respond in some way, and we don't know what damage to her head or back she may have suffered."

As Deirdre gave another little moan, Jenny became aware of the siren coming nearer. An ambulance turned into the school drive. Two men jumped out carrying what looked like a board. At that moment another car drove in and a third man got out of the car. All ran toward Deirdre.

Mrs. Stevens introduced the doctor to Jenny. "This is Dr. Purdy, the school physician."

As the two men from the ambulance knelt beside Deirdre, Dr. Purdy leaned over her. "What hurts, Deirdre?" he asked gently.

"My back," Deirdre whispered. "It hurts a lot."

The men put the board down. Dr. Purdy said, "Deirdre, they're going to have to slide you onto the stretcher with as little motion to you as possible."

"Can you give her something for the pain?" Jenny asked.

"I don't want to now because when we get her to the hospital we have to be able to learn from her what

hurts in which place." He glanced at Deirdre. "We'll
be as quick as we can, so hang in there."

The men laid the stretcher beside Deirdre. One of
them said to Jenny, who had been kneeling close to
her daughter, "Could you move back just a little,
please?"

When Jenny had moved the two men placed themselves so that one had her by the shoulders and the
other by the hips. Then, hardly lifting her, they slid
her onto the stretcher. Deirdre cried out once. They
carried her into the ambulance, followed by Dr. Purdy
and Jenny. The stretcher was placed in the back of
the ambulance. The doctor and Jenny sat on a bench
on one side.

In a surprisingly short time they were at the emergency entrance of a hospital set among trees.

"Here we are," the doctor said, and soon Jenny, the
stretcher, and the doctor were in the emergency room.

"We'll get a CAT scan," the doctor said to Deirdre,
"and then we can make you more comfortable." He
turned to greet the white-coated man who had just
come in. "Here's Dr. Whitby," he said.

Two men pushing a gurney came alongside Deirdre
and transferred the rigid stretcher on which she was
still lying to the gurney.

Dr. Whitby glanced up at Jenny. "She'll be back in
a minute," he said.

"Can't I go with her?"

"It'll be a tight squeeze. And as I said, it'll only be
a minute."

"Then I'll call my husband. Where is a phone?"

But the phone at their house didn't answer, and she
heard Robbie's voice come onto their answering tape.
She tried his office, but that didn't answer. Jenny then
dialed Summerstoke. Robert Senior.

"Dad-in-law," she said, addressing him as she always had, "do you know where I could reach Robbie?
I'm at the hospital near Deirdre's school. She's ...

she's had an accident, and I desperately need to talk to Robbie."

"I'm sorry, Jenny. I have no idea where he is. I hope Deirdre's accident wasn't too serious. How badly was she hurt?"

"She's off having a CAT scan now. I'll know more when that's done. You wouldn't know the last name of his secretary, would you? If I could call her at home she might know. Her first name, I know, is Marianne."

"I don't—yes, I do know. I think it's ... just a minute ... Simmons."

"Thank you. Thanks very much. If by any chance you hear from him, would you tell him to call this number—" and she read the number off the phone.

"Of course I will. Let us know about Deirdre as soon as you can."

When Jenny had left a message on her home answering tape, she called Providence information to see if she could track down a telephone number for Marianne Simmons. But there was no Marianne and the number for M.L. Simmons rang repeatedly without a reply. Finally she hung up. As long as there was something she could do, some act she could perform, she could keep at bay the full horror of what had happened. But now, at least for the time being, there was nothing.

She walked over to the cubicle where Deirdre had first been taken, sat down on a chair and closed her eyes. She tried to pray silently, but there were no words, only pictures of Deirdre going through the window and lying, legs splayed, on the lawn. Oh God, she thought, it's my fault!

At that moment she heard the sound of a gurney and opened her eyes again. Attendants were wheeling Deirdre back to the emergency room. Following were Drs. Whitby and Purdy. Deirdre's eyes were closed.

Jenny stood up. The gurney slid past her into its former place. Dr. Whitby turned to her. "We've given

Deirdre a painkiller and a mild sedative. She seems to have a collapsed lumbar."

"What does that mean?"

He smiled a little. "It means that one of her vertebrae has been cracked. We can operate and put rods in her back to hold her spine straight. With those, and since nothing else seems to have been injured, she can be up and about very soon."

Jenny had been aware of a phone ringing. Then someone answered it. A nurse came toward her. "Are you Mrs. Beresford?"

"Yes."

"Your husband is on the phone here. Can you speak to him?"

"Yes. And Dr. Whitby, I'm sure he'd like to talk to you, too."

When Jenny got to the phone she found an anxious-sounding Robbie. "What in God's name happened?"

"Deirdre ..." She paused. To her family she had said Deirdre had had an accident. But here in the hospital they knew different. Robbie had to be told the truth. "Deirdre jumped out of her window on the second floor."

"What?"

"Yes. Robbie, I don't have time to fill you in completely. I was there, and I'll tell you why later." She explained what the doctor had just told her. "Would you like to talk to him?"

"I certainly would."

Jenny motioned to Dr. Whitby, who went over to the phone. Obviously answering Robbie's questions, he talked about Deirdre's injury and what it implied. After that his end of the conversation was confined to yes and no and yes. Then he said, "There's a very good man there at St. Catherine's. We can certainly get her there either by ambulance or helicopter. Yes, if you can arrange for somebody to come from the hospital, that would be great. He can accompany Deirdre and her mother back to Providence."

That had been three hours ago. In short order Deirdre was put into the helicopter, followed by the doctor from the Providence hospital and Jenny. In what seemed like a few minutes they had landed on the roof of the hospital in Providence. As they got out, Jenny saw that Robbie was standing with one or two other men, all of them in white coats. Deirdre was wheeled to an elevator, followed by the doctors, Robbie and Jenny.

One of the doctors who had been waiting said, "We're taking your daughter to have another CAT scan and then to surgery. You go on down to the fifth floor. The nurse there is expecting you and will take you to the right room. As soon as we've finished with Deirdre we'll bring her down."

A few minutes later, Robbie and Jenny were sitting in a private room with an empty bed. The nurse, after one glance at their faces, had closed the door behind her.

"All right," Robbie said. "What happened?"

"As I told you, she jumped out of the window—"

"Yes, you told me that. I mean before. Why were you there at the school in the first place? What happened there?"

Jenny closed her hands into fists and stared down at them. Then she said, "When I got home from the hospital from seeing Mother Matilda, I found a message on our tape to call Mrs. Stevens at Hazelcroft. When I got her she said that they . . . they had reason to look for drugs in the rooms of some of the girls and they found some cocaine in Deirdre's room. She wanted us to come and get her."

"Drugs? Deirdre? That's unbelievable! Why?"

"She . . . Deirdre said she did it to be liked. That some of the other girls brought in the drugs and . . . and offered it to her and some of the others. So—"

"You mean she felt disliked, unpopular?"

Jenny nodded.

Robbie stared at her, "I know she had trouble at

the day school. But she was pretty popular there. Something else must have happened here. What was it? Did she tell you?"

Jenny opened her hands and continued to stare down at them.

"If you don't tell me," Robbie said, "I'll call up this Stevens woman tomorrow morning and ask her."

"She said the other girls thought she was . . . holier-than-thou, a goody-two-shoes. They . . . they called her Angel Puke." The horror of it pushed against Jenny again. She felt her eyes sting and her throat swell. "I knew she shouldn't have gone off to boarding school, but you and the rest of the family insisted—"

"This is because you'd filled her with your funda-mentalist jargon," Robbie said angrily, "where half the things most people do naturally is a sin punishable by hell. When she handed that out at the day school she didn't get a very good reception, either."

Jenny looked up. "She never said a word about it to me."

"Didn't she?" Robbie said. "She did to me. I'd ask her about some girl, daughter of an old family friend, and she'd finally admit that she and whoever it was didn't get on too well. And when I'd press her as to why, she'd say the girl thought she was too strict or some such. I spoke to you about it more than once, remember? And you always turned it off by saying children had to be brought up to do right—in the spirit of that saying from Proverbs or whatever you quoted the other day. Something about training up a child."

"Train up a child in the way he should go: when he is old he will not depart from it," Jenny said drearily.

"Neither of our children is old, but they're sure having their problems with it now. Our son is expelled and makes no bones about laying it at your door, and our daughter, also expelled, tried to commit suicide. That's some training."

Jenny stared at him, anger collecting in her. "And maybe if you'd been less set on a political career, you could have stayed home sometimes to be with the children instead of out half the time trying to drum up support. They could then have been exposed to your everybody-do-his-own-thing-just-as-long-as-it-is-in-good-taste Episcopalian mush."

"You haven't answered my question: Why the hell didn't you tell me about the phone call from the school? I'd have come with you, and I'd bet my bottom dollar Deirdre wouldn't have jumped out the window if I'd been around."

Jenny took a breath. "You didn't tell me about Three's being expelled and hitchhiking home, did you?"

"Oh, for God's sake—"

"All right," Jenny suddenly shouted, the scene in Deirdre's room coming back to her like a hammer blow. Her beloved daughter screaming, "It's all your fault, Mom! Just go away and leave me alone!" And then the unforgettable memory of Deirdre's body going through the window. . . .

At that point they heard the wheels of a gurney coming along. The door opened and Deirdre was wheeled in. She was unconscious. After sliding her onto the bed, the older of the doctors said, "She ought to be all right now."

"How long will she have to . . . to be here?" Robbie asked.

"Not too long. We'll get her up as soon as we can—in a day or two at most—and start moving her around."

Jenny glanced down at her daughter. "Can she walk with those rods inside her?"

"Oh yes. It'll be awkward, of course. She'll have to sit carefully and only in straight chairs and so on, and we'll give her a sort of plastic corset to wear as an extra hold. But if it heals as it should, everything will be fine. The good news is that nothing else seems to have been damaged. I guess she was lucky landing on soft earth." The doctor glanced at Jenny's drawn face. "I think you could do with a rest yourself."

Jenny ignored that. "When will she wake up?"

"In an hour or two. But she'll be sedated."

"I'll wait until she wakes up, then I'll go."

"Yes," Robbie said. "We'll be here till then." Then he went down to get her a sandwich from the cafeteria.

For the fourth day in succession Caleb called the desk clerk at the hotel where Julie had been staying before she left for New York. He used the public telephone in the back of the lobby of the same hotel.

No, the desk clerk said, she had not returned.

"Does she have a reservation to return?" Caleb asked.

There was a silence. Then the desk clerk said, "According to my record here, she did have a reservation for today, but she called and canceled that."

"When did she call?" Caleb felt his heart pounding.

"I'm sorry, sir, I don't know."

"It must have been some time since yesterday, because when I called then I was told she was due back in the hotel today."

"Yes. According to the record here, she was listed yesterday to return today, but probably this morning she called and canceled."

"I take it she paid her bill when she left."

"We really can't discuss that, sir. However, I don't think she would have been allowed to go without paying."

Caleb hung up. Julie had gone now, for good. He was sure of it. Why? Had she given up on the money he was due to get from the trust? Somehow, given her dedication—or, looked at another way, fanaticism—it was hard to believe. So why hadn't she returned to Providence? Why hadn't she called him?

The lobby, like so many others, looked almost mass produced in its furnishing and layout. Yet to Caleb it seemed entirely different from the day he had first entered with Julie. The difference lay, he well knew, not in the lobby but in himself. The Caleb who had joyously gone up to Julie's room on that first day here had been an ardent lover, in his own mind an ex-priest who had abandoned the anachronistic ways of the Church. Now he was—what was he?

Caleb paused in the lobby and looked around. After a moment he turned off into what looked like a bar, dressed up in wood paneling and prints to seem old-fashioned. Sliding onto a stool, he ordered a Scotch and soda.

The drink made him think of his mother, whom he had visited that morning. She was putting on a front of giving the rehab serious considerations, and he was fairly sure why. The fact that her second son, the only truly Catholic child she'd brought up, was about to leave the priesthood, was a final blow.

And how much, he wondered, staring into his drink, did that realization, combined with her obvious misery and suicide attempt, change him? Because he knew he had changed more than he would have considered possible when he arrived in Providence. Was it his mother who had effected the change?

The more he stared into his drink, the less, he found, he could answer that. And what did he feel about Julie? Pain was perhaps the most obvious feeling he could identify. But there was also anger and disappointment and a sort of numb bewilderment. Was it because he had come to see how much she was manipulating him? That their love which, for him, had been the central fact of his life and the main cause of his leaving the Church was for her just another maneuver in a political game? But hadn't he made the decision to leave the priesthood before her entry into his life? He couldn't really remember. She had been so tied up with everything.

Sitting there, the sort of despair he had known when he was a boy at prep school seemed to settle back on him. He had had no reason to remember that for a long time, but he found himself now recalling something that in the intervening years he had forgotten: That once or twice in those first miserable years at prep school he had even found himself thinking of suicide.

Andrew called Elizabeth from his house early in the morning. "We have to talk."

"Yes," Elizabeth said and added, "Graham's going to be here on Tuesday. I got the cablegram when I arrived home night before last, but our phones at Summerstoke are hardly private. So I waited to call the next morning and you'd gone."

"I'm sorry." He paused. "In view of what you just said about your phone, how about coming in for lunch? Capriccio's at twelve-thirty?"

"Fine. I'll see you then."

He was sitting at a table for two when she got there, a whiskey on the rocks in front of him. "I didn't order for you because I didn't know if you wanted a drink."

"I could do with one," Elizabeth said. "I'll have one of those," she said to the waiter who had sped up.

Andrew came straight to the point. "Do you think Graham knows about us?" he asked. "I mean, you weren't expecting him, I know. So why is he coming? Does he want to fight for you? Of course, from where I sit he'd be crazy not to."

Elizabeth put out her hand and touched his where it was lying on the table. His fingers closed around hers. "If this were the local diner," he said, "I could kiss you, but I'd better not here."

Elizabeth's hand tightened around his. "I wish it were the diner. But you're right." She released his hand and withdrew it.

Andrew looked at Elizabeth. "Have you thought about what I asked—divorcing Graham and marrying me? Since he's coming to see you, it seems, somehow the time to push for my own claim on you."

"Of course I've thought about it. Andrew, darling,

as I've said before, I worry what would happen to the children if I left Graham."

"Bringing them over here isn't the worst thing that could happen to them. They're young enough so that by the time they were teenagers they'd be acclimatized—Americanized."

"But would Graham let them go? He's a terribly devoted father."

"I thought he spent most of his time out of England."

"He does. But when he's there he's in many ways a better—more loving—parent than I am. Ailsa and I don't make out too well. She's much more at ease with him."

Andrew stared at his glass. "My temptation is to try to override all your arguments with better ones of my own—to make them up if necessary. But I don't think that's fair to you. I hope, my darling, that you'll decide to let us build a life together, to let me make you happy as you plainly haven't been before. But it has to be your decision as much as my pleading."

Elizabeth, near tears, didn't say anything.

When they were through, as though by mutual consent, they did not go back to his house, but parted by her car parked near the restaurant.

CHAPTER

20

"How's Ian?" Elizabeth asked.

They were in the room next to her own at Summerstoke to which she had shown him. The arrangement had been left to her by Robert Senior and the housekeeper, and this seemed the least controversial way of handling the matter. She could, of course, have put him at the other end of the big house or even on another floor. But since this was his first visit to the family and she had not spoken about her desire for a divorce, such a public statement of the state of affairs between them could be embarrassing.

"Doing unexpectedly well. He didn't, as you know, get a first, which disappointed him quite a lot. He's spent most of the summer with his mother's people and visiting friends. But it looks like he might have a job. He went to interview at one of the big auction houses and they seemed to like him."

"That's good. He should do well there. Art was his specialty at Oxford, wasn't it?"

"Yes. Although he actually read history." Graham paused. "I've thought a lot about ... well, about our problems, yours and mine, so many of which seemed to center around Ian. I think I've been unfair to you, probably because I felt guilty about Ian and his mother's family."

"Why? You didn't neglect him."

"No, but I didn't see as much of his mother's family as I might have. If I had, I might have made things easier for him and thereafter for you." Graham was looking at Elizabeth, his grayish eyes thoughtful.

"What do you mean?"

"I think I mean that I didn't like Fiona's family. It took me a while to admit that to myself, and to admit the reason. To be blunt, they made me feel inferior, the stable boy up from the ranks, presuming to have a relationship with an old and titled family like hers. So I avoided contact with them as much as possible, leaving it to Ian to do his own family connecting. Then when he seemed to take on some of their least attractive qualities, I must have felt it was my fault and therefore couldn't admit it to myself, or to you, an outsider."

Elizabeth was looking at Graham with surprise. "What made you see that?"

"I'm sorry to say the way I caught him talking to Duncan one day. He thought they were alone, and was busy denigrating you and everything American—which, considering the firm he wants to work for has offices in New York and does a great deal of business there, is rather amusing. I went in, told Duncan that everything Ian had said was errant nonsense. I then told Ian that if he ever talked either to Duncan or Ailsa that way again, I'd throw him out of my house, and let his would-be employers, who have many, many rich American clients, know what his views are."

"Wow!" Elizabeth said. "How did he take it?"

"He went red and then white and then walked out of the room."

Elizabeth glanced at his profile. "Are you sorry?"

"No, not really. Perhaps I came on strong out of my own sense of guilt that I hadn't really listened when you tried to tell me what Ian had been like to you. But there was something else. That girl you saw me walking with in Soho—she was a friend of Ian's, though I didn't know it at the time. I went to a party

I'd been invited to, probably drank more than I was accustomed to, and found myself alone at the end of the party with the hostess—that girl. She . . . well, she made it plain that it would be perfectly fine with her if I stayed the night—so I did. I have no excuse. Things weren't too good between you and me, and I suppose I was ripe for a fall. I went on seeing her, and finally learned that her brother and Ian were friends and they were connected with the Palfreys, Fiona's family. Ian had thought it would be a tremendous joke if what happened, happened. So he set it up. I'm not excusing myself, but when I found out I was very angry. Unfortunately, with my own complicity staring at me, I couldn't make too much of it to Ian, but it certainly fed my anger when I caught him talking to Duncan."

"How did you find out?"

"When I walked into her apartment one day, earlier than she was expecting me, she was on the phone giggling about something. In a minute I realized she was talking to Ian, and what they were giggling about was me. When she got off the phone I asked her a few questions. At first she was a bit evasive. Then she got angry and spilled the beans—all of them. I felt like the biggest fool on earth, and broke the whole thing off—not only because I'd been made a fool of, but because of you." He paused, then went on, "We all—the children and I—miss you so much, and they told me to tell you to come home soon. So did George Washington, in his dignified way. He's getting old, I'm afraid, Elizabeth. I took him to the vet before I left. His kidneys are not functioning perfectly. Other than that he seems to be all right. But every day he mews and walks around your bed and, unless some housemaid stops him, jumps on top of it."

"I hope nobody does stop him."

"That's what Duncan said. And I backed him up. So there he curls to snooze. I don't know how much time he has, but I think the sooner you get back to him, the better off he'll be."

"It's a terrible thing for a mother to say, but for some reason that gets to me more than what you said about the children."

"I thought it might," Graham said dryly.

Elizabeth said nothing for a moment. Then, abruptly, she asked, "Graham, why did you come?"

"To persuade you to come back to me, Elizabeth." As she stared at him, he went on, "I want that very much."

The headline was spread across the paper: BERES-FORD HOLDINGS LINKED TO MILITARY REGIMES.

Jenny had been the first down to breakfast, but Robbie was the first to open the paper.

"Jesus God!" he said.

Jenny, busy pouring coffee, looked up, opened her mouth to protest, then closed it again. "What?" she asked finally.

Robbie continued to stare.

"What is it, Robbie?"

"Surely my own son didn't do this."

Jenny put the coffeepot down and went around the table to where she could see the paper.

"What on earth do they mean?" she asked curiously. "And why on earth do you think Three might have something to do with it?"

"Because—Jenny, I don't have time to explain all this right now. They're talking about the All Americas Import and Export Exchange, which some radical left-wingers seem to think is guilty of propping up right-wing governments in Central and South America." Suddenly he pushed his chair back and went into the hall. "Three," he called upstairs. "Three?"

"Yes?" A sleepy voice sounded faintly. Then a door opened. "What is it?"

"I want you to come down here."

"Dad—"

"Do as I say. Now!"

In a few minutes feet in slippers went along the hall upstairs and then started coming down the stairs.

Robbie returned to the breakfast room. "Come in here," he called to his son. When Three came in, Robbie thrust the paper at him. "Is this your doing?" he asked.

Three looked at the headline, then took the paper and started reading the column.

"Well?" Robbie asked.

"Well, what?" Three asked belligerently. "So the truth about that company is finally coming out. So what?"

"You didn't answer my question. Did you give this information to the paper? I know that woman your uncle is involved with told you about it."

"No, I didn't. But I wish I had."

"You don't give a damn about me, do you?"

"Your plans ought to include getting that money out of a company like this. If people like you did that, maybe that could force that company out of places like Guatemala, the way American companies got out of South Africa."

"Let me get this straight. This news story didn't come from you?"

"I just told you. No."

"I'd like to believe you," Robbie said.

"I don't care what you think," Three said angrily. He glanced at Jenny. "I suppose Mom's been feeding you that I did it."

"As usual I must be the enemy." Jenny picked her handbag off the table, where she had put it preparatory to going out later. "I'm leaving. This fight's between the two of you."

Three opened his mouth.

"Just shut up!" Robbie said to him. Then, "Jenny? Jenny, wait a minute. Don't leave things like this!"

But Jenny had gone.

*   *   *

Terry stared at the phone. She'd been staring at it off and on for days, to the detriment of her work. The research and notes on her dessertation were about complete. What was facing her was the actual writing, something she'd been putting off.

Then, on impulse, one she'd had many times since she'd returned from Providence but always, at the last moment, turned back from, she picked up the receiver and punched out a number. As she listened to the rings, she glanced at her watch. It was nine in the morning. He probably wouldn't be home.

"Hello," David Stein said.

"Hello, David. This is Terry."

"Yes, I know. It's really great to hear from you. How are you?"

He sounded so much the same, Terry thought, yet there was a much more assured note in his voice.

"I'm fine. How are you?"

"Fine, too. What are you doing?"

"This minute?"

"Yes."

"Trying to talk myself into starting my dissertation."

"You never did like writing, yet you're good at it."

"Thanks. Maybe that'll help. You're with a law firm now, aren't you?"

"Yes. For the time being."

"Why only for the time being? Don't you like your law firm?"

"It's okay, especially financially, and I have a lot of debts to pay back. When they're gone, who knows? I'd rather go in for something more satisfying but less lucrative."

"Like public defender?"

"Or some outfit that specializes in that."

"You haven't changed, David. It's nice to hear that."

"Have you—changed I mean?"

"Yes. I left that little ladies' college and am at B.U., where I'm majoring in women's studies."

"From what my uncle reported to me you're a feminist."

"I am, although I don't know how he got that from our conversation."

The incredible part, Terry thought, was that they were talking as though they'd seen each other the past weekend, not seven years before. Then, realizing David was saying something, she replied, "What? I'm sorry, David, I was thinking how downright weird it was for us to be talking like this, like we'd seen each other last Saturday."

"I was thinking the same. Do you still like pizza?"

She caught her breath. "Yes."

"What's your new address?"

She gave it to him.

"I'll be by in twenty minutes."

Caleb saw the headline when he came down to breakfast at Summerstoke. "My God!" he said.

"What?" Elizabeth asked.

Caleb read out the headline.

"Isn't that the company you were telling me about?" she asked.

"Yes."

"Did you tell the paper?"

"No. The only other two people I knew of who could have are Julie and Three." He paused. "I don't think it was Three."

"You mean it was Julie."

"Yes."

"Just then Robert Senior came in and glanced at the paper Caleb had laid on the table. "What's all this?" He read the headline and skimmed the article. Then he glanced at his son. "Is this your doing?"

"If you mean did I give the paper that juicy bit of news, no. Did I know about the company, yes. I learned about it when I was in Guatemala."

"Then where did they get this?"

Both Caleb and Elizabeth went silent. At that moment Graham walked in the room. "Good morning," he said cheerfully.

Elizabeth glanced at him and smiled. "Good morning, Graham," she said. "I had Sarah fix tea for you. It's on the sideboard."

Graham looked at the tense faces—faces he'd seen for the first time only the night before—then quietly got his tea and sat down at the table next to his wife.

"What would you like?" Elizabeth asked him. "Eggs, bacon, cereal?"

"Cereal would be fine," he said and reached for the box in the middle of the table.

Robert Senior and Caleb were staring at each other. Robert Senior said, "Did you expect a disclosure similar to this?"

"Yes," Caleb said. "Or rather the threat of one."

"Why?"

Caleb took a breath. "I—and one other person—learned about All Americans Import and Export when we were in Guatemala. The plan was ... was to see if Robbie would donate some of his money from the trust to the freedom movement in Guatemala, the guerrillas, in exchange for not publicizing this."

"Do you mean to tell me that you would threaten your brother's chances of becoming governor just to have him contribute to a pet cause?"

"It's a hell of a lot more than a pet cause," Caleb snapped. "People are dying of hunger and malnutrition and bullets bought by money from this damn company. But you don't care about those, do you?"

"I care a great deal more about my son—or for that matter about any of my children—and what happens to them, than about some uncivilized country half a world away."

Caleb's face flushed angrily. "Spoken like a truly arrogant gringo. The whole point is that our money, Beresford money, is propping up the bullies in that country and for that we—not just the good old U.S.— but we Beresfords are responsible!"

"Graham," Elizabeth said dryly, "welcome to the Beresford family."

"It doesn't sound unlike parts of my own family," Graham said mildly.

Robert Senior turned to him. "I apologize to our guest."

"Well, I don't," Caleb said. "I'm not sorry to be a lone voice sticking up for helpless Indians in the hills of Guatemala."

Graham, spooning his cereal, looked up at him. "As far as I'm concerned, by all means say what you like."

"I suppose as an upholder of the British Empire—"

"Steady on, Caleb," Elizabeth said.

"That's past history," Graham said. "However, I'm perfectly willing to admit that we did our share of exploitation around the globe—as well as a fair amount of good."

"What—?" Caleb blurted.

"For God's sake, let's not get sidetracked," Elizabeth said. "Caleb, you say you don't think Three could have done this. Then it must be Julie?"

"What on earth does Robbie's son have to do with this?" Robert Senior said. "And who is Julie?"

"Julie is the woman I lived with down in Guatemala who is a member of the freedom movement. She was up here for a while. When Andrew wouldn't talk about how much money each of us would get, she left." Caleb took a breath. "I think this is her parting shot."

"I see," Robert Senior said. "So much for all those vows of celibacy."

"You don't have to belabor the point, Dad," Elizabeth said, instinctively trying to draw her father's anger away from her younger brother. "He's not the only member of the family to have broken vows."

Robert Senior turned toward her. His face was white and drawn. "I assume you're referring to yourself."

"Hey," Caleb said, glancing at Graham, "take it easy!"

Graham put down his spoon and looked up at Robert. "I also am guilty," he said. "As Elizabeth knows."

"Elizabeth is hardly in a position—" Robert started, and then stopped. The lines around his mouth seemed to tighten.

Elizabeth stared at him. Her mind seemed a jumble of thoughts and memories: Robert's face, with that same intent look, when she introduced him to Nigel ... his recent admission that all along he had known Nigel was gay ... Andrew's "He was having an affair with an older man ..." Her own careless statement, "Perhaps it was somebody he met at the party ..."

Like an explosion in her head, the pieces of a twenty-year puzzle came together.

"My God," Elizabeth said. "Of course. It was you, my dear father, all the time it was you!" Her eighteen-year-old agony and humiliation, the blow across her face suddenly made sense. "You took Nigel from me!" she said calmly. In the frozen silence that followed she drew a breath. "You—you unspeakable pervert!" She burst into tears.

CHAPTER

21

Robert Senior stared back at Elizabeth.

"Jesus God!" Caleb said.

"It's true, isn't it?" Elizabeth said.

"That I'm bisexual? That I fell in love with Nigel and he with me? Yes. They're both true. Whether that makes me in the classic sense a pervert, I'm not sure."

His voice was calm, Elizabeth thought, as though he were discussing a piece of historical research. "You're not even sorry."

"Why should I be? I saved you from the untold misery of discovering—probably after you were married—that he was also bisexual and was having affairs, or one-night stands, with half the attractive men he met. Do you think that would have made for a happy marriage?"

"You took him away from me," Elizabeth repeated. "And when I went to you for comfort, you humiliated me and then slapped me across the face. And now, twenty years later, you're acting as though you did me a big favor!"

"As I just explained to you, I did, whether you want to admit it or not. But I am sorry for humiliating and striking you. I've been sorry about that for a long time."

"Oh, you mean that letter," she said.

"What did you want? Bleeding knees as I crawled

to you for forgiveness? Nothing less would have satisfied your self-pity—apparently the only fully developed emotion you know how to feel!"

"Considering who—and what—you are, you have a hell of a nerve talking to me that way!"

Her father stared at her for a moment, then turned and walked out of the room.

"And he has the gall to criticize you and me!" Caleb said. "At least we go after the opposite sex."

After a few seconds Graham spoke, "He's not my father, and I in no way condone what he did to you, Elizabeth, but I feel forced to point out that he didn't make himself a bisexual. How or why it happens nobody knows. Everything that to a heterosexual comes naturally and society either puts up with or condones, carries a stigma when done with the same sex."

"Why are you sticking up for him? You're one of the most conventional—and moral—people I've ever met!"

"Somehow that doesn't sound like a compliment," Graham said dryly. "Besides being not entirely true."

"I'm your wife. You recently told me how much you wanted us to stay together. Yet you're justifying my father's abuse and ill treatment of me!"

"I'm not justifying it, Elizabeth. I think his treatment of you was unforgivable, and I will repeat now, in front of your brother, how very much I love you." He paused. "If I seem tolerant of your father's . . . of the problem itself, perhaps it's because . . ." he paused again and then went on, "because it has crossed my mind that Ian might be in the same category. When I realized that, I tried to find out as much about it as I could."

This admission abruptly deflated her anger. "I'm bound to say I wondered about Ian, too," she said cautiously. "But given how much you resented everything I ever said about him, I didn't dare put it into words."

Graham stood up and faced Elizabeth. "As I've told

you, I regret—very much—my lack of understanding about what Ian was doing to you."

Elizabeth stared at him for a moment, then reached out and touched his face. He put his hand over hers.

After a moment she dropped her hand and said lightly, "Do you think self-pity is the strongest emotion I have?" she asked.

"No, I do not. I think—" He stopped.

"You think what?"

"That in some ways the shoe's on the other foot. I've only been here a few hours, but I wouldn't be surprised if arrogant defiance is about the only method your father knows to deal with unacceptable feelings."

"You're probably right," Elizabeth said. She fished in her pocket for a tissue, then said, "Thanks," as Graham held out his handkerchief.

At that moment the phone rang. Caleb went into the hall and picked up the receiver. "Hello?"

Elizabeth, listening, heard the one-sided conversation that followed, punctuated by pauses.

After a minute Caleb said, "Yes, Robbie, I saw the damn piece. No, I didn't give it to the paper." Pause. "Since I haven't seen Julie for several days I don't know the answer to that. I wondered if it was Three." Pause. "I'm glad to hear he didn't." Pause. "No, I don't know who else could have done it, but, practically speaking, I don't see why Julie did it now when she could have used it as leverage later." Pause. "Yes, I told you that at your club." Pause. "No, it's not in the highest tradition of honesty, but then nothing that company does inspires integrity, and in a higher cause . . . Well, fuck you, too." And Caleb slammed down the phone.

He came back in. "I'm going into town," he said briefly. He paused at the door. "If the paper got even a whiff of all this about Dad, it could screw Robbie's ambitions even more."

"You wouldn't—" Elizabeth started.

"No, I wouldn't. But I can't help wondering what Dad's blue-eyed favorite son would think about it!"

After he left, Elizabeth stared at the remains of her English muffin. "For some reason I feel as guilty as hell for saying what I did in front of you and Caleb, although I don't know why I should. God knows, when I was a child Dad didn't hesitate to humiliate me in front of anyone."

Graham pulled the newspaper toward him. "I'm beginning to understand why you've never had any family pictures around our home." He paused. "It explains also, I think, some of the difficulties you may have had."

"What difficulties?"

"Well, perhaps with men. I've seen how defensive you are, how often and how quickly you get angry."

"I suppose so." Elizabeth reached for the coffeepot and poured herself some more coffee. Then she put it down and said in a strained voice, "Graham, I have to tell you I ... I, too, have been having an affair." Curiously, she hadn't expected to feel so bad in saying this. She somehow expected it to be easier.

"I thought ... I was afraid that might be the case."

"You mean, because I didn't come back while the trust was being settled?"

"Yes. Also the conversations we had on the phone. Guilt leads to anger—I should know, because I've felt it myself." He hesitated. "Elizabeth, are you in love with this man?"

"Yes."

"I see. That makes it difficult." Graham got up. "I think I'll go upstairs for a while. Perhaps we'll talk later."

When Robbie announced who he was, he was put through to the managing editor immediately. "I'd like to know where you got that news item about the All Americas Import and Export Exchange," he said.

"You must know, Mr. Beresford, that we have to protect our sources. I can't give you that information."

"I see. Thank you." Robbie was seething, but he had dealt with news people enough to know that he wouldn't be able to budge the managing editor. After he hung up, he dialed another number. "Kate," he said. "Did you read this morning's paper?"

"I did. I was going to call you as soon as I thought you'd be in the office. You're still at home, aren't you?"

"Yes. Is it as damaging as I think it is?"

"Yes, I'm afraid so. It's not going to hurt you among Republicans that much. But you need a lot more than just Republicans to win an election."

"What about the primary?"

"Since you're running on a liberal Republican ticket, it will hurt you more than it would your conservative opponent."

One of the things Robbie had always valued about Kate was her directness. She didn't fool around. She didn't pretend. At the moment he found it depresssing. "What can we do?"

"Get your money out of that company as fast and as publicly as you can. Once it's out, you can say, with some hope of people believing you, that you had just not been aware of what the company was doing, since your area of expertise is domestic rather than foreign." When there was a silence on the other end of the phone, she asked, "Is there some reason you can't move the money?"

"For one thing, it's not mine to move. It's administered by a board. Dad and I are on it, but we're not the only ones. I'll certainly speak to Dad. I'll also talk to our lawyer and our financial manager."

"Do, Robbie. You're going to have to be seen as moving heaven and earth to disinfect the Beresford money."

He put down the receiver, then picked it up again and dialed Summerstoke.

Robert Senior picked up the phone on the third ring. "Hello."

"Dad," Robbie's voice came over the receiver. "Did you see the headline in today's paper?"

"Yes. I did."

"This could be a blow. We're going to have to get rid of that stock—publicly."

"I was expecting a call from you about that, and I've already talked to our broker. We can move stock, all right, but we're going to lose a lot of money doing it."

"I see," Robbie said. "I take it this would affect everyone's income."

"Of course."

"How badly?"

"He's woking out the figures now. When he's done he'll let me know and we'll call a meeting of the board."

Robbie thought about the board. It consisted not only of Robert Senior, but also Robbie and Robert Senior's cousin, James Beresford and his two sons. Robert Senior had had no siblings. Elizabeth, Caleb, and Terry had never been on the board.

"I guess," Robbie said, "it really boils down to how eager they are—how much they'd sacrifice—to see me governor."

"I'm afraid it does boil down to that, Robbie."

Without quite knowing why, except that after all these years it was the one place he now found familiar, Caleb parked his car near the hotel and went in. For a moment he hesitated, then he made for the small, dingy bar. A number of drinks later, with a pocket full of quarters, dimes, and nickels secured earlier from a nearby bank, Caleb repaired to the bank of phones at the back of the lobby.

He had a variety of names and numbers of people connected in one way or another with the movement, and he started calling them. When somebody answered he'd ask, "Is Julie there?" When whoever it was said no, he'd ask casually, "Any idea where I could find her? It's important." If the answerer asked, "Who is this?" Caleb would usually give a fake name, adding, "We were together in Guatemala." Sometimes he'd get a slammed-down receiver as his reply.

At his sixth call he struck gold, but he was unprepared for the answer. "She went back to Providence," Carlos said. "She said she still had business there."

"Thanks." Caleb hung up and stood there for a moment. Then he called the hotel's front desk and asked for Julie Manners.

"Yes, sir, she's in room eighteen forty. I'll connect you."

"No, don't bother. I just want to surprise her with some flowers."

When the elevator let him off on the eighteenth floor, he found the room and knocked.

"Who is it?" Julie asked.

"Some flowers," Caleb said, muffling his voice through a handkerchief.

In a few seconds the door opened. "Caleb," she said, looking a little frightened.

"Surprise, surprise," he said, "May I come in?" Without waiting for her to answer, he pushed past her into the room.

"I was expecting you," she said, and closed the door.

"It was you, wasn't it, who gave the info about All Americas Imports to the paper?"

"Sure. Wasn't that our plan?"

"Yes. But now it's out, I'm curious how you think we could use it to get more money. Any clout it might have had is gone."

Julie shrugged. "You wouldn't have done it anyway. I could see how you were changing. Your family was softening you up."

"So how was giving that stuff to the newspapers going to change that?"

"It was the last dim hope. Seeing them rushing

around with their explanations might—just might—
have brought you back to where you were when you
and I came here, to your true loyalties." As she finished speaking, she crossed the short distance between
them and stood in front of Caleb. Putting her arms
on his shoulders, she leaned forward and pressed her
lips against his, letting her tongue slide into his mouth.
She could feel the almost immediate reaction in his
body, now pressed against hers, and moved her hips
tighter against his, sliding them back and forth as the
swelling thrust against her grew larger.

For a few seconds Caleb responded. His arms closed
around her, pulling her to him. His tongue went inside
her mouth. Then abruptly he pushed her away. "No.
I'm not falling for that this time. You betrayed me,
Julie. You sold me out with whoever you went to New
York to see, because I know it wasn't your sister. I
talked to her in California. Whose idea was this?
Yours or whoever you were staying with in New
York? Who's there now? Juan?"

For a second she stood there, looking at him, then
she walked away.

"Answer me, Julie. You at least owe me that."

"I was staying with Juan," she said over her shoulder. Then she turned. "The people down in Guatemala desperately need the money, and he'd come to
tell me that. When he called he wanted to know how
much longer it'd take to get your money plus anybody
else's we could maneuver."

"But still, you might have done better by keeping
your mouth shut. So why didn't you?"

"Because I'd come to despise you, Father Caleb."
Sarcastically she underlined "Father" in her voice.
"You talk about betrayal. You can't be faithful to
anything! You were all gung-ho for the Church when
you went down there, weren't you? Then you saw me
and read some of our stuff and you become gung-ho
for the revolution. As well as contributing your own
money, you couldn't wait to put the squeeze on your

brother. If that damn lawyer hadn't died, you might have done it. But he did and everything was held up, and by the time you'd been with your family for a while, you were back being a good little Beresford boy, including not telling them about me, even though you kept saying you wanted to marry me. I couldn't even meet your family. You were furious when I did meet Andrew whatever-his-name-is. Juan and I decided you needed a lesson."

There was a silence. "So why are you back?" Caleb finally asked. He could feel the rage gathering in him, but for the moment he was still able to hold it.

Julie didn't answer for a moment as her mind slid back to her conversation in New York with Juan. "Don't go," he had said. "It's a waste of time and money."

"No," she had disagreed. "There's always a chance I can get him back, long enough anyway, to get some of the money—even if it's only his share." She hadn't added, And I want to see his face when he knows how I used him.

"So you came to teach me a lesson," Caleb said now. "That's interesting. How?"

She was now at least getting part of her wish: seeing his face as he learned how he had been used. But it wasn't working quite as she had envisioned it. She had assumed that he would be pleading for a return to the relationship. Always he had before, especially following her sexual overtures.

"Caleb," she said, coming toward him. "Forget what I said. I didn't mean it. Let's go to bed—"

His open hand struck her face so hard her head snapped around as she was thrown onto the bed. Caleb stared at her. For a moment she was stunned, then she pulled herself up. "You—"

He struck her again. There seemed to be little connection with himself, as he had always known himself, and what was going on now. His hand had developed a life of its own.

When the cry came out of her mouth he grabbed her shoulders with both hands and started to shake her.

"You used me," he shouted. "All the time, all those hours and days, you used me. You despise me, but you used me." He was shaking her violently as he spoke. Somehow, between shakes, she slid out of his hands and lunged toward her open suitcase. As her hand folded on the gun Caleb was on top of her.

"Drop it!" He wrenched her wrist. The gun fell out of her hand. She opened her mouth. Caleb's fist came at her and struck her jaw, knocking her head back. She fell onto the floor.

Caleb stared at her unconscious form. He didn't know whether she was dead or alive. Then he picked up the gun, put it in his pocket and left the room. No one stopped him as he crossed the lobby and went to his parked car.

He drove until he found a deserted public phone. Calling the hotel and again disguising his voice, he said that someone should go to room eighteen forty because the person there might have had an accident and hung up quickly. Getting back in the car, he drove out of the city until he came across a deserted pond. Taking the gun out of his pocket, he wiped it off, took it to the edge of the water, made sure there was no one in sight and flung it in.

Then he turned the car around and started back to Providence. When he got there, he went to a church in the Italian section and walked in. It was filled with statues and lit candles, and there were people on their knees in the pews, praying, saying their rosaries, staring at the altar. Slipping into a back pew, he sat down.

He was there for a long time, looking back at the ruins of his life. Suddenly he understood, as he never had before, what had motivated his mother, not only in her suicide attempt, but in her cry when she was brought back, "Why didn't you let me die?"

Finally he got up and walked slowly to a confessional, pushed aside the curtain and knelt down.

CHAPTER
22

Jenny paced beside Deirdre, who had been told to walk up and down the hall outside her hospital room.

"How do you feel, darling?" she asked.

"Mom, I've told you three times today already. I feel okay. I'm not crazy about this damn jacket or corset or whatever it is I have to wear." She glanced at her mother as Jenny started to speak. "And you don't have to tell me I shouldn't say damn. I know that's what you think. But I've decided I'm going to say what I want. Daddy said I should."

"Darling, if I've given you the impression I'm trying to control—"

"What do you mean, trying to control? That's all you've ever done. You never leave me alone. You're at me all the time. Even here in the hospital you're always there."

"Deirdre, darling, you've had a horrible accident. I want to be with you—"

"I haven't had an accident. I jumped out the window. Stop trying to pretend." Deirdre raised her voice to a shout. "Everybody listen! I JUMPED OUT THE WINDOW!"

Nurses' heads appeared in doorways. One of them came up to Deirdre. "I know you're upset, but you mustn't shout like that, Deirdre. This is a hospital. There are people here who have to rest, and you're making it hard for them." The nurse glanced at Jenny. "Can't you—"

"No," Deirdre screamed. She turned and started to hurry back to her room. Catching her toe in her robe, she fell.

"Deirdre!" Jenny cried and bent over her.

"NO!" Deirdre screamed. "Go away!"

"Mrs. Beresford," the nurse said, "I think it would be better if you returned to the reception area. I'll help Deirdre up and make sure she does as little damage to the rods in her back as possible and then I'm sending for the doctor."

"I insist—"

"NO!" Deirdre screamed. "GO AWAY"!

"Please, Mrs. Beresford," the nurse said. "I'm going to get another nurse here to help me. It can be tricky."

"But I'm—"

Deirdre, lying on her face, raised her head and opened her mouth.

"All right," Jenny said shakily. "I'll go to the reception area." She turned and walked back down the hall to the room across from the elevator.

"Now," the nurse said in a calm voice, "can you get your right knee up under you? Good. MaryAnn, can you come and get on Deirdre's other side?"

As they were helping Deirdre up, the elevator opened and Robbie stepped out. Glancing to the left, he saw his wife sitting in a straight chair in the reception room, staring out the window. In front of him two nurses were busy getting Deirdre steady on her feet. He strode up to them.

"What happened?" he asked.

The first nurse glanced at him. "Mr. Beresford, if you can get on Deirdre's other side, MaryAnn can go back to monitoring her patient."

"Sure." Robbie slid into place and placed his hand under her arm. Deirdre was crying silently, the tears wetting her cheeks. Walking slowly, they got Deirdre back to her room.

"All right, Deirdre," the nurse said, helping her slide into bed. "I'm going to call the doctor to make sure you haven't thrown anything inside you out of whack. Mr. Beresford, I'd like to speak to you outside for a moment."

When they were in the hall, she said, "There was quite a scene before you arrived, and I think you ought to know about it." Quickly she told him what happened.

"I see," Robbie said. "Thanks for telling me." He paused. "Since I wasn't here, I obviously don't know what set her off. Do you?"

"No." She paused, as though she might say something more, but didn't go on.

"What are you not saying?" Robbie said.

"I have a feeling that Deirdre finds ... well, her mother is here all the time, from the moment visiting hours start until they close. You come, of course, when you're free from work. But no one else does. Deirdre has never actually said as much to me or to whatever nurse is on duty, but it's fairly plain her mother's constant presence, without anyone else coming in to relax it or change it, seems to upset her, although this is the first time she's made a scene. Sometimes I notice her pressure is up a little. There's no reason why others can't come to see her, although once, when I said that to Deirdre, she said, 'I don't want them.' "

Robbie was looking at her closely. "Anything else?"

"Yes. I hope you won't be offended, but I think she's in great need of counseling."

"Yes, I know that. You don't jump out of the window for nothing. We were just waiting till she got a little better. But maybe we should find a psychiatrist or therapist now." He glanced keenly at the nurse. "Any suggestions?"

"There's a wonderful woman connected with our psychiatric section, a Mrs. Weinberg. You couldn't do better than her."

The nurse nodded and went back to her station as

Jenny walked up. "I didn't see you at first, but I heard your voice. Was the nurse telling you about the bizarre episode that happened just now?"

"Yes. She said Deirdre and you were walking up and down the hall, when Deirdre started yelling at you to go away and then fell. Is that right?"

"Yes. More or less."

"What made her do it, Jenny?"

"I don't know, Robbie. I've no idea. I've been here every day since she was brought here. I have no idea what got into her."

"Have you been preaching at her again?" Robbie asked bluntly.

Jenny stiffened. "I suppose that's what the nurse implied."

"No, she did say that you've been here all day every day from the moment the visiting hours began until they closed. She also—please let me finish," Robbie said as Jenny started to interrupt. "She also said no one else has come by. I've told the others—Dad, Caleb, and Elizabeth—that Deirdre was here. Do you mean none of them has even dropped in when they're visiting Mother upstairs?"

"I didn't think—"

"You mean you told them not to—you wanted total control over her! No wonder she yelled at you. I'm going to go in and talk to her."

"We'll both go," Jenny said.

"No, I want to talk to her alone," Robbie said.

He went into the room and closed the door. Deirdre was lying on the bed, sobbing quietly. Robbie paused. He felt totally bewildered. Deirdre had always seemed so compliant, so close to her mother. There were even times he felt shut out. What was going on that he was too busy to notice?

Drawing up a chair he sat down beside his daughter and lightly took her hand. She withdrew it. He didn't try to take it again.

"Deirdre, you don't have to say anything if you don't want to, but could you tell me what happened?"

"I don't want to go to that school Mom said she wanted me to go to."

"Which school?"

"The religious one in Pennsylvania."

"First, you don't have to go to any school you don't want to, although the law says you do have to attend some school." He smiled a little. "If you didn't, you wouldn't be very employable afterward." He paused, but she didn't respond. "Do you have any idea where you'd like to go?"

"I don't want to go anywhere," Deirdre said stubbornly.

"As I've just explained to you, you have to go. There must be some school you'd find acceptable."

Deirdre sighed. After a minute she said, "An ordinary school like Wheeler, if I could get in, or maybe that Quaker school that Polly goes to. I went there once to pick her up when she was in a play and I liked the feel of it. And Polly says people—the kids there—are nice."

"All right, we'll look into it." After a minute he said, "Can you tell me what happened just now?"

"Mom had just said for the umpteenth time I'd had an accident and I didn't—I jumped out the window. She tries to pretend it didn't happen. And she's with me all the time. Nobody else comes. I guess everybody hates me."

"Nobody hates you, Deirdre. I'm sorry you think that. And other people'll be coming to visit, I promise."

He stayed there until the doctor came. The doctor talked cheerfully to Deirdre, examined her, his fingers probing the incision, then straightened. "You're a lucky young lady. You don't seem to have done any permanent damage. But try not to fall again!"

When he left the room Robbie followed. "I asked the nurse about a psychiatrist or counselor and she suggested a Mrs. Wienberg. Do you agree that she's good?"

"Very good, especially for adolescents." The doctor looked at Robbie. "Do you want me to call her today for you?"

"I'd be grateful. And I'd like to call her myself after that."

When the doctor had left, Robbie went back into the reception room.

Jenny was staring out the window. "Did she tell you I was making her life miserable by being with her all the time?"

"More or less. Why haven't you allowed some of the others to come see her? They'd have cheered her up considerably."

"I thought, given her rather fragile state of mind, that it might not be good for her."

"But good for her for you to be with her all day every day?"

"I was trying to tell her why I felt and thought the way I do, and to give her reason to feel the same. It's exactly what my father did for me when I got out of hand. I came to see he was right, and everything he said made me feel calmer and better."

"It's hard for me to imagine you ever getting out of hand, Jenny."

"Maybe so. But I did." She had her back to him, looking out the window.

"What did you do? Fail to go to Sunday school one Sunday?"

Jenny turned. "You really like to make fun of what I believe, don't you?"

"Hey, I just want you to back off a little with Deirdre. Come every day, but don't stay all the time. Give her some space."

"Who are you to tell me what to do? She's as much my child as yours."

"Do you want her to jump out of the window again?"

In a lower voice Jenny said, "You don't have to tell everyone in Providence what happened."

"It's a hell of a lot better than pretending it didn't happen. What's the matter? Why are you trying to cover it up?"

"I'm not trying to cover it up. Well, maybe I am. But I don't want it to be the first thing people think about when they see her. And according to my own beliefs that you have so little use for, to take your own life is a sin."

"It's also an expression of extreme despair. Look, I was talking to the doctor. I think she needs counseling, and he suggested a Mrs. Weinberg who is attached to their psychiatric wing. And I'm going to call her here later."

"I've already thought about that. There's a counselor attached to my old church—"

"No! Jenny, you've seen how she's reacted. Do you want to push her further?"

"Do I have no rights about this whatsoever?"

"You've tried your way, Jenny. Now let's try mine."

Robbie walked toward the elevator. Jenny watched him and then went in to Deirdre's room.

Deirdre was lying in bed. Her eyes were closed, but they opened as Jenny came in. Jenny walked to the end of the bed. "Well, Deirdre, I've been told by your father to leave you alone more. Is that what you want?"

"Yes." She paused, then added, "Please."

"All right, I'll do what you want." And Jenny picked up her coat and bag and walked out.

When she got back home, she found Three in the living room, watching a television show on animals. On his lap was an open book. As far as Jenny could tell from the title at the top of the page, it also was about animals.

When she came in, he glanced up and asked, "Mom, where's Patches?"

Something chimed in the back of her mind, and she

stopped. "I don't know. I haven't seen him for a couple of days. I assumed that you were taking care of him."

"But I thought you were taking care of Patches. I haven't seen him either." When Jenny didn't say anything, but seemed to be looking over the paper, Three went on, "You didn't put food out for him or anything?"

Her expression hardened as she looked at him. "No. I thought since you came home you'd be doing it."

"When did you last see him?"

Jenny put down the paper and thought for a moment. "I suppose when I went to pick up Deirdre."

"But that was three days ago! Where could he be? He might be lost or run over!"

"Well, why don't you make it your business to find out? He is, after all, your dog."

Three made an exasperated sound and slammed out of the room. Left alone, Jenny tried to think. The problem of Patches nagged at her. She had grown fond of the dog.

She went to the back of the house and the garden. She searched thoroughly everywhere, under the bushes, in the gardener's hut, in all the closets that Patches, when he was a puppy, tried to get into. There was no trace of him. And both his water dish and his food dish were empty.

Slowly Jenny came back to the living room. After a moment's thought she got out both the regular phone book and the yellow pages. Doggedly she started calling every animal hospital and clinic, asking if a reddish brown and white Cavalier King Charles spaniel had been brought in. It was at the third clinic that the receptionist said, "Yes. A dog fitting that description was brought in two days ago. He'd been run over. But he had no collar so we couldn't reach anybody, although we did put a couple of ads in the paper."

"But Patches wore a collar."

"Well, he didn't have it on when he was brought in."

"Is he there now?"

"I'm sorry to say he died this morning. The doctors here did all they could, but they couldn't save him."

Jenny took a breath. "Is . . . is his body there? I'd like to come and see if it is Patches."

"Let me find out." In a few minutes she was back. "Yes, all right, he's still here. If you come right away you can see if he's yours."

Jenny drove there. Automatically, out of habit, she prayed that it wouldn't be Patches, he would still be alive somewhere. But when she got to the animal hospital and was shown the body of a spaniel lying on a slab she knew it was indeed Patches.

"Well," the vet said, "is it your dog?"

Jenny, unable to speak, nodded.

"I wish you would have got in touch with us sooner."

"Would it have made a difference?"

"You never know." Then the vet added in a kinder voice. "Maybe not. He was badly hurt."

"It was my fault," Jenny said, and recognized the term as the theme of her life for the past week. She turned away and then said, "I'd like to pay for the care you gave him."

"That's all right," the vet said. "I'm sorry we weren't able to save him."

Jenny stood there, then got out her checkbook and scribbled a check and handed it to him. "Then this is a contribution. Thank you."

She started to drive back to College Hill but knew suddenly and absolutely she couldn't go back to the house. Turning the car, she headed for the hospital, but this time found her way to Matilda's room.

"Hello, Mother Matilda," she said as she went in.

Matilda, for once, was alone, and was reading a book. She put it down. "How are you, Jenny, and how's the rest of the family? How's Deirdre? I know she's in the hospital here, and everyone says she's doing well, but they don't want me to go and see her. What kind of an accident was it?"

Jenny stared at her for a moment. "It wasn't an accident. She jumped out the window. She said that everyone at school hated her for being so religious, holier-than-thou. She said they called her Angel Puke. So I've lost her, too, as well as Three. And now I've just learned that Patches is dead. Oh God! I've alienated both my children, turned them against what I've always believed, and made them into misfits. It's so awful! I meant to do the best, and I've done such harm! I'm a complete failure!" And Jenny burst into tears, sobbing as she stood there.

Matilda got slowly out of bed, slid her feet into her slippers and came over to where her daughter-in-law stood, her hands on her face, her shoulders shaking.

Matilda put an arm around her. "Well, Jenny, so am I. That's what I've always felt about myself. So I know how you feel. Come and sit down. We might as well be failures together."

CHAPTER

23

"Come back to the newsroom," the managing editor said. "I have an assignment for you."

When Tim was at Jock's desk, the latter looked up. "I think you should do another interview with our aspiring governor. He just called to ask how we found out about that All Americas Import connection. I didn't tell him about that gal who called it in, of course. But it'd be interesting to see how he thinks it might affect his political career."

Tim, who had slept poorly for the past week and hardly at all the previous night, was trying to focus on the matter at hand and was finding it difficult. Jock paused, then asked abruptly, "You all right?"

"Yes, why?" Even to his own ears his answer sounded as though it came from a distance.

"Because you don't look it. You look sorta weird."

Tim gave himself a mental shake. "I'm okay. I'll call up Beresford and set a date."

He called Robbie's office, got his secretary and requested the interview.

"Just a minute," the secretary said.

He then found himself talking to Robbie. "In view of the news today about the family investments, I thought another interview might be in order. How about my coming over to your office this afternoon?"

Tim was prepared for an explosion, but Robbie's

voice was cool and professional. He's not giving anything away, Tim thought, and reflected with a sense
of unreality that he was talking to his brother.

With a supreme effort he forced his attention back
to the phone conversation with Robbie and made a
date for the interview that afternoon.

Caleb left the church and walked to a pay phone
outside. From there he called the hotel and asked for
Julie Manners. He got the front desk instead.

"Who is this?" the desk clerk asked.

Caleb said formally, "I am a priest and I was told
she might be injured by ... by someone who told me
what had happened. Is Miss Manners all right?"

"I'll let you speak to the assistant manager," the
clerk said.

There was a murmur of voices. Then another voice
said, "This is the assistant manager. You were asking
about Miss Manners. She's in the hospital. She was
found in her room barely conscious. We called the
police and an ambulance took her to the hospital. You
are Father—?"

"Which hospital?" Caleb interrupted.

The assistant manager told him.

"Thank you," Caleb said, and hung up with the
other voice still sounding in the receiver.

In the confessional the priest had said, "I think you
ought to tell the police what happened."

"They'd crucify me and my family."

"And what do you think you did to her?"

"I gave that bitch her just deserts. She used me. All
the time she knew how I felt and she used me."

"That doesn't give you the right to attack her. You
know that."

Caleb waited a few seconds, then, "Yes, all right, I
know. But like I told you, Robbie, my brother, is running for governor. She's already screwed him up by
giving this item about the All Americas company to
the paper. I can't think of anything that she'd like

better than getting the family on the front page of the tabloids—and why? Because I didn't move fast enough to suit her on finding out how much money we're going to get."

The priest didn't say anything.

"All right," Caleb said. "I'll tell the police, but I'm first going to tell my brother, so at least he can be braced for the fallout. Oh God!" Caleb burst out, "It seems like I've done nothing but harm to everybody I ever cared about! What's it going to do to Mom? Send her over the edge?"

"I pray not. And I'll also pray for you."

"Come in," Robbie said.

To Tim's over sensitized eyes he seemed more tired—even older—than previously.

He put a tape recoder on the desk beside him, asking automatically, "Is this okay with you?" He had no idea how he would react if Robbie said, no, it wasn't.

"I suppose so," Robbie said. He watched while Tim clicked it on and sat down.

"How do you feel now after the disclosure in the paper, Mr. Beresford?" Tim asked.

"About the way you'd expect I would. From my point of view it couldn't have been timed worse." Robbie glanced at the dark-haired young man "As I'm sure you know, your managing editor refused to tell me who the tip came from. I suppose you're not going to tell me, either."

"You know I can't."

The interview went forward, with Robbie outlining how he intended to see the money disinvested and Tim numbly pretending to take notes. As Robbie was winding up there was a knock on the door. Marianne came in and said to Tim, "Your managing editor wants you to call him right away. You can use the phone at my desk if you want."

"You can use the one in here," Robbie said, and pushed the phone over.

Tim dialed the paper's number and asked for Jock.

"You still at Beresford's office?" Jock asked.

"Yes."

"Then maybe this is something you can talk to him about. The same female who gave out the news item about the All Americas company has called us, along, I gather with other branches of the media, this time from a hospital in Providence. She says that Caleb Beresford, younger brother of Robbie, with whom she has been living for the past couple of years down in Guatemala, where he was supposedly working as a missionary priest, beat her up because she told us about the family holdings in that company. She also told us we could send a photographer to the hospital so her picture, bruises, cuts, bandages and all, will appear with the story."

"My God!" Tim said.

"Well, get to it. It's a hell of a story."

"All right." Tim put down the phone. For a second he was astonished to find himself sorry for the obviously decent man in front of him, although to any journalist the story could hardly be more titillating. He cleared his throat and told Robbie what the managing editor had just said and added, "Jock implied she'd also told TV and radio." He paused. "Do you have anything you want to say about this, Mr. Beresford?"

"No. Certainly not until I hear my brother's side in this. But why—"

"I have to get back to the paper," Tim said. He knew, suddenly, that he had to get out of there.

"Just a minute—" Robbie started.

Almost knocking down the secretary who was crossing the outer room, Tim left the office and all but ran toward the elevator. He felt strange, unconnected with any self he'd ever known, as though everything about his life were coming apart.

"He sure seemed in a hurry," Marianne said indignantly. She glanced at her boss, who had risen and come out of his own office. "What did you say to him?"

"It's not what I said to him," Robbie answered grimly.

Marianne pulled open a file drawer. "You certainly can't ever tell about people. He looked like such a nice young man. Like he could be your younger brother."

Robbie, who'd been about to close the interconnecting door, whirled around. "What?"

She pushed shut the file drawer. "You don't have to bite my head off," she said mildly.

"Marianne, what did you say?"

She paused before answering, puzzled and a little upset. She'd never seen Robbie like this. "I just said he seemed such a nice young man—"

"Go on."

"Well, he does look like you—like both you and your father. What's so terrible about saying that?"

"Like he could be my younger brother, you said."

"Yes. I did. Have I committed some breach of—"

"Don't be an idiot, Marianne! I hope you know better than that!" Robbie went back into his office and closed the door. After he'd been sitting there a while, the phone rang again. He waited to let Marianne answer it. In a minute his buzzer sounded. He pushed the intercom.

"It's Kate on the phone," Mary said.

"Thanks. And Marianne," he said before she cut off the intercom.

"Yes?"

"I'm sorry if I snapped your head off. It wasn't . . . it had nothing to do with you. It's just been—I can't go into it now. . . ."

"I understand, and it's all right. Here's Kate."

Robbie picked up the receiver. "Hello, Kate,"

"What were you doing? Trying to find the right words for your withdrawal from the race?"

"Yes. Just about."

"We have a date for a drink. Why don't we have that now—before you send in your statement?"

"All right. I'm going to try to find Caleb, but I don't have much hope of succeeding."

"Meet me at Pete's in half an hour, Robbie. I'll be sitting at the back."

"All right."

He started with the obvious and called Summerstoke. His father answered.

"Is Caleb there?" Robbie asked.

"No. He left this morning. By the way, Andrew Treadwell called. He's ready now with the trust and will be here tomorrow at eleven to read it. You'll be here, won't you?"

"Yes." To Robbie the whole matter of the trust now seemed remote. "Dad, turn to the all-news station on your radio. It seems Caleb has beat up the woman who sent in the news item about our ownership of All Americas. She's in the hospital and is letting everybody—all the media anyway—know."

"Christ almighty!"

Robbie was about to hang up when another frightening possibility hit him. He caught his breath. "And Dad, better send someone over to make sure that Mom doesn't find out. We can't keep the news from her forever, but I think one of us ought to be with her when she learns."

Driving through Providence, Caleb turned on the radio in the car and hunted for a news station. A few minutes later, only half listening, he caught his own name. The announcer left little out. The words seemed to bounce off the wall of numbness that had closed around him.

Then, with a jab of horror, Caleb remembered his mother and how she loved to listen to the local news. When he gently teased her about being a news junkie, she'd said, "I know, Caleb, it sounds demented, but I find the voices soothing."

He'd have to get to her fast. Speeding up, Caleb turned his car toward the hospital holding his mother. An hour later he parked the car and rushed up to her room, not sure what he would find.

She was, as he had feared, listening to the news.

"Mom!"

She turned in the chair to face him. "Oh, Caleb, Caleb, what have you done now?"

"Mom—" He went over to her, sat in the chair beside the bed and took her hands in his. That close, he could see she'd been crying.

"We're a fine couple, you and I," she said.

"I can't explain—I don't know what happened. Except I've never felt rage like that."

She looked at him. "Had you been drinking, Caleb?"

He hesitated, then nodded.

"Oh, Caleb." Her voice was anguished. "Don't go down that road! I've been there. And all it leads to is dust and ashes and humiliation and loss—loss of everything. Most of all yourself." After a moment she said, "Did you ever know that your uncle Sean, the one nobody ever talks about, spent a year in jail for beating up somebody who'd enraged him? Over a woman, too."

"Mom, I'm so sorry. I shouldn't ever have been a priest. I've broken every vow I've ever made." He gave a groan and buried his face in his hands.

There was a long silence. Matilda gently rubbed his head, much as she had when he was a small boy. "Did you know that Saint Augustine used to go around with his illegitimate son when he was preaching the gospel?"

"Oh, Mom." Caleb gave a laugh that turned into a sob. "Only you'd think about that now."

What she thought about, with a ferocity that astonished her, was a drink—how it looked, how it smelled, how it would taste going down. Above all, how much she needed and wanted it. She had to have it. There was a hospital aide with whom she'd managed to establish a rapport. The woman, she knew, needed money. It would be an easy exchange: a few dollars and after her break the aide would slip back with a bottle.

Tim knew he should return to the paper, but he also knew beyond any question that he couldn't. He compromised by calling Jock from a pay phone and telling him that Robbie had refused to make any comment about his brother. He then added that he'd lied when he'd said things were okay with him. He was having to deal with a personal problem and would like a couple of days off.

"Sure," Jock said. He added, "Anything I can do?"

"Thanks, but I don't think so." Tim hung up quickly before the managing editor could ask any more questions.

Feeling strange, he walked slowly back to his car and got in. His chest was tight and he was having a hard time breathing. Idly, almost indifferently, he wondered if he was about to have a heart attack. It would certainly solve his problems.

Driving to his apartment building, he parked in front, let himself in and climbed the three flights to his studio. After going in, he stood with his back to the door, staring blankly into space.

Everything he owned about the kidnapping, every copied clipping and picture, along with the corduroy trousers, sweater, and toy engine were in the bottom drawer of the bureau. That formed the entire body of his proof and he knew it wasn't enough.

He'd met the Beresfords in all their arrogance and grandeur. It took no effort to imagine their scorn and ridicule if he showed up at Summerstoke carrying his pathetic bundle to back up an unbelievable tale that he himself couldn't really remember.

Now, for the first time, he wondered if he was crazy, if his belief that he was Mark Beresford was some kind of phantom in his sick brain. If that were so, the sooner he got out of here the better.

There were several routes. One also lay in the bottom drawer. Mark walked over, pulled the drawer open and looked at it. He'd had the .38 for a long time. He knew now that for him it was preferable to presenting himself to the Beresfords, only to have them reject him as they had the others who had claimed to be Mark.

Then he wondered if on some level he had always known it would end this way.

Caleb walked into the police station and announced his name.

"We've been looking for you," the policeman said. "A woman named Julie Manners has pressed charges against you for beating her up. She's now in the hospital. And you're under arrest."

"Is she seriously hurt?" Caleb asked. He knew he didn't greatly care, except as to how it might affect the rest of his family—especially his mother.

"Wait," she had pleaded with him when he told her he was going to give himself up. "Maybe—maybe it isn't as bad as . . ."

"As what, Mom? I did hit her."

"Oh, Caleb, do you have to?"

"Yes. You know I do. It's better than waiting for them to come for me."

Now he wasn't so sure.

"I don't know what you mean by seriously," the policeman replied. "Her face is black and blue. Her neck's in a brace. You sure did a job on her. Why?"

He had come of his own accord partly to avoid this. If he gave himself up, he'd thought, admitting everything, then he'd be spared what for him was more painful—explaining what Julie had done to him.

"It doesn't matter why I did it."

"Oh yes, it does. But now I'm arresting you."

None of this was going the way Caleb had imagined.

He could see Matilda was right. "At least call a lawyer," she had begged. He said now, "I believe I'm allowed a phone call."

"Sure. After we've done the paperwork." The policeman looked over at an officer behind a desk. "Joe, come over here. I want you to take down this guy's confession."

The second policeman came over, notebook in hand.

"Okay, start at the beginning. Where did you do this?"

"You know all this," Caleb said, "if you talked to Julie."

"It doesn't matter what I know. I want you to tell me."

Caleb went through the story, beginning with his phone calls around the country to locate Julie, and then his realization that she was in the hotel he was calling from. He paused.

"And then what happened?"

"I went up to her room." Caleb stopped.

"Go on."

"I got angry and hit her."

"Why?"

He couldn't bring himself to discuss with this semi-literate official his feelings of betrayal and watch them jot it down in a police notebook. "I don't see that the reason has any relevance. I came here of my own accord. Why are you questioning me like this?"

"Because we have to know if your story jives with hers. So go on."

Suddenly Caleb started thinking about the police in Guatemala. He had grown to hate them as vicious bullies. But he had never put law enforcement there and here in his own country into the same category. But police were police, he thought angrily. To come and voluntarily confess was one thing. What was happening now was another.

"I have a right to call my lawyer. Now."

The policeman looked at him. "I told you, after we do the paperwork."

"No. I want to call him now, and if you do anything to stop me, you'll see an account of it in the newspaper and over radio and television. My family isn't unknown."

The policeman stared at him for a moment, then pulled over a phone. "All right. Call."

Caleb called Andrew Treadwell's office, announced his name, and asked to speak to him.

"Just a minute," the secretary said.

"Hello, Caleb," Andrew said, coming on the phone, "what can I do for you?"

"Have you been listening to the news in the past few hours?"

"No. Why?"

"Julie Manners—you met her at lunch—has announced to the press that I beat her up. I did hit her. She's in the hospital."

"Where are you now?" Andrew asked.

"The police station," Caleb said. "I came down here of my own accord. Now they're trying to make me go into all the whys and wherefores, and I don't want to. So I insisted on calling you."

"All right. This is not the kind of law I handle, but I know somebody who does. I'll track him down and come down there with him."

"Look," Caleb said. "I did what Julie said I did."

"That may be, but what I said holds. Don't say anything more to the police. Just wait. We'll be there shortly."

Caleb hung up. "He'll be here soon, and he told me not to say anything more."

"Okay." The policeman got up. "I'm going to have to put you in the holding cell until he gets here."

"Look, Robbie, this isn't the end. You can run again—in another four or eight years."

Robbie stared into his glass. "No. I don't know why

I'm so sure of this, but I'm convinced that it's now or never. You're probably right—this whole scandal about Caleb will put off a lot of people—"

"Like the entire Catholic population of the state, which is most of the state. Catholics, at least the working-class kind, don't easily forgive a priest gone bad. And—I don't mean to belabor this more than I have to—you can't get much badder than Caleb right now. What got into him?"

"I don't know," Robbie said wearily. "Sometimes I think Dad was right—he did it just to get back at Dad and me!"

A waiter came to the table. "Mr. Beresford?"

Robbie looked up. "Yes?"

"Your secretary is on the phone. You can use the phone over there."

Robbie glanced at Kate. "Excuse me." He went over and picked up the phone. "Yes, Marianne."

"Your father called, Robbie. He wants you to call him back."

"Thanks." Irritatedly Robbie punched out the Summerstoke numbers. The phone was picked up on the first ring.

"Hello," Robert Senior said.

"Dad, you wanted me to call you."

"You have an efficient secretary. I won't ask where she found you. You heard the news about Caleb and this girl, Julie whatever-her-name-is?"

"Yes."

"Well, according to Andrew Treadwell, who called me, he's gone to the police and given himself up and is now under arrest."

"God in heaven!"

"Yes. You're nearer to him than I am, so could you get over there and see him? Andrew tells me he might have to stay in jail overnight until the arraignment tomorrow. He's got Roger McNair to take the case. For God's sake, if there's any question of bail, we can supply that! Why he couldn't have talked it over with me—but he's always been much closer to his mother."

"Have you talked to her?"

"Yes. Although I didn't get to her before she heard the news on the radio. From what she tells me, he went to see her right before he went to the police."

"Okay, I'll go on over."

"I'm afraid there's more bad news. That woman Caleb beat up has now retained one of the top litigators in Providence, Joe Newton, and is pressing a five-million-dollar suit against not only Caleb but the family."

"But she has no case!"

"Maybe not. But I guess she thinks she can get one whale of an out-of-court settlement."

"I wonder if we'll ever get rid of this," Robbie said wearily.

"I don't know," his father replied. "I'm sorry, son."

Robbie went back to the table and told Kate what had happened.

Kate started to slip back into her coat. "If anybody can get him off, Roger can."

"And Julie-whatever has now retained Joe Newton to sue us all."

Kate paused and stared at him. "That could be bad—really bad."

"Tell me about it!" Robbie took the coat from her and held it for her. "I'm sorry to have to hurry, but I have to go over to the jail."

Kate slipped into her coat. "How's Deirdre?"

"Coming home tomorrow."

"How's Jenny bearing up under it?"

"She seems to have retreated from her . . . well, her evangelizing, I suppose you'd call it. I think the whole thing has wounded her badly. And I'm afraid I didn't do anything to help."

Kate looked at him. "I can't imagine you adding to her problems."

Robbie took her arm. "Can't you? I can. It'd be a

lousy thing to do to her right now." He looked directly into Kate's eyes. "But I can all too easily imagine it."

Robbie, Andrew, Roger McNair, and Caleb soon stood on the pavement outside the precinct.

"I don't know how you did it, Roger," Caleb said. "I thought for certain I'd be spending the night in jail."

"I did it by pointing out that since Julie Manners has not been seriously hurt—and I checked with the hospital before coming—what you did is really a misdemeanor and not a felony. And by swearing to have you in court by nine tomorrow. Can you spend the night in town?"

"He can spend it with me," Robbie said. "I'll make sure he's there."

Caleb looked at his brother, started to say something, and then shrugged.

"What about the reading of the trust?" Robbie asked Andrew.

"I called your father and told him we'll do it day after tomorrow."

"One more day won't matter," Robbie said, almost to himself.

"Are we in that bad shape?" Caleb asked ironically.

"Your shindigs haven't been exactly a boost for my campaign, Running for office costs money. Furthermore, your former friend, Julie Manners, is pressing a five-million-dollar suit against not only you, but the family, on the grounds that we didn't sufficiently discourage you from beating her up."

"But I didn't know myself before I got there that I was going to do that!"

"Don't be naive, Caleb," Andrew said. "What she's interested in is a hefty out-of-court settlement."

Caleb stared at him. "Will she—can she get away with it?"

Robbie answered, "If you mean, can she drain a large amount of money from the family—yes. If not in winning the suit, then in forcing us to defend it. Litigation costs a lot of money. And Joe Newton, who'll probably get a third of anything she wins, will see to it that the out-of-court settlement is as near to what they want as he can make it."

Caleb turned toward Andrew. But would you ..." His voice trailed off as he realized the naïveté and impropriety of what he was going to say.

"Would I charge a whacking great fee?" Andrew said sarcastically. "No. Because I'm an old friend of the family. But I'm not a litigator, either. I would advise getting somebody who's on a par with Joe Newton, and who is not an old friend of the family. There's no way, Caleb, that it's not going to cost your family one hell of a lot of money. That was an expensive temper tantrum you had."

There was a silence. Then Caleb said, "My god, I'm sorry. I'm sorry. What can I say?"

Andrew said, "I want you to think carefully. Is there anything you can tell us that we can threaten her with? It would have to be something so terrible, or frightening to her, that she'd abandon this suit, and I can't imagine what it'd be."

Caleb stared at the other three men.

"Is there anything—anything at all you know that we could stop her with?" Robbie asked.

Caleb went on staring. To give them what they needed would violate everything he had fought for, every loyalty he had felt for the past years. He needed time to think, but there was no time. Julie had already shown how fast she could move. He was prepared for the arraignment and to pay the penalty for having hit her. But she had shown that that wouldn't satisfy her. She was going to take her revenge on his family as well.

"I'll have to think," he said finally.

"You do that," Andrew said.

CHAPTER
24

It took very little time for Tim to pack up everything he owned. Keeping busy was what saved him from using the gun that was still at the bottom of the bureau drawer. His mind, his escape hatch, had finally opted out. He thought of nothing. He just packed. He had no idea where he was going to go, but he knew he had to leave Providence if he was to hang onto what sanity was left him, and if he was not going to kill either himself or the Beresfords. He'd phone the managing editor later. He'd made no friends. His cronies at the bars he'd drunk at would, after he'd been absent a few nights, spend a little drinking time wondering why he hadn't shown up. After that, they'd forget. Carrying his bags downstairs, he put them in the trunk of his car and got in. He'd also have to phone the superintendent of his building at some point, but that could wait. Putting his car in gear, he headed out of the city.

The transatlantic phone call this time was for Graham. He and Elizabeth were finishing up dinner with Robert Senior when they heard the telephone and a servant came in and spoke to Graham.

"It's London for me," he said and got up.

If it were the children, Elizabeth thought, they'd ask for me, wouldn't they? "I hope to heaven it's nothing to do with the children," she said after Graham had left the room.

"I hope so, too," her father said evenly. A wealth of unspoken territory lay between them.

Graham was out of the room for what seemed a long time. Finally he came back. Elizabeth took one look at his face and got up. "Graham, what is it?"

"It's Ian. He has pneumonia. He's in hospital and they're not sure ... they don't know whether he'll make it. I have to go back as soon as possible. I made a reservation on the Concorde for tomorrow. I'll have to leave here tonight. I'm sorry, Elizabeth." He sounded distracted.

"Graham, I'm so sorry." As she said the words they sounded false to her. "I really am," she said. And then, "Was he ill when you left?"

"Not like this. I called him before I took off. He said he was feeling a little under the weather and might be getting a cold. But since this was true of almost everybody else in London, I didn't pay much attention. I'm going to pack. I've got to get to New York tonight." He turned and started to leave the room.

She went up to him at the door. "I'm going with you." The words came out of her mouth without her thinking about them.

He paused. "No. I want more than anything else in the world for you to come back to England, to me. But I don't want it to be like this, out of sympathy. Besides, you still have reason to be here when that family trust is finally read, and I have to leave in a few minutes."

Elizabeth took a breath. "All right. I can drive you to Boston and you can take the shuttle. It only takes an hour. But we'd better go pretty soon. I'm not sure how late the shuttle runs."

"The last one leaves at ten," Graham said. "I inquired. Do we have time to make it?"

"Yes, if we leave in a few minutes."

                        *   *   *

Robert Senior, alone in the house, except for two
of the servants, was trying to concentrate on a book
when the phone rang. He picked up the receiver.

"Dad!" an excited voice said.

"Yes, Terry. How are you? You sound excited!"

"I'm better than that. I'm married! David and I
were married this afternoon in the registry office. I
know . . . I know I didn't let anyone know. But I didn't
know myself. It was so sudden. Daddy, congratulate
me!"

Robert Senior took a breath. It had been a long
time since any of his children had called him Daddy.
"I do indeed congratulate you and also David. Is he
there?"

"Yes."

"Put him on the phone."

There was a faint murmur at the other end. Then
a young man's voice he remembered well said, "Good
evening, sir. I hope you don't mind too much."

"I wish I'd had the opportunity to give her away.
But other than that, I'm extremely happy for you
both."

"Thank you." Robert Senior could hear the faint
note of surprise in his new son-in-law's voice.

"Come and see us soon," Robert Senior said.

There was another muffled exchange. Then Terry's
voice asked, "How's Mom?"

"Coming along."

"I could call her. But somehow I'd rather you'd tell
her and the others."

"I will. God bless you both."

Robert Senior hung up, surprised that he really was
happy about Terry's marriage. Whatever else could be
said about him, David Stein was a bright young man.

Caleb lay on his bed and stared up at the ceiling of
the guest room.

He and his brother had not talked as Robbie drove

them both to his house in College Hill. Caleb had nodded to Jenny and Three, who were in the sitting room, but hadn't stopped to talk. Now, as he lay there, still fully clothed, he could hear the faint murmur of voices from below. What he saw in his mind with a vividness that made him sick at heart were the faces of the Indians of Chichicastenango and Quetzaltenango, the beggars sitting on the steps of the cathedral in Guatemala City, the tired, patient faces of the children and their parents who had only corn to eat and not enough of that, of those who died too young because the medical attention they desperately needed was not available to them.

He saw also the faces of those in the movement, those who had trusted him. If killing himself would solve the family's problems he knew he would do just that. But his death would solve nothing. Julie would press her suit against his family anyway. It was useless for him to try to draw some kind of balance of relative importance between his brother's losing the election and the terrible condition of so many innocent children thousands of miles away. In theory, of course, there was no comparison. But for the first time in his life he confronted the difference between theory and concrete fact. His brother was his brother. The money he would lose—the entire family would lose—belonged to them, not to him.

Sourly Caleb remembered his defiant resolution to blackmail Robbie into giving up his inheritance. With Julie and her singlemindedness cheering him on, it had seemed so right. What a fool, what a terrible fool, he had been! Father Donnelly was right. His whole life had been spent in reacting—against his popular, successful brother, swinging to the Catholic right against the WASP Beresfords, then to the Catholic left against the powerful few in a land of desperate poverty. Was he incapable of doing anything simply for its own sake?

But there was no question, really, now as to what

he had to do. He got up and went to the head of the
stairs. "Robbie," he called.

His brother came out into the hallway. Caleb went
down the stairs. The brothers faced each other. "I
think I know what would stop her," he said, and knew
he would never forgive himself as long as he lived.

They drove almost in silence. Elizabeth knew Graham was right, that she should return to England of
her own accord, having had time to think about it.
Yet she felt almost hurt that he had rejected her offer
to fly with him. This is stupid, she thought angrily.

"I'm really sorry about Ian," Elizabeth said. She
reached out her hand toward him in the passenger
seat. But evidently he didn't see it in the dark, or
perhaps didn't want to see it, Elizabeth thought. She
withdrew her hand. No matter what Graham had said
to her at dinner the previous evening, Ian was his son.
He loved him as a father loves a son. This was something that did not involve her. I have to stop making
some kind of a personal rejection out of this, she
told herself.

They seemed to get to Logan Airport in no time at
all. "You go in," Elizabeth said. "I'll park the car."

When she went in, she saw him sitting in one of
the seats in the shuttle waiting area, along with other
passengers. Never before had she seen him looking so
dejected. She glanced at the clock and saw he had a
good half hour before the shuttle would leave. Going
over, she sat down beside him and decided the most
considerate thing she could do was not to talk to him,
or make him talk.

She didn't know how long they had been sitting
there when he suddenly reached over and took her
hand. "Elizabeth, I love you so much. In the midst of
all this I keep thinking about that."

Her hand closed around his, returning the pressure.
"And I love you, Graham. I didn't realize . . . I didn't
think." She was shocked to admit that it was true. But

it was. She knew beyond any doubt. How much his vulnerability that she had never before seen had to do with this, she didn't know. But her love for him surged through her. "I wish to God we weren't in a public airport," she said desperately. "I'm so sorry now about—"

"It doesn't matter. Not now. Do you really love me?" Graham asked.

"If we weren't sitting here, before God and everybody, I'd show you." Suddenly she saw a small area around a corner that didn't seem to be occupied. "Come," she said.

They went there and were for a moment alone. Then their arms were around each other. He was kissing her with a passion she couldn't remember before, and her own body seemed on fire. She felt as though she were melting into him when, through everything else, she heard his shuttle flight being announced and realized that it was not the first time. She sprang back. "You have to go," she said.

He stared at her. "Elizabeth—"

"Graham, darling, your plane's leaving. Ian!" she said. She saw his eyes change and suddenly focus on the present. He snatched up his bag. She almost ran with him to the door where the other passengers were filing through.

"I'll be over as soon as I can," she said.

He smiled. "I don't know that I can wait that long. Try to make it even sooner."

Caleb and Andrew stood at the end of Julie's hospital bed. Confronted with her bruised face and the neck brace she was wearing, Caleb found he was amazed at the damage he had done, yet oddly untouched by it.

"I'm sorry I did this to you, Julie," he said, and realized as he spoke that it was true, but only because of the harm she could do him and his family. God forgive me! he thought. He took a breath. "Julie, I'm here with Andrew, who as you know is a lawyer, to let you know that if you make one more statement to the media or go on with this civil suit, I have information about you and everyone you work with in Guatemala and elsewhere in Central America that I will give to the Guatemalan Embassy—places, names, identities, plans. Many of your people will either die or go to prison, which, as you know, down there can amount to the same thing."

She stared for a long moment. Then, "And I thought you were wholeheartedly for the movement. You lying pig! You don't care about anything except for your lousy family and its loathsome, ill-gotten money."

"You were pretty interested in it yourself," Andrew said.

"For the people!"

"And that excuses everything, doesn't it? I'm here to make certain you understand exactly what Caleb is saying. I have here a statement, which you're going to sign, about your activities and your friends down there and about your agreement not to talk. If you refuse, then we will publish this statement and Caleb will carry out his threat."

"You—" The stream of invective startled even Caleb, who had heard her use langauge like that, but directed against people they both opposed.

"Well," he said when she seemed to run out of breath, "you want me to talk about Juan and Carlos, and Ricco and their safe houses and those who help them in the mountains and the villages and their next targets?"

"They'll be long away before any of your clubfooted friends get there." She looked at Caleb. "And I actually believed that you cared about the movement and the people in it."

"I did. I still do. It's you that's threatening them. All you have to do is sign this and they'll be as safe as they were before."

"You're a liar!"

"You can always talk to the media and see if he is," Andrew said.

Julie stared at the two men for what to Caleb seemed a long time. It was extraordinary, he thought. When her capacity for rage and hate was directed against an enemy they both opposed, it had seemed to him like a knight's sword, raised in righteousness against the monster of evil. Now she had become an evil in her own right. And yet part of him was on her side, not because he had any of his old illusions about her, but because of the cause they had both served. He hated the fact that to him his family came before those people he had sworn to help.

Julie snatched the paper and signed and threw it at Andrew.

"Thanks," Caleb said. "If there is one more word about me or my family in the press emanating from you, and if your lawyer is not in touch with Andrew tomorrow withdrawing your suit, then I will go to Washington to the Guatemalan Embassy. A lot of our ... of your friends can run and hide some other place. But not all. I can still identify a few the Guatemalan government doesn't know about. So, keep your promise! Let's go," he said to Andrew.

As they left, he felt sick with pain. My God, he thought, as they went down in the elevator. What do I do with my life now?

Matilda lay in her hospital bed and stared out the window at the lights she could see. In the bottom drawer of the bureau in the single room were various articles brought from home by members of the family: a heating pad, a spare robe, a box or two of tissue, some books. Hidden behind the robe was the bottle the aide had brought to her. She had put it there and waited until the hospital was quiet—as quiet as a hospital ever was—and then she would take it out and drink in the relief, the surcease, the ease, that her soul and body longed for.

Visiting hours were almost over. She still heard voices from the various rooms, and occasionally a scrap of conversation from the nurses' station. But the vast majority of friends and relatives had gone back down the hall to the elevators, chatting volubly. After a while, she knew, when everyone had left, one of the nurses would check on her, but by then she would have had what she had desperately wanted. She hadn't had a drink now for almost a month. There'd been tranquilizers and occasional sleeping pills, but none of these ever did for her what alcohol did.

After a while she got up and pushed the door, not making the mistake of closing it all together, which would alert the nurses immediately. Slipping on naked feet to the bureau, she opened the bottom drawer and took the bottle out, and in the light coming from the bathroom she gazed at the familiar label. Then she got back into the bed, holding the bottle to her chest.

Images chased themselves in and out of her mind. What she wanted to do, what she'd been fantasizing about, was unscrewing the bottle top and drinking, drinking, drinking. For some reason she hadn't done it.

"Oh God," she said aloud. "Please help me."

She didn't know how long after that she drifted off to sleep or how much later it was when she became aware that the nurse was in the room.

"When the doctor comes in the morning," Matilda said, "please tell him I want to see him."

"All right, Mrs. Beresford. Do you think you'll be going to the rehab?"

There were no secrets anywhere, Matilda decided. "Yes. I've decided to go to the rehab." She thought, this time it will work. Why she felt that she didn't know. And it didn't matter. After the nurse had turned out the light she lay there, saying an extra rosary for herself and her son, Caleb. The last things in her mind before she drifted off to sleep again were Honey I, Honey II, and Sweetpea, and she half said, half dreamed another Hail Mary that they'd be there and well when she finally got home.

Driving back from the airport, Elizabeth, happy beyond memory, felt as though she and the car were soaring several feet above the highway. For a while all she could think about were those moments in that little dead-end hallway, Graham's mouth on hers and the pressure of his body against her own. She couldn't remember ever feeling that way before—not with Nigel all those years ago, not with Andrew, not even with Graham himself in the months following their marriage.

But as she drove the name Andrew dropped into her consciousness, started to darken her happiness.

She knew she had to tell him what had happened between her and Graham and somehow make him believe that it had come as a total surprise to her. But it would not be easy. Driving along, she tried to think of various ways to go about it and under what circumstances it should be done. Also, there wasn't much time. She would be returning to England as soon as she could—right after the reading of the trust, which was tomorrow.

Making a sudden decision, she went past the exit that would take her to Summerstoke and made for College Hill. She dreaded what lay in front of her, but knew that the sooner she did it the better.

Stopping at the first pay phone, she dialed Andrew's home number, hoping he wouldn't be in. But he was, and the delight in his voice was the worst reproach of all.

"Andrew . . . Andrew, dear, I have to talk to you. Can I . . . can I come now?"

"Of course! You know you don't have to ask. Are you all right?"

"Yes, yes, I am. I'll be there in about half an hour." And she hung up before he could ask any more questions.

It was not an easy meeting.

He greeted her at the front door, pulled her to him and kissed her. He knew immediately that something was wrong.

"What is it?" he asked.

"Andrew," she said, and put her hands up against his chest. At that moment she would have given anything to be somewhere else.

He pushed her a little away from him. "What is it?"

She took a breath. "I saw Graham off this afternoon."

There was a silence as she tried frantically to find words that would convey the truth with as little pain for him as possible. "I don't know how this happened, but I . . . I'm in love with him again."

He stepped back. "You're going back to him, aren't you?"

"Yes," she whispered.

"My God," he said. "And I thought you really meant it—all those things we said."

"I'm sorry," she whispered.

"Sorry! What did he do? Offer you a better contract?"

"Andrew, please don't!"

He paced around for a moment, then turned and faced her. "I've met a lot of women since Althea and I broke up. I thought I knew women, at least enough to be able to tell who was on the level and who wasn't. Obviously I was wrong!"

Unable really to blame Andrew, Elizabeth was nevertheless fighting to keep her temper. "You may not believe this—"

"I can't imagine why not!" She'd never heard that biting note in his voice.

She took a breath. "You may not believe this, you probably won't, but I was as surprised by what happened to Graham and me as . . . as you could be. I didn't do this deliberately. Truly—"

"Oh, spare me, Elizabeth. You played a good game.

You came over here out of love with your husband. I was handy and easy game and you played me to a fare-thee-well. Graham got anxious, as you plainly intended him to, and came after you. That was the intention all along, wasn't it?"

Elizabeth turned and went to the door. "No. But you're in no frame of mind to listen to anything I have to say. Whether you believe it or not, I'm sorry. Good night." And she left.

As she walked to her car, she reflected that in one way, at least, Andrew had won: her love for Graham was untouched, but her joyous mood was destroyed.

When Robbie and Caleb got home, Caleb muttered good night and went to his room upstairs. Robbie started into the sitting room and then stopped. Jenny was sitting in an armchair addressing a golden brown, long-haired dog of mixed ancestry in front of her. "Now sit," she said, and when the dog lowered its hindquarters to the carpet and thumped its tail she said, "Good dog!" and gave it something she was holding in her hand.

"What on earth is that?" Robbie asked.

She looked up. "This is Tootsie. Come in and meet her."

Robbie stared at his wife as he walked in. Finally he said, "Where did you get her?"

"From the shelter. I was passing there today and something made me go in. Tootsie was there, waiting to be adopted. I was going to talk to you about it first, but when you and the others left, I knew the shelter was about to close, so I went and brought her home. Isn't she beautiful?"

"Are you sure you want to do this?"

"Yes. I have to have something or someone I can fuss over, and I can fuss over her. From what the people in the shelter told me, she's had a pretty hard life so far, so she won't mind being fussed over. And she's housebroken."

Robbie stood there uncertainly. "About the other morning—" he started.

"It doesn't matter," Jenny said quickly.

"It has hurt you, so it does matter," Robbie went over and put his hand on her shoulder. She sat absolutely still for a second, then got up. "I have to take Tootsie for her walk," she said. The dog by this time was jumping around. "Come along, Tootsie," she said and clipped a leash onto the dog's collar. When she got to the door, she turned. "By the way, I've decided to go back to school. I think I'm going to go to the School for Social Work at the college and start on my MSW."

Robbie was irritated at her rebuff, although he understood it. "What about Tootsie, your latest acquisition? Who'll walk her?"

"I will. I'll arrange school so it won't interfere with my various responsibilities, which will include Deirdre until I can hire someone to help look after her as long as she needs it."

As she left, Robbie had a sudden memory of his meeting with Kate Malloy this afternoon and his final words to her. They more than hinted at his interest in a more intimate relationship with her, but also stated that any involvement between the two of them would be a lousy thing to do at this time to Jenny. Was he a little late in that realization? Had the harm been done? A small voice within him told him that Kate was still there. He pushed it away. But as he sat down in the living room with a book, he had a sudden image of his mother's dachshunds and her, to him, faintly ludicrous devotion to them. Had the relationship between her and his father anything to do with that? The idea was distasteful to him. All his life he'd looked up to his father. Whether or not his father had had affairs he didn't know. But given his mother's alcoholism and its unmistakable toll on her mind and body, he wouldn't have blamed his father if he had.

Robbie sat there, thinking about it. He and his father had never had that legendary father-son talk about sex. They hadn't needed to. He'd learned all he needed to know in school, in college, and through various experiences. He had never even been tempted to talk the matter over with his father. Was there anything odd about that? He himself had talked to Three. But then Three had asked him questions. Was there something about his own father that had somehow foiled in him the impulse to ask questions before they could surface?

Robbie, never comfortable with the abstract was relieved to hear Jenny open the front door. "All right, Tootsie," he heard her say. "Come on in."

Tim had left the main part of the city and was heading north when he found he was slowing his car, although he was not conscious of any decision to do so. After a few more yards he stopped altogether and stared into the blackness. The houses here were sparse and the streets not well lighted.

What was it that snooty Lady Paterson had said about her mother? Something about being under a suicide watch. Was there anything, anything at all she could tell him about that fateful day twenty-six years ago that had not been covered exhaustively by the press?

She's a drunk, he thought angrily to himself. She was a drunk then. That was why she'd gone back to the car. What could she possibly remember or tell him? Anger at her irresponsibility and at Elizabeth Paterson's indifference to what had happened to her five-year-old brother filled Tim as he sat in the stationary car and brought him relief. He was used to anger. It had motivated him most of his life, and he welcomed the surge of energy it brought. He'd go back to the hospital and have it out with Matilda Beresford. Turning the car, he headed back toward Providence.

CHAPTER

25

Andrew got out of his car, closed the door and stood looking up at Summerstoke. Knowing the explosive nature of the information he was carrying in his brief-case, he wondered how much longer he would be visiting it. Then he reflected that such a thought was irrelevant. Somewhere in the course of a sleepless night he had decided to return to Seattle as soon as possible. Glancing around, he noted the other cars, the ones belonging to Robert Senior's first cousin, James Beresford, and his sons.

His mind then slid to Elizabeth. He was still angry and desperately hurt, but the long, sleepless night had made him realize that some of his accusations were unjust. By morning he knew that everything that had passed between them had not been a ploy on her part to get Graham back. Being a just man, he was aware he had to tell her this, and he dreaded it.

After a minute or two he walked up to the front door and rang the bell. Robert Senior opened the door to him.

"We're all expecting you, Andrew. Come in."

The tall, aging man was obviously excited, and Andrew's heart, already heavy, grew heavier.

Robert Senior led the way to a large room toward the end of one wing. From former years Andrew recognized the formal dining hall, a larger and grander room than the small one adjacent to it, used when only the family was present. The oak table had been lengthened by several segments and chairs had been placed on both sides and at the head and the foot.

Most of the family, including spouses, were gathered there. The most obvious absentee was Matilda. Andrew looked around for Graham Paterson, whom he had never met but whose picture he had seen, but he wasn't there. There was one stranger, standing by Terry.

"Andrew, I don't believe you've met David Stein," Robert Senior said. "He and Terry were married in Boston two nights ago."

Andrew went over and shook hands with the slight, intellectual-looking dark-haired young man. "Congratulations," he said.

"Thanks," David said, and smiled.

Andrew glanced at Terry, "And best wishes." She looked livelier and prettier than he remembered.

"Hello, Robbie, Jenny, Caleb." He nodded to each.

Quickly he greeted James Beresford and his wife, Carol, and their two sons, Malcolm and Jonathon, and their wives, Margaret and Roberta.

Andrew walked over to where Elizabeth was standing by the window. "I have to talk to you." As she gazed at him he said, "Later," and in a lower voice, "alone. All right. Yes, all right."

"Shall we all sit down?" Robert Senior said. He himself went to the head of the table. "Andrew, why don't you sit at the other end?" Andrew went there, opened his briefcase, took out the legal papers inside and placed them on the table. Then he sat down. The others ranged themselves in the chairs on each side.

For the first time in his life Andrew wished violently that the task that lay in front of him belonged to somebody else.

A half hour later there was a tense silence. Then came the explosion.

"Are you telling me, Andrew," Robert Senior said, "that the woman I've always considered my mother was not my mother? That I was born to my father, the first Robert Beresford, by an Irish housemaid, with my mother's full knowledge? I don't believe that for a minute."

"I'm sorry, Mr. Beresford. The documentation is all here—your father's statement, which I have just read, signed and witnessed by your father and by two staff members in my grandfather's office, your birth certificate and the adoption papers." He paused. "I realize the statement is a considerable shock, but would you like me to go over it again?"

Robert Senior's face, Andrew thought, was like a piece of carved stone. Then, unexpectedly, Carol Beresford, James's wife, suddenly spoke up. "I would."

"So would I," Robbie said.

Robert Senior gave the barest of nods. "Please," he said. His voice was neutral.

"All right. Your parents, that is, your father and his wife, Pamela Langley Beresford, were married for ten years with no children. Your father's wife, Mrs. Pamela Beresford, went, over several years, to a variety of specialists in the field. For a long time no one could—or at least would—say definitely, with scientific proof, that she was unable to bear children. Then, finally, a group of doctors in New York gave her the unhappy news at about the time she discovered that her maid, Eileen O'Gorman, had become pregnant by her husband, Robert Beresford. She was, as you know, very family minded, very proud of the Beresford name. Whatever her personal feelings about the matter were, she told your father, to his great surprise, that if the child were a boy she would like to adopt that boy as her own if she could persuade the maid to give him up and return to Ireland.

"Two months before you were born your father, his wife, and your birth mother came out here to Summerstoke. They brought no other servants from College Hill, so there was no one around to notice Eileen's growing size and, conversely, the fact that your father's wife remained as slender as she always was. According to a letter from your father to his lawyer, my grandfather, also among the papers here, it was a difficult way to live, almost like camping out, and, of course, lonely for Pamela Beresford, who could not see anyone, friend or family member, and had to give out that because of her pregnancy she had been told to stay in bed and keep completely quiet. Such extra domestic help as was needed was brought in by the day only and kept away from the part of the house occupied by your father, his wife, and Eileen O'Gorman. The only person who was aware of Eileen O'Gorman's pregnancy was the family doctor who delivered you and who was sworn to secrecy. His signed statement that he would divulge to no one that he had delivered Eileen O'Gorman of a son is also among the documents here.

"When you were born and appeared to be healthy your parents turned over to the maid the sum of twenty thousand dollars—quite a handsome sum at that time. She went back to Ireland and died there five years later from pneumonia. A skilled baby nurse was brought in for you, and your father started adoption proceedings. The only person who tumbled onto the secret was your father's brother, John Beresford, which he did by accident, simply turning up at Summerstoke unexpectedly one day, walking through an open garden door and seeing both women, Eileen O'Gorman and Pamela Beresford, together. Which of the women was pregnant and which wasn't was obvious. He asked some pointed questions."

Andrew paused. He and Robert Senior, with the length of the table between them, were staring at each other. Everyone else was silent.

Andrew took a breath. "Your father, sir, took his brother into his confidence, asking his support and silence. When you turned out to be a boy and your uncle knew that your father's plan to adopt you—and thus legitimize you—would go forward, your uncle said that he wanted to be reassured that this would not cut him or his own son, James, from their share of the family inheritance as set up by your grandfather, Peter Beresford, for his heirs. Your father, sir, was well aware that behind this statement was a genteel threat of, well, blackmail. John and his heirs would inherit, no matter what. In fact, if you could be proved illegitimate, they would inherit the whole bundle, not just their half. By adopting you, of course, your father would make you as legitimate as John's son, James, and you would be assured of your family inheritance. What he wanted to avoid at all costs, though, was to have the birth arrangement with Eileen O'Gorman and the adoption made public. So your father agreed to place a sum of money in a living trust not to be opened for sixty-five years. The money placed in the trust would be left there untouched, and when the trust was opened, the money accrued would go to John Beresford, your father's brother, or his heirs, which are, of course, James Beresford and his sons, Malcolm and Jonathon."

There was another long silence. Finally Robert Senior spoke. "So after all this, we, I and my family, won't get a goddamn thing!"

"I'm afraid not."

James Beresford, a blondish, stocky man, cleared his throat. "Tell us again, how much is now in the trust?"

Andrew looked down and shuffled some papers. "Fifty thousand was placed in the trust sixty-five years ago. It's had ups and a few downs—notably during the Depression. But the amount now in the trust is about twenty-four million."

Looking around the table, Andrew thought that even if he didn't know who was going to benefit and who wasn't, he would be able to tell by the expressions on the faces—or rather, in the cases of Robbie, Jenny and Caleb, the lack of expressions. The others were murmuring excitedly to one another. Their efforts not to seem indecently happy were not entirely successful.

Then the atmosphere in the room was sliced by a

laugh. Caleb, sitting at Andrew's right, was laughing almost hysterically. "If you only knew some of the people who were counting on this bundle."

Andrew knew, of course, that he was thinking of Julie.

"That's enough, Caleb," Robbie said. "It's really not funny."

"Isn't it? I think it's hilarious! And from everything I can gather we don't have enough now to support our wonderful lifestyle." Pushing his chair back, he got up and went out of the room.

There was another, slightly embarrassed silence.

"What gets me," Terry said, "is that all this wouldn't have happened if Dad had been a girl. I suppose Eileen O'Gorman would have had her baby and had the job of bringing it up herself. Talk about sex bias."

Andrew said, "There's no question that there was plenty of that going around sixty-five years ago."

He glanced at the faces of Robert Senior and of his son, Robbie. "Any other questions or, er, statements?" he asked, and looked at the members of Robert Senior's family who hadn't spoken. When no one said anything, he addressed James Beresford. "The details of the trust, the bank used and where the money is invested and so on are all here, and I am now going to turn them over to you. If you"—he glanced down at James's sons and their wives—"any of you, have any questions I will, of course, be glad to answer them."

There was a murmur from the James Beresford contingent.

Robert Senior's voice, sharp, demanding attention, cut across the murmur. "Is there any way to break the conditions of the trust?"

"Now really!" James Beresford said.

"You're free to try," Andrew replied, "though of course you would have to do it with another lawyer.

But I don't think so. The old man—my grandfather—knew how to draw up a binding legal document."

"Is the family—" Elizabeth started. The others at the table turned toward her. She flushed. "Never mind."

Robert Senior said, his voice flat, "Let's go into the living room for drinks ..." He paused, and then went on, "so this room can be readied for our lunch."

An elaborate, festive lunch had been planned to follow the meeting. Eleven people, still minus Caleb, followed Robert Senior out of the dining hall and across the handsome central hall. The six members of James Beresford's family were chatting quietly to themselves, trying, Elizabeth couldn't help thinking, not to appear too happy. Twenty-four million dollars to be divided among three families was not bad, she thought.

Now that she knew she was returning to Graham—and at the mere passing reflection of that fact she felt happiness leap through her—her own disappointment at not inheriting seemed minor. But the others? She looked around. Robbie and Jenny were standing with Terry and David Stein. Andrew, who had just come in, was talking with James and Carol Beresford. Elizabeth drifted toward Robbie and Jenny. She assumed the conversation would be about the trust, but she discovered she was wrong.

"What made you choose social work?" Terry was saying to Jenny.

"Yes." Robbie was staring down into his glass, but he looked up. "I, too, meant to ask you that."

"Because it's a first step toward, maybe, pastoral counseling—something like that."

"Are you going back to school?" Elizabeth asked, surprised.

"Yes," Jenny said. "I was thinking first of getting a job, but then this occurred to me—at least, it came up in a conversation I had with the rector of our church. His exact words," she recalled, spoken with a smile, "were, 'You need somewhere useful to put all that energy and drive.' "

David said, "My uncle's a psychiatrist. I'm sure you have plenty of contacts here in Providence, but if not, or if you're thinking of training in Boston, I know he'd be glad to talk to you."

Jenny smiled. "Thank you, David. I'll remember that."

"Where's Three?" Elizabeth asked.

"He had an appointment this afternoon at Moses Brown school," Robbie said. "Whether they'll suit him or he'll suit them I don't know. But he was clear he didn't want to come here anyway for the reading of the trust. It may well be," he went on, irony in his voice, "that he'll be the only person in our branch of the family who'll be happy with how the trust turned out."

"As I started to ask and then decided not to," Elizabeth said, "are we—our branch—getting squeezed financially? It certainly hasn't seemed so since I've been here."

"Yes, we have been feeling the pinch," Robbie replied, "and no, we didn't pay much attention to it because the glorious trust was going to bail us all out."

"Do you think you'll go on with your plans to run for the election?"

Robbie hesitated, then said firmly, "Others run with no private means. It'll be a lot harder. But yes, I'm going on."

Elizabeth smiled. "Good for you."

Jenny touched his arm. "Anyway, it's not the worst thing in the world," she said. "We're all alive and well. That's the main thing."

"Ms. Positive Thinking in person," Caleb said, coming up to the group.

Robbie turned to him. "It's at least preferable to your self-involved, self pitying goings-on. And, forgive me for mentioning it, but you're not exactly in a position to throw the first stone, are you?"

Elizabeth, standing right in front of Caleb, had smelled his breath. She turned to face him. "You've been drinking, haven't you?"

"What d'you think you're doing?"

"But you had more than just a glass of white wine, didn't you?"

"Mom drinks, why the hell shouldn't I?"

"Our mother is in the hospital trying to confront the process of stopping," Robbie said coldly. "Is this the way you plan to end up—getting drunk and beating up women on the way?"

"All right, all right," Elizabeth said. "Let's at least try to keep the peace."

Caleb, who had been holding a glass, put it down on a side table and walked out again.

The lunch was strained, with bursts of talk alternating with silences. Everyone was glad when it was over.

As they got up, Andrew came up behind Elizabeth. "May I speak to you for a moment?"

She led him into the hall and toward the long porch.

When they were there he said abruptly, "I owe you an apology. I came to see ... don't think you'd ... well, set this whole thing up, use me to get Graham back."

"I didn't, Andrew. Truly, I didn't."

"Yes, I accept that. I'm not any happier about it. But it makes things ... not easier, but more manageable."

"You're going back to Seattle, aren't you?"

"Yes. As you know, the boys are there." He looked at her. "Good luck, Elizabeth. Please don't take it amiss if I say I hope I don't see you again."

"No, I won't." She held out her hand. He didn't take it, but gave her a wave from the door into the hall where the others were picking up their handbags and coats preparatory to departing.

There was something so bleak about Robert Senior's face as Robbie and Jenny were leaving that she forgot her resolutions and said, "Don't look so depressed, Dad-in-law. God never closes a door without opening a window."

A look of distaste came over her father-in-law's face. "Thank you, Jenny, but I really can't cope with this *Reader's Digest* brand of religion. If there is a God, which I doubt, I don't think He wastes time making people feel better. Robbie, we'll talk when I've had a chance to digest all these happy tidings. Good night." And the tall, good-looking, aging man walked away.

He was finally put through to the provincial. "Father Gilbert? This is Caleb Beresford. I'd like to ... I think I'd like to come back. Is that at all possible? Is it too late?"

"I can't answer that till I talk to you. Come and see me tomorrow. But I must tell you that if by any chance you do come back, I think you should stay here and work in an ordinary parish. It's less glamorous, but it should help you find out what you should do, what you are fitted to do, and what you want to do. The probationary period will be much longer. And there will be no family influence to speed up the process."

"Yes, all right. I'll come and see you tomorrow. What time, Father?"

"Come around eleven. With your bag."

"All right." Caleb hesitated, curiously unwilling to hang up. The hangover that he knew he was going to have had already started. "Goodbye," he said finally.

"Goodbye. I'll see you at eleven. God bless you."

Thank God they're all gone, Elizabeth thought, seeing the last car go down the driveway. Now that she'd decided to return to London the following day she knew she had, later, to go back to the hospital in Providence to see her mother. But first she thought she would pack.

She was about to go upstairs when she passed her

father's study. He was in there, his back to her, staring at something on a side table. For a moment Elizabeth wondered what it was, then remembered: it was a silver-framed photograph of his mother, his adoptive mother, Pamela Langley Beresford. A matching picture in a similar frame to the side was of his father, the first Robert Beresford.

Elizabeth walked in sloly. "That was quite a shock."

"Yes." Her father turned around. "It was."

Seeing the bleak, desolate look on his face, Elizabeth hesitated. "I don't mean to sound like Jenny, but it's not the absolute worst thing in the world."

"Objectively speaking, I suppose not." He moved across the room and stared out the window. "But speaking of the worst thing in the world, I hope you won't get angry when I ask you this, but after our, er, conversation at breakfast the other day I realize that besides you, Caleb and Graham, are now privy to my ... my bisexuality." He turned and looked at her. "Am I to take it that you're going to enlighten Robbie?"

Yes, Elizabeth thought, he had always loved Robbie more than any of the rest of them. If she wanted revenge she knew now where it lay. A sense of triumph at her weapon blazed in her. How she could wound him! Then, inexplicably, she found herself thinking of Graham and she knew she wouldn't use it. With that realization much of her bitterness seemed to flow away.

"No, Dad, Robbie will never hear it from me. And I doubt very much he will from Caleb. Caleb's had a rough time. His life and everything he thought he was and believed in has been pulled from under him. But I think he'll be all right."

"What gives you such confidence?"

"I don't know. But I have it."

He turned back to the window.

Elizabeth made a sudden decision. "Dad, I've decided I'm flying back to England tomorrow. I've been too long away from Graham and the children."

"All right."

"You're happier with me over there, aren't you?"

After a moment he said, "Until now I have been. I'm sorry."

"It's all right. After all, I was happier being away over there, too."

"I like Graham. He's a good man. And he loves you."

"Yes, I believe he does."

"Elizabeth, you're my daughter, and though you probably don't believe it, in my own perhaps warped way I love you. I realize I haven't shown it. I'm sorry I've been such a rotten father to you."

It was too painful. Elizabeth looked down. The English, she thought, were right in their dislike of emotional scenes. "Yes, well, I think I'll be getting upstairs now. Since I've decided to go back to London tomorrow, I have a lot of packing to do. And after that I want to go to the hospital and see Mom one final time."

They stared at each other across the space between them. Then he crossed over to her, put his arms around her and hugged and then kissed her.

All her life, she had thought she wanted that. Yet all she wanted now was to get away. Hastily she pecked his cheek. "Good night, Dad."

Tim hesitated until all the staff at the desk looked thoroughly preoccupied, then he simply walked into Matilda Beresford's room.

As before when he had come, she was lying with her eyes closed. He went in and approached her bed. She opened her eyes, and in a repetition of the previous time, said, "Mark!"

Whatever he was going to ask or say went out of his mind. This was the woman he'd spent most of his life hating. Now, looking at her, all he could think about was the pain so visible in her face—a face so much thinner and more drawn than when he'd first met her at Summerstoke.

"Mark," she said again. "It is you, isn't it?"

"I don't know," he said. "I thought I did, but now I'm not sure."

Everything he had been preparing to say, all the reproaches, vanished. He felt as though he were breaking apart inside. He put his hands over his face and was only aware that he was crying when he felt the tears. But he couldn't stop them, and he couldn't stop the sobs. His hands still over his face, he sank down into the chair beside the bed.

"Mark, Mark," she whispered. "I knew it was you. You're alive. You're all right. Talk to me, my son!" Slowly, painfully, she got out of bed and went over to him. "Why didn't you tell us sooner? Why?"

It took him a while to answer. "I don't have any proof. Only the little engine and the clothes, and they don't prove anything. The lawyers sent away the others who claimed they were Mark."

"But they weren't Mark. You are."

He looked up at her. "How do you know?"

"You look like Mark would look. And anyway, I know. Of all people, I should know. It's my fault you were kidnapped. I went to get the flask."

"Yes, I know. Ever since I've read about it I've hated you for it."

"I don't blame you. I've hated myself for it. I can't tell you how much."

Tim looked at her curiously. "Is that why you drank?"

She hesitated. "I'd like to say yes. It certainly took off then, but I was drinking before." She paused, her hand on his shoulder. "But you aren't sure about being Mark, are you?"

He shook his head. "No. I've told myself I am. But I'm not, because I can't remember anything. Nothing."

"You remembered MacDougal."

"I could have read about him. I looked it up afterward. There was something about him in one of those women's magazines."

After a moment's silence Matilda said almost timidly, "Please tell me something about ... about your life. Where you grew up. And what first made you think you were Mark."

He took a deep breath and passed his hands over his cheeks, drying them. Then he got up and started walking around the room. "That would take a long, long time. Longer than I have."

"Why, why?" she cried. "We can have all the time we want. I want to know everything I can."

He was gripped with astonishment that it was so different from what he had envisioned. In his imagination he would be towering over a guilty family, taunting them with his suffering and poverty and what he'd been denied. He'd be demanding the money—the trust money—that would rightfully be his. But this broken, pathetic woman made that impossible.

Suddenly he found himself thinking of the woman who had called herself his mother. Her hated voice sounded in his head now the way it had sounded through the closet door: "You don't know how much I love you. That's why I have to keep you in there. So I won't lose you."

I must be going crazy, he muttered to himself. The two women almost seemed to merge into one in front of him. Yet one was mentally deranged and had literally imprisoned him in a closet, and the other an alcoholic whose need for a drink had facilitated his kidnapping.

"What did you say, Mark?"

Timidly she reached out and touched his arm as he passed.

After a moment he took her hand. "Mrs. Beresford," he said as gently as he could. "I knew from as long as I could remember that the parents I had were not my real parents. They said—in my father's words—that I'd been taken. I had no reason to think I was Mark Beresford except for a coincidence of the dates. They said—" He paused. "It's too long to go into now. But I looked up a lot of stories and because of the dates I decided I must be Mark." And he told her about the significance of the date, December 17.

"That is the day," she said eagerly.

"But it doesn't really mean anything."

There was silence for a while. Then she said, "If you don't really think you're Mark, and you won't let me, then why did you come? What did you want?"

He thought immediately of the Beresford wealth, and more recently, the trust money, and felt curiously ashamed. "Well, there was the trust money."

She was looking at him. "And if there is none—at least for our branch of the family?"

He turned. "Is that true?"

"Yes. My husband phoned me shortly before you came. It seems the trust fund was set up for his uncle and his family to repay them for not ... well for not revealing that my husband was really adopted. If that's why you came ... if that's all you wanted, then, I'm sorry, but it's no use." She stared down at her hands. "I was so sure."

"So was I. And it wasn't just the money. That ... well, that always represented to me whatever it was I'd lost. It became sort of a symbol. My father, my adoptive father, was an old-time radical. He said the rich got their money by stealing from the poor. He could never hang onto a job, and we never stayed in any place very long because we had to go to another town so he could look for more work. But every time he lost a job or got laid off or fired, he'd make a speech about it being the fault of the rich.

Matilda looked at him. "How did they come to have you?"

He told her what his father had told him. "My parents—the ones I thought of as my parents—were driving through Providence and went past a store. They said I was outside crying. Apparently my mother said something like"—Tim glanced down at Matilda— " 'That child's being neglected. We have to take him.' I may not have the words right, but that's how it happened."

After all these years, Matilda thought, after all these years, she knew now what had happened. "She was right. You were neglected that day. We—Elizabeth and I—had taken you to Shepard's to buy you a Christmas present. You ... well, like any child, you ran from one toy to another in the toy department— stuffed animals, Piglet and Eeyore, I think—and finally hit on the toy engine." She glanced up at him. "You say you still have it. Did you bring it here?"

He walked over to his briefcase, opened it and took out the small bundle wrapped in paper. Unwrapping the paper, he unfolded the clothes and put them on Matilda's lap and stood in front of her, holding the engine.

She picked up the trousers excitedly. "I remember getting these for you. I've forgotten which store, because every children's department had more or less the same. But I remember now being irritated because when I got them home and started to fit them on you, I noticed the seam at the top of one of the legs had come apart. So I mended it."

She opened up the small garment and peered inside. "Look," she said, her voice rising. "Here's the place. I didn't have thread to match exactly, but since they were dark brown I used black. Here, you can see, the rest of the seams are brown but this bit is black."

His heart beating rapidly, he went over and took the trousers from her. Inside was about an inch and a half of seam stitched in black thread instead of the matching brown of the others. Slowly he lowered them and stared at her. "Do you remember anything about the sweater, or the engine?"

She shook her head. "No. I think the sweater was

a present from one of my friends, but I can't remember who from. Do you have it there?"

He handed her the sweater.

"No," she said. "I remember you were wearing a sweater like this and this color, but nothing else."

"Here's the engine," Tim said, and handed it to her.

She closed her eyes. The scene came back with appalling clarity: her growing impatience, standing there while Mark ran from one thing to another, Elizabeth's eyes on the cosmetic counter halfway across the store, her own compelling physical need to restore herself with a drink, the knowledge of the flask in her car parked nearby, the conviction that she had to go and drink from the flask ... had to ...

"I'm sorry, I'm sorry." Tim patted her shoulder as she sobbed. Reaching out with her hand, she grasped his wrist. "Oh, Mark, Mark, I know it's you. I wish you believed it. It would be so wonderful!"

"I wish I did, too," Tim said, his voice shaking. What he truly wished was that, one way or another, it would be over. The doubt, the constant doubt, was more painful than anything else.

Matilda was feeling the left wrist she was holding. "Mark, do you have a scar under the watchband?"

He stared, then unbuckled the watch, revealing the scar.

"I can tell you how you got that," Maltida said, her voice breathless. "You and Elizabeth were having one of your fights—you used to have a lot of them. She got mad and pushed you and you fell backward. You were near the shed in the garden on College Hill, and some idiot had left a board with a nail sticking out of one end. The nail went into your wrist. It was a nasty cut and got infected."

He stood there, staring down at his wrist.

At that moment there was a step in the doorway. Both looked up. Robert Senior stood there. All three stared at one another.

"Robert," Matilda said in the same voice, "this is Mark."

Robert Senior walked slowly in, staring at the tall young man who so resembled him. "It seems inconceivable," he said after a long silence. But—looking at you, it doesn't."

"Remember the scar Mark got? How it was infected? Show him your wrist, Mark, and show him the trousers. Those were the ones I mended."

Tim held out his left wrist. Robert took it. "Do you remember anything, anything at all?" he said.

Tim shook his head as he handed him the trousers. "Nothing," he replied.

"Look inside where it's mended, Robert," Matilda said. "Don't you remember, I was sitting in the living room with you when I did that. We were watching the news. Don't you remember?"

Robert was staring at the seam, running his thumb over the thread. "Yes," he said finally. "I do remember." He cleared his throat, put down the little trousers. "With all the others I knew right away it wasn't true, that they weren't Mark. But now, looking at him. And then this ..." He passed his hand over his face.

He turned to Matilda. "After the reading this afternoon, when we learned we'd been left nothing, Jenny made one of her fatuous comments, about God never closing a door without opening a window. I thought it was inane and told her so. Perhaps ..." He paused, seem to choke a little, then cleared his throat. "Maybe I owe her an apology. I'm not at all religious, but perhaps she was right. This is so overwhelming, I can't seem to think." He gave something oddly like a sob, put his hand up to his eyes for a moment, then glanced down at his wife. "Well, Matilda?"

"All I know," she said, her voice thick with emotion, "is that this, our son, was dead and is alive again, was lost and is found."